WASTING PERFECT CONDITIONS

Wasting Perfect Conditions

A Novel

B. Clement Williams

iUniverse, Inc.

New York Lincoln Shanghai

Wasting Perfect Conditions

iUniverse books may be ordered through booksellers or by contacting:

iUniverse
2021 Pine Lake Road, Suite 100
Lincoln, NE 68512
www.iuniverse.com
1-800-Authors (1-800-288-4677)

Because of the dynamic nature of the Internet, any Web addresses or links contained in this book may have changed since publication and may no longer be valid.

This is a work of fiction. All of the characters, names, incidents, organizations, and dialogue in this novel are either the products of the author's imagination or are used fictitiously.

ISBN: 978-0-595-45956-8 (pbk)
ISBN: 978-0-595-69882-0 (cloth)
ISBN: 978-0-595-90256-9 (ebk)

Printed in the United States of America

To My Father, Everett L. Williams

The Finest Man I've Known

Book One:
Atlanta

CHAPTER 1

▼

The sight of the new Buick almost made Heyward Jennings physically ill. It wasn't so much the fact that it was a Buick in itself or even that it was the smaller LeSabre; the truth was, he liked the body style and the way it rode and handled in the heavy Atlanta traffic. What bothered Heyward, to the point of anguish, was the fact that the car was gray and he was just plain sick of the color and tired of everything it stood for.

It was a long-held tradition at First Mercantile Security Bank that all of its executives would drive corporate-owned cars and those cars would be gray Buicks. It was believed by the bank's president those particular cars projected the conservative and sensible nature of his bank, and he supposed that to be a good thing. The one exception to gray Buicks, and only a few people knew the real reason why, was the car driven by the chairman of the board of directors.

Custom held that the chairman must drive a white car, and it had to be the biggest model Cadillac made at the time it was leased. It was as if the white Cadillac was the bank's flagship vehicle and all other cars, and their drivers, were somehow less special.

So, scores of past and present bank executives—aside from the chairman— were required to drive cars whose dreary color made everyone gloomy, even on the sunniest of days, at least in Heyward Jennings's opinion.

As he walked toward his new car, he realized he had made a decision months ago, although he had not previously acknowledged it, even to himself. There was no specific discussion of it with anyone, none that he could consciously recall. Without a doubt, the Fortson computer incident had some bearing on it. He would be turning in his old car today but wouldn't be picking up a new one, at least not that one.

Changing directions and feeling better already, he walked across the parking lot used by the bank's executives to the small security hut where James Rimini was standing outside recording the license plate number of an exiting courier van. Heyward entered the small building to hear the ever-present radio delivering a hellfire sermon on the evils of money and greed. James and Heyward had known each other for more than twenty years and had often gone fishing together in James's old wooden boat at a time when Heyward still fished, and he, on occasion, had gone to watch James's son play high school football. Heyward Jennings, prominent banker, was the only white face in a sea of black faces, yelling at the top of his lungs and waving a foam-rubber number-one finger in support of Thomas Rimini and the Weston County High School Fighting Cougars.

"How's it going, Mr. J.? Nice day to pick up your new car," James said as he walked in and turned down the volume on the radio.

"After all this time, why don't you just call me Heyward? Rhymes with *wayward*, like the sinners that radio preacher is always fussing about."

James grinned a wide grin. "Your name is Mr. J., or better yet, Mr. Jennings, as long as your office is in that big building over there and my office is this little shack." He reached over to an old coffee percolator. "How about some coffee? I made some fresh just now."

"No, thanks, but I do need a telephone book if you've got one." Heyward looked at the old percolator. "One that doesn't have coffee stains all over it?"

James reached into a drawer and pulled out a worn and dog-eared telephone book and handed it to Heyward. "Here you are. Alexander Graham Bell gave this one to me himself when I first started with the bank."

Heyward thumbed through the pages, pulled out his cell phone, and began to dial. "Hello? Yes, I need a cab. I'm over at the FMSB's back parking lot." He hesitated for a second. "By the way, are your cabs really painted yellow or is that just your company's name?"

As Heyward finished his call to the Yellow Cab Company, James's office phone rang, so Heyward stepped outside into the brightness of the April morning sun. He caught a partial reflection of himself in a window. *I really need a haircut,* he thought to himself.

At sixty years old, he still had his hair, though now, it was mostly gray and white, but it was all still there. He was pleased with himself that he had not gained any weight since his early thirties, largely thanks to his habit of walking four miles each morning before work. Looking at his reflection in the window, he wondered if he was still a little over six feet tall since he'd seen a television show the week before about people losing height as they aged.

James hung up and stepped outside. "Mr. J., I couldn't help but overhearing you talking to the cab company. Is something wrong with your new Buick? Wouldn't start?"

Heyward turned and looked back at the new car, which was parked no more than fifty feet from where they stood. "No, everything's fine with it. It just doesn't suit me at the moment, that's all."

"Well, would you rather borrow my old car if you need a ride? I know it's not something an important executive like you normally drives," James said. There was no sarcasm in his remark.

"Thanks, James, I appreciate it, but I'll just take a cab. It's kind of a personal thing for me right now. Besides, if people saw me driving that big limousine of yours, they might think I'd won the lottery and ask me for some money."

Seven minutes later, Heyward got into the back seat of a Yellow Cab driven by a dark-bearded, serious-looking man wearing a turban. Heyward leaned forward and said, "I want to go to Antonio Washington High School over on Green Street. Do you know where that is?"

"Yes, sir, of course I do. It'll only take us about fifteen minutes, maybe twenty at the most, depending on the traffic," the driver said in a pronounced Southern drawl, which startled Heyward. He'd heard Southern accents all his life—he just didn't expect it from someone wearing a turban.

Twelve minutes later, the cab pulled up at the front door of the high school.

"Can you wait here for me a little while and just keep the meter running? This shouldn't take long at all," Heyward asked the cabbie, as he reached into his back pocket and took out his billfold. Carefully, he pulled out a one-hundred-dollar bill that had been folded up between his credit cards for years. Being a cautious man, he had kept the bill there just in case of an emergency. He never knew when he might be caught in a situation where he was short on cash or when credit card terminals might be down or he got caught driving too fast in a speed trap and had to use it to pay the fine. In all the years he'd carried the bill, though, he'd never needed to use it.

Heyward tore the bill in two and gave one half to the driver. "You keep this half and wait here. When I get back, I'll give you the other half." Not waiting for a reply, he got out of the cab, walked through the front door of the school, and went into the administrative office.

Heyward had not been to the Antonio Washington High School in a very long time. His wife, Elizabeth, was a science teacher and had taught there off and on for a good part of their marriage. She could retire at any time now—with state benefits—but said she enjoyed teaching and, for the most part, had pretty good students.

Elizabeth, like teachers everywhere, complained of too much needless paperwork, too much emphasis on standardized testing, and too much government interference. And Heyward, like husbands of teachers everywhere, could almost tune her voice out when she complained about those things but seemed like he was, in fact, listening to what she was saying the whole time.

"Hello, stranger, we haven't seen you in ages," a vaguely familiar-looking woman said from behind a counter. "How are you, Mr. Jennings?"

"Yes, it's been quite a while, hasn't it?" replied Heyward. He was embarrassed that he couldn't remember the woman's name. "I need to go see Elizabeth, if I can."

"Sure thing, but I'll need to issue you a visitor's pass first. Things have changed quite a bit since the last time you were here." Then, as an afterthought, she asked, "By the way, you don't have any type of weapon on you, do you?"

Heyward followed the woman's directions to Elizabeth's classroom. As he walked down the halls, he wondered why all schools seemed to smell the same way. Was it chalk dust or the cleaning supplies used on the floors? Maybe it was the smell of hundreds of children crammed together for seven or eight hours? After getting back on track after he had taken a left at the library when he should have taken a right, he spotted the closed door to his wife's classroom, which was identified by a plaque that simply read: "Mrs. Jennings, Science."

Sitting in the hall in an uncomfortable-looking chair was a rather small boy with bushy, blond hair. The kid looked up and, out of the blue, surprised Heyward by saying, "You look like you're rich."

"Well," Heyward answered, "I look like I'm smart too, but that doesn't mean I am smart, now does it? Why are you sitting out here in this hall by yourself?"

"Mrs. Jennings told me to sit out here and think about my behavior. She says I speak out without raising my hand and I don't think before I start talking."

"Well, don't worry about it; she says the same thing about me on occasion. What's your name?"

"Riley Daniels."

"Well, Riley, how about you do me a favor? Would you go into the class and ask Mrs. Jennings to come out here for a minute, please?"

"Yes, sir, I will. But why don't you just go in and ask her for yourself?"

"I guess I could, but I don't want to scare her in front of the class. You see, Riley, I'm her husband, and I'm afraid when she sees me, she'll think somebody in our family died and that I'm here to tell her who. Nobody did die, I'd just like to talk to her about something else."

Riley shrugged, got up, and entered the classroom. Heyward noticed he seemed to do so with a considerable air of importance, as if he had been called for a special assignment. Through the partially open door, Heyward could hear him talking.

"Mrs. Jennings," Riley said, "there's some old man outside the door that wants to see you. Oh, and just so you know, nobody died."

Elizabeth Jennings was an exceedingly patient and tolerant woman. In all their years of marriage, Heyward could only recall a handful of times when they had argued and couldn't recall a single time that she had raised her voice to him.

It was Heyward that credited Elizabeth for the good way their two children, Lucas and Charlotte Anne, had turned out and gave her even more credit for staying married to him all of these years. It wasn't that he was a difficult or annoying or boring person; it just seemed to him that he had married "above himself" at the time. Heyward had had a slight tendency to underestimate himself in his younger age.

As Elizabeth opened the door and saw Heyward waiting in the hall, she immediately steeled herself for bad news. In all her years teaching, she could never remember a single instance he had come to her classroom during normal school hours.

"Oh, my God. Who died?" she asked.

"Nobody, nobody's died. Didn't you hear what Riley said?" Heyward looked at her anxiously. "I just wanted to tell you something that couldn't wait until later. I've decided to quit my job and want to know how you feel about moving to the beach permanently?"

"Quitting your job? When?" she asked.

"Today, right now. I've had enough. How do you feel about leaving Atlanta for good and moving to our beach house as soon as we can?" Heyward asked. At the time, he thought it was the most normal, reasonable question in the world.

"I guess I knew this was coming at some point soon." She hesitated a few seconds, as if she was thinking. "You know, we would have to wait until this school year ends the first of June, but that would be fine with me, I suppose. Are you sure about this? Don't you want to think about it more?"

"Elizabeth, I've never been more sure of anything in my life. There's nothing more for me to think about, not today, not tomorrow, not ever."

"All right, then. Right now, I've got to get back to my class. We'll talk about it more tonight when I get home, but it is okay with me."

Heyward gave her a quick kiss on the forehead, turned, and walked down the hall that smelled exactly like halls in schools everywhere; this time, he didn't make a single wrong turn.

Elizabeth watched him for a moment before she remembered. Today was the day he was supposed to get his new Buick.

CHAPTER 2

▼

The Yellow Cab was waiting in the visitor parking area, positioned where the tur-ban-headed driver could see Heyward as soon as he walked out of the school. Within a matter of seconds, the cab pulled up, and the driver got out and smartly opened the back door. It was as though Heyward was a visiting dignitary from another country.

"Back to the bank, sir?" the cabbie asked.

"No. Turn left out of this parking lot and head out that way for a while. I'll tell you where to go as soon as I'm able to recognize the road," Heyward instructed.

After a short ride and several turns, they arrived at the Orchard Valley Car Supermarket, which advertised on television as the largest Metro-Atlanta car dealer; it boasted the lowest prices, the biggest inventory of new and used cars, and, above all, a soft heart for buyers with bad or poor credit.

"You can let me out right here," Heyward told the cabbie and looked at the ticking meter. "Here's the other half of the one-hundred-dollar bill. It looks like this covers the fare and tip, doesn't it?"

The meter showed a charge less than half of that.

"Oh, yes, more than covers it. It's a pleasure having someone in my cab who appreciates my time and driving talent. Thank you very much, my good man."

After he got out of the cab and began leisurely strolling through the new cars, Heyward was approached by a personable-looking salesman sporting a big Orchard Valley Car Supermarket smile, who, to Heyward, didn't look old enough to drive himself.

"Now, that there's something a car salesman likes to see. A man getting out of a taxicab at a car lot has got to be a serious car buyer," the amiable young man said in a friendly way. "An *earnest* car buyer."

"Well, maybe so and maybe not. Maybe I *am* a serious car buyer, or maybe I just lost my driver's license and have to take Yellow Cabs everywhere I go. Maybe I just go to dealerships to remember what it was like to have a car." Heyward grinned. He always liked to bullshit a bullshitting salesman, that is, if they seemed likable and honest.

"No, sir, I don't expect you really lost your license. My name is Eddie Waller. Welcome to Orchard Valley." Heyward introduced himself, and the young man gave him a good, firm handshake. "What can I do for you today, Mr. Jennings? You look like you might be in the market for a big Cadillac or the gold-edition Yukon. We've got some real good deals on 'em, you know, with our big spring-time sale going on."

Heyward immediately changed his smile to a deliberate, no-nonsense look. It was a talent he'd perfected over the years, and he used it whenever he wanted to let people know he was the man in control of a situation.

"I've got two questions for you, Eddie. If you answer those two questions right, I'll buy a car from you today, this afternoon. One, do you have a new forest green Jeep Wrangler with big tires on the lot, and if you do have one, what's the best deal you can give me on it?"

Less than an hour later, Heyward and Eddie were signing sales papers on a new forest green Jeep Wrangler with extra big tires.

After all of the paperwork was done, they walked outside to wait for the Service Department to give the Jeep a complimentary wash and fill the tank with gas, something that Orchard Valley Car Supermarket did with all new car purchases.

While they were waiting, Eddie casually remarked to Heyward, "You know, Mr. Jennings, you really got a good deal on that Jeep. I can't remember my sales manager ever agreeing to discount a car that much. I bet you saved ..."

Heyward waved his hand and politely cut the young salesman off. "Eddie, I'm going to give you some valuable advice. Over the years, some very smart people have routinely sought my counsel, and through my job, I was paid handsomely for it." Heyward had Eddie Waller's attention. "Now, I'm going to give you some priceless advice, at no charge, just because you seem like a really nice guy.

"Eddie, after you make the sale, stop selling. Don't talk any more about the deal you've done once it's done. If you do, the only thing that can possibly happen is you talk someone out of buying a car when they've already agreed to buy it."

With those words of wisdom hanging in the air for the young salesman to contemplate, the carwash man drove up with the shiny new Jeep. Eddie went over the car's gauges, features, and maintenance schedule with Heyward to make sure he understood them and had no questions. Then, together, they put the canvas top down.

After the perfunctory "Thank you for buying your car from Orchard Valley" and the "Please keep me in mind for your next car" from Eddie, Heyward put the Jeep into gear and drove out into the heavy afternoon traffic, the sun shining on his longer-than-normal gray hair.

The drive back to the bank's corporate office was largely uneventful, although Heyward stalled the Jeep more than once while trying to get used to using the manual transmission and a tight clutch. He did feel a little funny, though, as he was waiting at stoplights; he felt it was as if everyone was staring at him from other cars since there were no tinted windows or a roof to shield him from their view. "Go ahead and stare while you can," he said out loud at one stop. "It won't be long before I'll be looking at the Atlantic Ocean, and you poor sods will still be stuck in Atlanta traffic."

It was just after three-thirty when Heyward turned on to the street where the bank's executive parking lot was. He drove down the street in his new Jeep, past the executive lot and the security shack where James Rimini was curiously watching him, and pulled into another parking lot used by the bank's downtown customers. It was usually hard to find an empty parking spot in the customer's lot because it was common for people to go into the bank for a transaction then proceed through the front of the bank and walk to other places downtown they wanted to go. Why wouldn't they? It didn't cost them anything to park there, and they knew the bank wouldn't alienate a customer by towing their car. Besides, parking in downtown Atlanta was a major hassle most customers reasoned, and FMSB owed them something for banking there anyway.

Heyward didn't want to park his new Jeep in the executive parking lot out of respect for Mr. Horace Beauchamp Parker III's rules. Mr. Parker was the bank's president and a direct descendant, the only grandson, of the bank's founder, Mr. Horace Beauchamp Parker. Horace Parker III, or Parker the Third, as he was known to bank employees, was a stickler for correct protocol, and Heyward clearly understood the executive lot was for corporate-owned cars only, specifically the gray Buicks.

In fact, Parker the Third was so adamant about proper procedure and courtesy that years before, he required every employee of the bank to take a series of etiquette courses. He did this simply because he once saw a teller use her finger to point a customer to the department she was looking for; he felt that pointing a finger was rude. He had his own faults, of course, but impoliteness was usually not one of them.

As he drove into the customer parking lot, Heyward noticed a clear spot two rows over from the entrance. Pleased with his good luck, he began to turn into the empty parking place when he saw that a gold Mercedes sports car was parked directly over the white line, taking up two parking spots.

"That son of a bitch! How arrogant can some people be?" he said as he put on his brakes. As he put the Jeep in reverse to back out, Heyward noticed the car had a vanity license plate that read: "MRS DR G."

After a couple of minutes or so of driving around the lot, a man came out of the bank and got into his car. Heyward waited as the man pulled out and drove away, then he pulled in, carefully parking between the white parking lines. He walked across the customer parking lot over to the security shack where James Rimini had been watching him.

"Goodness gracious!" James said. "Is that your new set of wheels, Mr. J.? I didn't think they would sell a sporty car like that to an old fart like you."

"They didn't sell it to me, James; they gave it to me because I'm so good-looking." Heyward smiled broadly at him. "I hope you don't expect anyone will give you one for the same reason."

They both turned and looked across the customer parking lot at the Jeep. "No more gray Buicks for me. They can have them for all I care. Let's talk later. I've got to go see Mr. Parker right now."

Heyward had started toward the corporate tower when he turned around and asked James, "Did you see that Mercedes taking up two parking spots? Somebody ought to do something about that."

CHAPTER 3

▼

Horace Parker III liked to know every employee's name in every branch and every department of First Mercantile Security Bank, and there could literally be hundreds of people working for the bank at any given time.

It was not unusual for him to leave his imposing office—some people said it even smelled like money—on the fifteenth floor of the FMSB tower for hours on end, just to visit with the bank's personnel. Parker the Third also liked to make unannounced visits to the bank's branch offices, and those offices extended all over the state of Georgia; he felt unannounced visits were the best way to insure everyone was performing by the high standards he, his father, and his grandfather before him had set for the bank.

In general, he was proud of the bank and its employees, but woe to the manager who was not prepared to discuss, in minute detail, all of the operational aspects of his or her responsibility. Horace could be tough on incompetence. But although he could be tough on incompetence, he could also be incredibly supportive, almost to a fault, of dedicated and loyal employees. It was his philosophy to give employees—team members, as he liked to call them—a great deal of latitude to perform their tasks, particularly if they showed initiative and good judgment in all their dealings.

His seventy-two years on this earth had given him an appreciation for hard work and the financial rewards that came as a result of that effort. Horace also had an appreciation for Adelaide, his wife of forty-nine years, who was always glad to venture her advice or opinions when he was troubled over a difficult decision. But in a most particular sense of appreciation, Horace took special delight in his current girlfriend, Gracie, and his four girlfriends before her. Horace

Parker III not only liked his conservative gray Buicks but also his not-so-conservative blondes.

Heyward had, in one way or another, met two or three of Horace's girlfriends over the years. It was not that he wanted to meet them; it was a matter of a brief introduction here or there as a few of them had enough audacity to turn up at Horace's office from time to time.

Heyward himself was never romantically interested in blond-headed women, or any other women for that matter, after he met Elizabeth. It wasn't the way he did things, and besides, Elizabeth, for all her patience and tolerance, would probably have killed him if she found out he did stray. Heyward just accepted his boss's peculiarities about blond women—what choice did he have?—but he liked Adelaide Parker and hated to see her debased.

So, the afternoon he turned away from the gray Buick and bought his Jeep, as he left James Rimini in the parking lot to contemplate the situation with the Mercedes, Heyward made his way into the FMSB tower to his own office on the eleventh floor. He was immediately met by his secretary, Miss Emma Belavedo, who began waving a handful of various papers at him as soon as she saw him.

"When you get settled at your desk, Heyward, I need you to sign this contract for the Davidson deal," Miss Emma said. Heyward always referred to his secretary as Miss Emma, a throwback to his Southern upbringing which required addressing an older, never-married woman as "Miss So-and-So." It wasn't that Miss Emma was necessarily older than Heyward; she just seemed that way.

She continued, "I need to get it out by FedEx today, and also, you need to call Leon Campbell as soon as you can. He's called for you twice already, and you know how impatient that man gets sometimes."

"Okay, let me have those papers, and I'll sign them now. Do me a favor. Call up to Horace Parker's office and see if I can meet with him today. I need to talk to him before he goes home tonight."

*   *   *   *

"Leon, how're you doing? Believe you called me," Heyward said into his phone.

"Well, hello, Heyward. Guess what? A little bird just called and told me he saw you drive up in a Jeep. Are you having an identity crisis, or are you just starting a second career as a forest ranger?" Leon asked. "How about taking me for a ride after work and maybe letting me drive it? My insurance is paid up through the end of this month if the check didn't bounce."

Leon Campbell was one of Heyward's oldest and closest friends and had been working for the bank only a few years less than he had. Leon was a good banker and had a healthy sense of humor but tended toward the boisterous and somewhat bawdy side of behavior. Elizabeth Jennings could only take Leon in small doses, as she often said, "A little bit of Leon goes a long way with me," and the fact that he had been divorced twice didn't exactly further a favorable opinion with her. Elizabeth always winced when Leon referred to his ex-wives as Plaintiff Number One and Plaintiff Number Two.

"Can't do it today. I've got an appointment with Horace at five o'clock. I wanted you to know, Leon, I'm hanging it up. I'm tired of all of this, and I expect everyone is tired of me. That's what I'm going to talk to Horace about," Heyward said in a low voice so his secretary wouldn't overhear him. "I think Elizabeth and I are going to move to our beach house at Wexler Island as soon as she finishes this school year."

"Well, I'll be damned." Leon sighed. "I guess it doesn't surprise me. I've sensed that you were heading in that direction. So when do you think your last day will be?"

Heyward thought before answering. "The sooner the better. I want to do this before it gets to be a big ordeal for everybody, and I suppose, too, it depends on my meeting with Horace. Don't tell anyone about this yet. Especially don't say anything to Miss Emma. I want to talk to her about this first, before she hears it from anybody else, and reassure her that she will be fine after I'm gone. I don't want her any more upset than she will already be."

"You got it, buddy. Call me after your talk with the old man. Oh, by the way, what's with the Jeep?"

"I'll use it at the beach. I kind of figure it will be good to have down there. I think I may start doing a little surf fishing. Who knows? Maybe I'll actually catch a fish or two, maybe even buy a little boat," Heyward said. He was already beginning to feel satisfied with himself.

✳   ✳   ✳   ✳

The five o'clock meeting with Horace Parker III was not short in duration. Horace showed little surprise that Heyward was ready to retire, but he was a little taken aback that he wanted to be gone as soon as possible.

"I guess he sensed it was coming," Heyward later recalled to Elizabeth.

Horace wanted to make sure that Heyward had made adequate preparations for his upcoming life of "being a beach bum," as Horace phrased it, after a lifetime of work, meetings, and commitments. He voiced his desire to make sure there would be a smooth transition of Heyward's responsibilities to his successor—which would probably be Elliot Coleman—and asked Heyward about having a formal retirement party for him at the Executive Club downtown, which he declined.

"I'm sure we'll talk again before you leave, but I want to tell you right now that this bank would not be what it is today if it hadn't been for you. You are a man who gets things done, and your people respect you. Not only that, they like you, Heyward, and that's important too."

Horace paused. "I do want to ask you one thing, and it will be totally off the record, just stay between you and me. I've heard rumors of it. What really happened between you and that Robert Fortson guy?"

Heyward thought a moment and said, "Well, first of all, thank goodness nothing bad came of it. I suppose I could have been sued or the bank sued. I really thought I might have even been fired over it."

As briefly as he could, he detailed the story of the incident, an event which caused him many sleepless nights, as he was concerned about legal action that could be brought against him and the bank; even more worrisome, though, was what happened to him that day.

*   *   *   *

About four months earlier, one of Heyward's department heads casually mentioned during a routine staff meeting that one of his associates, Henry Pyatt, could not get the bank's computer department to fix a problem in his email program. The trouble had been going on for some time, and there was little, almost no, response from the computer technicians. Heyward said he would be in another meeting later that day with the computer department manager and would ask her about Henry's situation.

That afternoon, the computer department manager related to Heyward that a Robert Fortson had been assigned to fix Henry's problem and would do so promptly.

Two days later, Heyward himself checked with Henry Pyatt to see if his email problem had been addressed. He found out it had not, and no one had even bothered to contact Henry about it.

Near the end of office hours on the third day, Heyward took the elevator to the fifth floor where Henry Pyatt's office was located and stuck his head in the door.

"Henry, yes or no, has data processing fixed your email problem?" Heyward asked, trying to keep his growing frustration in check.

"No, sir. I have called Robert Fortson twice today and left messages in his voice mail, and he won't even return my calls."

When Heyward heard that, he exploded.

Henry Pyatt was the bank's softball captain, and during the playing season, he would store a bag or two of the team's equipment in his office on days the team was scheduled to practice. Heyward dumped one of the bags on the floor and picked up a bat that fell out among the gloves and balls.

"Stand back, Henry! Stand back, now!" he shouted and proceeded to pound the computer with the ball bat. Within seconds, in five violent blows, Heyward beat the processor, printer, and monitor into a mangled heap.

Henry almost went into shock at the scene, and for a moment, it appeared he would faint as he watched one of the bank's top executives viciously attack what was really just a piece of business equipment.

Heyward threw the bat on the floor and slammed the pieces of what was left of the computer into a cardboard box Henry used to store old printout reports. "Come with me. We're going to get this straight right now," he ordered.

Heyward strode through the corridors of the fifth floor carrying the box filled with the crushed computer, while a still-disbelieving Henry trailed behind at a safe distance. They went to the stairwell and up to the seventh floor, that level being where the computer technicians had their offices.

"Where is Fortson's office?" he demanded of the first person he saw, a startled young woman with oversized glasses. The woman, too astonished to speak, could only point to an office at the end of the hall.

Heyward started towards the office then abruptly stopped and turned back to her. "Quit using your finger to point. Goddamn it, don't you know that's rude?"

At the office the woman had pointed to, a man looked out the door and then ducked his head back in. The man, Fortson, had heard the commotion in the hall, heard his name connected to that commotion, and looked out to see a very angry, gray-headed man coming in his direction.

"Are you Robert Fortson?" Heyward demanded.

The man, with his arms wrapped tightly around his chest, could only nod. Heyward slammed the box onto his desk, knocking some reference binders and a potted plant onto the floor.

Leaning across the desk, not more than two feet from the sweating bald man's face, Heyward shouted, "Get this fucking computer fixed, and get it fixed today!

Do you understand me? If you don't, it's going to be you and me in the fucking parking lot tomorrow morning and only one of us will walk away."

Heyward turned and walked away at an unhurried pace with Henry Pyatt following but gasping for air.

∗   ∗   ∗   ∗

When Heyward finished the account of himself, Henry Pyatt, and Robert Fortson, Horace leaned back in his plush chair and put his hands behind his head. "That's about the way I understood it. You're absolutely correct: The bank could have been sued by this guy, and you could have been sued too. I tried my best to avoid knowing about it, you know, in any official manner, because if I did, I would have had to make some very unpleasant choices. One of those choices would have involved your limited future with the bank, Heyward. The other choice would have been to pay Mr. Fortson a ton of money to make the problem go away, I'm sure, but I felt like you were owed some," then he paused as the image of Gracie, his blond girlfriend, crossed his mind. He, Horace, was well aware of his own history of what might be considered a lack of good judgment by most people. "Well, Heyward, I felt like I owed you a little leeway for your one occurrence of imprudence."

Heyward shifted in his seat. So his boss *did* know all about it.

"I guess you know, Heyward, the man quit and moved back to Wisconsin or Michigan, wherever he was from. Took a job at another bank up there, I understand. He told somebody he wanted to move away from the South because the people down here were crazy." He halted briefly. "Anyway, it's over, I guess."

Horace came from behind his desk and sat next to Heyward. "You've told me a story, and now I'm going to tell you one. Do you know why my father hired you all of those years ago?"

"No, not really. I was kind of surprised I got the job, if the truth be known," Heyward said.

"Well, my father, Horace Junior, you know, once told me a story about that. He said he only had one job opening at that time, and it was between hiring you or Harold Davenport. I'm sure you remember Harold. As it turned out, he decided to go with Harold and one morning, told him he was hired. Horace Junior was going to meet you right after lunch that same day just to thank you for applying at the bank. But he was going to tell you he couldn't hire you because your grades in college were so bad and you scored so poorly on the bank's employment aptitude tests. As I recall, he said you just barely graduated from school."

"Yes, it took me a long time to get out of college because of my grades. One professor told me he passed me just to get me gone and out of there," Heyward replied.

"Anyway, back then, my father always went home around noontime to eat lunch and take a short nap. As he was driving back to the bank that afternoon— that's when his office was over at the old building on Oak Street—he saw you changing a flat tire for some black lady that had three or four little kids standing around the car. He knew that probably wasn't your wife and children, so he figured you were just helping a stranger out of a bind. I recall he said it was really hot that day too."

Heyward vaguely remembered changing the tire, but it was a very long time ago.

"To make a long story short, my father said he decided to hire you that afternoon and somehow would make a job for you in the bank. Something about you must have had pretty good character, bad grades and sorry aptitude scores aside."

Heyward could feel his face turning red and stinging, mostly out of embarrassment.

I was not even supposed to work at the bank much less spend all this time here, he thought, numb with shock. *My whole career was based on a fluke.*

CHAPTER 4

▼

Elizabeth Jennings was not only an exceedingly patient and tolerant woman, she also tended towards habit; years of teaching school, science in particular, gave her an appreciation for structure. The day Heyward came to her school, a Wednesday, was the day she devoted to running errands after her last class, always in the same order of travel and always with the same sense of purpose.

This day, she went directly home from school. For all she knew, Heyward might be there already, packing for the move to the beach. While his pronouncement to quit—maybe he actually meant retire—*surprised* her, she was not *shocked*. For the last three months or so, he had somehow seemed to stay agitated, she had thought.

She knew he was not sleeping soundly; his tossing and turning kept her awake more nights than not. And oddly, he seemed to be using curse words often, and, to her, it seemed like he enjoyed using them when he did. Normally, Heyward never swore. In fact, he once told her that swearing was a sign of ignorance and lack of self-discipline.

He did still have his sense of humor about him, though, and he was still in good health, she thought, thanks to her sensible cooking and his habit of walking four miles each morning. She knew his job was stressful, but he always seemed like he handled that stress well.

As soon as she got home, Elizabeth called their daughter, Tootie, whose given name was Charlotte Ann. Everyone, including her parents, called her Tootie. There were at least three or four stories of how Charlotte Anne picked up her nickname—her older brother, Lucas, still, to this day, claimed it was because she farted and burped a lot as a baby—but regardless of the true reason, the nickname somehow stuck.

Tootie answered on the fourth ring after she recognized the number on caller ID; Elizabeth knew she didn't always want to be bothered by just anybody who called her.

"Hi, Mom, what's going on?" she asked.

"Nothing much, Tootie. I was just wondering if you and Josh still wanted to use the beach house next weekend? I'm trying to get the schedule worked out for the spring, and you know Lucas always wants to use it right after April 15." Lucas was a certified public accountant and liked to go to there to recuperate after tax season was over.

Tootie hesitated then said, "I doubt it. Remember, Josh has that big case going to trial next week, and he's been working late every night getting ready for it. Don't plan on us going that weekend or any other weekend for a while. I guess you can let Lucas use it as long as he wants."

Tootie's husband, Josh, was a young attorney and worked long hours. Tootie loved her brother, Lucas, very much, but if a person paid close attention to some of the things she said, they could sense that she was counting on her lawyer-husband to make a lot more money than her accountant-brother. She and Josh had two children, a set of fraternal twins, Charles and Hannah, who were three years old. Tootie and her family lived on the other side of Atlanta from Elizabeth and Heyward, which was close enough for the grandparents to baby-sit when needed but far enough away for each family to have their own space.

"Alright, I'll cancel you for next weekend," Elizabeth said. "By the way, Tootie, have you talked to your father lately?"

"No, not really. He never calls me anymore just to talk to me like he used to. If he does call, all he wants to do is talk to the twins, and then he tells them some big story about a monster fish he almost caught when he was a lot younger." Tootie sounded aggravated. "You know, he doesn't realize it, but sometimes he scares them when he talks about catching some fish that's bigger than them. I really wish he wouldn't do that."

"Well, you need to be patient with your father, Tootie; he seems to be going through something right now. I'm not sure what it is but …"

Tootie interrupted her. "Sorry, Mom, but I've got to go. The furniture store is beeping in. I've got to get off the phone with you so I can give them directions. We're getting a new hutch cabinet delivered today. Call me later," she said, and she promptly hung up.

So, Elizabeth thought, *Heyward has not mentioned anything about retiring or anything about moving to the beach to Tootie.* If he was going to tell anyone, she knew, it would have been their daughter.

*   *   *   *

Heyward and Elizabeth had owned a nice vacation home on Wexler Island, South Carolina, for a little over ten years. By all standards, Wexler Island had become one of the premier seashore vacation destinations along the East Coast before and during those ten years. As baby boomers began to age, the barrier island became a retirement Mecca as well.

They had talked about retiring to Wexler before but always in general terms, always prefaced with the word *someday* and usually only on the seven-hour drive home from a vacation.

Heyward actually paid little attention to his own financial matters—although he paid a great deal of attention to the financial well-being of FMSB—and left it to Elizabeth to take care of the Jenningses' household finances. It was only on the long drives back to Atlanta, that Heyward would ask her details of their financial status like how much money they had in their accounts, where the accounts were located, how much they had in retirement, and if they had received the last statement of what his pension would be when he did retire.

It was on their last trip coming home from the beach, a month before he showed up at her classroom, that Elizabeth felt like Heyward actually began to understand how much money they had, both in savings and in investments. He'd made a lot of money over the years, particularly once he reached the upper levels of executive standing at the bank, and in turn, Elizabeth, to her credit, had made sound investments as well as saved almost all of her salary during the years she taught.

It was on that trip, the last one coming home from Wexler Island, that they both realized they had enough money for the rest of their lives, although neither one said it out loud.

CHAPTER 5

▼

All things considered, Elizabeth, too, was ready to retire, ready to move to the beach, and now that Heyward had brought it up, she was ready as soon as it was possible.

If anything did bother her, it was the way he surprised her with the idea and the fact he wanted to make it happen so suddenly. Heyward Jennings, above everything else, was a conservative banker and not a man given to impulsive behavior.

He did have certain idiosyncrasies about him, though. He had little interest in his own personal wealth, even though money was his business. He liked to talk about fishing but never fished. He always wore black socks, and despite everything Elizabeth said to the contrary, he claimed that there was a right and left sock. He had subscriptions to three boating magazines and read each one cover to cover but didn't own a boat. He had to eat dinner the minute he got home from the bank, before doing anything else, and insisted Elizabeth heat the plate in the oven before putting his food on it. He did a great deal of charity work but would never accept even the smallest token of appreciation for his work, no plaques, no trophies, no testimonial dinners; he considered them "showy."

But for all of his ways, it was his relationship with his dog, Peaches, that was the most curious. He treated her like a little person, and when Elizabeth couldn't see him, Heyward would actually cook the dog her own meals.

It all started when Heyward saved Peaches' life one day. First Mercantile Security Bank, as one of its many benevolent causes, donated money to different animal shelters around Atlanta on a regular basis. On the day he saved Peaches' life,

Heyward, by sheer coincidence, happened to walk by an Accounting Department desk and saw a bank check made out to a shelter not too far from where he lived.

Heyward volunteered to drop the check off on his way home. While he was there, he saw a small, sad-looking dog sitting alone in a cage on a bare concrete floor. The dog looked like it might have had a slight case of mange, and Heyward asked about it.

"That one's a pretty sad case," one of the shelter workers told him. "Nobody has wanted to adopt her, and she's been here way too long now," she said. "Look at her. I hate to say it, but she's just too ugly for most people."

Heyward stepped up to the cage and looked in. "What do you mean she's been here too long?"

"You know how it is, Mr. Jennings, they can't keep dogs here forever. There's just not enough room for all of them that come through a place like this."

"Well, if no one adopts her and you all can't keep her, what's going to happen to her?" Heyward asked. The woman looked at him, looked at the dog, and made a face.

"I'll tell you this, lady, that's not going to happen to that little dog today," Heyward said and opened the cage door himself. "It's not going to happen to her."

From that point on, the little dog and Heyward were almost inseparable. One of the neighborhood children suggested the name Peaches, in honor of Georgia, and a year or so later, the same child's father told Heyward he believed Peaches knew that he'd saved her life. "That," the man said, "is why she's such a good pet to you."

Heyward didn't answer him, but deep inside, he was positive Peaches was smart enough to know what he'd done that afternoon.

*   *   *   *

On the day that Heyward came to Elizabeth's class at Antonio Washington High School, the same day he'd told her he was quitting his job, it was Peaches who alerted Elizabeth that Heyward had bought his new green Jeep.

The little dog liked to bark at any strange car that might pull into their driveway—Heyward claimed she could tell the differences in car shapes and sounds—and barked wildly at the unfamiliar sound of the Jeep.

Elizabeth, with Peaches at her side, opened the door to the driveway and saw Heyward standing beside the new car. When he saw them looking at him, he reached in the car and blew the horn a couple of times, just for effect.

"Well, how do you like it?" he asked. Elizabeth was not exactly sure if he was talking to her or the dog.

"Where did you get this? Did you buy it, or is it the bank's company car?"

"I bought it today for me—for us. This is what I am going to drive when we move to the beach," said Heyward, smiling proudly. "You can drive it too, if you want."

"Thanks anyway, but I think I'll stick with my Camry. You're not afraid to ride in this thing, Heyward? It looks, well, exposed to me."

While Elizabeth talked to her husband, Peaches walked around the car, pausing at all four tires to sniff each one. Then, as if she was satisfied with the choice of a Jeep, she looked up at Heyward.

"You can ride in it, Peaches, but you can't drive it. You don't know how to change gears," he said to her. He sometimes talked to the dog, just to acknowledge her presence so she didn't feel left out.

"I guess if you're happy, then I'm happy for you. Did you get your new Buick today too?" Elizabeth asked.

"Hell no. I'm not driving those damn gray things anymore," he said.

Once again, she thought, *There he goes with that cussing.*

CHAPTER 6

▼

"Why don't we call that real estate woman that's always sending us something in the mail about her selling so many houses?" Heyward asked Elizabeth after he parked the Jeep in the garage. "You know who I'm talking about, don't you? That short, fat lady that I said looked like a fireplug in her picture."

"Who?"

"You know who I'm talking about, Elizabeth, that real estate lady agent that I said had plump little legs and had no neck ... Butter somebody." Heyward couldn't remember the woman's name, but he did remember she seemed like she would be aggressive, if her mailings were any indication. "We'll get her to sell our house."

"Oh, you mean Butterfield, Janie Butterfield." Elizabeth knew who he was talking about.

In short order, they decided to sell their Atlanta home and live in the existing house they already owned—and had paid for—on Wexler Island. Heyward may not have cared about their personal wealth, but Elizabeth did, and whenever she could, she made extra payments on the vacation home whenever extra cash came through the household.

In less time than it took to drive from Atlanta to Wexler Island—seven hours—Heyward and Elizabeth decided on how much they wanted for their Atlanta house, what furniture they wanted to take to the island, what furnishings they wanted to offer to Tootie and Lucas, and what they wanted to give to the Salvation Army.

"We'd better ask Lucas and Samantha what they want before we let Tootie have her pick. If not, I expect she'll want most everything, probably," Heyward said. Samantha was Lucas's wife. They had only been married for a couple of years and lived in Knoxville, Tennessee, where Lucas had his accounting practice.

"All right, then. I'll call Janie Butterfield tomorrow about selling the house. We'll need to tell the kids, and I'll need to tell my principal I won't be teaching next year," Elizabeth said.

Heyward's simple decision that he couldn't drive an FMSB gray Buick any longer touched off a new chapter in their life.

It was settled. They would leave Atlanta and move to Wexler Island and the beach.

✳   ✳   ✳   ✳

Later that night, as they were lying in bed almost but not quite asleep, Elizabeth finally brought up the question that had been bothering her since Riley Daniels told her there was an old man wanting to talk to her outside in the school hall earlier in the day.

"Why now, Heyward? Why now, and why all of a sudden?"

"Well, I've been thinking about it for some time, but I just wasn't sure. I guess it's just one of those things. You know, it kind of hits you all of a sudden." Heyward thought better of trying to explain in too much detail because, all said and done, he wasn't exactly sure himself.

"Let me ask you something, Elizabeth, something that's been on my mind for a good while now. Why is it that you married me in the first place?"

"What do you mean, Heyward? I'm not sure I understand what you just asked me."

Heyward propped himself up on his elbow. "Why did you marry me? You had other choices. I thought you were making a big mistake at the time."

"Are you serious? Why would you ask me such a question after all these years?" Elizabeth didn't understand.

He hesitated. "I don't know. You were so lively and pretty, and you had a much better education than I did. Really, at the time, my job prospects weren't too good either."

"I loved you then, and I love you now, Heyward. That's why I married you, and nothing else matters, then or now."

Elizabeth turned on the light on the nightstand. "Are you okay, Heyward?"

"I'm fine. It's just that, somehow, I don't know why, but in some ways, I feel I let everybody down."

"Let everybody down? You've never done that in your life. You're a good hus-band and father, the grandkids adore you, and you provided well for your family. Why on earth would you think that?"

All of a sudden, Heyward regretted saying anything. "No reason." The truth was that he felt like he'd let himself down too, but he wasn't going to bring *that* up now.

Elizabeth turned off the light. "Nobody feels like you let them down, no way. You've done very well for us and for you too, and you did it playing by the rules."

By the rules, he thought, *always by the rules.*

"Let's go to sleep," Heyward said. "I guess it's just one of those things an old fool thinks sometimes."

CHAPTER 7

▼

Heyward woke up earlier than usual the next morning, skipped his morning four-mile walk, and arrived at his office in the FMSB tower long before Miss Emma showed up. It was important, he felt, that he talk to her about his decision to leave the bank before she heard it from anyone else. It didn't take long for the office grapevine to circulate that kind of information, and somebody somewhere always seemed to embellish news with an unfounded rumor or two. He needed to assure her that everything would be alright for her, given the proper time and patience.

Miss Emma had been his secretary for many years, and as things sometimes happen in long-term work relationships, their connection went far beyond normal job responsibilities. She was not only his secretary but had become, for all intents and purposes, his gatekeeper, scheduler, protector, critic, and occasionally, a substitute mother figure when she thought it was needed. Miss Emma was meticulous and thorough, conscientious and dependable, and handled many of the technical particulars of Heyward's job which were, for him, some of his weak points; her strengths in those areas allowed Heyward to concentrate on his strong suit, dealing with people. Together, they made a good team.

On the other hand, Heyward destroying the computer and his physical threat to Robert Fortson scared Miss Emma because she knew it was common knowledge all over the bank. What would happen to her if the bank fired Heyward over this? Would she be fired too, just because she was so closely associated with him? If she lost her job, who else would hire her at her age? She had a little bit of money saved away but not near enough to live on the rest of her life. She had to work, had to have money coming in, and could suffer little disruption of her income stream.

On this morning that Heyward arrived at the office early, Miss Emma was in for a rather unpleasant surprise, and she knew it as soon as she arrived and saw him standing by her desk.

"Good morning, Miss Emma. Can we talk a few minutes before you get started on your work? Let's go into my office," Heyward said. His dread of what was coming made his throat dry, and his voice cracked.

"Oh my, Heyward. Is this what I've been afraid of? Have you been fired?"

For the next forty-five minutes, Heyward tried to explain to Miss Emma his decision to leave and that, no, he wasn't being forced out of the bank. As she alternated between outright crying, sniffling, and blowing her nose—Heyward had to give her his handkerchief—Miss Emma began to understand the situation.

Heyward assured her that she would still be employed by the bank and that she would be assigned to work with Elliot Coleman, his successor in responsibility and job title. Mr. Parker III himself had guaranteed that, Heyward said. Besides, he continued, Elliot Coleman respected Miss Emma. In fact, he was one of the few young executives who referred to her as "Miss" and knew he needed her help if he was going to be successful. Not only was her employment and status guaranteed, she would be getting a raise.

Upon hearing that bit of news, Miss Emma stopped sniffling. Almost immediately, she began talking about how much she liked Elliot and all the different ways she could probably help him. "Maybe this was all for the best after all," she said, wondering how much her raise was going to be.

Heyward got up and opened his door then pausing just a moment, closed it again.

He sat down next to her in a nearby chair.

"Miss Emma, I want you to do me a favor before I leave the bank. I want you to call your sister, Lucy, and make up with her. It's been over thirty years since you all had your falling out, and as a favor to me, I want the both of you to reconcile and get back to being sisters again."

"Heyward, that woman stole my boyfriend, and I'm never going to forgive her for that. It was my one chance for happiness, and she took him away from me. I hated her then for doing that, and I just won't forgive her now." Miss Emma crossed her arms. "No, I can't do that, even as a last favor to you."

"Miss Emma, she's your sister, your only sister, and neither of you are spring chickens, if you know what I mean. Think of all the years you all have wasted not being together because of this thing. She didn't even marry him anyway. Do yourself a favor and call her, please."

"I've got to get back to work if I'm going to keep my job with Elliot Coleman," she said and stood up. "Heyward, you're a kind person, and you've got a good heart, but I'm never going to forgive that woman for what she did to me, and you need to understand that." And with that, she walked out.

After some time to let things settle down, Heyward buzzed her on the intercom.

"Miss Emma, would you call Kevin Pasko in Materials Management and Doreen Shumar in Human Resources and set up a time for me to meet with them, please?"

As Heyward was finishing his appointment instructions to his secretary, Leon Campbell tapped on the open door and walked into Heyward's office.

"Let me be the first to congratulate you," Leon said with a big grin, offering a handshake. "Not many men have your good fortune."

"I don't know, Leon. Everybody will retire one day, I suppose," Heyward said shaking Leon's hand.

"Who said anything about retiring?" Leon asked. "I was talking about your good fortune to be meeting with Doreen Shumar."

Leon had a thing for Doreen. She was tall and thin but was incredibly well endowed and had cropped blond hair. Even though Doreen wore a wedding band, no one had ever met her husband, who was rumored to be a welder or carpenter or brick mason, and she kept no pictures of him—or anyone else for that matter—in her office. She never attended any type of bank social function, not an office Christmas party or Fourth of July picnic, and she never volunteered any information about him or her family to any of her bank associates.

Any time Leon was near the Human Resources Department, he would invent almost any excuse to walk by Doreen's office just so he might see her and her big breasts. By lucky coincidence, Leon once bumped into her as she rounded the corner of some cubicles, and for days, he could speak of little else.

Leon sat down and glanced out the window. With an air of certainty, he looked back at Heyward and said, "You know she's a cooter-muncher."

"A cooter-muncher? She's a what?" Heyward asked. He had never heard that expression before, not even from Leon, and he'd heard a lot of things from him over the years.

"She's a cooter-muncher. You know, a lesbo." Leon was now looking back at the window.

"A lesbo? Are you telling me Doreen Shumar is a lesbian?" Heyward was shocked.

"Yep, she's a lesbian. I know that for a fact."

"You've got to be kidding me. She's married; she wears a wedding band," Heyward said. "She can't be both, married and a lesbian."

"Sure, she can. I know about these things," Leon said, as if just saying it made it possible. "Anyway, give her my regards when you see her, you lucky dog."

When he'd made sure his request had been registered, Leon continued, "How did your talk with Horace go yesterday? I guess you talked to Emma about it too. She looks like she's been crying."

Heyward, glad to be off the subject of Doreen Shumar and her sexual orientation, whatever it may be, related his conversations with both Horace and Miss Emma. "Actually, I think everything is going to work out okay for everybody," he said, not bothering to bring up his lack of success in getting the Belavedo sisters back together.

"Well, you know everyone will miss you, myself included. Of course, I do expect to be invited to come down there to eat your food and drink your liquor." Leon brushed some lint from his shoulder. "Seriously, Heyward, how does it really feel to be finally leaving this place … You know, how does it feel to think you won't be working anymore?"

"Leon, all I can tell you is that it feels very strange. I haven't really thought too much about the future or what I will do to occupy myself. There's nothing I can think of that I really want to do. Maybe fish some."

"You fish?" Leon said and laughed. "I'd like to see that happen."

"To tell you the truth, Leon, mostly what I've been thinking about is everything that's happened over the last … what is it, thirty-something years, and I have no feelings about a lot of it … none at all, almost numb about it. It's like, for the most part, I wasn't actually there, more like it was somebody else instead of me."

Heyward lowered his voice. "I can tell you this, but keep it to yourself." He looked around his office like he was making sure no one had come in without his knowing it. "I've been having some weird feelings lately. Sometimes I feel like I've let myself down—and everybody else too—and in some ways, I just feel completely pissed off." Then he added, "And I don't really know who or what I am pissed at."

Leon Campbell had his faults; that was for sure. All you had to do was ask Miss Belavedo or either of his ex-wives. But if he was anything at all, he was Heyward's friend and from time to time, worried about him.

"First of all, I don't know why you would feel like you let anybody else down. I can't understand that. You're probably one of the best executives this bank ever had; that's for damn sure. In my opinion, you letting other people down should never be an issue for you."

Heyward shrugged.

Leon continued, "Tell me one time you didn't do a good job—better than anyone else could do—on any project you were in charge of? I can't think of one, and I bet you can't either. Then, too, look how loyal the people who worked for you are to you, as a person. Think about how many people you've helped over the years."

Heyward looked at him a moment, then at the floor, then the ceiling. "I don't really recall—"

Leon cut him off. "Your problem, and it could be a big one, is you always did everything by the book. You just told me you feel pissed off and don't know why. You're probably pissed off at yourself and just don't realize it—always by the book and what everyone expected of you."

Leon was beginning to enjoy saying some things that he had wanted to in the past but never did because he didn't want to hurt Heyward's feelings. "I swear to God, Heyward, sometimes you just have to go up the down escalator, just for the fun of it. Sometimes you have to drive one hundred miles per hour in a fifty-five zone, just to thumb your nose at everything. I'm going to tell you something: I was actually proud of you for beating that computer up and threatening to do the same thing to that little asshole programmer. Proud, I was, real proud."

"That was a dumb thing I did," Heyward said. "I could have gotten fired over that and probably sued too. Crazy. I'm ashamed I lost control like that. By the way, I didn't say anything to Elizabeth about it, and I would appreciate it if you never mentioned it to her, okay?"

Leon ignored his question. "Heyward, let me ask you something. If you got fired or got sued over it, couldn't you live with that? I mean, couldn't you handle either one of those things if they happened; they're not going to kill you, are they? Fuck it, you're sixty-two years old. They aren't going to cut your arm or leg off or put you in jail, are they? What's so bad about being pissed off and showing it occasionally?"

Leon stood up. "I'll leave you with those brilliant thoughts. I'd better get to work now or that Elliot Coleman may try to cut my arm or leg off." Leon grabbed his crotch. "Good luck if he tries. Both of my ex-wives have wanted to cut my balls off for years, and they haven't been able to yet. See you later," he said and walked to the door.

"Before you go, Socrates, one thing: I'm only sixty years old, not sixty-two," Heyward corrected his friend.

Leon looked at him one more time. "When you see Doreen, how about a look down her blouse for me, will you?"

CHAPTER 8

▼

For the rest of the morning, Heyward worked on a detailed outline of his job responsibilities and the projects he had going on. Elliot Coleman, if he wanted to, could use it to prepare for the complexities of his new job title.

When Heyward had assumed the position years ago, there were no guidelines or procedure manual for him to follow, and he felt like he'd wasted weeks that could have been productive. Horace Parker III simply told him he was responsible for what happened, good or bad, then left it to Heyward to figure things out the best way he could. Heyward wanted to help Elliot hit the ground running, as they say, because he liked his successor, and besides, he just felt it was the right thing to do.

Heyward told Miss Emma to hold his calls and discourage anybody from interrupting him, if that was possible. He wanted to concentrate on writing his outline for Elliot and wanted to finish it as quickly as he could; the sooner he finished, the sooner he could retire.

A few hours after lunch, Miss Emma knocked on his door. "I'm really sorry to bother you, Heyward, but there's an attorney on the phone, and he's adamant that he speak to you right now. I don't know what he wants, but his name is Matthew Rabon and he is very insistent that he speak to you immediately."

"Alright, Miss Emma, go ahead and put him through to me, and please close my door on your way out."

Heyward felt sick to his stomach. *This must be Robert Fortson's attorney,* he thought. *Here comes the start of a personal lawsuit, just when I wanted to be through with all of this.*

"Hello," Heyward answered. He tried not to sound upset.

"Hello, Mr. Jennings. My name is Matthew Rabon. I don't believe you know me, but I am an attorney representing your father's brother, Mr. Walter Jennings. Mr. Jennings is your uncle, of course. It is important that I speak with you. May we do so now?"

"My uncle Walter? Yes, I can talk now. Please go on." Heyward felt immediately relieved. Whatever this man wanted with him, it was not to sue him for threatening to beat up Fortson.

"Mr. Jennings, your uncle has been ill for some time and is presently in the Sheridan General Hospital here in Sheridan, Alabama. The medical staff advises me that his condition has worsened and his death is imminent. They are reluctant to be specific as to the amount of time he has left, but they imply it could be in the next twelve hours or so." Matthew Rabon spoke in a carefully measured tone.

Heyward was surprised. It had been years since he even thought about his father's brother and much longer since he had seen or talked to him.

The attorney continued, "Your uncle would like to see you before he passes on. It is essential to him that he talks to you, and his condition is so bad that conversing with you over the telephone is not practical. Would it be possible for you to come here today, without delay? I cannot overstate how important it is to him." There was a pause. "Please."

Heyward said nothing. His thoughts went to a very distant memory of a man that he could scarcely remember. He could visualize his uncle Walter's face, but he could remember little else of him.

"Mr. Jennings?"

"Yes, I'm here, Mr. Rabon."

"Mr. Jennings, I know this is highly unusual. I also realize that it could be a hardship for you, but please, can you come now?"

"All right, I'll come. I'll leave my office in a few minutes and come straight there, there to Sheridan General Hospital."

Heyward hung up and then called Antonio Washington High School. He left a message with the woman at the front desk—he still couldn't remember her name—for Elizabeth to call him on his cell phone when classes changed and she had a minute or just to call after school.

He opened his office door and told Miss Emma the gist of the brief conversation with his uncle's attorney. "I'm not sure how long I'll be gone, but I'll call you as soon as I know something definite. How about canceling my meetings with Kevin and Doreen, please?"

Heyward continued, "I don't know what this is all about," more to himself than to his secretary.

It would be almost a three-hour drive from Heyward's Atlanta office to Sheridan, Alabama. Miss Emma, efficient as always, had gone on the Internet as Heyward prepared to leave and printed out directions to the small Alabama town. Then she printed another set of directions on how to get to the hospital once he got into Sheridan.

By Atlanta standards, traffic was relatively light, and he pushed his new Jeep up to cruising speed on I-20, toward the Alabama state line; the car was considerably rougher riding than the Buick he was used to. To the best of his knowledge, Heyward had never been to Sheridan and couldn't seem to remember if he even knew his uncle lived there.

Why would my uncle want to see me? he wondered.

∗   ∗   ∗   ∗

Heyward was born and raised in a small town, Rawlins, in the southwest corner of Georgia. His father, Robert, and his brother, his dying uncle Walter, were from Rawlins County too, but his father never moved from the area and seldom traveled out of the state.

Ruth Sikes Jennings, Heyward's mother, was born and raised in the northeast Georgia mountain town of Lost Springs which sat astride the state line between Georgia and Tennessee. There was a Lost Springs, Georgia, and a Lost Springs, Tennessee, because the state line ran down the very center of Main Street.

Both of Heyward's parents were long deceased, his father dying from what was sometimes called the brown lung disease, an illness common at one time to textile mill workers. His father worked his entire life as a loom operator in the local textile plant. Ruth moved to Rawlins when she married Heyward's father and worked all her adult life as a dime-store clerk. Heyward had an older sister, Barbara, who died in a car accident when she was a senior in high school; his parents never really recovered from the loss and somehow seemed to be in a perpetual state of sadness the rest of their lives.

After Barbara's death, Heyward's parents were determined that he would attend college and have opportunities they never enjoyed. His high school grades were miserable—all of his teachers said he wasn't "living up to his potential"— but a sympathetic school counselor convinced a small liberal arts college to give him a chance. There, Heyward's grades were less than acceptable, actually well below average, but with the urging of several perturbed professors wanting to be rid of him, the college president allowed him to graduate.

For years after he finally received his college diploma, Heyward always felt a little guilty that his parents' hard-earned tuition money had been wasted on him. Although he held jobs all during his school years, Heyward's parents footed the large majority of the cost of his education, insisting that he not be forced to take out student loans. Good parents, they didn't want their son saddled with debt as he started life on his own if he, indeed, ever did graduate. Unfair to himself, Heyward couldn't help but feel that his sister, Barbara, would have made her parents prouder had she lived.

Not really having any idea what he wanted to do after graduation, Heyward joined the United States Coast Guard, telling his parents he thought that military training would be good for him and would provide an opportunity to see the world beyond south Georgia. It was in the coast guard that he began to realize he may be just as intelligent, and in many cases a lot more intelligent, as other people, no matter if they were military or civilian. It was also during the time of his coast guard enlistment that he met Elizabeth who was in graduate school in Virginia. They married shortly after they met.

His uncle, who was now in his last hours of life, moved from Rawlins before Heyward was born and had only visited the area and his family occasionally, now that Heyward thought about it. In fact, he could hardly recall hearing his father talk about his distant brother, and the few times he did, it was brief and in passing conversation, as though he were speaking of someone who had already died.

As he drove west on the interstate, Heyward thanked God that his children, Lucas and Tootie, and their families liked each other and seemed to have a good relationship. They had had their moments, though, when Lucas and Tootie were teenagers. They could get on each other's nerves and found unique ways to irritate each other, just for the sake of irritation.

Lucas, in particular, seemed to thrive on making his younger sister's life difficult, aggravating her and her friends and intimidating any boy who asked her out on a date. Lucas was a big kid, and he, along with some of his football friends, took special pleasure in hiding behind the bushes to wait for Tootie's dates to show up. They would let the boy park his car, then as he walked to the front door, Lucas and his friends would mass around him and threaten the boy with what they would do to him if he did not treat Tootie right or didn't get her home on time.

In an effort to even the score with Lucas, Tootie once emptied a full bottle of cheap perfume on the dashboard of his car, and for weeks, Lucas would go to school smelling like a "Paris whore," at least that's what his friends began calling him, not that they or Lucas had ever met any prostitute at that time in their lives, much less one from an exotic place like France. Then too, none of them knew what any whore, American or European, might actually smell like.

Still, all in all, Lucas and Tootie remained close, and Heyward and Elizabeth were always grateful for that.

CHAPTER 9

▼

Night was beginning to fall when he reached the town limits of Sheridan. About a half hour into the trip, Elizabeth called, and he told her what little he could remember of his call from the attorney, Matthew Rabon. She made him promise to call when he arrived at the Sheridan hospital. "I'm not real comfortable about you driving that Jeep, you know," she told him.

From the parking lot, Sheridan General Hospital seemed more modern and a good bit larger than Heyward had been expecting. Somehow, he imagined in rural Alabama, all hospitals would be tired and rundown, with elderly doctors practicing behind-the-times medicine, just waiting until they retired or died. He didn't have any real reason for thinking that way other than associating Alabama's entire medical community with the faded memory of his uncle Walter, and it embarrassed him just a little.

With a great deal of effort, Heyward climbed out of his Jeep and stretched his back and legs. Every muscle in his body ached from the rough ride of the Jeep, and before he called Elizabeth to let her know he'd actually found little Sheridan, Alabama, he made a mental note not to mention those aches to her. Some things she just didn't need to know, he thought, especially things about his Jeep.

Once he could move his legs without the muscles almost cramping up, he entered a contemporary, softly lit lobby where, at a round information desk, a petite older lady directed him to his uncle's room.

She cheerfully told him, "Walter K. Jennings, Room 401. Take the elevators to the fourth floor. There'll be signs directing you to his room, but if you get lost, just ask somebody where to go. They'll tell you."

Heyward tried his best not to stare, but the woman's hair seemed to be tinted dark blue which complemented the light blue hospital frock she was wearing. He'd heard jokes about old ladies' hair being blue but had never really noticed it before on anyone else. As he thanked her for the directions, Heyward thought that would be a good job, working at a hospital information desk, for Miss Emma Belavedo when she decided to retire.

When the elevator door opened on the fourth floor, Heyward realized the palms of his hands were moist, and he could feel his pulse quickening to the point that a slight feeling of light-headedness came over him. At his age and level of experience, few situations intimidated him; still, he always seemed to feel ill at ease in a hospital or around doctors. All hospitals seemed to have the same smell, he thought, the same way all hallways of school buildings seemed to smell alike.

Just off the elevator, directional arrows pointed left or right to the corresponding room numbers, and Heyward found his uncle's room, Number 401, much more quickly than he wished. Outside the closed door, he breathed deeply a few times, softly knocked on the door, and entered a dimly lit room, which was much colder than he would have expected.

It took a few moments for his eyes to adjust to the low level of light, but the smell of the room hit him immediately, and he almost gagged. There was an unmistakable smell of illness about the room. After choking back a wave of nausea, Heyward made out the image of a small man standing by the window.

On the bed, he could see a face—he thought it was a face—but the features seemed all melted together. He couldn't recognize any shape on the bed that could be a body; the bed seemed flat, like it had just been made up. The only way he knew somewhere under the covers there had to be a human being was that there were clear tubes and wires snaking out to medical equipment and hanging bags of liquid, all coming up from the sheets. Those tubes had to go into someone. He recognized the chirp of a heart monitor and the steady, slow hissing of what must have been a respirator.

The small man came around the bed and whispered, "Mr. Jennings? Let's step outside for a moment." The man was older than Heyward, and he, too, was dressed in a business suit, the only difference being that he was wearing a sweater vest as well. The very first impression Heyward had of the man was that he appeared to be distinguished and polished. *Dignified,* he thought.

"Thank you for coming, Mr. Jennings. I'm Matthew Rabon. I know this is highly unusual, and I appreciate your cooperation," he said as they shook hands.

"Mr. Rabon, it appears that time is of the essence so I will be blunt: Just why am I here?"

"Indeed, Mr. Jennings, time is of the essence. I, too, will be blunt and to the point. Your uncle, Walter Jennings, and your father entered into a partnership to purchase some land here in Sheridan many years ago. This land had a stand of timber on it, and they were going to have the timber cut and eventually use those proceeds to help, to an extent, pay for the land. I am going to be very brief here, Mr. Jennings. Your father was in Georgia. Your uncle was here in Alabama and made the actual deal to buy the land and then the deal to cut the timber. The deal he made and the deal he told your father he made were far apart in reality. Your uncle cheated your father at every step of the way, and your father was forced to sell his portion of the land back to your uncle at a reduced rate. I assure you, Mr. Jennings, I was not any part of this process, and it was only much later that I met your uncle. Just recently, I learned that he cheated your father out of his portion of the land."

Heyward thought about how hard his father had worked over the years with so little to show for it. The thought that somebody—his own brother—had cheated him flooded him with anger.

He held his temper in check. "So? What's that got to do with me?"

"Your uncle wants your forgiveness, you being your father's proxy, in a manner of speaking. Walter Jennings wants to die with this settled. He wants to die with what he feels would be a clear conscience." Matthew Rabon continued, "If you offer your forgiveness, you must do it now, right now. There is no time to deliberate. I'm truly sorry to put you in this position."

Heyward breathed out deeply. *I hate to be put in this spot,* he thought to himself.

"All right, Mr. Rabon. My father was a good man and taught me to be a decent person in all things. Knowing him, I expect he would want me to grant his brother his dying wish."

Heyward put his hand on the door. "Let's get this over with."

Both men entered the room. This time, Heyward didn't notice the cold, any smells, or the sounds from the equipment. He walked directly to the bed, leaned over close to the face, and said, "I'm here, Uncle Walter. I'm Heyward Jennings. I'm your brother's son."

For several long seconds, there was no movement or acknowledgment from the face, and Heyward, relieved, thought he might have been too late. Then, with a sudden jerk, his dying uncle turned toward him and slowly opened then closed his mouth. No sound came from him.

Heyward became aware of a stench coming from somewhere, from deep in the dying body only inches away. It was all he could do to stand the smell.

"It's me, Uncle Walter. I'm Heyward Jennings, son of Robert Jennings, your brother. I forgive you, Uncle Walter. I forgive you. Your conscience can be clear now."

CHAPTER 10

▼

Heyward brushed past Matthew Rabon, found a men's room just off the corridor, went inside, and threw up. When he thought of the smell coming from inside his dying uncle, he threw up again.

It took a few minutes before he was able to wash his face, but he couldn't seem to shake the odor that had apparently followed him in. He waited a few seconds to make sure his queasiness had passed and, to steady himself, held on to the sink and focused on a single tile on the restroom floor. He felt that if he took his concentration from that tile, he was sure he would be nauseous once more, and Heyward Jennings did not like to vomit.

After standing there for at least five minutes, he felt his head clear, and he walked out into the hall and to the elevator. Heyward punched the down button three or four times in rapid succession, as if that somehow made the elevator come faster, and waited for the door to open. Heyward sensed Matthew Rabon standing behind him, but he didn't want to look at him or talk to him and he certainly didn't want to look in the direction of his uncle's room.

A few seconds later, the elevator came, and together, they rode in silence to the first-floor lobby.

Heyward strode through the lobby, past the cheerful lady sitting behind the information desk, and out into the night air. Matthew Rabon seemed to be right behind him, but as in the elevator, Heyward completely ignored him.

It was only after they had walked out from the hospital's portico that Heyward stopped. He towered over the attorney. "Look, Mr. Rabon, you seem like a nice man. But, you know, that was a bit much, don't you think? I mean, really, give me a break."

Mr. Rabon calmly replied, "The situations we find ourselves in can be difficult, especially when they are not of our own making. Still, I thought you handled that rather well, if you don't mind me saying so. I expect your uncle has already died just in the time it took us to walk out here, don't you?"

"I hope the son of a bitch is dead and reaping his rewards in hell right now."

Matthew Rabon put his hand on Heyward's shoulder. "He was an old man, Mr. Jennings. Old just like you and I will be one day, me sooner than you, I might add. We still have some unfinished business, the two of us. Can we chat a minute? Please?"

Heyward noticed a small, well-landscaped, ornamental lily pond with a couple of unoccupied benches. He didn't say anything, just pointed at a bench, and they walked over to it and sat down in the cool, evening air. The pond was lighted and threw off just enough light for the two men to see each other.

"You know, my father worked his whole life in a textile mill and my mother in a dime store. They were what you would call 'good people,' Mr. Rabon, 'good people.' I never heard either one of them complain about anything—and, believe me, they didn't have it easy. They just worked hard, paid their taxes, and raised their children, or children until my sister, Barbara, died. Now, I hear his brother, his own flesh and blood, cheated him. And I sent him off to eternity with a clean heart."

They sat in silence. Matthew Rabon let Heyward speak his mind without pressing or hurrying him.

After a while, Heyward continued, "My father and mother set good examples for me. I've tried to be a good man, you know, do what I felt they would expect of me."

"I did not know your parents, but I would have to assume they would be proud of what you did tonight. It was a great act of kindness, don't you think so, Mr. Jennings?"

Heyward ignored the question. "You said we had some unfinished business, I believe." Heyward snorted. "What else do you want me to do now? Pardon an ax murderer or worse yet, you want me to excuse a crooked politician?"

"Walter Jennings named you as his sole heir in his will. Your uncle ..." Matthew Rabon paused for a moment as if he were thinking how to phrase something. "Your uncle had some very expensive habits. There's really no point in delving into all of that now or any of his other behavior, unless you are particularly interested. The long and short of it is that you will probably inherit somewhere in the neighborhood of $415,000. And that, unless I'm mistaken, should be a non-taxable event."

"I'm sorry, Mr. Rabon, I'm not sure I heard you right." Heyward asked incredulously, "Did you say $415,000? Me? $415,000?"

"In the neighborhood of $415,000."

"Well, damn," Heyward said. He forgot, for the moment, about throwing up. "I'd say that was a pretty pleasant neighborhood, wouldn't you?"

"Pleasant, indeed." Matthew Rabon continued, "Everything will have to go through probate, of course, but I don't anticipate any significant problems. It will take a while for me to tie all the loose ends together so I caution you to be somewhat patient, please."

Heyward didn't ask him any questions about his uncle's life and avoided the subject of how Walter Jennings made his money. He certainly didn't ask anything about his expensive habits; there was really no point in it.

He did ask if Walter had any more relatives—he did not—and asked if any funeral arrangements had been made. Matthew Rabon said he would handle the burial according to his uncle's instructions, those things having been taken care of some time ago. Tactfully, the attorney let Heyward know that all of his professional fees had been satisfied at the time Walter Jennings had made his own funeral arrangements.

They stood and shook hands. "If you please, Mr. Rabon, don't call or contact me directly. When you need me, call this person at this number, and she will let me know. Then, I'll get back to you." He took out one of his bank's business cards and wrote Miss Emma Belavedo's name and telephone number on the card. "I don't plan on telling anyone about any inheritance for now, and I would appreciate it if you didn't either."

The attorney put on his reading glasses and looked at the card. "I keep everything I do in confidence, Mr. Jennings. Is this the woman I spoke to today at your office?"

Heyward nodded.

They shook hands again. Heyward headed to his Jeep, and Matthew Rabon walked back into the hospital.

CHAPTER 11

▼

For the next few days after his trip to Alabama, things began to settle down for Heyward. He still went to the bank every day, as usual, and he and Elliot Coleman began shifting responsibilities from one to the other. Heyward liked the younger man and wanted him to be successful; Elliot liked Heyward too and listened intently to his advice and respected his experience. Miss Emma was now fully on board working with her new boss and went out of her way to support him, although she did say to Heyward more than once, "He seems so young to me."

A week or so after he cancelled his appointments with Kevin Pasko in Materials Management and Doreen Shumar in Human Resources to make the emergency trip to forgive his dying uncle, Heyward finally caught up with them.

His meeting with Doreen was pleasant and productive. She knew Heyward was leaving the bank and in her efficient way, had all the information already put together that she thought he would want. Together, they went over all of the benefits he would be receiving in retirement, and she carefully reviewed each section of the FMSB Employee Separation Manual given to every departing employee, whether that departure was voluntary or not.

Despite himself, Heyward could not help himself from looking at Doreen's wedding ring and thinking of what Leon had told him about her. He looked around her office but didn't see any pictures of her husband—the one nobody at the bank had ever actually met—or any pictures of a family or friends or even a pet. There were no cute knickknacks that women employees sometimes decorated their offices with. Doreen's office was exactly as she was, professional and pleasant, but to the point.

Most of all, he was careful not to stare or even take a random glimpse at her big breasts and quickly averted his eyes any time he thought they may come into his line of sight. Heyward wanted to look but didn't. Leon, he thought, would be greatly disappointed in him, but he wasn't Leon and certainly didn't want to be like him.

Doreen ended their meeting with a handshake and smile and asked him to be sure to let her know the exact day he would be leaving the employment of FMSB, because she would have one or two additional forms for him to sign on that day.

His meeting later that day with Kevin Pasko was far from pleasant.

If any one person was universally disliked by the other employees, it was definitely Kevin Pasko. Kevin was responsible for purchasing the supplies for the entire bank and responsible for all of the bank's physical properties—the buildings, the landscaping, and the furniture in the buildings. His job was not easy, and it was his duty to keep costs in line and to secure the lowest cost service contracts to maintain those buildings.

There were essentially two traits for which Kevin was so disliked among his fellow associates at FMSB and a third thing that sometimes made him the butt of their jokes.

Kevin had a certain amount of authority delegated to his position, and he made sure that he used every bit of that authority to fulfill his job responsibilities, or at least those of his formal job description. There was no leeway, no flexibility—in reality, no common sense—in the way he interpreted any guideline regarding bank property. Over the years, many employees had had run-ins with him, mostly unnecessary confrontations over minor issues.

The other matter that, for some odd reason, irritated people was that Kevin would wear a long-sleeve, crew-neck sweater over his shirt and tie almost every day of the year. It didn't matter if it was winter or summer, Kevin would wear a sweater, and it seemed that the sweaters were limited to red, burgundy, or dark green colors. If he was not so unpleasant in the wielding of his limited authority, his sweater-wearing may have been characterized as an eccentricity instead of an irritant to everyone.

Despite all the gossiping about how annoying he could be, it was the picture of his wife, which he prominently displayed on his credenza that most bank employees associated with Kevin Pasko. The fact was his wife was fairly attractive and to most people, normal-looking. But the photograph, for whatever reason, caught her image the wrong way, and no matter from which direction a person viewed the picture, she looked like she had a growth of fine, dark brown hair all over her face. Leon Campbell put it best when he said it "makes her look like a fucking monkey."

Miss Emma had set an appointment for Heyward at 2:00, and he arrived at Kevin's office door exactly on time. Kevin was on the telephone and kept Heyward waiting about five minutes which Heyward simply chalked up as another little irritating power play from the materials manager.

"Come on in," Kevin finally said. "What can I do for you?"

"I guess you know I am leaving the bank, Kevin." Heyward looked at the man wearing a red sweater across from him. He waited a moment, receiving no visible sign that Kevin had heard him and continued, "I would like to buy my desk from the bank and take it with me when I leave. I assume it was fully depreciated years ago."

"Why do you want your desk?"

"Well, I've had that same desk for at least sixteen years. I got it when we remodeled the interior of the bank way back then. Actually, I inherited it from Horace Junior. He asked me if I wanted it when he changed his office around. I like the desk, and it means a lot to me, sentimentally, of course."

Kevin looked at Heyward as if he had lost his mind. "I don't know, Heyward. We've never had a request like this. I can tell you the bank probably won't allow that to happen because it's never been done before and it would set some type of precedent."

"Are you kidding me? The desk is at least sixteen years old. Who in the hell else would want it?" Heyward felt like he wasn't going to be able to control his rising anger.

"I told you, it sets a precedent. Can you imagine if we let you buy that desk how many people would want to buy bank property if they ever left the bank? I mean, we would have tellers wanting to buy their calculators or staplers or that sort of thing or janitors wanting to buy their favorite mops."

"I'm not a teller or janitor, you little prick," Heyward said, starting to shake with frustration.

"Look, Heyward, my answer is no, and I'm in charge of those things, but if you want to take this to Mr. Parker, we'll see what he says."

Heyward stood up and glared at the smirking Kevin Pasko.

"Be careful and don't do anything stupid, Heyward. I mean, I don't think you have your baseball bat with you, do you?"

Heyward stared at him, his frustration mounting by the second. Over Kevin's shoulder Heyward could make out the picture of the man's wife, and in an instant, without being conscious of it, his mind created an insult about the woman, something about her being a goddamn monkey and eating his banana. But Heyward was still Heyward, and he let the cheap shot pass.

He walked to the office door, turned, and looked at Kevin. "I'll tell you why I wanted to take that desk with me. It represents something to me that you wouldn't understand. Things that Mr. Parker Junior taught me—things like decency and honor and respect. Those are things you hardly see in people anymore, especially people like you."

Heyward walked out of the office, his face as red as the sweater Kevin Pasko was wearing that day.

*   *   *   *

Still stewing an hour after his meeting with Kevin Pasko, Heyward called Elizabeth.

"You know something, Elizabeth. I've decided to take a little time off before my last official day. I think I'm going up to visit my old cousin, Dewey Sikes."

Elizabeth looked at the phone receiver and could only say the first thing that came to her mind: "Uh-oh."

CHAPTER 12

▼

Dewey Sikes of Lost Springs, Georgia, could be the poster child for the expression "good old boy," although he would fight anybody, with or without knives, who called him a redneck. To Dewey, the term *redneck* was an insult and insinuated a lack of class and education; while it may be debatable if he had any class or not, he did have a high school diploma and nearly one year of technical school.

Heyward Jennings and Dewey Sikes were first cousins. Heyward's mother, Ruth, had been the younger sister of Dewey's father, Ned. Dewey was exactly one year younger to the day than Heyward and had an older brother, Louis, who was about two or three years older than his cousin.

While Heyward and Louis were close, Dewey was more like a brother to Heyward, although they were as different as night and day in almost every way. A person would imagine Heyward was a high-level corporate executive simply by looking at him. Tall, slender, his white hair clearly styled in some type of salon, he was polished and cultured in his appearance. Dewey, on the other hand, was short and round with what looked like baby fat in his face and stomach. He had his hair partially bleached and cut in the style of a mullet: short in front, long in the back. But the one thing strangers first noticed about Dewey was that he always seemed to be grinning or laughing or always be in a good humor.

As children and early teenagers, Dewey and Heyward spent most summers together at their grandmother's farm in Northern Georgia. Me-maw, as they called their Grandmother Sikes, was a typical country grandmother who cooked anything the boys wanted to eat, let them play all day long without any bother, and when they were about thirteen years old, let them drive the old blue Chevrolet pickup truck their deceased grandfather bought in 1954, or at least let them drive it on the many rural dirt roads that crisscrossed the hills of Springs County.

Louis would come to the farm too, when Heyward was there, but not quite as often as Dewey. Together, they all would have a picture-perfect summer in the country, sneaking cigarettes, lying about how far they went with their girlfriends, and shooting the .22 rifle their grandmother kept hung above the front door on two bent nails.

It was Louis who gave Heyward his nickname of Hick, just to make him feel good. Even in their early years, it was obvious to everyone that somehow, Heyward was different from his two cousins, even different from his maternal grandmother. Heyward, bad grades and all, knew that he would go to college and become some type of professional, although no one could quite understand, certainly not articulate, why that would be so. It just seemed to be an unspoken understanding among the family.

Louis and his younger brother somehow sensed their path in life would be more like their parents', that being more of a blue-collar world. Heyward was proud of his nickname, Hick, because even though everyone knew he was going to be different, it gave him a feeling of acceptance by his country cousins.

But while Heyward would become a prominent banker, and Louis would eventually own his own plumbing company, it was Dewey Sikes who would become very rich.

In his early twenties, it occurred to Dewey that he could accumulate wealth faster if he didn't have to pay taxes—those being federal, state, or local. And while everyone complained about those taxes, Dewey actually did something about it. His first venture in business was to buy a couple of beat-up mobile homes that were on their way to the scrap yard and rent them out to people who didn't necessarily want records kept of their whereabouts, legally speaking. He put those trailers on a remote area of his grandmother's farmland that couldn't be viewed from the highway and could only be accessed by a dirt road perpetually scored with deep ruts. A couple of trailers here and there grew into many trailers at different locations, all providing a *stream* of cash money that over the years, turned into a *river* of cash money, all virtually untraceable and therefore tax-free.

From time to time, a renter would tear up a trailer, and Dewey would have to threaten to bring in "John Law" unless he was somehow compensated for the damage, but Dewey would just as soon not bring legal authorities into the equation, mostly for his own benefit.

Every year around New Year's Day and Fourth of July, Dewey would open up illegal fireworks stands around the county, again, all cash transactions. He had come across some derelict horse trailers one day as he was negotiating the purchase of some old mobile homes and thought they would be perfect for his fireworks. They were old and worn out, but then, it would not really matter if there was an accidental explosion and any of them were destroyed in the blast.

While the sale of fireworks was against the law, Dewey was adamant his part-time employees issue a stern warning to children about the dangers of improperly handling rockets and firecrackers and even had a sheet printed with cautions and instructions to be given out with each unlawful purchase. Dewey once told one of his workers, "I just couldn't live with myself if some little child got hurt using my sparklers," although that particular employee couldn't understand what he said because the man was conversant only in Spanish. Of course, Dewey didn't pay employer taxes on that worker or sales taxes for any pyrotechnics sold.

Every stand flew an American flag on a makeshift flagpole and active military personnel received a fifty-percent discount on anything they purchased. Veterans received somewhat less of a discount, depending on which branch of service they had been in and if they served overseas or not; Dewey would determine the amount of discount from year to year, depending on what he perceived the state of the world at the time. "It's my way of saying 'thanks' to our men in uniform for keeping the American way of life strong," he would often say. Most times, when he remembered, he would add "our young ladies in uniform, too".

Dewey also had eight catfish farms. He would find some worthless scrubland that no one wanted to farm and negotiate a lease—always on a handshake, never in writing. If he could pay the owner in cash, he was willing to pay a higher amount; if the payment had to be paid by check, Dewey would find some credible reason not to lease that particular tract of land.

Some type of running water had to be available on the property. He would bring in huge bulldozers and have them dig ponds about four feet deep or so and fill them with water. With a little bit of aeration equipment and a lot of commercial catfish food and scraps from certain local restaurants, Dewey could raise catfish in that dirty water and sell them to a broker to be wholesaled all throughout the state of Georgia.

The labor was provided by undocumented immigrants who were paid in cash and all the catfish they cared to eat. Dewey was once invited to speak at an aqua-agriculture convention on his successful process of raising catfish, but he declined because he didn't want to catch the attention of certain legal authorities. His wife, Donna Sue, heard about the invitation and was upset that he turned them down because the convention was in Dallas, Texas, and she had never been to the Lone Star State or even Oklahoma, for that matter.

Of all the enterprises that Dewey Sikes was involved in, both lawful and questionable, nothing gave him greater pride or pleasure than his establishment, The Barkin' Bitch Bar and Grill. The name of the bar was a direct result of Dewey's continued aggravation with Donna Sue's pet dog, Barbie, a mean little Chihuahua, that one of Dewey's illegal workers had given her. The dog was jealous of Dewey and anytime Donna Sue showed her husband any attention, Barbie would bark and growl and flash her pointed little teeth at the man who weighed at least fifty times her weight.

If anyone wanted to catch up with Dewey, all they had to do was to go down to The Bitch, as most locals called it, and sooner or later, he would show up. Dewey himself was a teetotaler and looked down on anyone who did drink; he saw it as a character flaw. He always had new bartenders and waitresses thoroughly instructed on how to tell if a customer had had too much to drink, and they had strict orders not to serve alcohol to anyone who appeared to be getting too intoxicated to drive their pickup truck or motorcycle. Just as he was concerned with children being injured by his illegal fireworks, he was concerned that none of the bar's patrons be put in harm's way driving home and that no innocent motorist or pedestrian be injured on account of his bar. He wasn't too concerned with the legal responsibility he would face if an accident occurred, Dewey had plenty of layers of legal protection for that sort of annoyance, but he genuinely wanted everyone to be safe when leaving the bar.

Fistfights at the bar were another thing altogether. Dewey loved to see people fight in general, and nothing pleased him more than to see women brawl, particularly if it was over a man. If they pulled each other's hair or maybe one jerked a wig off and hit the other woman with it or even tore a blouse open, it was all the better. He had been known on an occasion or two to "accidentally" remark to one woman that he had seen her rival talking to her boyfriend in an overly friendly way, knowing that in a short while, there would be two women wrestling and clawing each other on the beer-soaked floor.

From time to time, there would be a knife fight between men, but the bar's bouncers would put an end to it before too much serious damage was done to one or the other fighter. It was remarkable to Dewey that people could be fistfighting one minute and then be drinking and laughing together the next minute. He simply chalked it up to human nature.

*　　　*　　　*　　　*

Heyward and Elizabeth would go to Lost Springs to the Sikeses' family reunion, normally held every July at the local state park. It was almost always unbearably hot and humid, and every year, it seemed that the attendance waned slightly as the older relatives died off.

But Heyward enjoyed seeing all of his mother's relatives—those few still alive—and the satisfying connection to his childhood, the summers he spent on his grandmother's farm with Dewey and Louis. Elizabeth was never very excited about going because she was, even after all these years, considered something of an outsider, she being from the state of Virginia. She had very little in common with the other reunion attendees, most of whom were country people, but she did enjoy hearing the family gossip about this relative or that family member, and she took some pleasure in hearing the differences in speech between the Sikes family and the world outside of Lost Springs, Georgia.

The Sikes called children *youngins*. They would *cut* a light off instead of *turn* a light off. They *mashed* a button instead of *pushing* it. A paper bag was called a *paper pocket*, and a fly swatter was known as a *fly flap*. She noticed that Dewey and Louis took the language difference to even another level when they spoke to each other.

And so, when Heyward told Elizabeth that he was going to take a few days to go see Dewey, she knew he was going to a place far different from the executive offices of First Mercantile Security Bank in downtown Atlanta.

CHAPTER 13

▼

The trip from Heyward's house in Atlanta to Lost Springs was just shy of three hours if a person wasn't in a particularly big hurry. Heyward put the Jeep's top down and edged out of town a little after lunchtime, taking the two-lane back roads that eventually wound their way towards the hills of Springs County. This part of Georgia was mainly rolling farmland with small country towns every twenty miles or so, spaced apart just enough for farm people to be able to make it to town every Saturday afternoon back in the old days. Heyward noticed there seemed to be a lot of small Baptist churches in this area of Georgia, most of them with the word *new* as part of their name: New Bethel, New Hope, New Ebenezer, New Zion. All of them had a small cemetery nearby, and most had some type of a covered picnic area for church homecomings or celebrations. Seeing the churches reminded him of the small Baptist church his grandmother had attended when he or Dewey or Louis could drive her after their grandfather's passing, their grandmother having never learned to drive.

On this spring day, more than a half century later, he could remember seeing her, his grandmother, sitting in the pew on the left side of the church, which was the women's side. Husbands and wives did not sit together in church; all women sat to the left of the center aisle, all the men on the right, and it embarrassed Heyward when he was a young boy that his grandmother insisted that he and his cousins sit by her and all her women friends and did not let them sit with the grown men.

The church wasn't air-conditioned in those years, and most of the congregation kept cool by fanning themselves with small paddle fans donated by the local funeral parlor—an advertisement on one side, a picture of Jesus praying on the other side. It puzzled him that the choir was made up of people from the congregation who did not wear any type of choir robe like they did in his own home church in Rawlins. At the beginning of the service, about fifteen people, usually old women, would leave their pew seats, go up into the choir loft, and sing the same songs as the congregation. When it was time for preaching, the choir would separate and go back to the seats they originally occupied in the pews. Heyward asked his grandmother why they did this, and she was never able to give him a good explanation because she too did not know why this was the way it was. It was the same way when she was a little girl.

The preacher, who usually farmed on the side, always scared little Heyward—and everyone else in the congregation, grown men included—with his sermons, talking about burning for eternity in Hellfire and the wily ways of Satan and that men who lusted after women were bound for damnation. As Heyward got a little older, he developed an inclination for tuning the preacher and all the warnings about Hellfire out and would look around the congregation for country girls about his age that he and his cousins would talk about the following week. When he got a little older, he grew interested in the possibility of hooking up with one of these girls in his grandfather's pickup truck; he decided he would worry about damnation later. But the hookups never happened, at least for Heyward and Dewey. Louis, being a little older and a lot bolder, did make it to the truck a time or two but never would tell them any of the details.

Thinking of his grandmother made Heyward incredibly sad although he could not understand why. The summers he spent with her on the farm were some of the best times of his life, and the pleasant memories stayed with him all through his adult years. Now, as he was facing retirement, he sensed that he was returning to a time that might be similar in some ways to his childhood: a general lack of concern for time or money, with no responsibility for almost anyone or anything.

I wonder what my grandmother would say about all the years I spent between then and now, he thought to himself. *Did I turn out to be the kind of person she would have been proud of, or would I have been a disappointment to her?*

As he drove along reminiscing about his visits to the country, Heyward thought about his mother and father and the way they sacrificed for him. Neither of his parents lived long enough to see his success in the business world, and he felt bitter disappointment that they died before his own children were born and never got to know them. He could never remember his parents ever voicing or showing any disappointment in him, but a sense of guilt overwhelmed him nonetheless as he drove along the highway, guilt that he had somehow never lived up to their expectations or the hopes they may have had for his deceased sister, Barbara.

By all accounts, he would be considered a success. He had a happy and long marriage. He had raised two normal and well-adjusted children, and he had supported his family in what would be considered an above-average lifestyle. His family never really wanted for anything. They loved him, and by and large, he had earned the respect of the people he worked with.

Why was he questioning himself? Was that normal for a man facing retirement? Was it his imagination, or did people at the bank not really seem all that interested he was leaving? Of course, there was a certain amount of the standard "We'll miss you" and the "Thanks for everything you did for me" but now it was all beginning to seem trite and not really heartfelt, like the bank employees were saying those things only because it was expected of them. When he refused Horace Parker's offer for a retirement party, it now seemed, as he drove along, that Horace didn't push the point or absolutely insist on it like Heyward would have done for his boss or any of his close associates. Even Miss Belavedo seemed in some way to be ignoring him now that she knew her position and continued employment was certain with Elliot Coleman.

Heyward was not expecting the bank employees to wear a black mourning band on their arms because he was leaving or put his portrait on the wall or anything like that, but it did seem to him there was very little sadness in the fact that he would no longer be gracing the halls of First Mercantile Security Bank any longer. At least, the bank should allow him to take his old desk with him, and even that wasn't going to happen. Now, as he was driving along Georgia Highway 393, he remembered that according to Parker III, he was not even supposed to be hired at the bank in the first place.

Just thinking about all of this made him feel somehow that something just wasn't right. Despite all logic, he felt like a failure.

*   *   *   *

Dewey Sikes was not the least bit surprised when his cousin walked into The Barkin' Bitch. After all he had seen in his bar, he wouldn't have been surprised if the Pope himself in all his flowing white robes and tall, pointed hat strolled in at any time and ordered a plate of spaghetti and a jar of moonshine liquor. What did startle him a bit was that Heyward, or Hick, was dressed in blue jeans and an old gray T-shirt.

"Well, God Almighty, looked what the durn cat drug in," Dewey said to no one in particular. "I didn't realize today was a bank holiday." He came over and warmly shook hands with Hick.

To anyone witnessing the two men greet each other, it was obvious they liked each other and genuinely so. After a while of catching up on family news, including Heyward's imminent retirement and pending move to the beach, the two walked out of the bar to look at Heyward's green Jeep Wrangler. The only comment Dewey made about Heyward's plans to quit was, "It's 'bout durn time."

Heyward showed his cousin around the car and demonstrated how easy it was to engage the four-wheel drive by simply shifting one lever. Dewey seemed impressed, particularly with the oversized tires. Heyward pulled out some accessories he'd bought for the car in Atlanta, those being sidesteps, a special grill for the front, and lights that were supposed to attach to the top of the Jeep somehow.

"I tried to put these steps on the car, but I scraped my knuckles a couple of times when the wrench slipped." Heyward held up his hand for inspection. "By the way, that hurts like hell. So I threw all this stuff in the car and brought it up here to you. Do you think your body shop could put all this on for me?" Heyward asked.

Dewey was slightly amused. One of the few legitimate businesses Dewey operated was Sikes's Body Shop, where he employed several men exceptionally competent in automobile body work and a few mechanics to do engine repair. The company was profitable and enjoyed a good reputation around the area, plus, Dewey could use it to clean money from some of his other off-the-record enterprises. For the most part, the body shop kept him in good standing in the Lost Springs community, but Dewey, just being Dewey, preferred to hang out at The Bitch and listen to the jukebox and, if he was lucky, catch a catfight between two crazy women.

"I expect they can handle all of this without too much trouble. You know, most kids that get these Jeeps put this kind of stuff on themselves," Dewey reminded Heyward.

Heyward, in the Jeep, followed Dewey over to the body shop. Dewey was driving a rusted-out Chevrolet pickup truck that seemed distantly familiar to Heyward.

"I guess you recognize this old thing, Hick. It was Granddaddy's 1954 pickup, the one we used to drive all over those dirt roads when we was growing up. I'm going to fix it up myself. I just kind of wish I had a kid of my own to pass it on to." Dewey and Donna Sue never had children, if you didn't consider her Chihuahua, Barbie, a child. Dewey didn't consider himself to be the "father-type" and, in the back of his mind, thought he would probably be doing some serious jail time at some point in his life. He felt that a stretch of incarceration wouldn't exactly make him a responsible father.

Heyward looked in the truck and at Dewey's urging, got in the driver's seat.

"This steering wheel is a lot smaller than it was fifty years ago. My right foot can actually reach the foot-feed without me leaning forward." Heyward referred to the gas pedal as a foot-feed in deference to the local way of speaking. "Maybe we ought to go down to Me-maw's church and see if we can get any of those girls to come out and sit in the truck with us."

"Hick, most of them girls we made eyes at are all using walkers by now. If they ain't using walkers, they got them big, old, ugly sunglasses for their cataracts. Besides, if they still go to church, I wouldn't care a whit about them anyways."

While Heyward sat in the truck and reminisced, Dewey walked into the body shop and gave two of the mechanics instructions about the placement of the Jeep's accessories. He took one of the mechanics to a closet in the back of the shop and retrieved a long box that he had been saving for some time. Dewey talked a while to the mechanic, both of them grinned, and he came back outside to the old pickup truck.

"Okay, Hick, let's get going. You drive. Let's go out to the old farm."

CHAPTER 14

▼

There was really not much left standing at their grandparents' old farm place. The dirt road running by the original site of the house was about washed out, and weeds and a few saplings had taken root here and there. It had been a long time since the county sent any graders to scrape the road smooth; the post office no longer sent a rural mail carrier down that way.

The two cousins walked around the fallen ruins of what was at one time, the house, a barn and, farther out, a smokehouse. They could make out the corner foundations and recognize the general layout of what were once the floors and walls. Now, pine trees and dogwoods grew in the spots where their grandmother cooked and sewed and said her evening prayers.

"Everything looks a lot smaller now than it did when we were kids, doesn't it?" Heyward asked.

"Either things got a lot smaller or we got a lot bigger," Dewey replied. "It always makes me a little sad to come out here. Sometimes, now, on a summer night, I swear I can hear Me-Maw singing church songs to herself like she used to do."

"Do you still own this land, Dewey?"

"Yeah, Hick, I do, but I won't never do anything with it. Won't never put no trailers on it or never sell it. I'll leave it just as you see it now until the day I die, I guess."

They walked around quietly, pausing occasionally at different points to remember some of the different things that happened summers a long time ago.

"Do you remember the time that old mule got out of the pasture and came up here and poked his head through the window that night? We thought it was some kind of ghost or man from outer space coming to get us," Heyward asked. They both laughed.

The sun was getting lower on the horizon, and Dewey looked at his watch.

"Hick, we got to go. I'm supposed to meet Louis at the airfield here directly. You drive, if you will," Dewey said.

"Do you all still fly? I almost forgot about that."

Seven or eight years ago, Dewey won an old, worn-out single-engine Cessna airplane from J. T. Gooch in a poker game that was held on Friday nights in the back room of The Barkin' Bitch Bar. Dewey didn't fly at the time, never considered owning any plane himself, and really had no use for one, particularly one that didn't have at least a spare engine—kind of like a spare tire—in case the main one sputtered out, he said.

Nonetheless, he let J. T. Gooch throw the title to the Cessna in the pot when he ran out of cash, and Dewey won the hand, and the plane, fair and square.

Since the ownership of an airplane was now in the family, both Louis and Dewey decided to take flying lessons, and each earned his pilot's license. As it turned out, both brothers couldn't fly in the little plane at the same time because their combined body weights far exceeded the plane's load certification.

Louis, in particular, became a very skilled and proficient pilot by anyone's measure; Dewey slightly less expert than his brother. Eventually, Dewey traded the Cessna won from J. T. Gooch, and he and Louis went in together and bought a larger, twin-engine plane in which they could fly together and flew it all around the Southeast. Even so, neither of their wives would travel with them, despite the fact that Dewey offered to get them both some tranquilizers from some of his special sources.

The county airstrip was a ragtag affair consisting of a patched-up runway, a few corrugated hangers, and a wind direction sock that, at that time of the early evening, hung limp and lifeless. The farmland which surrounded the airport was relatively flat, by northeast Georgia standards, and the few crops grown there were mostly corn and a few pitiful acres of soybeans.

About a mile from the airport, Heyward spotted a small speck coming up the road at them, five or six feet above the blacktop, and directly in front of their pickup truck. In less than an instant, the speck morphed into the front profile of a twin-engine airplane; the spinning propellers on each side of the plane were clearly distinguishable in the dim evening light.

Heyward jerked the pickup to the side of the road, turned on the headlights, and began blinking the high beams off and on. Panicked, he furiously blew the horn, but even in his fright, he felt foolish for doing so; he knew the pilot couldn't possibly hear the horn over the plane's two gunning engines.

Only at the last possible instant, the plane lifted over the cab of the truck, which shook back and forth from the vibration of the plane's engines. Heyward realized he had clinched his teeth so hard his jaw ached, and he became aware that his forearms were beginning to cramp from holding on so tightly to the steering wheel. For a moment, Heyward thought he'd wet his pants, just a little.

A few seconds ticked by, and there was no sound of an explosion that Heyward expected from a crashing airplane; the only sound in his ears was a loud ringing as if one of his eardrums may have erupted. The very corner of his left eye caught a movement.

Turning his head, he saw the plane climb, twisting, and in a few seconds, it dove down less than ten feet above the ground and crossed the road, left to right, just in front of the stopped truck, and then it disappeared from his field of view.

"Holy shit, that was close!" Dewey screamed. "That sorry son of a bitch is going to kill me yet."

Heyward was shaking. "What was that, Dewey? What was that?" It was all Heyward could gather himself to say.

"That's my asshole brother. He doesn't have the sense God gave a green apple," Dewey said. "You know something, Hick? I think I peed in my pants."

Heyward was able, just barely, to limp his grandfather's truck up to the old building that served as a hanger.

Louis climbed out the pilot's side door as the pickup pulled to a stop. "I thought that was you, Hick. I couldn't tell for sure 'cause you looked like you was screaming pretty good when I went over y'all."

Heyward shook Louis's hand, but he didn't have much strength left in his arm from gripping the steering wheel so hard and he gave his cousin a limp handshake. Dewey acted upset.

"Thanks a lot, Louis. You ain't never got that close before," Dewey said.

"That close before? I did done it," Louis replied.

"You ain't done it."

"I did. I did done it."

"You ain't. You ain't done it."

Heyward managed a half smile. "Good to see things haven't changed since last time I was here." He liked the way his cousins sometimes fussed. "Nice plane."

Dewey answered, glaring a little at his older brother, "Louis and I bought this one a while back. As you can see, it's a twin-engine and can carry six people. We use it to fly all over the place, and we're thinking about taking a trip out to Vegas as soon as we can get the wives to fly with us."

Then he added, still glaring at his brother, "Of course, it's not supposed to be used for aerobatics."

Louis looked back at him. "It is. It is done it."

CHAPTER 15

Donna Sue Sikes, Dewey's wife, cooked them all a big, old-fashioned country dinner. Donna Sue was always glad to see Heyward and treated him like some type of minor celebrity, their "big-city banker relative," she would call him from time to time. But while Donna Sue rolled out the royal treatment, her little pet Chihuahua dog, Barbie, actually nipped Heyward on the ankle and broke the skin just to remind him that he was only a visitor and that Donna Sue belonged entirely to her.

After supper, they all debated about going down to The Barkin' Bitch Bar for a while but opted out to rest on the front porch and rock "a spell" on their custom rocking chairs. Dewey had the chairs specially made by a man down in Mississippi who built wooden furniture to order; they seemed to accommodate his large size. Normally, if Heyward wasn't visiting, Dewey would be at the bar this particular night.

It was the third Wednesday of the month, and Dewey, being the world's biggest fan of Jerry Lee Lewis, had declared a year or so ago that every third Wednesday night would be considered "In Honor of Jerry Lee Lewis Night." As the sole owner of The Barkin' Bitch, he proclaimed that on that special night each month, only Jerry Lee Lewis records would be played on the jukebox, no other singer or band—only Jerry Lee Lewis records all night, period.

Sometimes, this created a little conflict with the occasional visitor but most regular customers knew of Dewey's fascination with the rock and roller from Louisiana and accepted it for what it was.

Dewey liked to try different ideas and promotions at The Bitch, just to keep everybody interested in coming back to drink and spend money. At various times—mainly whenever the mood struck him—Dewey sponsored different contests like Sexiest Grandma Night or Best Legs in Springs County Night or Most Hairspray and Makeup Night, but he drew the line on karaoke. "We don't get a lot of those damn Japs in here anyway," he once explained to Donna Sue.

One time and only one time was there any real trouble in the bar as a result of the contest nights. Some good old boy from the next county over put forward to Dewey that he should promote a Best Elvis Impersonator Night and that he, the good old boy himself, would be a contestant and most likely win. But when the man ventured that Elvis was actually a bigger star than Jerry Lee, Dewey set about fighting with him and sent the man home with a broken nose. Around Dewey, it was wise not to say anything disparaging about the United States of America or about his favorite singer. No one ever brought up the irony that as patriotic as Dewey Sikes was, he never paid any taxes.

On this night, however, Dewey was perfectly content to stay at home with his visiting cousin. Louis's wife, Sadie, stopped by, and all five sat on the front porch and talked until late in the evening. No one was much interested that Heyward was retiring, but they were fascinated that he and Elizabeth were moving to the beach. The Lost Springs relatives loved the beach, and one week every summer, they would drive either to Daytona Beach or Panama Beach and more often than not come back seriously sunburned. They always had to travel down by car since the two women wouldn't fly with their husbands, even though it would have been a short hop in their plane.

Sometime around ten, Dewey's telephone rang. He excused himself to take the call, talked a minute, and came back out on the porch. "No problem, they just had a question down at the bar," he said to no one in particular.

"Hey, Dewey, let me ask you something," Heyward said. "How can you call your place The Barkin' Bitch Bar? Don't the local authorities have some type of problem with the name? I mean, I'd have thought by now, they'd have made you change it."

"Sure, the town has a problem with the name," Dewey told him. "But the fact is, *bitch* is a real word. It's even in the dictionary. Anyone can look it up if they're smart enough to know how to spell it. Plus, my regulars seem to like it okay."

Donna Sue jumped into the conversation. "Heyward, I wish you could make him change his mind. It embarrasses me." Donna Sue never called him by his nickname, Hick.

"Oh, I've had everybody in the world try to make me change it, but they can't. There've been all types of petitions brought to me and politicians wanting to create some kind of laws about it. Never works."

Dewey continued, "The worst people are those Bible thumpers and those sorry hypocrites I call 'Country-Club Christians.' They're the ones who come around in their big, fancy cars trying to save my soul and then go back to gossipin' and being mean to each other and cheatin' poor people. If they meet me on the street, they just turn their noses up at me and act like they didn't see me at all, you know. I don't fit in with their high-society types. Damn hypocrites."

Then he added, "Some of those religious people are good, though, real good people. It's just those high and mighty women who claim they're so religious and then look down at regular folks that are shameful to me." After a few seconds, he muttered, "Two-faced bitches."

Everybody laughed.

Dewey continued as if he was defending himself, "No kidding. I'm a-telling you. When somebody starts bragging about what a big Christian they are, you'd better lock up your pocketbook real quick-like."

The next morning, Heyward woke up to the smell of bacon frying. He got dressed and came down to the kitchen where Donna Sue poured him a cup of coffee and cooked him eggs, bacon, grits, and homemade biscuits. As she worked at the stove, she told him that Dewey had gone to see how the body shop was coming along with adding the accessories to his Jeep and would be back after while. Finally, she sat down across from him with her coffee.

"Heyward, I want you to know something about Dewey you may not know. I'm going to tell you something, and you have to promise never to let on that I told you."

"All right. I'll keep it between you and me, promise."

"Last night, Dewey said some kind of ugly things about church people. Don't pay him any mind about that. Dewey has his faults, Lord knows, but he has a real good heart." She shifted in her chair and took a sip of coffee. "What you don't know is that he is very generous with his money. Did you know he has paid the cost for a lot of underprivileged kids, both black and white, to go to college? A lot of kids. Paid all their expenses. And he did so without telling a soul."

That was news to Heyward. "Really? I didn't know that. I knew deep down he was a good guy, but I didn't know he did that."

"Well, Heyward, that's not all he does," Donna Sue continued. "That airplane of his and Louis's, they fly little sick kids to special hospitals and fly their families back and forth. Never charged anybody one red cent, ever. Never takes credit for it. That's what Louis was doing yesterday, flying a sick child and his parents up to a hospital in Tennessee."

Heyward didn't know what to say.

"Dewey pays for a summer camp for sick kids with cancer to go to up here in the hills. He don't tell anybody he does that. All the money goes through his lawyer, and the lawyer gives it to the camp. Most of them kids have it real bad, but they all feel better when they go there."

They heard the Jeep coming up the driveway. Donna Sue added, "Please, Heyward, don't say anything to Dewey about what I told you. Don't tell Elizabeth either. I just thought it was important for you to know all that."

CHAPTER 16

▼

"Okay, Hick, your Jeep's all fixed up now. You can take her on to the beach."
Dewey beamed. He got a cup of coffee for himself and Louis who had followed
him into the kitchen.

"I think the boys did a real good job on it," Louis added.

The three men walked outside to look at the handiwork of Sikes's Body
Shop's mechanics. Donna Sue came out to look too, holding the little chihuahua
close to her chest. Heyward thought the car looked sharp; with the addition of
the special grill, the sideboards, and the lights added to the roll bar, it looked
almost custom-made.

Dewey showed Heyward where they added switches for the lights and placed a
few speakers just behind the driver's seat so he could hear the radio better, especially if he had the canvas top down.

"All right, let's take her out for a test drive," Dewey said. "I told old Parson
Gibbons we would stop by and give him a ride into town. Hick, you can drop all
of us off at the same time, if you will."

Heyward was going back to Atlanta after his Jeep was ready, so he thanked
Donna Sue for her hospitality and told her that he looked forward to all of them
coming to stay at the beach for a week, if they could. Donna Sue hugged Heyward good-bye, but when he tried to pet Barbie—a gesture of conciliation—the
mean little dog nipped at his hand, and he barely jerked it back before blood was
drawn.

The canvas top was already down, and the sun was shining brightly on them.
Dewey told Heyward how to get to Parson Gibbons's house which, being a little
further out in the country, meant they had to take a narrow country road. Every

so often, they would pass a farmer out in his field or driving his tractor, and it seemed to Heyward that Dewey and Louis must have known just about everyone they saw.

After several miles, Dewey, in the front passenger seat, spotted a man carrying two grocery bags walking along the side of the road and told Heyward to slow down a little as they came up behind him. Out of the corner of his eye, Heyward saw Louis tap Dewey on the shoulder, and as they drew abreast of the walker, Dewey leaned forward and pressed a button in the glove box.

The right side of the Jeep exploded in sound, almost as loud as when the plane buzzed over them the day before. The man, a young Hispanic, jolted away from the blast and stumbled down a steep drainage ditch. Heyward was so startled he stopped the Jeep.

"Get on out of here, Hick! Get out of here!" Louis yelled from the back seat. "That Mexican'll want to stick a switchblade in us if he can climb out that trench."

Heyward pulled a couple hundred yards down the road then slowed down but didn't stop and looked back. He didn't want to be stuck with a knife, but he didn't want the man to drown either. Dewey and Louis were laughing so hard they could hardly catch their breath and eventually, Louis had to fish his asthma inhaler out from his pocket and give himself a few puffs of spray.

The man climbed out of the ditch and with both hands, gave them the finger.

"Listen, Hick, I had the boys put on a little accessory that might not be considered entirely legal in all fifty states. We took off an air horn from a wrecked Mack truck and bolted it to the bottom of your Jeep. It's rigged up so you can blast somebody by just pushing this button here in the glove box."

Dewey opened the compartment and put his finger on the button. "They hid that horn real good, so I don't think you have to worry about any cops seeing it, unless'n you decide to blow it in downtown Atlanta."

"You ought to have a lot of fun with that, Hick," Louis added.

For the rest of the trip to Parson Gibbons's house, Heyward kept looking in the rearview mirror, nervously expecting a car full of Mexicans with knives to be coming after them or maybe a county deputy running them down with his lights flashing.

"Okay, okay, slow down, Parson's house is down this dirt road." Dewey pointed to a turn.

Parson Gibbons lived in a dilapidated mobile home in the middle of nowhere. A small, wiry man, well over seventy, pushed the front door open then closed it only after he kicked the bottom part a few times. Heyward couldn't help but notice the man's front teeth were grimy, he needed a shave, and from the way he smelled, he could use a good bath.

Dewey got out and moved to the back seat next to Louis. Parson stuck his hand out to Heyward, and as he was introducing himself, Heyward wondered how long it would be before he could wash his hands with some type of disinfectant soap. Heyward felt that Parson Gibbons had to have some type of communicable disease. They pulled back onto the road and headed back towards town, going a different way so they could avoid the angry Mexican should he still be walking in their direction.

Feeling a little embarrassed about how quickly he judged the man, Heyward thought he ought to make an effort for some small talk.

"So, Parson, are you the pastor of some church around here?" Heyward asked.

Parson Gibbons turned to his left and looked back at Dewey and Louis. The men in the back started laughing again; it was as if Christopher Columbus himself had just announced to them the world was indeed flat and he was sailing back to Spain.

"I ain't no preacher, never have been, never will be," Parson said, disgusted. "My daddy just named me Parson because he wanted me to grow up religious and be a preacher man, that's all."

"Well then, Parson, what would he've named you if he wanted you to be a fornicator?" Louis asked.

They rode along in silence pondering Louis's question when Dewey tapped Heyward on the shoulder and said, "Pull over a minute, Hick. I hear some kind of noise coming out from under the car. I think you might have picked up a branch off a tree or a stick or something."

Heyward hadn't heard anything, but he pulled the car to the side of the road and stopped.

"Parson," Dewey said, "jump out and look under the car. There must be a branch caught up under your seat."

As Parson got out of the Jeep, Louis leaned forward and opened the glove box.

Grinning at Heyward and Dewey, he said, "Hold your ears, boys. This is going to be real good."

CHAPTER 17

▼

Heyward felt relieved when he got back on the highway to Atlanta later that afternoon. Between being almost killed by Louis in his crazy airplane stunt and making a Mexican mad enough to knife him, he had had enough excitement in the last twenty-four hours to last him a while. Added to that, he felt really bad about them scaring Parson Gibbons with the air horn.

Parson had taken the trick with a good attitude even though the surprise blast of sound literally knocked him to the ground. He simply got back up, dusted himself off, and smiled. He spent the rest of the trip into town smiling, but he didn't say anything to anyone and didn't respond in any way to any questions the three of them asked him; they all figured he just couldn't hear anything for the time being. Oddly, Heyward thought Parson Gibbons wasn't offended or angry at their practical joke; he just took it for what is was.

Some time after they let Parson out on the town square, Heyward commented that maybe they should have taken the man to a doctor to have his ears checked for possible damage.

"Hick, let it go. It was a joke, that's all. Quit worrying about it. Not everything you do has to be levelheaded or make sense," Dewey said.

Louis added, "What's he going to do, try to kill me? Have at it, if he wants to try."

Heyward knew his cousins were, for the most part, right. He was well aware of his tendency to worry about the consequences of every action, just look at how he agonized over bashing Henry Pyatt's computer and threatening Robert Fortson. Even Leon had pointed it out. Still, it was hard to make a major personality adjustment, especially after living a lifetime of caution. Maybe, just maybe, walking away from that new gray Buick was a good start.

Elizabeth called and interrupted his thoughts. Janie Butterfield, the little fireplug real estate agent, had gotten an offer on their Atlanta house and for the amount they wanted. It was another good start.

When he got out in the countryside and no other cars or trucks were around him, Heyward reached into the glove box and pushed the air horn button. The horn blared. No Mexicans with knives and no Parson Gibbons came to kill him. Satisfied, he blew the horn three more times.

After a while, he called Miss Emma Belavedo.

"Miss Emma, this is Heyward."

"Hello, Heyward. Can you hold on a minute, please?" She put him on hold and left him there for what seemed an eternity to him but in actuality was about forty-five seconds. When she came back on the phone, it seemed to him that she had her mind on something else and he was simply a distraction to her.

"I'll be in the office tomorrow morning. Tomorrow will be my last day, and then I'll be through. How about letting Doreen Shumar know to get my final papers together to sign?"

"All right. Well, we'll see you tomorrow then," was all Miss Emma had to say.

"Wait, a minute, Miss Emma. Has a Mr. Matthew Rabon called me, by any chance? Does anybody at the bank need me for anything?"

No, he had not received a call from a Mr. Rabon, and no, no one at the bank needed him.

Miss Emma Belavedo, his secretary for over fifteen years, a woman he had looked after and protected, a woman whom he counseled to reconcile with her sister, couldn't wait to get off the phone with him. Heyward felt like an old shoe that had lived its useful life up and was no longer needed by anybody. It irritated him to the point he said, "Fuck you," out loud and to no one in particular. He rode the rest of the way home in silence, except for a short laugh when he thought about the Mexican giving him the bird.

*   *   *   *

Later that evening, Heyward took a piece of masking tape and wrote the words, "Do Not Push" on it and placed it over the button that triggered the air horn. He knew it was just a matter of time before some hardhead pushed it just to see what would happen, even with the tape on it.

*   *   *   *

On the last official day of his working life, Heyward woke just as he had for the last thirty-plus years and walked his four miles just as he had done most of his adult life. With no particular excitement, he drove the same route to his office as he had for many years, but for the first time, the traffic didn't really bother him.

When he got to the bank, he loaded the few remaining personal items from his office into the Jeep, sat at his desk one more time, and rubbed the top in appreciation of their time spent together. It reminded him of an old Western movie where a cowboy patted his faithful horse as they parted forever, and it made him very, very sad.

There was a pleasant but low-key going-away party for him in the Executive Conference Room where more than a few people teared up. Miss Emma finally realized Heyward was really leaving for good and cried like a baby. Everyone gave him a small present of some kind and then together presented him with a rod and reel specifically made for surf fishing. Horace Parker III gave a little speech and then excused himself saying he had a plane to catch. After Horace left, Henry Pyatt presented Heyward with a wrapped box, and everyone laughed when Heyward opened it to reveal the baseball bat that he had used to destroy Henry's computer. Everyone had written a short message on it and signed their names. Horace did not sign it or write a message, but Heyward did see a small "HPIII" initialed on the end of the bat.

Then, it was over. Everyone went back to their desks, each waiting for their own time to retire, be it one more year or twenty-five.

Leon helped Heyward take all of the presents to his Jeep and then, as if he didn't want him to leave, asked him to come up to his office, one last time, and have a drink of liquor just for old times' sake.

He pulled a bottle from his bottom desk drawer and poured each of them a good, stiff drink. The two old friends sat in silence for a long time, every now and then mentioning some person's name or a one-sentence remembrance of some event, at which the other smiled and nodded.

After twenty awkward minutes, there was a knock on Leon's office door, and Doreen Shumar walked in with an ink pen and a couple of personnel forms for Heyward to sign.

"I'm glad I caught you before you got away," she said. "Would you mind signing these two forms? Then you'll be officially retired."

Heyward took the forms and pen from Doreen, leaned forward from his chair to the desk, and signed his name where she, standing by him, indicated with her index finger.

On his last signature, she gathered the forms and looked down at him. She was still standing and, being somewhat on the tall side, towered over him as he sat in his chair.

"Heyward, I have a little going-away present for you and for you only," and with that, Doreen Shumar lifted her blouse and bra to expose two huge breasts. Before Heyward—or Leon—could react, Doreen put her hands on each side of his head and rubbed her large breasts on and around his astonished face and all through his white hair.

When she had rubbed him all she wanted, which couldn't have been more than five seconds, she removed her hands from his head, stepped back, and put her clothes back in place.

"I've been wanting to do that for at least five years," she said, looking at him. "Happy retirement."

Heyward was too startled to speak or move; he just sat there and looked at her. Leon stared at Doreen, not quite sure if he understood what he had just seen.

Doreen picked up her pen, gathered the two signed forms, walked over to the closed office door, and put her hand on the doorknob. Then she turned and looked at the two men.

"Close your mouth, Leon. You look like you never saw a pair of boobs before," she said as she opened the door.

Leon, with absolutely none of his normal bravado, could only squeak, "Those aren't a pair of boobs, lady, that's a set of titties!"

Book Two:
Wexler Island

CHAPTER 18

▼

Thaddeus Wexler was an unusually wild sailor, even by the brutish standards of his fellow crewmates. The ship on which he served, known for a brief time as *The Flying Cloud*, was a small but successful pirate ship that sailed the waters off the coast of what would later become the colonial states of Virginia and North and South Carolina. It would be Wexler's name that would be remembered by future generations while the name of the ship and that of the captain would quickly pass from history's memory.

In fact, the name of the ship was often changed due to the superstitious nature of captain and crew. They thought it was possible for spirits and ghosts to inhabit a ship and by repeatedly changing the name, they felt bad and evil spirits would be confused and go elsewhere to a ship more easily identified by a permanent name. For the most part, good spirits seemed to find this ship, whatever the name, without difficulty because their opportunity to capture and loot merchant ships in the years before the American Revolution was considerable.

The crew of this pirate ship was made up of violent men, and they were never known to show mercy to any of their unfortunate victims or to each other, for that matter. And so, one day when Thaddeus Wexler began to show some unexplainable behavior patterns, the ship's captain and crew became bothered with him.

At particular moments—and no one could predict them—he would begin hissing and screeching like a wildcat. He would arch his back and extend his arms, and with his fingers bent like claws, he would cling onto the ship's rigging. He would grasp onto the ropes and shriek at the top of his lungs until his fellow crewmembers beat him into unconsciousness using sticks and the butts of their pistols to end his fit. Most times, a few of the crew would give him some extra thumps, just for good measure. When he awoke from his trance and beatings, he would exhibit rather normal behavior, as normal was known in the world of his companions.

After four or five occurrences of his cat-like behavior, it was decided by the captain that Thaddeus Wexler must be possessed by some type of evil spirits and would have to be killed or exiled from the ship. In reality, it was not evil spirits that caused his fits; more than likely, it was the result of some contaminated liquor he drank or possibly the result of a serious venereal disease picked up in the West Indies during a previous voyage. After a long discussion between the captain and crew, it was decided to cast him off the ship to isolation on an island where he could live or die as cat or man.

On a bright spring morning, Thaddeus Wexler was put ashore on a small, uninhabited barrier island on the coast of what would later become South Carolina with two goats, a few bottles of rum, and, of all things, a small handbell taken from a looted ship.

A historical account of the event was never recorded in written form, and the eventual fate of Thaddeus Wexler remains unknown, but the small barrier island became accepted to all mariners as Wexler Island, and eventually future maps would identify it as such. For the next several centuries, the island remained pretty much as it had been on that day with the exception that, at any given time, several dozen wild goats could be found roaming the woods and sand dunes.

*   *   *   *

Some three hundred years after Thaddeus Wexler was put ashore on the island that would eventually be named after him, Heyward and Elizabeth left Atlanta for good and, like Thaddeus Wexler, became full-time residents of the island.

All in all, the move was easy. They already had a house, and it was in one of the best sections of the island in The Three Oaks development. Over the last ten years, Elizabeth had taken great pains to furnish and decorate it in a style that was upscale but with a distinct sea motif.

Since their resident status changed from part-time vacationers to full-time residents, The Three Oaks Welcoming Committee felt it necessary that they formally welcome the Jennings to their little slice of the coast.

Elizabeth liked the group. Heyward thought they were nice enough too, just different somehow from them. He'd lived in the South all of his life and spent most of his time there. His only extended period away was during his stretch in the coast guard. Like most executives, his job did require him to occasionally travel to different areas of the country, but those trips were almost always by plane, and while he enjoyed traveling for the most part, he was always glad when he came home.

Most of the people on the welcoming committee had not lived on the island more than three years, and most of them were from "up North." Heyward recognized some minor cultural differences in speech and customs but was not particularly disturbed by them. One older man, a Mr. Wilenski, pulled him aside from the others and explained that he and his wife had moved from Pennsylvania, and he was glad to meet a real Southerner and to find out he was as normal as himself. Mr. Wilenski confided that he thought the South still put criminals in chain gangs and that he had expected to see Confederate flags flying from every pickup truck on the highway.

Then and there, Heyward made a mental note never to introduce his cousins to the man, should Dewey and Louis ever take the notion to leave the hills of northern Georgia for a visit. But if elderly people from Pennsylvania liked Jerry Lee Lewis, if only in a small way, there might be a slim possibility that they'd all get along with Dewey, at least for a while.

CHAPTER 19

▼

In less than two months after the move, Heyward and Peaches had established such a custom of walking on the beach that if they hadn't gone by a certain time of the late afternoon, Heyward claimed Peaches would begin to sulk. The little dog seemed to keep her own timetable; if Heyward hadn't pulled the Jeep out of the garage for the short ride to the beach by the prescribed hour, she would simply go to the door, lie down, and begin whimpering.

"I swear," Heyward said once to Elizabeth, "she's acting like I forgot her birthday or something like that."

There was always something interesting to see on the beach. Peaches liked to watch the seagulls and sniff at all the smells; Heyward liked the open space and the way the breeze felt coming off the ocean.

But of all the things that Peaches enjoyed, she was most partial to the attention that children—and adults—gave her. It was rare that any child playing on the sand would not come over to her and pat her head or rub her back. Peaches, with her calm demeanor, was particularly good with shy children and seemed to sense and understand their caution.

Most people would first ask what her name was, then most, having never seen a dog quite like her, would question what breed she was. Every now and then, someone, with no intention of purposely hurting her feelings, would say they had never seen a dog as homely as Peaches. Heyward would immediately speak up for her, much like a father who defends the esteem of a daughter too plain to be asked to her senior prom.

She was also good when she chanced on other dogs walking on the beach; like them, most dogs and owners had their own rituals and routines to their walks.

After a while, Peaches could recognize certain dogs from a far distance and Heyward got to know the owners by sight. He could never remember their names, but he could recall, without any hesitation, the names of their dogs—Nellie, Katie, Bo, Sammy, Rufus, Lulu, Willy, Sheck, Roscoe, Carmen, Manfred, Pebbles, and Wendy.

Of all the dogs on all the beaches on Wexler Island, Peaches was the smartest, the most well-behaved, had the best personality, and was the sweetest, at least in the eyes of Heyward.

*   *   *   *

Over the span of many years, the Town of Wexler Island's town council had created special ordinances as guidelines to what they felt was appropriate behavior for anyone using the island's beaches.

The town council had metal signs made, which the town's maintenance department posted at every beach access point. If you went to the beach, it was a certainty that you would walk right by one of those metal signs, although in reality, very few people even noticed, much less read, any of them.

NO OVERNIGHT CAMPING ON BEACH
DO NOT LEAVE CHAIRS, UMBRELLAS, ETC. ON THE BEACH OVER-
NIGHT
NO CONSUMPTION OF ALCHOLIC BEVERAGES ALLOWED ON
BEACH
DOGS MUST BE ON A LEASH EXCEPT BETWEEN THE HOURS OF
6:00 AM TO 8:00 AM AND 7:00 PM TO DUSK
NO FIREWORKS PERMITTED AT ANY TIME

By Order of the Town of Wexler Island

Every summer, some teenager would scratch in at the bottom of the sign that topless and nude sunbathing were permitted, but anyone caught urinating in the ocean would be subject to a one-hundred-dollar fine. By the end of summer, almost every sign would be gone. By late September, they would be tacked on the walls of college dormitories along the Eastern Seaboard.

Almost no one paid the slightest attention to the ordinance pertaining to the consumption of alcoholic beverages, even the strictest Baptist. On vacation, certain church rules were meant to be broken. Besides, didn't Jesus himself turn water into wine on occasion?

The ordinance about fireworks was waived for two days of the year: Fourth of July and New Year's Eve. On the eve of those holidays, the town council bought space in the island's weekly newspaper announcing the temporary suspension of the fireworks ordinance and wished everyone a safe and happy holiday, knowing all along they really couldn't stop anyone on those days, even if they really wanted to. Usually in that same edition of the weekly paper would be a notice by some do-gooder that volunteers were needed to clean up the spent fireworks that washed up on the beach the following day.

The town tried to enforce the ordinance about dogs being on leashes when possible, which was most of the time, and that was only because every Wexler Island policeman liked riding up and down the beach on the department's four-wheel ATV. The ATV was the only practical option to patrol the beaches because of the soft sand. There was no shortage of officers volunteering for that particular duty; in fact, each summer, there would be at least one heated argument between three or four officers about who rode the ATV and whose turn was next. Being out on the beach wearing a WIPD T-shirt, shorts, and wrap-around sunglasses sure beat sitting in a sweltering patrol car keeping an eye out for the occasional speeder.

Riding the ATV was a bona fide babe magnet, according to certain patrolmen, although the reality was that most women sunning on any of Wexler Island's beaches were either much too old, much too young, or if they were in the right age range, were married to rich men and wouldn't give a poor town cop the time of day from their Gucci watches.

Neither Peaches nor Heyward would know it those first few months, but it would be something that happened on one of their afternoon walks, an incident, that would begin a change in the way Heyward looked at life in general.

CHAPTER 20

▼

The incident—a fight—happened late on a Thursday afternoon and involved four people and Peaches. The people, Heyward, a Michael Castillo from New Jersey, his mother-in-law, and a Wexler Island police officer named Roberto Ramirez, had all had an aggravating day up to the point of the confrontation.

Heyward had started his day as he normally did, with a four-mile walk just after dawn. In the faint light, he saw that the newspaper boy had, for the fourth straight day, thrown the newspaper in the middle of the lawn, which was covered with a heavy dew, which meant the paper itself was covered with the same heavy dew. Every home in their development was required to have the same mailbox, which was supplied by The Three Oaks Homeowner's Association for a charge. Every mailbox was exactly the same, painted dark green—by coincidence, the exact color of Heyward's Jeep—and each mailbox had a slot built under it specifically designed for newspapers.

It annoyed Heyward that the paperboy wouldn't put the newspaper in the slot.

"It's not like the end of the world or anything like that," he told Elizabeth after his walk. "It's just aggravating to get those ink smudges all over my hands."

Later that morning, he tried to call Matthew Rabon, his uncle Walter's attorney, but was told he was in court and would be unavailable for several days. There had not been any word from the Sheridan attorney since they last shook hands in the hospital parking lot, and despite his better judgment, Heyward was beginning to feel uneasy that a big problem, or problems, might be brewing. He made an effort not to dwell on the potential inheritance, but $415,000 was a whole lot of money by anybody's standards, and in his mind, he could see dozens of unprincipled people trying to get their greedy hands on *his* money.

Then Tootie called and told Elizabeth that the twins, little Charlie and Hannah, had come down with some kind of rash on their behinds, and they couldn't come visit for the weekend as they had all planned. Heyward didn't particularly care if Tootie and Josh had cancelled, but he was terribly disappointed that he wouldn't be able to play with his grandchildren. He didn't say so to Elizabeth, but he felt like Peaches was disappointed too.

He was upset, but again, said nothing to Elizabeth about it, that no one from the bank had called him, other than Leon Campbell. He thought somebody, at the very least Miss Emma, should have called by now, just to check to see how he was doing or tell him they missed him or—in his wildest dreams—that the bank couldn't operate without him and ask him if he would please come back to work at once or they would all be out of a job and be out of it soon. Heyward had no intention of going back to work in Atlanta; he just wanted someone to tell him he was missed and missed more than anyone else that had ever left FMSB.

Feeling aggravated about the wet newspaper and feeling low that he wouldn't be seeing the grandkids and that no one at the bank seemed to miss him, Heyward decided to call Leon. Leon never failed to lift his spirits, either with a dirty joke or by telling him the latest gossip about Doreen Shumar.

Leon's assistant, Becky, took his call. "Mr. Jenkins, Mr. Campbell is not in at the moment." Becky was a stunning brunette who had worked as a waitress at a downtown diner where Leon and Heyward sometimes ate lunch. Leon thought she would make an agreeable secretary for him and suggested that she apply at the bank, even though she had no real secretarial or administrative experience. It seemed to Heyward that Becky was a better waitress than secretary, but then, that really was not his problem.

"Could I take a message or have him return your call, Mr. Jenson?"

"Jennings. It's Jennings, Becky, Heyward Jennings. Can you tell me when you expect him back?"

She hesitated a few seconds. "No, sir, he had another doctor's appointment, and I don't really know how long he'll be. Would you like to leave a message in his voicemail?"

He told her that he thought that might be a superb idea, and when she transferred him to Leon's voicemail, he spoke quickly, like he was in a hurry or being pressed to get off the phone.

"Leon, this is Heyward. I've got to talk fast. I just wanted to let you know I'm sitting on the beach right now drinking a cold beer. It's real sunny out here. Tons of good-looking women walking around in little, tiny bikinis. If fact, there's some kind of movie company down here on the beach right now shooting one of those 'wild women' videos where all the girls take their tops off for the cameras. By the way, I caught a great big sailfish yesterday, and I'm going back out fishing later. Just wanted to let you know what retired life was like, and I hope you are working real hard. Bye."

Heyward was speaking from his easy chair in his den at the time, and even though leaving a smart aleck message like that made him feel a little better, it irked him that he couldn't actually talk to his friend.

The last straw in Heyward's aggravating day was when Elizabeth asked him, "Heyward, does it seem to be getting warm in here to you? It feels stuffy to me, and listen to the way the air conditioner is sounding kind of funny. I think there must be a problem with it."

The air conditioner was definitely making a strange noise, and the thermostat in the house was registering seventy-nine degrees.

✳   ✳   ✳   ✳

Two miles from Heyward, Michael Castillo from New Jersey was becoming aggravated too. Michael Castillo and his wife, Sonja, had rented a condominium at Wexler Island for a week from Sonja's brother, Francis, who also lived in New Jersey.

Francis was often overextended and in an effort to make the payments on his overpriced condo, rented it out to friends and relatives during the peak summer months. The condo, supposedly bought as an investment, had a great deal of hidden costs associated with it that Francis hadn't counted on when he signed the mortgage papers and in an effort to save a little money by cutting expenses, Francis scrimped on having the condo cleaned each time a renter departed. By the time Michael and Sonja Castillo opened the condo's front door to start their two weeks of a relaxing beach vacation, the place was not clean and it had a funny smell.

To make matters worse for Michael, Sonja had invited her mother to fly down without telling her husband until the very last minute. Three days later, Sonja's mother showed up and loudly announced she was there to eat, shop, and drink piña coladas to her heart's content.

Michael Castillo did not like his mother-in-law when she was in New Jersey, and she didn't particularly care for him either. When she showed up on *his* vacation at the dirty condo in South Carolina, he liked her even less. He was not too happy with his wife on top of that.

To make things even worse, when he put his old bathing suit on, he realized just how much weight he'd gained in the last twelve months.

By late Thursday afternoon, Michael Castillo was more than a little drunk and more than a little sunburned. But when the thought occurred to him that his mother-in-law could live another twenty or twenty-five years, he was bound and determined to stay on the beach and out of the condo as long as possible that day.

*   *   *   *

The Town of Wexler Island's Patrol Officer First Class Roberto Ramirez was having problems of his own.

The very first thing Thursday morning, the mayor himself—George Washington Patton—summoned Officer Ramirez into his office and demanded to know just how it was that he had issued a parking ticket to his wife, Mrs. Clarice Patton. The mayor's office was small and cramped and located in the back of the Wexler Island Town Hall, which in itself was quite small and cramped.

The position of mayor shared space with the town clerk, a part-time paid position, and the chief of police, a full-time paid position with limited benefits. The chief oversaw the five full-time policemen under his responsibility.

"Don't you recognize Mrs. Patton's Cadillac by now, Officer Ramirez? Who told you a patrolman could write her a ticket?" the mayor questioned.

G. W. Patton always referred to his wife as "Mrs. Patton" to anyone outside his family, even among their friends; he referred to her as "Dear" the rest of the time. G. W., as his close cronies called him, had been elected mayor without interruption for the last twenty-five years, starting back when there was only a small number of full-time residents living on the island. Now that Wexler Island was experiencing an influx of new residents, most of them from "up North," G. W. knew his reign may be coming close to an end and was telling all his friends that he wouldn't run again. His decision not to seek reelection was just to save face in case all of the new population didn't exactly appreciate his service over the last two and a half decades.

Officer Ramirez left the mayor's office with Mrs. Patton's traffic ticket in his left chest pocket, torn up and placed there courtesy of the mayor himself.

Outside the town hall, the flustered patrolman noticed he had a voice mail on his personal cell phone. His ex-wife had left a message informing him, in a not-so-polite manner, that he was late on his child support and that she was turning him in if he didn't pay it by late afternoon Friday.

He was not exactly having a stellar day, but when he checked out the WIPD's duty roster, he found he was fortunate enough to pull duty patrolling the beaches on the department's ATV. The sun was shining, so he thought the beach ought to be full of women interested in checking out his vehicle.

Even that plum assignment had its own aggravation: The ATV was out of gas, and he had to use his own credit card to fill it up. The town's gas card had expired two days before.

CHAPTER 21

▼

On the beach, Michael Castillo was working his way through his last six-pack of the day and growing increasingly tired of his mother-in-law's constant yammering. Down the beach a mile or so, Police Officer Ramirez was still stewing from his meeting with the mayor, as he gathered up the pieces of a Styrofoam cooler that had blown off the back of a fishing boat and been broken apart by the ocean. The pieces of the cooler had finally made their way onto the beach.

"I'm taking Peaches to the beach for her walk," Heyward told Elizabeth. "Maybe the air conditioner repairman will be here and gone by the time we get back." With that, he helped the dog into the passenger seat of the Jeep before Elizabeth could ask him to run an errand or two. Heyward adjusted the window so Peaches could stick her head out and catch the wind or bark at any cats or squirrels that she might happen to see on the way.

In less than six minutes, they pulled into the paved parking lot, the one specifically assigned to The Three Oaks residents. Before he turned the Jeep's ignition off, Heyward noticed it was a little after seven according to the dashboard clock. He had not worn his watch one time since leaving Atlanta and had no intention of ever wearing it again, along with his intention of never again wearing a necktie or suit or any type of shoe that had to be laced up, at least until his own funeral.

It was already past the time that the local town ordinance required dogs to be on a leash so Heyward decided to let Peaches roam around free. She was a good dog and she never bothered or jumped on anybody. She was sociable around other dogs, and she always came promptly when Heyward called her. This evening, Peaches was looking forward to wandering the beach at her will and she, in her special way, knew there would be thousands of different scents lingering in the sand, and if she was lucky, there might be the remains of a horseshoe crab or fish that washed up with the tide.

There was almost an hour of daylight left when they parked the Jeep, and despite the cool sea breeze, most people were beginning to pack up their beach chairs and head in for the day. As usual, some people would stop gathering up their things long enough to call Peaches over and pet her then wave to Heyward and ask him what her name was or what kind of dog she was. Heyward could set his watch by those questions, if only he still wore one.

"Let's head this way today, Peaches, up the beach, if it's all the same to you," Heyward said to the little dog. "If I rightly remember, we went the other way last night, although it doesn't really matter to me, and I doubt it does to you." It seemed like a fine idea to Heyward that he consult the dog; after all, she was smart about those types of things, he reasoned.

They walked together for a while at the edge of the ocean, then Peaches would run up to the dunes and investigate some sight or scent that caught her attention. She minded her own business and her manners, just like she always did. Then, after about twenty minutes of walking, Peaches caught a blur of movement from a small crab up where the dunes met the beach, and she went over to investigate.

The crab couldn't have been more than ten feet from the sulking man and two chatting women who were all slumped down in their beach chairs.

✳   ✳   ✳   ✳

Michael Castillo wasn't normally a mean or cruel man, but after eight hours of steadily drinking beer under a hot summer sun and listening to the nonstop chatter of his wife and mother-in-law, and on top of everything, eight hours of thinking how his brother-in-law had rented him a dirty condo, Michael Castillo had passed being in a bad mood and was slowly becoming furious.

Peaches, meanwhile, was busying herself by staying out of the way of the crab's front pincher claws.

"Go on. Get away from me, you damn ugly mutt," Michael Castillo yelled at the dog from his beach chair.

Heyward, who had been walking along the edge of the ocean, was watching Peaches carefully, just as he always did. It took him a second or two to understand it was *his* dog that was being yelled at by the pot-bellied man.

"I said get the hell away from me!" Michael Castillo threw an empty beer can towards the little dog, just missing her and the crab.

Heyward couldn't believe what he had just seen take place. For a split second, he thought he might pass out from a rush of blood to his head, as if his brain needed a blast of oxygen to process the information his eyes had just relayed to it. Immediately, a rage he had not ever felt before—not in his youth, not in his adulthood, not even close to the anger he felt when he trashed Henry Pyatt's computer—took over him. In a flash, he was standing over the man in the chair, his finger pointed not more than three inches from the nose of the beer-can-throwing man.

"Don't you ever throw anything at my dog, you motherfucker! I'll kill you with my bare hands if you ever as much look at her again!" Heyward screamed. "Goddamnit, I'll kill you if you do, understand?"

It took a few moments before Heyward's rage subsided enough for him to turn away. "Let's go, Peaches. Let's go before I hurt this man," he called out to the dog.

He hadn't taken more than three steps when he felt the pain of a fist pounding the back of his head. The impact dazed him and knocked him to his knees. Then, he felt another blow, this one catching him, again from behind, on his jaw, just below his right ear.

Heyward struggled to get up. It only took a moment for his head to clear, and he shook his head twice as if he was trying to shake off, not the pain, but the incomprehension of what had just happened to him. Somebody, he finally understood, somebody had hit him.

In something of a hypnotic state, what some people might claim to be an "out-of-body" experience, Heyward felt a calmness come over him. As if he was watching someone else, Heyward balled his hands into fists and hit his attacker in the cheek and hit him hard; Michael Castillo's eyes glazed over.

With his left fist, Heyward punched him again, this time in the nose.

Michael Castillo fell backwards, and as he did, his mother-in-law came at Heyward with one of her flip-flop sandals and began flailing it at him. She wasn't inflicting any pain on him, but she was definitely trying to hurt him. Heyward yanked the shoes from her hand and she staggered back toward her daughter.

Police Officer Roberto Ramirez watched the whole episode unfold. The officer had just parked his ATV not more than forty yards away before any of the action took place and had been listening to a woman explain that she had left her car keys on her beach towel, and now they were gone. Was it possible that some sea gulls might have carried them off somehow?

When Officer Ramirez heard the first shout from Michael Castillo, he instinctively looked up and saw the entire confrontation. The policeman, realizing exactly what was happening, started his ATV and roared toward the fight.

The woman with the lost car keys continued talking to herself about where they could possibly be, even though no one was around to hear her.

CHAPTER 22

▼

It took almost thirty minutes and the sunlight had mostly faded away before Officer Ramirez had sorted everything out about the fight. Since he had witnessed the incident, he didn't have much problem with the "who did what to whom" and didn't have to, or want to, listen to any testimony from the family from New Jersey or from Heyward. He did record the names of some people that were on the beach at the time of the incident, but most witnesses slipped off before they became involved. No one needed medical assistance so Officer Ramirez had no reason to call for an ambulance.

The officer duly recorded the events, carefully writing the details in his patrol book. He wanted Heyward to press simple assault charges against Michael Castillo and for good measure, press charges against the mother-in-law, but Heyward said he didn't think that would be necessary. They both had learned a lesson, he felt. Unable to get assault charges on them, at least for the time being, the officer did issue a ticket to Michael Castillo for littering. Throwing an empty beer can on the beach had to be a violation, even if the man intended to pick it up all along.

"You sucker-punched Mr. Jennings, I saw it myself. I wish he would press charges against you and that woman you call a mother-in-law. Nothing would please me more than to lock you both up in a cell overnight." The Wexler Island police officer was not in a good mood.

The old woman started to say something then thought better of antagonizing the officer. She had seen movies of women in jail—sometimes Southern jails—and didn't think that was something she would like to experience.

"If I catch you going over the speed limit or if you even sneeze the rest of the time you are on this island, your ass is mine. Understand?" Officer Ramirez said, pointing his finger in Michael Castillo's face just to rile him.

Since it was almost dark and since Heyward was a good mile from his Jeep, Officer Ramirez offered him and Peaches a lift on his ATV. Heyward appreciated it. The back of his head and his face were beginning to ache a little, and he seriously doubted that a twenty-minute walk would make it feel any better.

When they got to the Jeep, the policeman took Peaches and offered a hand to Heyward. He was, after all, sixty years old and had just been in a fistfight with a much younger man. Heyward stumbled just a bit getting off the four-wheeler, due more to the darkness than the fight.

"Careful, Mr. Jennings, easy does it. You seemed to survive the fight all right. I don't want you getting hurt getting off an ATV," the officer said. "Mr. Jennings, let me ask you something. You seemed to know what you were doing when you hit that man back, twice that is. Do you do this sort of thing very often? I mean, were you ever a boxer when you were younger?"

Heyward could see the face of the officer now that the parking lot lights were beginning to glow. "I don't guess I've been in a fight since the first or second grade, then I probably got beat up anyway. In fact, I can't remember ever being in a fight."

Heyward paused a moment then added, "Before today, I couldn't ever imagine fighting someone. I was just a banker and had a pretty boring life actually."

Police Officer Roberto Ramirez cranked up his ATV and extended his hand to Heyward. "Well, if you don't mind me saying so, sir, it was a thing of beauty to watch, even as quick as it was over." He revved the engine. "I'm on early shift tomorrow. I might drop by your house just to check on you, if it's okay with you and your missus?"

✳   ✳   ✳   ✳

Elizabeth burst into tears when she saw Heyward come through the garage door. By the time he drove home, the right side of his face just below his ear was beginning to swell a bit and was turning bright red where Michael Castillo's fist hit him with the second blow. She had never seen him injured or really hurt during their entire marriage, no traffic accidents, no gashed fingers from carving knives, not even a black thumb from a misplaced hammer blow, and what she saw frightened her. Heyward had a time convincing Elizabeth that he had actually been in a fistfight and that overall, he had won the fight. She had never known him to take physical action against any person or any object—he never told her about smashing the computer—and as far as she was concerned, her husband was incapable of hurting a fly, much less another human being.

It took him a good half hour to convince Elizabeth that he was not seriously hurt and, no, she didn't need to take him to the local clinic or call an ambulance. She did make him put a piece of steak on the swollen area of his face, even though, for the life of him, he couldn't understand how that could possibly reduce any puffiness.

He decided a hot shower might make him feel better and thought if Elizabeth saw him doing something normal, something like taking a shower, she might begin to feel that he wasn't about to die after all. In the shower, Heyward examined the knuckles on both hands, how the skin was slightly split on the right hand and on his left, how the knuckles were beginning to bruise. Standing buck naked in the shower at sixty years old, he began to feel for the first time a sense of pride, a sense of self-respect. He—not because of the bank's influence or his job title—he was finally a man to be reckoned with.

*   *   *   *

True to his word, the policeman pulled into the Jenningses' driveway the next morning, just to check on him. Elizabeth met the young officer at the door.

"He's in the den sitting in his easy chair if you want to arrest him," she said. "But then, I doubt there's a law against being old and foolish, is there?"

"No, ma'am, I'm not here to arrest Mr. Jennings. I just want to make sure he's doing alright. You ought to be real proud of him," he said.

"Well, Officer, he's seems to be proud enough of himself for the both of us; how about I just leave it at that?"

Heyward was sore and a little stiff but overall seemed to be in good shape considering he had been in his first fistfight in nearly six decades. As soon as he saw Officer Ramirez, he stood up and in the process had to suppress a groan. He and the officer chatted for a while, almost like old-time acquaintances until Roberto Ramirez received a radio call that he was needed to direct traffic around a car that was broken down near one of the beaches.

Heyward walked him outside to the police cruiser and thanked him for checking on him.

"Are you sure you don't want to press charges on Mr. Castillo before he leaves the state? You might even launch a lawsuit against both of them and sue 'em for some kind of damages," the policeman said.

"No, I don't expect so, but thanks. I suppose they learned a lesson from this whole thing," Heyward said.

They shook hands again, and Heyward watched the cruiser pull away.

There, standing by himself on the driveway, he said out loud, "No, I don't want to press charges against them or anybody else. Those people may have done me the biggest favor of my life. Being in a fight might hurt, but it just doesn't hurt that much."

It hurts, but it just doesn't hurt that much.

CHAPTER 23

▼

Heyward laid low for the next couple of days, piddled around the yard, and stayed out of Elizabeth's way. At some point every day, she asked him if he was feeling okay, if there were no signs of internal bleeding, and if he was absolutely sure that a trip to the doctor was still out of the question. He and Peaches took a few walks on the shore but always went down the beach, away from the direction of where the altercation had taken place. He wasn't particularly worried about running into Michael Castillo, but he saw no reason to press his luck. It was better to leave things as they ended the other night, him coming out on the best end of the deal.

With the help of some extra-strength pain relievers, Heyward lost any remaining soreness and muscle aches, and the little discoloration of the skin below his right ear soon disappeared. Elizabeth was careful to write on a small notepad exactly how many pills she issued him and followed the directions on the bottle's label closely. He may not have been too smart getting in a fight, but she was smart enough not to let him overdose on pain medications.

"Heyward, you know these drug companies do studies on how many pills people are supposed to take within a certain period of time," she said. "I know you never read any instructions about anything, but trust me on this one."

"Believe me, I'm perfectly fine. I've had teeth filled that hurt more than this," he said. "See, look at how steady my right hand is when I hold it out," he added, sticking out his left hand and, at the same time, his left foot, shaking it like he had some kind of old-fashioned nervous disease like Saint Vitus, all just to aggravate her.

"Not to frighten you or anything like that, but the weird thing is since I took that little hit on the head, all I want to do is speak in Latin. Is that something I should be worried about?"

Elizabeth put down the book she was trying to read. "Heyward, I saw you messing around the other day with that rod and reel the folks at the bank gave you as a retirement gift. Maybe you feel good enough to go fishing now and try to do something constructive instead of trying to annoy me."

"Well, *E Pluribus Unum* to that."

*   *   *   *

Heyward didn't realize it until he had moved to the beach, but the employees of FMSB had given him a really nice and expensive, top-of-the-line rod and reel made specifically for surf fishing. They had also chipped in and bought a tackle box that to him looked like a small suitcase, and they'd put in all the different kinds of tackle needed to do some serious surf fishing. All that Heyward needed was bait, and he'd seen a fishing-tackle shop not too far away that he supposed could supply almost any kind of bait, if he had any real clue as to what kind he needed.

As a boy growing up in Georgia, Heyward fished the small ponds that dotted the area, most of them nothing more than ponds to irrigate cotton or peanuts which were the only crop farmers in the area seemed to grow. Back then, all he could afford was a long cane pole and, for bait, worms and crickets he gathered himself. For the most part, it didn't really matter what kind of bait he used because the small bream and catfish, the only fish that could live in the murky water, weren't choosy what they ate and seemed to be hungry all the time. Heyward knew how to handle a simple cane pole and cork in the small country ponds; using a rod and reel like the one sitting in his garage was going to take some getting used to.

When he pulled up to Dilly's Bait and Tackle Shop and saw all the faded signs advertising the different baits they carried, Heyward got the fleeting feeling that maybe he was in over his head. Surf fishing looked like it might be complicated.

A familiar-looking elderly man pushed through the store's screen door carrying a small paper bag. It took a second for Heyward to recognize him as one of the group who had come to welcome him and Elizabeth to The Three Oaks, even though they had had a house there longer than most of them. He remembered talking to the man that day and recalled he had moved from Pennsylvania and something about him being a bit apprehensive about moving South because of wild stories about chain gangs and Confederate flags and such.

The old man looked at him. "Haven't we met somewhere before?"

"I believe we have. You came with your wife and some other people to welcome my wife and me to The Three Oaks the day after we moved in. If I remember correctly, you said you were glad to be living in the South now." Heyward sometimes liked to rib certain people, just to entertain himself, just like he did with Eddie Waller, the salesman who sold him his Jeep.

"I doubt I said that. But that doesn't matter anyway." He walked around, looking at the Jeep. "That's a good-looking vehicle you have here."

"Thanks," Heyward replied, trying to think of something to distract the man if he got too curious and noticed the air horn Dewey Sikes had installed under the car.

The man seemed to study the front grill for a moment and then looked at the spotlights bolted to the top of the Jeep's windshield. "I sure could've used that back home in Pennsylvania, back when I did some bear hunting when I was younger and could still see." The man turned his head slightly, eyeing Heyward. "Do any bear hunting?"

"No, I can't say that I've ever been bear hunting," Heyward said.

"Deer hunting? Ever go deer hunting or hunt birds?"

"No, no deer hunting, no bird hunting. I'm not much of a hunter, never have been, probably never will be."

"You don't use this Jeep to go bear hunting. You don't hunt deer or birds. It never snows here on this island, so you don't need that four-wheel drive for that. What do you need a Jeep for? Seems like a major waste of money to me," the man said.

As much as he tried not to, Heyward could feel himself getting a little irritated. The man had essentially said he was foolish for buying a four-wheel drive vehicle, and he got the feeling the man looked down on people who didn't kill animals for enjoyment or sport.

"Listen," Heyward said, "I like this Jeep. That's why I bought it, plain and simple."

"I'd never waste money on something I didn't use," the old man said.

"Well, I have enough money I can buy any kind of car I want to, a Jeep, a Mercedes, a Jaguar, a Lexus, a Cadillac, doesn't matter." The old man was beginning to aggravate Heyward; he quickly changed from good-natured kidding to goading, something he didn't normally do. "Besides, I may need this Jeep because I might get myself a part-time job guarding a chain gang. Did that where

I used to live. You know, in some of these real small country towns they throw people from up North in jail for all kinds of traffic violations and make them work their fines off clearing ditches along the highway. These good ol' boy sheriffs like to do that if they're in a bad mood, sometimes."

Heyward felt like the man had it coming to him. Let him worry a while about getting caught speeding and put on a chain gang and his decision about moving South instead of questioning his, Heyward's, intelligence about buying a Jeep.

✳   ✳   ✳   ✳

For one reason or another, Heyward had been in bait shops like Dilly's before, but exactly why, he couldn't remember, certainly never to buy fishing bait. If he had earlier thought that he might have been in over his head, now he was absolutely sure of it. There were rows and rows of sinkers, different sizes and colors of hooks, fishing line, swivels, red-and-white corks shaped like cigars, Styrofoam minnow buckets, and beer coolers, rods and reels, crab nets, knives, and a big cooler with glass doors that at one time had been used for dairy products in a grocery store. Over in a corner was a concrete tank divided into three sections, each with its own whirring aerator and each with a pronounced odor of fish.

Above the counter, there was a handmade sign which read, "We and the bank have an understanding. They don't sell fishing tackle, and we don't make loans or give credit." Under the sign, next to an old cash register, sat a fat woman who had to be close to Heyward's age. She swatted a fly and then flipped it over the counter. Heyward saw her but quickly turned away; she was wearing an old, torn T-shirt that, in its earlier life, must have been white instead of yellow, and from what he could tell from that first glance, she may have once had teeth, but now he couldn't be sure.

"How's about it?" the old woman said from behind the cash register.

"Good morning," Heyward said. "Mind if I look around for a minute or two? I'm not sure what I'm really looking for."

"Help yourself. Take your time. I ain't going nowhere; that's for dang sure. Just you don't do what that old man you was talking to outside did, though. I told 'im not to open that jar of stink bait, but he wouldn't listen," she growled. "Made him buy it, I did."

Heyward gave a small laugh and looked at the woman's eyes, and when he did, she, too, gave a small chuckle. "Yeah," he said to her, "some people. I guess some things never change."

He took his time wandering around the shop, picking up different lead weights and placing them in the palm of his hand as if he were gauging the heaviness of each, looking into the glass cooler at all the different boxed and bagged fishing bait, and in general, just browsing. After a while, he said to the woman, "I'm going to try some surf fishing. Can you tell me what kind of bait would be best?"

The old woman suggested he use some cut-up squid and some frozen shrimp, which he should peel and cut in half. "You really won't catch much of anything this time of the year. Maybe some spots, or if you're lucky, some red drums. Nobody's doing much right now. Conditions aren't too good, and besides, surf fishing is always iffy at best."

"I don't expect I would catch much. I'm mainly interested in trying. If I catch something, that means I'll have to clean it, and I don't want to have to do that."

"Well, at least you're honest about it," she said as she wrapped the bait up in some brown paper and gave him back change.

"By the way, I see your sign about bankers not selling fishing tackle." Heyward pointed above her head. "I hope that's working out for you."

"Don't have much use for bankers. They hand you a life jacket when the ocean is calm and want it back when the water gets rough. Don't really like 'em," she replied.

"Me either. I bet that old man that opened the jar of stink bait was probably a banker. Kind of smelled like one, now that I recall," Heyward said.

She took the fly swatter back in hand, and he went out through the screen door.

C H A P T E R   24

▼

The old woman at Dilly's was right. Heyward didn't catch much of anything surf fishing, but then, he didn't expect to catch much and didn't really care.

He spent the first afternoon just standing in the surf, trying to keep his bait—a piece of cut squid—from being pushed back on the beach by the tide. It was only after he changed to a heavier lead sinker that the problem seemed to be solved. He also changed the size of the hooks four times thinking that maybe he was using the wrong size and fish either saw the hook or couldn't take the bait because it was either too big or too small. Eventually, he switched bait from squid to shrimp and when he had no bites, went back to squid.

He walked up and down the beach looking for the signs that a sandbar or slough had somehow formed just offshore, thinking either of those might bring in fish, though he was not real sure what a sandbar or slough might actually look like, especially from his perspective on the beach. To him, everything in the water looked the same.

The final affront happened when he made his very last cast of the afternoon. With the intention of throwing his bait just beyond the breaking waves, Heyward held his finger a split-second too long on the line as it came off the spinner reel's spool. The line sliced his index finger, and before the sinker hit the waves, he had blood on his shirt and shorts and smeared all over his fishing reel. The cut itself hurt and hurt bad, and the salt in the ocean water made it sting even worse.

On the second day of surf fishing, Heyward stopped by Dilly's to buy a sand spike he'd seen other fishermen using. A sand spike was nothing more than a section of hollow PVC pipe that could be pushed deep into the sand. The rod and reel could be placed in the open end. That way, a person could set his fishing rod in the spike and not have to hold it all day long.

When he walked into Dilly's, the old woman was still sitting behind the counter as if she hadn't moved in the last twenty-four hours, not even to change her dirty T-shirt.

She laughed at Heyward when she saw his bandaged finger. "I see you cut your finger. What'd you do, hold your line too long casting?" She laughed again and swatted at a fly.

"Yeah, I did," he said. "And it hurts like hell, to tell you the truth."

Heyward asked her if she had any sand spikes for sale.

The woman pointed to some in a wooden crate. "I knew you'd come back and get one of them stakes, providing you kept up your surf fishing. I'd thought about mentioning it yesterday, but that's something most folks have to figure out for themselves, if they got any smarts about them."

She stood up and reached behind her. "Here, I'm going to give you this because I like you." She handed Heyward a folded pamphlet, laminated on both sides, with pictures of different types of fishes. "This might help you one day tell the difference between a croaker and a shark, if you ever catch one. Oh, and if you cut your finger again, blood won't hurt it none. It's covered with that plastic stuff."

For the next several days, Heyward fished, or at least his rod and reel was in the sand spike. He idled away his time and mostly thumbed through the guide the old woman gave him and looked at the color pictures of the fish.

When he wasn't looking at the images of the fish or checking his bait, Heyward sometimes thought about what might be happening that very moment at the bank or wondered who was driving the gray Buick he left behind. Sometimes, he thought about how scared he was when Louis flew the plane at him in their grandfather's old truck. But mostly, Heyward thought about Doreen Shumar and her large breasts.

It didn't pay for him to think about Doreen too much because it would cause him to go into a slight funk.

On one bright, sunny afternoon, he even said out loud, loud enough that anybody walking behind him could have heard, "To think, I probably could've had sex with her if I'd just had the damn nerve."

Disgusted with himself, he packed up his fishing gear and went home.

✳   ✳   ✳   ✳

Elizabeth met him at the door. "You had two phone calls while you were fishing. Emma Belavedo called and so did Horace Parker."

Heyward felt his pulse quicken when she told him Miss Emma had called him. Maybe Matthew Rabon had finally finished his uncle Walter's estate and was trying to get in touch with him about where to send his inheritance check.

"Heyward, Leon Campbell had a heart attack, and it doesn't look good for him," Elizabeth said, her lower lip quivering.

Heyward was stunned. Did he hear her right? Leon, heart attack?

Elizabeth inhaled deeply and then exhaled the same breath, as if that movement was the only thing that could get the next words from her. "Emma said that he was at work when he got sick, and they called an ambulance for him ..." Elizabeth was still talking, but Heyward couldn't distinguish the words she was saying. To him, only noises were coming from her lips.

Heyward Jennings was not a drinking man and had never been a drinking man to speak of, but while Elizabeth was still talking, he walked over to a cabinet and pulled a bottle of bourbon from the shelf. He poured two glasses, one for him and one for Elizabeth, and then in three gulps, emptied his glass.

As the liquor settled him, Heyward began to understand that Leon had had a heart attack and that it was sometime around mid-afternoon in his office. He was in an intensive care unit of a hospital somewhere in Atlanta, and the prognosis was not good, not at this point in time.

"I guess Horace was calling with the same news?" Heyward asked.

"No, I don't think so. Horace called just after you left for the beach, sometime around eleven this morning. That had to be before Leon ..." and she started crying.

Heyward was a little surprised that Elizabeth was so upset; she was not particularly partial to Leon because of his ways, and she had never met either of his two ex-wives either. Maybe it was that he was about the same age as his friend and she knew the same thing would probably happen to him one day. One thing that was for sure was that Heyward couldn't handle a crying woman.

He called Miss Emma. She, like Elizabeth, didn't much care for Leon, but she was upset and crying on the telephone. Heyward was finally able to get the name of the hospital out of her and told her he would probably drive on to Atlanta that night. He would rather fly, but there were only a few commercial flights out of the Wexler Island Airport and someone had told him they were only morning flights anyway.

"Oh, Heyward, things seem to be so different at the bank now. I don't want to burden you on top of Leon getting sick, but I've wanted to call you several times and stopped myself. Things are just, well, they're bad for me." Miss Emma was starting to cry again.

"Really? Besides Leon, what's wrong?"

"I really shouldn't say anything now, but Kevin Pasko is giving me a hard time about everything, and Elliot Coleman doesn't seem like he wants to do anything about it. I think they are trying to run me off," she sobbed, "and I have to have a job, you know that."

"Okay. Let's not worry about that right now. I'll be on my way to Atlanta shortly, and we'll talk about things after I check on Leon. Until then, try not to worry about Pasko or Elliot."

Heyward looked at Elizabeth. "Do you want to go to Atlanta with me or would you rather wait here and see what happens with Leon?"

CHAPTER 25

▼

Elizabeth decided she would stay at home to look after Peaches, but if events turned worse, she would come later. Heyward assured her that he was fine to make the long drive, even after being out in the sun and wind all day, but that he would prefer to take her Camry instead of his Jeep.

"I didn't really want to tell you this, but that Jeep about beat me to death when I drove it here when we moved," Heyward told her. "It's fine for short trips but not for hours at a time, at least not for me, a man of my age, and not tonight."

Elizabeth helped him pack, and after a quick shower and a sandwich, Heyward was on his way to Atlanta. As he was walking out the door, Elizabeth told him, "I want you to promise me that if you get too tired driving tonight, you'll stop at a hotel and not push yourself to get there. I just don't think Leon will die from this … I expect God wants him to pay a whole lot more alimony to those poor ex-wives of his before he dies."

Not long after he crossed over the state line into Georgia, sometime around midnight, Heyward was pulled over for speeding, something that had not happened to him in so long he couldn't remember the last time. Dull gray Buicks had their own special way of slowing him down.

The Georgia State Trooper, Officer Malcolm Stewart, was a sturdy-looking man but to Heyward, seemed almost too young to be patrolling the dark expanse of Georgia interstate all by himself. Heyward immediately thanked God that his son, Lucas, was a CPA working in a safe and comfortable office, probably now sleeping in a king-size bed, instead of pulling over who-knows-whats on I-20 in the middle of the night.

The trooper asked for Heyward's driver's license, car registration, and proof of insurance, which thankfully, Elizabeth had pressed him to promptly change to their new South Carolina address not long after they moved. Proper paperwork and documentation wasn't going to be a problem. The patrolman walked back to his cruiser to check to see if Heyward had any outstanding warrants or APBs on him or if there was any reason he needed to run him in to the local county jail.

It seemed appropriate, almost a tribute to his sick friend, that Heyward thought about Leon and how if he was in this same situation, he would have been thinking about all the logical—meaning excusable—explanations to the cop for why he had been speeding and why he shouldn't be issued a fine.

Leon never seemed to mind being pulled over for any traffic violation; he considered it an obligation, a duty, to talk his way out of a ticket, almost like it was a badge of honor to get any fine reduced or changed to a warning. If Leon had been in Heyward's place, it would have been so easy for him to talk his way out of a ticket, starting with *going to pay last respects to a friend dying of a heart attack*; it would almost have been beneath Leon's talents.

The trooper came back to Heyward's window. "Mr. Jennings, I clocked you going ninety-three miles per hour in a seventy-mile-per-hour zone. Is there any credible reason you were exceeding the speed limit?"

The officer was polite and spoke in a flat and measured tone intended not to incite or agitate a traffic offender unnecessarily here on these isolated backwoods roads of Georgia. It almost seemed to Heyward, at the time, that the patrolman was wanting to hear an original excuse, or if not entirely original, at least one he hadn't heard a hundred times before.

"You want to know why I was driving ninety-three miles per hour? I'll tell you plain and simple—I wanted to, that's why."

State Trooper Stewart peered closely at the white-haired man in the Camry. "Sir, did you say you wanted to?"

"That's right, I wanted to," Heyward repeated himself.

"Well, Mr. Jennings, I'm going to issue you a citation for speeding, and I'll trust that you'll *want to* pay this ticket. Do I need to give you a breathalyzer test? Sir, have you been drinking?" The officer shined his flashlight in Heyward's eyes.

"Officer, I had one drink over five hours ago at my home on Wexler Island, South Carolina. Since that drink, I have eaten a meal and haven't had any other alcoholic beverages of any kind. I'm stone-cold sober, and that one drink in no way has impaired or influenced my reflexes or my judgment."

State Trooper Stewart put his hands on his hips but said nothing.

Heyward continued, "I was exceeding the posted speed limit and got caught. I'll take the ticket like a man and not whine about it, if it's all the same to you. Also, I want you to know that as soon as I am out of your sight, I will more than likely drive ninety-three miles an hour again, just because I want to. Look, I'm not trying to be a smart-ass, Officer, I'm just telling you the gospel truth."

The trooper tore the ticket from his citation book and thrust it through the open driver's window. "Here's your ticket. There're instructions at the bottom of the form how to pay the fine, or if you want to go to court, there's information for that too. Goodnight, Mr. Jennings, and just so you know, I'm going to follow you for a while. Don't exceed the speed limit, or you'll be looking at another ticket."

Heyward watched in his rearview mirror as the trooper walked back to his car. He balled the ticket up and tossed it out the window. "Follow me all you want to, Georgia State Trooper Stewart or whatever the hell your name is. You mess with me again and my good friend, Officer Roberto Ramirez of the Wexler Island Police Department, and I just might have to straighten your ass out."

There was something about getting a speeding ticket and not caring about what the cop thought about you or the fine or, for that matter, worrying about how it would affect your next car insurance bill. There was also something about bloodying a drunk's nose on the beach and, even more, something about having your face massaged by a lesbian's big breasts, even if you didn't try to get her in bed.

There was something about knowing your best friend may be on his deathbed and there was nothing you could do to help him.

Damn, Heyward thought to himself, *I might have to become a badass after all.*

✳   ✳   ✳   ✳

He arrived at the Wall County Medical Center a little after two in the morning and immediately went up to the cardiac intensive care unit, where, in the waiting area, Leon Campbell's two ex-wives were napping on a couch together.

Gina Campbell was Leon's first wife. She divorced him when she caught him running around with Jean Arbus, who later became wife number two, Jean Campbell. Jean Campbell was the same woman lying on the couch with her head on Gina's shoulder.

The similarity of their names proved to be quite confounding to almost everyone, especially Leon. After he married Jean, he sometimes mixed their names up and called her Gina at the most inappropriate times. Jean would, more often than not, get Gina's mail, and Gina would get mail addressed to Jean; insurance companies stayed in a state of confusion as to exactly which Mrs. Campbell they were covering, and there were many embarrassing mix-ups at cocktail parties and Campbell family reunions.

At first, the original Mrs. Campbell—Gina—hated the second Mrs. Campbell—Jean—for stealing her husband, even if he was a "no-good, double-timing scumbag," in her exact words. Then, when Leon later got involved with an insurance adjuster, Jean divorced him over that little incident, and the two ex-Mrs. Campbells begin talking to each other about Leon and all his many faults, and soon, the two women became good friends. No matter how mad they ever were at Leon or how much he hurt them with his straying ways, both women *liked* him and came to the hospital as soon as they heard about his condition. "Besides," Jean told Gina, "we have an obligation to warn the nurses about him, just in case he comes through this all right."

Even if the two women liked Leon, they more or less detested Heyward. It was Heyward, they assumed wrongly, that covered up for Leon when each was still married to him and enabled him to get away with his dalliances for so long. Heyward could never seem to convince either of them that he was completely innocent of his friend's actions and that he was just as naïve about Leon as they were. "His best friend didn't know? Please, spare me," Gina told him once when he tried to plead his lack of involvement.

Jean Campbell stirred when Heyward entered the dimly lit waiting area and when she saw him, nudged Gina. Both women looked tired and drawn to Heyward, but even in that condition, they could still be sassy. "Gina," she said, "wake up. Titty-ears is here."

Gina stretched her arms and twisted her neck to get out the slight kink she'd developed lying on the hard couch. "You're on the wrong floor, Heyward. Plastic surgery is on the second level, but you'll have to wait until morning. All the women with boob jobs have gone home—no one's going to rub your face tonight."

Good old Leon, Heyward thought. *Can't keep anything to himself.*

"Hello, ladies. Now that you both have had your little shot at me, how's Leon?"

CHAPTER 26

▼

The fact was, Leon was not all right, and from what the women told him, it looked like he may never be totally all right again.

Although they weren't too thrilled that Heyward was Leon's accomplice, or so they thought, they both hugged him anyway. Any animosity they held for him had vanished for the time being, and in a few minutes, they explained everything they knew that had happened after the point of his collapse, including the condition Leon was in at that particular time of the night. Heyward had to piece bits and pieces of words and sentences together because everything the two women said was between them crying and blowing their noses, all while they were both talking at the same time.

At one point, in the middle of the commotion, Gina stopped crying and looked at him. "Heyward, you really have a nice suntan," she said and went back to crying and blowing her nose.

Leon had indeed suffered a massive heart attack and hadn't regained consciousness since the EMS people restarted his heart with their electric paddles while he was lying on his back on his office floor. The two women said doctors had been very good about coming out to the waiting room to let them know his condition since they were his only living family, or in their case, ex-family. "The doctors keep saying it doesn't look good for him," Jean told him. "It just sounds so bad."

Heyward looked around the waiting room. In the dimmed lighting, he could see there were other people, tired-looking people, propped up in chairs or lying on couches all waiting to visit someone in the intensive care unit.

"Heyward, you go in to see him when they let us back in there," Gina told him. "I'll go with you, if that's okay with you, Jean." Jean nodded her head. "The hospital only lets two people go in at a time and only for five minutes. They're real strict about that and visitors can only go in at the top of every hour."

At 3:00 AM, a nurse came out and said something, although Heyward couldn't make it out. Four or five people, who seemed to be asleep, immediately got up and went through a set of double doors, passing a yellow sign with big red letters declaring, "No Visitors."

Gina jumped up, grabbed Heyward's left arm, and held him tightly against her. She hurried him through the doors. "Five minutes," the nurse told her.

The smell of the CICU made him gag, but not so much that Gina noticed. It was familiar to him, just as were the sounds of the respirators and the monitors; it all reminded him of the dark hospital room in Sheridan, Alabama. Heyward immediately thought about his uncle's inheritance and in the same moment felt ashamed. All that passed out of his mind as soon as he saw Leon.

Leon didn't look all that bad to Heyward, nothing like the emaciated body of Walter Jennings. Leon looked like he was sleeping, like Heyward would imagine him sleeping had he been in his own bed without a small clear tube in his nostrils, some type of intravenous fluid going into his right arm, and a small pulse monitor slipped over the index finger of his left hand. Heyward felt if he just shook his friend's arm, he would wake up and ask what all the fuss was about and then ask Gina why she was there, if was he late on an alimony payment or what had he done now to incur her wrath.

Heyward and Gina, arm in arm, stood silently by the bed.

So this is it? Heyward thought to himself. *This is how it ends? After all that, this is it?*

Their five minutes were over faster than he thought possible. Gina guided him away from the bed and back into the waiting room. Jean saved them a place on the couch and patted her hand on the cushion for them to sit down.

"Heyward," Gina said, "I just want you to know, right now, I forgive you for helping Leon when he was cheating on me."

He stood up, fully upright and awake, and looked down at her. Without saying a word, he went down the hall until he found the door that opened to a stairwell. In the privacy of the empty stairwell, Heyward began crying uncontrollably and without shame, something he had done only on one occasion since he was a boy in grade school.

The only other time was on Charlotte Anne's, Tootie's, wedding day. He had cried alone in the church's stairwell, a stairwell that looked almost identical to the one he was now in.

✳   ✳   ✳   ✳

Just before seven the next morning, he was nudged awake by Horace Parker III himself.

Heyward didn't fully wake within the first four or five seconds, but he did immediately feel his exhaustion. It took him a little longer to comprehend he was in a hospital waiting room and longer than that to realize it was actually Horace standing in front of him, already dressed for work in a dark three-piece suit.

"Good morning, Heyward. I'll tell you, this is one tough reason to have to come back to Atlanta," Horace said. "How's our boy doing?"

Heyward felt as if his body had been beaten with sticks. His joints and muscles felt like they did when he once had the flu, and that was the sickest he had ever been in his life. There was an awful taste of stale coffee in his mouth, and when he tried to talk, his tongue stuck to the roof of his mouth.

Finally, Heyward was able to relate everything he knew about Leon's medical condition to his old boss before a nurse came out and announced that visitors would be permitted to come into the ward for five minutes and five minutes only. Horace looked at Heyward, who nodded his head in the direction of the nurse, and together, they went to see Leon, leaving Jean and Gina to shift positions on the couch.

The two men stood beside the bed for only a couple of minutes. Horace was solemn, but he didn't seem to be particularly upset or shocked at Leon's condition. He didn't speak at all until they returned to the hall in front of the waiting area.

"He doesn't look too good, does he? I expect time will tell, one way or another," Horace said then changed the subject. "Heyward, I need to ask you to do me a favor, if you will. I called your new house before Leon had his attack, but I figured you'd be coming here when you didn't call back. By the way, you've got a great suntan."

Heyward was still aching all over, and his mouth was even drier than when Horace woke him up, dry as if he was entering the first stages of dehydration. "What kind of favor?"

"Thomas Pennington—you may have heard me talk of him before—is an old friend of mine, and we're thinking about adding him to the bank's board of directors. If he gets on the board, it would sure help me out a lot."

"What does that have to do with me? I mean, I have nothing to do with who gets on the board and who doesn't," Heyward asked, looking around for some type of water fountain. He really needed something to drink.

"No, no, I didn't explain. Thomas is a big-time financier, but I guess you know that already. He has a daughter who lives down on that island where you do, what is it, Wexler? Anyway, his daughter is married to a young man who inherited some kind of boat company there on the island. Apparently, they make the boats there and ship them around the country. Thomas Pennington said his son-in-law is in over his head with this company and that he's not a good manager or something to that effect. I think Pennington wants the boy to sell the company."

"What does that have to do with me?"

"Pennington doesn't seem to like his son-in-law, and the boy doesn't like him. Besides, Thomas Pennington is busy, very busy, and doesn't have a lot of time to help out a little boat company, especially one that he doesn't own."

"He's too busy to help out his own daughter and her husband?" Heyward asked. He saw a water fountain, pointed to it, and walked over to it with Horace trailing behind him.

Horace waited for Heyward to drink then pulled him by the arm to a part of the room where no one could hear him. Horace looked around to make sure no one was within hearing range. "Look, Heyward, Thomas Pennington is as big a son of a bitch as they come. He may be an SOB, but he is my friend in spite of that. And, I want to get him on the board."

"All right, I understand all that, but what does this have to do with me?"

"Look, I know you're retired, and you deserve to do the things you want to do without getting involved with this. But, as a big favor to me, could you go over and meet this couple and just see if you can recommend anything to help them and this boat company? You always show sound judgment, and you know how businesses are supposed to work. Could you do it for me, as a favor? It would sure help me, and if you could, at least act like you are helping his daughter. Thomas Pennington should be appreciative and support me if he gets appointed to the board."

"I don't know anything about building boats or selling a boat company, and I doubt I would like to help someone like Thomas Pennington, if he's a son of a bitch. But I'll tell you this, Horace, I'll look into going by to meet this couple if you will do me two favors?"

"What're the favors?" Horace asked. He didn't usually bargain with bank employees, but then, he realized Heyward was no longer an employee of FMSB.

"One, I want Miss Emma to be taken care of. I've not talked to her yet, but I understand she's being given a hard time at the bank. You personally guaranteed me before that she would be looked after when I told you I was going to retire."

"Yes, I did. I don't know what's going on with her situation. I certainly haven't heard about anything, but I will guarantee she will be taken care of. What's the other favor?"

"I want my old desk back, the one your father gave me." Heyward paused. "Oh, and I want you to make Kevin Pasko personally pay the charges to have it shipped to my house on Wexler Island."

"That's actually three favors, Heyward, but consider all three done. I'll have my secretary get the information to you about these people at the boat place. Keep working on that tan."

They shook hands. Horace left for the bank, and Heyward went back to the water fountain.

CHAPTER 27

▼

Heyward thought it might be wise to get a hotel room within walking distance of the hospital. "Not to make light of Leon's condition, ladies, but if I have to spend another night on that waiting room couch, I'll be in such bad shape, they'll have to put me in intensive care too," he told Jean and Gina. "I'll get you all a room too, if you don't mind sharing one."

Tootie called him on his cell phone as he entered the lobby of a downtown hotel that one of the nurses recommended and asked him to come over to their house and stay with them. He thanked her but said he wanted to stay close to Leon; what he didn't tell her was that he didn't want to drive the forty-five minutes to her house and that he didn't want to have to deal with Atlanta traffic any more than he absolutely had to. Besides, as much as he loved his daughter and her family, just being around the commotion of the little twins without Elizabeth there to settle them down would've been almost as hard to deal with as the traffic.

He felt a little better after a hot shower and breakfast, good enough to go back to the hospital but not good enough to take his normal four-mile morning walk. From his room, he could see the FMSB's corporate tower several blocks away and way in the distance, the area that Elizabeth and he had lived in for so many years.

Funny, he thought, *I lived here almost my whole adult life and don't miss any of it at all—none.*

Entering the hospital, he decided to go into the big gift shop on the first floor and there, bought some chocolate for Leon's two ex-wives, just to let them know he had no hard feelings about their little digs about his face massage. It occurred to him that neither of Leon's exes had remarried, and they both apparently came to the hospital as soon as they got news of his condition. As he walked out of the gift shop toward the elevators, Heyward formed a mental picture of Leon getting all well and once out of the hospital, marrying both of his ex-wives. *A threesome of wild sex,* thought Heyward, *might just be worth having another heart attack for.*

There was no change to Leon's outward condition during the morning, but the doctors did tell Jean and Gina that an EEG showed he had normal brain function and that, in time, he should regain consciousness, which was a very good sign. They couldn't be certain without running more tests how much actual damage had been done to his heart muscle, but the doctors didn't seem to be as pessimistic as they had been the night before.

After spending the morning in the waiting room, Heyward suggested they all go down to the hospital food court for lunch or, if not lunch, at least for a change of scenery. They were becoming restless; they had read every magazine from cover to cover and were growing tired of the waiting room's television which had been tuned permanently to the hospital's information channel. An elderly woman sitting near them kept asking Heyward every few minutes if he was a relative of hers, her niece's husband. At first, Leon's ex-wives thought the question was funny, but after an hour or so, the three failed to see any humor in the old woman or her questions.

Down at the food court, they all got hamburgers and soft drinks which seemed to put everyone in a better mood. Gina and Jean asked Heyward how he liked retirement and kept telling him how lucky he was to be living at the beach, how it must be nice to spend all day out in the sun and get such a good tan as he had.

"I'll tell you, if I didn't have to work, I'd move to the beach too," Jean told Gina. "I'd get tanner than a brownie and marry me someone rich like Heyward."

Heyward told them he spent a lot of his time surf fishing and that he hadn't caught the first fish yet and wasn't really sure he would ever catch a fish. "But that's okay, I just enjoy watching the waves and the seagulls. Hey, do y'all want to hear something funny? Believe it or not, I got in a fistfight not too long ago," he told them. "Won it too," he quickly added.

The fight was big news to the women. They asked him all about it, how it was that a conservative guy like him could get involved with any kind of fisticuffs and if he got in trouble with the law for beating up somebody from New Jersey. Jean asked him if Peaches got hurt by the thrown beer can, and Gina asked him if Elizabeth was upset with him about the turn of events. Neither of the women had met Elizabeth, but Leon had talked about her before when he was married to each woman, explaining that he didn't think she liked him for some reason.

"Yeah, she was upset. She kept wanting me to go to the doctor to be checked over, but I never did," he said, puffing out his chest as if not seeking medical attention was some type of manly badge of honor. Heyward leaned forward, put his elbows on the table, and crossed his arms in front of him. Taking an exaggerated amount of time, he looked both women in the eyes. "Of course, with my reputation as a tough guy, people ought to know better than to mess with me."

They all laughed out loud when he said that, like they were young and back in junior high school, which was kind of a nice break from worrying so much about Leon.

"By the way, no real reason for me to ask, but do either of you ladies know what happens if you don't pay a speeding ticket in Georgia?"

*   *   *   *

By midafternoon, Heyward felt much better about everything. Leon's prognosis seemed more positive than anyone could have predicated the night before, and after lunch with the women, Heyward walked over to his hotel and took a short nap. Right or wrong, he sensed a feeling of admiration from the women. He had defended himself and his dog, and he had gotten the better of a younger man with a couple of well-thrown punches. Not only that, he had a good tan, and, as one of the women said, he was looking fitter than he had in years.

He was sure that if asked their opinion of him twenty-four hours earlier, they both would not have spoken too highly of him; in fact, they both would have spoken of him with some derision because they supposed wrongly that he had helped Leon in covering his affairs.

On the downside, he decided he'd better walk over to the FMSB's corporate tower and visit Miss Emma Belavedo.

Before getting a visitor's pass at the information desk, Heyward walked around the building to the executive parking lot to say hello to his old friend James Rimini. There were several gray Buicks in the lot, and despite himself, Heyward couldn't help but look at his old parking spot. There was a car parked there, a gray Buick, which put him in something of a somber mood, as if it was a conditioned reflex, like one of Pavlov's dogs.

"James Rimini doesn't work at this lot anymore, sir," a young man with a military demeanor told him. "He was reassigned to the custodial staff and works the night shift cleaning offices over in the corporate tower."

"What?" Heyward was speechless. James liked being in charge of the executive lot. He liked joking with all the executives, and he had told Heyward more than once that he liked being able to walk in and out of the guard shack whenever he wanted to just to be outdoors, even if it was outdoors in downtown Atlanta.

"James loved this old shack. Why would he change jobs?"

"No, sir, you don't understand. James didn't make the change himself. Some responsibilities changed in the bank within the last few months, and James works under Mr. Pasko now," the guard said. Heyward felt like the man had scoffed when he said, "Mr. Pasko."

Heyward said nothing more. He walked over to the corporate tower and got a visitor's pass from the information desk, even though the three women at the desk knew him by sight and by name.

"I'm going up to see Emma Belavedo," he told one of the women. Heyward knew bank procedures required the woman to call Miss Belavedo to see if she was expecting a visitor, regardless of who the visitor was. The bank didn't need some lunatic person wandering the corporate halls; there were problems enough just with the employees.

Miss Emma met Heyward at the elevator and hugged him as the elevator doors closed behind him. She started crying, and he, not her, lead the way back to her office.

"Now, now, Miss Emma, everything is going to be just fine. I've already spoken to Horace. But tell me, what in the world has gotten you so upset?"

✳   ✳   ✳   ✳

Kevin Pasko was wearing a dark green crew-neck sweater on the day Heyward came from the hospital to visit James Rimini and Miss Emma, even though it was still warm outside. He had spent all day going in and out of meetings and always carried a clipboard wherever he went. For some reason, he thought his clipboard gave him an air of authority.

When Kevin got back to his office, Heyward was sitting in his chair behind the desk and was holding the picture of Kevin Pasko's wife he had taken off the credenza. Heyward was studying the photograph as if he were looking for some type of missing detail in the picture.

Heyward sensed, rather than saw, Kevin Pasko walk in.

"You know something, Kevin, I don't know what makes me madder ..." Heyward said, not looking up.

"Madder? What are you talking about, Heyward? You're not supposed to be in here," Kevin Pasko said, clearing his throat. He was a little nervous. He hadn't expected anyone to be in his office, much less sitting at his desk, and he certainly had not expected Heyward Jennings. In fact, he never expected to see Heyward again after he'd retired.

Heyward gently set the picture back on the credenza, taking his time to adjust its position so that it was placed at exactly the right place and exactly at the correct angle to the office door.

"I'm talking about what makes me madder, Kevin, what makes me madder. Is it the fact that you are using my old desk, the one that Horace Junior gave me, that you insisted the bank wouldn't give me when I retired? Or is it the fact that you have been harassing Miss Belavedo or that you reassigned James Rimini to a night shift cleaning offices. I'm sure you did that because they're my friends." Heyward turned and looked at Kevin Pasko, who hadn't moved and was still standing on the threshold of the office door.

Heyward leaned back in the chair. "I don't know, Kevin, do you? What would make you madder, say, if you were me?" Heyward paused just a second then continued without giving Kevin a chance to answer. "Would those things make you mad, Kevin? What about the fact that you wear a sweater when it's eighty degrees outside? Apparently, that doesn't make you mad. It makes me mad for some reason. In fact, it makes you look like someone who would throw a beer can at a little dog on the beach."

Kevin Pasko looked down at his chest to make sure he was wearing a sweater then looked at Heyward. "Look, Heyward, you don't work for the bank anymore, and you can't tell me what or what not to do. I think I'd better call security."

Heyward didn't seem to hear him. "You know, Kevin, all those things make me mad, but not mad enough to hurt you. But I'll tell you what does drive me over the edge. How can a little weasel like you marry an attractive woman like your wife then keep a picture in your office that makes her look like a damn monkey? Tell me, Kevin, why do you continue to keep a picture that insults the looks of your wife? Tell me, why is that, Kevin?"

Kevin Pasko took a step toward his desk. "You're mentally unstable, Heyward. You should have been fired over that computer incident, but the old man looked out for you. I'm not afraid of you. What can you do to me?"

Heyward stood up behind the desk. "I can hurt you, Kevin. Beat you with my baseball bat, just like I did that computer. Would you like me to do that, hurt you? Just keep bothering Emma Belavedo or keep James Rimini away from his old job. I can't tell you how much I want to bash your face in. Just give me a reason."

Kevin Pasko suddenly turned and left his office. Heyward could hear him talking to someone outside. "Call security, and call them now. This man has threatened me."

He stuck his head back in his office but stood outside, his body shielded by the wall. "Security is coming, and you're in big trouble, buddy, threatening me that way. I'm going to have you locked up."

Heyward picked up the picture of Kevin Pasko's wife again and acted like he was studying it. "Kevin, no one is going to believe I threatened you—me, a high-level executive who drove old gray Buicks and never hurt a fly in his life? Look at you, you're an insect, that's all, a little insect that someone needs to step on and squash."

Heyward put the picture down, and Kevin Pasko looked over his shoulder to see if a security guard was anywhere near. "Kevin, you have a choice; that's all there is to it. Leave Miss Belavedo alone, and reassign James Rimini to his old daytime job. You do that, and we'll go our own ways. Don't do it, and I'll come back and catch you away from the office. Simple choice for a simpleton like you."

He walked out of the office and to the elevators.

CHAPTER 28

▼

Heyward figured the little insect, as he had called Kevin Pasko, had waved off the security guard because he made it down to the lobby of the FMSB corporate tower and past the information desk without being stopped or questioned. He felt like he had handled himself pretty well in Kevin's office, as far as intimidating the man, and he especially liked that Kevin felt like he had to call security. No one had ever been afraid of him before, at least not physically afraid.

But what do I do if he doesn't stop bothering Miss Emma? What if he doesn't put James back to his job on the lot? he thought. *There's no way I'm going to beat him with my ball bat or any other way. I might not be exactly mentally straight right now, but I haven't reached that level of depravity yet.*

When he was an executive, he always liked to plan for every contingency possible, even those unlikely to ever happen. On significant projects, ones that committed the bank to some type of exposure, either financial or its reputation, Heyward always had at least two backup plans if he could. Sometimes, he would have to opt to one alternative or another, a detour here and there, to reach the end result that was always the objective in the first place; he never bragged to anyone about those displays of good sense, but despite his own recent questions about his success or failure, his track record with the bank was perfect. With Kevin this afternoon, he had backed the man into a corner; what was he going to do if his conditions weren't met?

Although he felt good about scaring Kevin, it did bother him to be called "mentally unstable." It was one thing if he himself had questions about his own state of mind; it was something altogether different for someone like a Kevin Pasko to bring it up.

Heyward didn't feel he was mentally unstable. Maybe he was a little worn out and maybe he was a little off center about his growing dislike for gray Buicks. And maybe retiring on the spur of the moment, without any forewarning to anyone, especially his wife, showed some level of idiosyncrasy, but those were mostly age related. They didn't mean he was off in the head or some type of whacko or nutcase. Smashing Henry Pyatt's computer with a baseball bat and threatening Robert Fortson *might* show some signs of volatility, but those were one-time occurrences, not full-time mental instability, he reasoned.

When he finally got back to the hospital, Leon's condition hadn't changed for the better, but it hadn't taken a downturn either. Gina and Jean were still there, still going to see their ex-husband each hour, and to Heyward, they both looked exhausted. He suggested that they go over to the hotel room he had gotten for them and rest for a while. He promised to go in to see him every hour, just like they did, and he also promised to call them if anything changed.

He walked them to the elevators and gave Jean the key to the hotel room. "You all take showers and get cleaned up. Why don't you all order a good meal from room service? Get a steak, lobster—get anything you want—and just put it on my tab. Get a good night's sleep and in the morning, go down and get you some new clothes to change into. There's one of those high-class boutiques just off the hotel lobby and put those on my room bill too. Leon always told me you all had expensive taste in clothes."

They both gave him a small hug without saying a word, and when the elevator doors opened, it seemed they could barely walk in. Heyward watched the doors close, and as he walked back to the hard couch, he wondered what Leon did to deserve such devotion from the two women. When they divorced him, they wanted—at the very worst—to murder him or at best, neuter him, but still, neither woman ever remarried, and apparently, they continued to love him or at least it seemed so to Heyward.

Heyward thought it might be a prudent thing to do to call Elizabeth and casually work into the conversation that Gina and Jean were going to be using a hotel room that was rented under his name. He had called her several times since leaving the island and told her where he was staying. But he could just see her calling the hotel for some reason and asking to be connected to his room only to have the phone answered by a strange woman. That reasoning certainly was not one of a man who was "mentally unstable," he thought, just smart.

When an intensive care nurse let the waiting room visitors in for a five-minute visit just after midnight, one of the head nurses pulled Heyward to the side. "Mr. Campbell's eyes are open now, but he may not be fully awake or totally conscious. We're going to run some more tests on him in the morning, and we should know more then. Be careful what you say to him, he might not know where he is or he may not be able to comprehend everything that's happened to him." Then she added, "He's still not able to talk."

When Heyward walked up to his bed, Leon's eyes were open, and it looked like he was staring at the ceiling tiles. At first, he was not sure if Leon was able to focus, but when he touched his arm, Leon's eyes moved to Heyward's face.

"Hello, Leon. It's me Heyward. You've had a heart attack, and you're in the hospital, but everything looks good. You are going to be just fine, they say."

Leon blinked once and closed his eyes but didn't open them again for the rest of the five-minute visit.

When he got back to the waiting area, Heyward decided not to call Gina and Jean. They needed to get some sleep, and besides, there was nothing anyone could do or say to Leon until the next hour's visitation.

Leon didn't open his eyes at all on the next time Heyward was allowed in the intensive care unit or the four times after that. At the six o'clock visitation, Leon seemed to be awake, and as weak as he was, he tried to speak. Heyward could tell that he was trying to form something on his lips and leaned over the bed, just as he had done for his uncle Walter, to see if he could make out what Leon was trying to say.

Heyward wasn't sure, but he thought he made out the word *can't*.

He caught the eye of a nurse and waved her over to him. "He's trying to say something," he told her, but she just nodded, checked the flow of the intravenous fluids, and walked away.

Heyward called Jean and Gina and told them the latest news.

Then, two days later, the doctors declared that Leon had not only suffered a major heart attack, but at some point, he had also had a stroke that left him paralyzed on his left side. It appeared that Leon was going to have a long recovery, if indeed there was any real possible recovery.

Gina and Jean told Heyward that they would look after their ex-husband and for him to go on home. "Men just don't do well hanging around a hospital. Go home," Gina told him. He paid his hotel room bill and checked out after prepaying the ex-wives rooms for five more nights.

Despondent, he drove back to Wexler Island, neither caring one way or another if he did or didn't get another speeding ticket.

CHAPTER 29

▼

Elizabeth knew her husband was a little down, Leon being in the condition he was in and all, and she let him mope around a couple of days before she let on about the air horn.

About the only thing that kept Heyward's spirits up after he got back from Atlanta was admiring his tan in the mirror, that and watching The Weather Channel for hours on end. Watching weather nonstop kept his mind off heart attacks and strokes, but looking at his tan did make him feel good.

"You know, I had several people tell me I had a great tan, Elizabeth. I didn't really notice it until people started mentioning it to me. What do you think?"

"I think you need to stop watching TV and go fishing or something ... anything. Just how many times do you need to see the weather forecast? It's not going to change every eight minutes, is it?"

He knew when she was getting aggravated with him, and when she did, he liked to egg her on. "I have to know the weather conditions at all times. Don't forget, Elizabeth, I'm a surf fisherman, a famous surf fisherman, and all surf fishermen have to know how the ocean is going to behave. The weather affects the ocean; therefore, I have to know about it." She just looked at him like he was senile. He continued, "We might get a temperature inversion or an air mass moving down from Canada and not even know it if I'm not watching out for it ... those could really screw up my fishing."

"Oh, is that right? Do you even know what a temperature inversion is?"

"No, not really."

"How about an air mass moving down from Canada?"

"Nope, not that either. But it could be serious if it happened and affected my fishing."

"Well, Heyward, since you don't have a clue how weather affects the fishing, let me ask you something else. What's that air horn doing on your Jeep?"

"Uh-oh."

"Yes, Heyward, uh-oh. I expect Dewey Sikes had a hand in that one. Thanks to that horn, there's a little old man walking around here somewhere that I scared years off his life. I took Peaches to the beach while you were gone and saw that button in your glove box." She made sure she had his complete attention at that point in the conversation. "We had just pulled in the parking lot, next to this elderly man, when I reached into the glove box to see if there was a cloth in there to clean my sunglasses. I saw the button and the label, and I pushed it anyway."

"No kidding? I guess I know what happened next."

"You know partially what happened next. It scared me so bad that my foot slipped off the clutch, and the Jeep lurched forward and hit a lamppost. If you look closely on your front bumper, you can see a small dent in it where I hit it."

"Well, why did you push a button that was clearly labeled not to push it?"

"Curiosity, Heyward, curiosity. Remember, I taught science."

✳   ✳   ✳   ✳

It was two days later that Heyward received a letter from Horace Parker with the contact information for the boat manufacturing company, the one he asked him to see about helping when they ran into each other in the hospital waiting room. Two days after he received Horace's letter, Gina called about Leon; two days after her phone call, a freight company delivered Heyward's old desk from the bank.

For someone who liked FMSB to project conservativeness, Horace Parker used some mighty elegant stationary. The letterhead, stating it was from the president of the bank, was engraved on some very expensive-looking paper, and the bank's logo had been woven into the paper stock so that it appeared as a special-made watermark, something Heyward had never seen before. The envelope matched the letterhead perfectly and had the name and address of the bank embossed in gold across the upper left corner.

Heyward remarked to Peaches, who had accompanied him out to the mailbox, "I've got to hand it to old Horace. He likes his fancy stationary and his blond girlfriends while we all had to drive those plain old Buicks. But I suppose he can do whatever he wants to, being the boss and all."

Horace had written the letter by hand, using an old-fashioned fountain pen. He simply wrote the name of the boat manufacturer, South Island Boat Company, the name of the owners, Danforth and Lauren Jackson, and the company's telephone number. Horace wrote a little note of how appreciative he was that Heyward would take the time to do him such a large favor and hoped that the fishing was good on Wexler Island.

Gina telephoned to let Heyward and Elizabeth know Leon had been moved to a nice rehabilitation center outside of Atlanta, close to her home, and that she and Jean would look after him the best they could. Leon had not improved much and still could not speak, at least nothing they could understand, and he could not move any of the left side of his body.

"All we can hope for now is for some good therapy and medical care and pray that he doesn't have another heart attack or stroke," she told Heyward. Heyward promised to come visit Leon in a couple of weeks, but he would come immediately if she needed him, all she had to do was let him know. As soon as he got off the phone with Gina, he sent Leon a card that Elizabeth had bought him for that purpose and signed his and Elizabeth's names at the bottom of the inspirational message. After he thought a moment, he signed Peaches' name too.

Two days after Gina's phone call, Eastern Freight and Shipping Company delivered Horace Junior's desk to the Jenningses' residence. The two men who brought the desk put it in the small office that Elizabeth had set up, and they were nice enough to remove all of the packaging material off the desk.

When the packing was removed, one of the delivery men let out a low whistle. Someone had, in big letters, scratched into the top surface of the desk: "ASSW-HOLE."

"Not only is Kevin Pasko a little prick, he can't spell worth a damn either," Heyward said as he rubbed his hand over the scratched-in letters.

CHAPTER 30

▼

When Heyward first received the letter from Horace Parker, he looked up South Island Boat Company on the Internet to see what kind of information he could find on the company, then he did a search on the young owner, Danforth Jackson. He already knew a little about Thomas Pennington, the man was in the financial news occasionally, but Heyward ran an Internet search on him too, just to see if anything interesting turned up.

South Island Boat Company did have a Web site. It was well designed and provided general information about the company and its products, which was very limited because the only thing they made was a line of small wooden fishing boats. The Web site had an interesting page that related the history of the company and explained that the boats were made by hand, by craftsmen who, for the most part, learned their craft from previous generations of island boat builders.

He found almost nothing on the Internet about Danforth Jackson other than an obscure article written by him that appeared to have been published in some type of academic journal which Heyward had never heard of before. The article written by Jackson had something to do with the findings of a statistical analysis of an archaeological find, but the subject matter was so complicated to Heyward that he didn't attempt to read the article beyond two paragraphs. He thought it odd that anyone as intelligent in the fields of statistics and archaeology as the young Jackson must be would be interested in running a boat-building company.

There was nothing on the Internet about a Lauren Jackson or a Lauren Pennington or a Lauren Pennington Jackson, which Heyward assumed covered all the names the woman might have, she being the daughter of Thomas Pennington.

There was, however, plenty of information about Thomas Pennington, the financier. Apparently, Pennington was very well known in the international field of finance and had held some prestigious positions—all congressional appointments—in the government of the United States. From everything he could read about the man, Pennington was extremely wealthy, but nowhere could he find any information about him personally; Heyward was interested in why his old boss, Horace Parker, said he was a son of a bitch and felt it odd that Horace would be friends with anyone he described that way.

Heyward did another search on the Internet: a map and direction inquiry on the physical address and location of the South Island Boat Company. The plant was indeed located on Wexler Island and was only about eight miles from Heyward's house, as the crow flies.

"Are you going to call this person, Jackson, first or just drop by and introduce yourself?" Elizabeth asked Heyward. "How are you going to explain why you contacted him?"

"Quite frankly, I don't really know what the best way is to handle this sort of thing. This fellow might be none too happy to hear from me since, according to Horace, he doesn't like his father-in-law. He may consider me a meddler in his business, and quite frankly, I don't need that," Heyward said.

"Or, Heyward, he might be glad to have an outsider's help if his company is in trouble like Horace supposed it is. He might just welcome you."

Later that afternoon, after two hours of unproductive surf fishing, Heyward went home and asked Elizabeth to ride by the boat company with him, just to see the outside appearance of the building and get a feel of the area before he called Danforth Jackson.

"Plus," he said, "we can stop and get some ice cream on the way." Heyward had found an old-fashioned ice cream shop, the kind of place he took Elizabeth on dates before they were married, and whenever he was anywhere in the area, he would stop by and get a banana split.

It wasn't hard to find the South Island Boat Company, but then, it really wasn't hard to find any place on the island, depending if a person didn't mind the fact that a lot of the older roads didn't have any type of street sign.

The location of the company was stunning. There were at least twenty live oak trees—Elizabeth said they had to be hundreds of years old—that shaded two buildings: a small one, out front, like it was an office of some type, and another building that was larger, but not large in the sense of a manufacturing plant. Behind the oak trees, there was a wide expanse of marshland that seemed to stretch as far as Heyward could see.

Both buildings were made of some type of old bricks, but neither Heyward nor Elizabeth had ever seen anything quite like them before. The windows on the larger building were long; they extended from just below the roof to just a few feet from the ground, and they were open, swiveled out as if positioned that way to catch any kind of ocean breeze.

"Look at those trees and that view of the marsh. Have you ever seen anything so beautiful?" Elizabeth said. "And the Spanish moss hanging down from them makes this look like a picture from some type of travel brochure."

"It looks like something to me out of a history book, Elizabeth. I'll bet these trees were planted before the Revolutionary War. Who knows, maybe even George Washington himself walked around under them before he signed the Emancipation Proclamation."

"Uh, Heyward, it was Abraham Lincoln who signed the Emancipation Proclamation, not George Washington."

They sat in the Jeep and just looked at the scene, the two old buildings under beautiful live oak trees with the marsh behind them.

"Do you notice anything strange?" Heyward asked his wife.

Elizabeth stared for a few moments and said, "Bicycles. Look at all those bicycles; there must be ten or twelve of them. That looks a little weird to me."

"That's what I was thinking too," Heyward said. "Two cars out front and all those bikes around the side building."

Heyward gave the Jeep some gas, and they headed home. "Something tells me, Toto, we're not in Atlanta anymore," he said to no one in particular.

*   *   *   *

The next morning, Heyward placed a call to the South Island Boat Company, to Danforth Jackson in particular, in order to fulfill his promise to his old boss.

The phone rang eight or nine times before it was picked up. It sounded like a man who answered the phone, "South Island Boats," and in the background, Heyward could hear some type of machinery running, like a compressor or a power sander; whatever it was made it hard for him to hear or understand the person on the other side of the line.

"I'd like to speak to Danforth Jackson, please," Heyward said.

"Who?" the voice on the phone asked.

Heyward repeated himself, but this time, much louder. He could hear the telephone receiver being set down on a counter. After at least two minutes, a voice came back to the line. Horace Parker was going to owe him big time for this, possibly more than what he asked for in the hospital waiting room, he thought. Besides, even though he got his old desk, it had the word "Asswhole" scratched on it, and what good was that going to do him?

"Dan Jackson." A loud sound, like a table saw, drowned out anything else the voice may have said.

This is very awkward, Heyward thought but then proceeded to try to explain who he was. He explained how Horace Parker III had asked him to call as a courtesy to Thomas Pennington, but that he himself did not personally know Mr. Pennington. He asked if he, Heyward, could come over just to introduce himself in person.

Dan Jackson was not especially friendly, but Heyward expected that; no young man, or a man of any age for that matter, wants to be offered help from his father-in-law, especially one he doesn't like. Nonetheless, they set up an appointment for ten o'clock the next day, at least Heyward thought that's what they agreed to, but he could hardly hear over the sound of the loud background noise.

*   *   *   *

Danforth, or Dan, Jackson as he introduced himself looked like he may have been in his late twenties. Horace said he was young, but still, Heyward was a little startled at how young. Dan presented himself well, and when he shook Heyward's hand, he noticed the man had a good, firm handshake. Heyward considered a firm handshake absolutely essential to being a person of substance, either man or woman; both were the same to him.

"Mr. Jennings, I would like to ask you a couple of questions before you sit down, if you don't mind," Dan said, after he showed him into his small but neat office.

"Ask me anything you want to," Heyward answered.

"Are you being paid by my father-in-law, Thomas Pennington, for coming here or are you being compensated by him in any fashion for doing this?"

"No."

"If Thomas Pennington is not paying you, is Horace Parker or anybody else paying you or influencing you?"

"Thomas Pennington is not paying me. No one is influencing me. Horace Parker is not paying me for coming here, at least not financially paying me. I agreed with Horace to come meet you and see if I could be of any help to your boat company, if he would do a few simple things for me. First, I wanted him to make a certain person at FMSB quit harassing my old secretary, and I wanted him to have an old friend at the bank reassigned to his old job responsibility, if he wants it back. Also, I wanted Horace to give me my old desk that I used at the bank. That's it, nothing else."

Heyward continued, "Pretty much, I'm doing this as a favor to Horace. He wants to look like he's helping your father-in-law so if he gets on the board of FMSB, he'll look out for Horace's interest. Does that answer your questions fully? Anything else you want to know?"

"Thanks for telling me that, and I hope I didn't insult you," Dan said. "If we come to some type of arrangement for you helping me, I'm not sure what to pay you."

"Let's get one thing straight since you were so interested if your father-in-law was behind all of this." Heyward continued, "From what I hear, I understand that Thomas Pennington is a son of a bitch, and I personally have a thing against SOBs. I won't work for them or with them, okay?"

"Understood, Mr. Jennings," Dan told him.

"All right, Dan, I see we need to get some other things straight as well. I'm Heyward, not Mr. Jennings, and I don't want any pay from you, period. I might not be of any help to you, anyway. Okay, again?"

Dan nodded and stuck out his hand, and the two men shook hands on everything they had talked about up to that point.

"Now," Heyward said, "tell me all about the South Island Boat Company and why all those bikes are parked out on the side of the building."

CHAPTER 31

▼

The South Island Boat Company had been in existence for almost fifty years. It was started by Danforth Jackson's grandfather, William Jackson.

William Jackson was a commercial fisherman long before Wexler Island became an upscale beach resort and before it had attracted well-to-do retirees like Heyward. Fishing on the scale that William Jackson did was not a very lucrative way to earn a living or a reliable way of providing for a family, but it was a way of life and it was his way of life.

After a particularly nasty storm destroyed his small fishing boat, he had no choice but to build another one in order to support his family, or else he would have been forced into earning his living by farming or moving from the island. He built his replacement boat himself and to that boat added some small features that his original one didn't have, features that made his fishing much more efficient.

The local fishing community took notice of his boat, and while the other fishermen might have been able carpenters, none could match the natural talent William Jackson had for boat construction. Soon, William was making boats for other fishermen and crabbers on Wexler Island, and in the tradition of the American entrepreneurial spirit, started a bona fide boat-building business to supply small wooden fishing boats to commercial fishermen up and down the Eastern Seaboard. When his boat manufacturing business prospered to the point that he could no longer fish, he turned the business over to his son, Stewart, who was Dan Jackson's father.

The South Island Boat Company prospered for many years.

Dan Jackson grew up in the company and worked in the production end of the operation but his heart was never really in the business like his father and his grandfather before him. Eventually, Dan went off to college, majored in archeology, went to work for a prestigious museum outside of Philadelphia, and married a girl, Lauren Pennington, who was finishing up her college career.

Stewart Jackson died unexpectedly, and Dan, being an only child, was forced to come back to the island and run the company for his mother who was suffering with a debilitating illness. Dan knew how to produce boats, but he had never been interested in the administrative part of the company. Events forced him to learn at an accelerated pace.

"I want to keep this company going, for one thing, for the sake of my father and grandfather. My mother is financially set, so she is taken care of okay. The other reason is because of the people who work here. Most of them inherited their skills from their fathers and, in some cases, from their grandfathers. We pay well, a lot more than they can earn working in the resorts, and here, they have dignity in their work. Over there," Dan said pointing in the general direction of the big resorts on the other part of the island, "over there, they're service workers, nothing more."

Heyward nodded.

"These people are counting on me to run the company and keep their jobs viable. I could sell the company to one of those large fiberglass boat manufacturers, but everything here will be changed and I don't want that. Or I could do like my father-in-law wants me to do."

"What's that?" Heyward asked.

"I could close the company and sell the property to some developers. I could get millions of dollars for the land, especially with these old oak trees and the view of the marsh—millions."

"Why don't you do that? I expect you could get millions for this property. Then you could go back to your archeology without any headaches or responsibility," Heyward said.

Dan Jackson looked at his watch. "Are you hungry? Why don't we grab a bike and go get some lunch? It might help you understand why I don't want to sell."

*   *   *   *

Dan told Heyward he needed to make a few quick phone calls before they left the building for lunch, and Heyward, taking the hint, excused himself from the office to give the young owner some privacy.

Heyward turned his cell phone on—he always turned it off before going into any kind of meeting—and noticed he'd had a call from Miss Emma Belavedo.

Under the shade of a big oak tree, he called Miss Emma who, true to form, answered the call before the second ring. Heyward liked that about her—she answered a phone promptly. They talked several minutes about Leon Campbell and how bad it was that he had had a heart attack and a stroke, and Heyward got the feeling that Miss Emma might be having a twinge of regret that she had spoken so critically of Leon every time she'd had the chance.

Eventually, she got around to telling him the purpose of her call. The attorney, Matthew Rabon, had called her and asked that she get in touch with Heyward with the message to call him back, preferably today around four o'clock, if Heyward found that convenient.

Heyward wrote the telephone number down on a piece of paper he carried to remind him of some errands. The area code and phone number she gave him was definitely for Sheridan, Alabama.

"Miss Emma, before you hang up, I need to ask: How is it going between you and that sorry-ass, sweater-wearing Kevin Pasko now? I mean, has he been leaving you alone since my visit?"

To his relief, Kevin had stopped bothering her.

Heyward stared for a moment at the telephone number on the paper. In his mind, he could visualize the small, distinguished-looking Matthew Rabon sitting in what he supposed would be his well-appointed office, holding a check for $415,000 made out to one Heyward Jennings. *Maybe all he needs is my new address here on Wexler Island so he can overnight the check to me,* Heyward thought.

Heyward rubbed his eyes. *Durn,* he thought, *I should have talked to Elizabeth about this before now.*

Dan walked out of his the building and said, "I'm buying lunch, and I hope you're hungry. Remember you asked me earlier about those bikes?" He pointed one out to Heyward. "I hope you can ride that one because that's how we get to Sunny's Diner around here. I feel sure you'll like it."

As it turned out, just riding a bike to lunch explained a lot of things about Dan Jackson, South Island Boat Company, and some of the people on Wexler Island that Heyward eventually would meet.

*   *   *   *

"There's no one actually named Sunny or even Sonny for that matter," Dan said to Heyward as they rode their bikes down a narrow, two-lane paved road, which was shaded by big oaks. "You'll see."

The diner's owner, Mazelle DuPont, he explained, apparently just liked the word *sunny*; when she first opened the diner years ago, she thought it would be a pleasant name, friendly, for working people looking to have a good meal, breakfast or lunch, at a price they could afford.

"She closes the place at two o'clock and too bad if you haven't finished eating," Dan said. "Mazelle is going fishing, come hell or high water, and you'd better be gone or else she'll lock you up in there for the night." Mazelle enjoyed a local reputation for being a skillful and patient fisherman along the tidal creeks that backed up to her restaurant.

"She's a fine person. From what I heard, she was the first black woman on the island to open up her own business. And that was years ago when, on this island, both black and white women didn't much work outside their homes. Imagine how hard that must've been."

Like the boat company, Sunny's Diner was built around and under some large live oak trees. As they parked, but didn't lock, their bicycles, Heyward noticed that there must have been ten other bikes parked under the same tree. Dan saw him looking at them.

"The folks that work out back in production use the company bikes to ride down here to lunch every day. Some of then ride home to eat, just depending on what they want to do that day. It's something my grandfather started," Dan explained. "Most everybody that works in the plant lives close around here, you see."

They opened a well-worn screen door that reminded Heyward of the screen door on Dilly's Bait Shop and were greeted by a tiny black woman with close-cropped salt-and-pepper hair. Heyward, who was still at least six feet tall, seemed to loom over the little woman.

"Good afternoon, come in, come in," she said in a voice that seemed to warble out of her small frame. She looked up at Heyward through the bifocal part of the lens of her eyeglasses and said, "I haven't seen you before, have I?"

"This is Heyward, Miss Mazelle."

Heyward was really beginning to like Dan. He had a good, strong handshake. He was straightforward about not wanting help from his father-in-law, and now, he was addressing an older woman the same way Heyward did Miss Emma Bela-vedo.

The woman shook his hand firmly too, like Dan, but Heyward felt a little awkward about being too firm back; he didn't want to crush or injure her small hand.

"If you're okay with Dan, you're okay with me too," she said as they followed her to a table with a red plastic tablecloth that a younger woman was wiping off with a damp cloth.

On the way to their table, Dan returned the waves and nods from different people sitting around the diner, almost all of them black and all of different ages. They all wore dark blue shirts with the words *South Island Boat Company* stenciled over the front pocket.

"If you decide to help me for a while, you'll meet most of these folks," Dan said as they sat down at a table with mismatched chairs. On the table were salt and pepper shakers that were shaped like little fish.

Two men came over and introduced themselves to Heyward as they made their way to the cash register. "We're Monroe and Boney," the tallest one said. They shook hands with him and with Dan.

"That's Mon-Roe, Mr. Jennings. Dan calls me Monroe like educated people are supposed to do, but all my ignorant friends call me Mon-Roe."

"Well, I guess if it's all the same to you, I'll call you Mon-Roe. I'm not very well educated to speak of, anyway."

The two men nodded at Heyward and left to pay their dinner tab.

"You'll see, Heyward," Dan said, "the people that work at the company are good people. I just hope I'm up to the task so they can keep their jobs."

CHAPTER 32

▼

After lunch at Sunny's, Dan and Heyward rode their bikes back to the plant, and together, they walked around through the production area where about ten boats were in different stages of completion.

Dan introduced Heyward to all fifteen employees, one at a time. As he introduced each person, he told him a little about their background and how long they had worked with the company. Most people had worked there their whole adult life; it was the only job they had ever held. Some employees worked beside their fathers, learning the skill of wooden boat building that was passed down to them from *their* fathers. Several people told Heyward that their fathers, or mothers, had retired from South Island Boats and they, themselves, planned to retire from there too.

"Is that true what some of those folks told me?" Heyward asked Dan as they stood out behind the building in some shade. "Sons working alongside their fathers now and those others had family members who retired from here?"

"Yep, this is a family business in that sense. Fathers or mothers worked here and then their sons or daughters came to work here when they were old enough. It's always been that way as far as anyone can remember."

He continued, "I'm proud that my father and grandfather were good employers and proud of everybody who works here too. Can you imagine that sort of loyalty in a big company?"

"Shoot," Heyward said. "I liked working at the bank, but I swore if either of my children got into the banking business, well, let's put it this way: I didn't want them working there."

Dan rubbed his hand along the painted side of a finished boat. "There is very little opportunity for people on this island for work. Like I told you before lunch, there're service jobs over in the resorts, but nothing that pays hardly anything more than minimum wage."

Heyward nodded. Up to now, he had never really considered that there were people living on Wexler Island long before The Three Oaks had been carved out of the island's forest.

"I guess there are not many companies that furnish bicycles for employees to ride to lunch on," Heyward finally said.

"Or to ride back and forth to home on either," Dan said. "Would you want to be the one who told these people they were out of a job because I wanted to sell this land and have someone build condos on it? My father-in-law says he wouldn't mind telling them they're fired. Said he wouldn't have any problem telling them. In fact, he has already lined up a developer and had him draw up an artist's conception of villas overlooking the marsh. He thinks he can somehow get me to sell if he does that sort of thing, I suppose."

Heyward couldn't think of much to say to that. The land, he figured, was extremely valuable, probably a whole lot more valuable than the worth of the boat company, at least as he could tell from the little information he'd seen so far. Of course, to the employees, the company was very valuable; it put food on their tables, and apparently, it was a way of life too.

"Oh, off the subject of land development and condos and back on the boat business for a minute, Dan, why are all the hulls of the boats painted navy blue?" Heyward asked.

"For good luck. According to my grandfather, a boat with a dark blue hull brings good luck, so we've always kept that tradition up."

✳   ✳   ✳   ✳

The phone call he was supposed to make to Matthew Rabon had not been off his mind since he had spoken with Miss Emma earlier in the day. This thing with his uncle's estate had been going on for a while now, and Heyward was ready to get it settled one way or another. It seemed like his inheritance—it was the only time he knew he would inherit anything in his lifetime—was almost too good to be true, and in the long run, he really expected to be disappointed somehow. It was almost like misreading a lottery ticket, seeing your number match the winning combination only to later realize you had made a terrible mistake and no lottery proceeds would be forthcoming.

It had been a hard thing to keep to himself all this time, but he still had not said anything to Elizabeth about being named as his uncle's sole heir or about the attorney estimating they could be on the receiving end of a small fortune. Now, it appeared the day of reckoning was near; he wasn't sure exactly how she would take the news or exactly how he would break it to her.

Heyward called the attorney from the little office that Elizabeth had set up just off the den in their new house. She had put his old desk, the one with the word "ASSWHOLE" scratched in the top, in the room and covered the word with a blotter. Matthew Rabon's secretary put his call through, and without any small talk, the attorney got right to business.

"Mr. Jennings, everything with your uncle Walter Jennings's estate has been settled, and all the documentation has been filed in the county courthouse. I'm pleased to tell you all obligations have been duly fulfilled."

He continued, "I will overnight a copy of all the documents to you for your files. Then there's the matter of getting the funds to you. We can wire them into your account today or send a check if you prefer a check."

"Mr. Rabon, were there any problems on getting the estate settled?" Heyward asked, still not absolutely convinced that some obscure law or last-minute claim was not going to upset his inheritance applecart.

"There were a few little things to take care of, there almost always are in something like this, but everything has been satisfied. In the packet you receive tomorrow will be a detailed listing of all the 'ins' and 'outs' of what we did. Would you prefer us to cut a check, or would you prefer a wire transfer?"

"A wire transfer would be fine with me, Mr. Rabon." Heyward gave the attorney his bank information and bank account number.

There was a slight pause on the attorney's end of the phone as if he was looking at a clock or his watch. "Ah, let's see. Yes, the funds can be wired today and will be in your bank account after midnight tonight."

Heyward's mouth was completely dry. He wished he had a glass of cold water, or warm water, for that matter. Despite the fact that his parched tongue was sticking to the roof of his mouth, he asked, "Mr. Rabon, exactly how much money, excuse me, how much funds are you going to be wiring me?"

"Hold on, let me look again just so I get the exact amount … Yes, the final amount of settlement is $421,577.90."

Heyward thought he said thank you before he hung up but really didn't remember even saying good-bye.

Heyward walked slowly from the den. He went to the kitchen sink and drank directly from the faucet then splashed his face with cold water. When he had gotten enough to satisfy his thirst, he went into the den and sat down in his favorite chair, which seemed extraordinarily comfortable to him.

Elizabeth, who was sitting on the couch reading a magazine, asked him, "Who were you talking to on the telephone?" Peaches had been watching some squirrels playing on the wooden deck and trotted over for him to pet her.

"Elizabeth," Heyward said, "you need to sit down." Then, he realized he must be in something of a daze because she *was* sitting down. "We need to talk. I've got some good news for you."

CHAPTER 33

▼

For a time, Elizabeth didn't say a word. She didn't ask a question. She didn't clear her throat or even blink her eyes. Heyward thought she comprehended everything he told her. He knew she would remember his trip to see his dying uncle, but she looked like she was in a state of complete bewilderment.

"Did you say $421,577?" she finally asked.

"And ninety cents. The exact amount is $421,577.90. We may need the ninety cents to buy a pack of chewing gum or mail some letters someday," he replied.

"And when should we get the money? I know you told me already, but I went blank there for a minute."

"It should be in our checking account after midnight tonight. All of it," he realized that he did tell her before but understood this was a lot to take in.

Elizabeth coughed three or four times, then blurted, "Holy ... well, holy fuck is all I can say!"

Heyward was almost as shocked to hear her swear as he was when Matthew Rabon had told *him* the amount. In all their years of marriage, through everything they had gone through together, Heyward had never heard his wife use bad language in any form or fashion.

Just to be on the safe side, Heyward explained to her, once again, that he thought it best not to tell her of the possibility of an inheritance when he returned from the trip to Sheridan. He didn't want any hint of suspicion that might later surface that somehow, he had been keeping the information from her for some other reason than to save her from disappointment should the whole thing fall through.

"Well, what do you want to do with it? Have you given any thought to that?" she asked.

"Nothing special. I might want to buy a boat, a nice boat. I had a figure of around $150,000, or so. Keep it at a marina around here somewhere, and we'd go out on it for fun. A big enough boat would have room for the kids and the twins too." He paused before he got excited. "I'll be Captain Jennings … Commodore Jennings—those have a nice ring to them—or, better yet, Admiral Heyward Jennings, sailing out of his home port on Wexler Island, South Carolina. That sounds even better."

"Maybe you could become a pirate, Heyward, and get a parrot and a wooden leg too." It didn't take her too long to get a little saucy with him.

Heyward looked at Elizabeth. "Well, what about you? What would you like to buy?"

Elizabeth made a face that Heyward took to mean she didn't know at the time or would have to think about it and let him know later. His thoughts drifted from his wife to trying to remember if he still had any of his old coast guard uniforms in some of the boxes they moved from Atlanta. He would look snappy in them at the helm of his new boat.

Just after midnight, they went to their computer and pulled up their bank information on the Internet. There was a wire transfer of $421,577.90 credited to their account.

"Thank goodness," Heyward said. "They didn't forget the ninety cents. Now we can buy that chewing gum."

"Heyward, let me ask you something." Elizabeth looked up from the computer screen to her husband. "How did your uncle Walt earn his money?"

He just shrugged his shoulders.

CHAPTER 34

▼

After Heyward had been around for two days, his first real impression was that South Island Boat Company had most of the fundamentals in place to be a going concern, one that would last for at least another fifty years. The company had good relationships with its distributors, and those distributors actively and successfully promoted South-Island-made boats. The boats themselves enjoyed a good and long reputation for quality and strength among people who were knowledgeable about boats in the niche they filled. The employees of the company seemed to be accomplished, and most seemed to be grateful to have the jobs. Although there was not a big market for small wooden fishing boats like they made, the company had a small but steady backlog of work.

In Heyward's opinion, Dan seemed to be capable of running the company, even though he was young. He had grown up in the company, working with the skilled craftsman in making the boats and learning about the materials that went into construction. It was obvious that his employees liked and respected him and that he, in turn, tried to look out for their well-being. Dan just needed a little help in the accounting end of the business and a dose of confidence that he could run the company without his father's or grandfather's help.

Around noon on Heyward's third day, Dan came out into the production area and, above the sound of a sanding machine, shouted out to Heyward, "Let's go to lunch. I have somebody that's going with us that I want you to meet."

Heyward brushed some sawdust from his shirt and walked up to the office to see a tall, slender man wearing khaki pants and a long-sleeve khaki shirt folding some type of paperwork into his front pocket. The man had gray hair, which he wore cut a little on the long side, and his face and hands were weathered and seemed like worn leather. Heyward thought he looked like he spent all day out-doors, and unless the sun aged him much faster than most people, he had to be in his early to mid-seventies.

"Heyward, I'd like you to meet an old friend of the company. This is Leland Tiller. Leland, this is Heyward Jennings." Heyward shook the older man's hand and got a firm handshake back, just as he expected he would.

Dan continued, "Leland owns Tiller Lumber Company, and they have supplied us with wood for a real long time, at least as long as before I was born."

Heyward knew he was going to like the lumberman after having lunch with him and Dan. Leland moved slowly and deliberately, and he seemed to speak just as slowly as he moved. He was careful in the words he chose, as if he was weighing the meaning of every word and as if he was only allowed an allotted amount of words to use on any given day.

Over lunch, at Dan's suggestion, Leland explained to Heyward about the kinds of wood used to make South Island boats, the characteristics of the wood, and why each type was important to strength and durability in boats. Heyward liked the way Leland explained things. He never talked down to him. He patiently answered his questions, and then, once he had answered the specific question, he seemed to anticipate what Heyward was going to ask about next.

"Do you fish, Heyward?"

Heyward told him of his unsuccessful surf fishing and the surf casting rod and reel he had received when he retired and told him about going to Dilly's for bait.

"I guess when you went to Dilly's, you met Edna. She's that old gruff woman that works there, and she always wears a dirty T-shirt," Leland said then laughed. "Be careful not to let her get you in that bait room in the back; you might come out of there wearing that T-shirt around your head."

Leland continued, "I'm going fishing on the Black Oak tomorrow. Why don't you go with me?"

Then he added, "We'll be fishing in fresh water in the river, not salt water, so you might like that a little better. I'll bring you a rod and reel. The one you use in the ocean isn't what you want to use where we're going. Lauren is coming too."

Heyward looked at Leland, then Dan, then Leland again as if he was trying to tie everyone together in his mind. "Lauren? Dan's wife?"

"Oh, yeah. She likes to fish and catches more than I do most days."

*   *   *   *

When Heyward first saw Lauren Jackson, he was so shocked by her good looks that he stuck a hook in the tip of his finger. Even at seven in the morning, she was stunning; she was tall and thin and looked like he expected a top fashion model would look in real life, even though he had never seen or met an actual model before. She had long brunette hair, which she wore in a ponytail that she stuck through the back of a New York Yankees baseball cap. She sported a long-sleeve, blue denim work shirt that had the words "South Island Boat Company" embroidered over a pocket. Heyward had noticed some of the production workers wearing the same type of shirt, but none of them wore it like she did; the sleeves were rolled up stylishly, like women sometimes wore them, and she had turned the collar up like he did if he wanted to avoid a sunburned neck. She wore a pair of faded blue jeans and white tennis shoes. Heyward tried not to stare but, in spite of his best efforts, couldn't take his eyes off her, she was so beautiful.

She extended her hand, and they shook. "You must be Mr. Jennings. Dan said you had gray hair and drove a green Jeep Wrangler with big tires. He didn't tell me you were so young looking or so handsome."

Heyward was completely tongue-tied, and when he tried to speak, it sounded like gibberish. At last he blurted out, "Yes, I must be him. You must be Lauren Pennington."

She laughed. "No, not Pennington, Lauren Jackson. Pennington was my maiden name." She smiled at him. "Do I look like a Pennington to you? They're all business types and so important looking."

Heyward could not recall a time he was so embarrassed. "I'm sorry. I thought … I mean … I didn't mean …" and his voice just trailed off. He wished for the moment that a great tidal wave would wash him off the boat landing where Leland Tiller was putting his boat in the water, but he knew they were on a freshwater river and a tidal wave was highly unlikely to appear.

"I like your Jeep," she said, pointing to his car. "Maybe you'll take me for a ride in it one day. Let's make a bet right now. If I catch more fish than you today, you've got to let me drive it!"

Heyward took the car's ignition key from his pocket and held it out to her. "If that's the bet, I might as well give you my car right now. Catching fish is not something I do particularly well. In fact, seafood restaurants won't even let me order fish off the menu."

They laughed again, and by that time, Leland had the boat in the water and was waiting on them.

"Leland, isn't Joey going with us this morning?" Lauren asked as he cranked the engine and the boat began to move away from the launch pier.

"No, not today. Joey's not going to make it today," was all Leland said.

Despite Leland's help, and pointers from Lauren, Heyward didn't catch a fish all morning, even though Leland caught a couple of smallmouth bass and Lauren caught three, all bigger than Leland's fish. Heyward did manage to hook himself again in the finger and despite the pain of the barbed hook, was glad he did because Lauren climbed over the seats and helped him get the hook out of his finger and put a bandage on it.

When they got back to the boat-launch ramp, Leland looked at Heyward's wrapped finger. "Heyward, you didn't have much luck today, but at least you didn't get seasick or hook Lauren or me. What do you think, Lauren? Think old Heyward scared some fish today?"

"Be nice, Leland. After all, Heyward's a city boy. Let's just hope he can help Dan out more than he can fish, though. If not, I suppose there'll be bulldozers pushing a certain boat company out of the way for some condos, don't you think?" she said.

Heyward didn't care if Leland kidded him about his lack of fishing skills or if he got another hook stuck in his finger or even, for the moment, if bulldozers pushed South Island Boat Company and all of those bicycles off the face of the earth. All he cared about was when he would be able to see Lauren Pennington Jackson again.

CHAPTER 35

▼

The following Monday, Heyward offered Dan Jackson his suggestions for the South Island Boat Company.

"As I see it, Dan, there're only two things that I see are important for you to do. They're so simple I didn't even write them down."

Heyward made sure he had the younger man's attention. "I think it's pretty straightforward. From everything I've seen, I believe you have a solid company here and I believe you are more than capable of running it, but you need to learn more of the accounting side of the business." Heyward paused. "You've got someone doing your books now, but they just give you the month-end figures. Go take some accounting courses at the community college over in Marshfield. Learn everything you can about why the accountant does what he does. That will give you more insight into things and help you make good decisions."

"Accounting?" Dan asked.

"Yes, accounting. Learn it inside and out and how it affects your business."

"All right. You said there were two things. What's the other one?"

"Ever since we met, you've talked at great length about whether to sell or close the company and develop the land, you know, whether to develop it into condos and such. You seem to be fixated on whether to sell or not. Actually, you seem to be tormented by it." Heyward looked at him for a response. Dan frowned.

"My second recommendation is for you to make a decision, once and for all, and put the issue behind you one way or another. You can't run a business with a big question like that on your mind all the time."

"Well, Heyward, what would you do if you were me? Sell? Not sell?" Dan asked.

"That's your decision to make, Dan. I shouldn't suggest you doing either one. But let me ask you something. What is it *you* want to do? Do you want the money for selling to put in the bank? You could go back to the museum or go on archeology digs. On the other hand, the company your grandfather started, the one you grew up in, goes away if you do that. All the folks back there," Heyward waved his hand in the direction of the production area, "all those folks get on those bicycles and ride away forever. Probably Miss Mazelle will have to close Sunny's because y'all are her main customers, and if you're not here, whose going to eat over there?"

Heyward continued, "Think about old Boney back there. He told me he was trying to get custody of his little boy, Monty, from his ex-girlfriend, Monty's mother. I'm sure you know the story: The mother is a drug addict and takes any money Boney gives to her for Monty for drugs. If his job goes away, any chance he has to get custody of Monty goes away with it. Personally, I'd hate to have that on my conscience, and I expect you would too."

Dan got up and went over to the only window he had in his office. He put a hand on each side of the windowsill and looked out over the marsh. "I remember one time when I was a little boy, my father came home one night and told my mother that Retha Radwin's house—she used to work here at the company before she died—anyway, her house burned down, and she didn't have any insurance. Lost everything. My father and mother helped her rebuild her house and gave her a bunch of our furniture. My father raised money from other businesses on the island to help her out. Leland Tiller was a part of all that too."

"Dan, if you sell, all that goes in the history books and ends."

Heyward stood up.

"Anyway, it's my opinion that you could run this company and do well for yourself and be someone everyone looks up to. Learn a little bit about accounting and get some confidence in it, and you'll be more than all right," Heyward said.

He put his hand on the young man's shoulder. "Now that I put all of that on you, I'm going to meet Leland for lunch at Sunny's and then, don't get your feelings hurt now, but I'm going to start looking for a big Sea Ray cruising boat. South Island boats are for fishermen, and I don't think I qualify for that title."

*　　　*　　　*　　　*

Heyward was waiting on Leland at Sunny's. He was sitting back in an alcove of the restaurant reading the menu for the lunch special when the man who was fast becoming his friend walked in.

"Have a seat, Leland. It looks like they've got some shrimp and grits for the lunch special today," Heyward said.

"Sounds good to me, Heyward, but do me a favor: Let's move to another part of the restaurant. I don't like sitting over here; the walls are too closed in for me."

They moved to another table out in an open area where Leland could look out the windows.

Leland spoke. "Sorry about that. I just don't like being closed in. I know it sounds weird, but being closed in, in any kind of place, reminds me of being in a coffin, and I hate that thought. I'm what my grandson, Joey, calls claustrophobic."

Heyward nodded. "I guess a lot of people have things like that about them—idiosyncrasies. I have one or two myself; for instance, I hate gray Buicks. They'd probably get you in a coffin before I got in another gray Buick."

Leland picked up the saltshaker that was shaped like a fish. "I'm real bad about being closed up. Over at the lumberyard, we occasionally get shipments of wood from South America—Brazil, Argentina, places like that. The wood is shipped from overseas in one of those metal shipping containers you see on ships, the kind of metal containers that stack real high on those freighters. When a truck delivers those metal containers to our lumberyard, I can't go in them. Just can't force myself to go in a tight place like that."

He continued, "In fact, when I die, they know to cremate me and spread my ashes in the river. No coffin for me. My lawyer knows all about it and so does my family. No, sir, no coffin for me."

"Well, let's eat and talk about things we like then. What do you think about Sea Ray boats … cruisers? A big one, a lot bigger than the South Island boat we fished from Saturday?" Heyward asked Leland, who was still staring at the saltshaker.

While Leland was thinking, Heyward wondered if Lauren Jackson would like to go out for a cruise. Of course, Dan and Elizabeth would have to go, and he would probably take Peaches too. *I'll bet old Peaches would like Lauren,* he thought. *Who wouldn't?*

Leland was familiar with all types of boats, and over lunch, they talked about big boats, about local marinas around the island where Heyward could berth a boat, and the benefits and drawbacks of buying a new boat over a used one.

*   *   *   *

Heyward knew that he didn't have much more reason to be at the South Island Boat Company. Dan had agreed that his assessment had a great deal of merit and that he would take his suggestions under consideration.

"You've certainly earned whatever favors Horace Parker was going to do for you in exchange for helping me," Dan told him later that day. "My father-in-law is coming for a little visit next week to see Lauren. Thank goodness it's supposed to be a short visit, but then, he doesn't ever spend much time with her."

"Are Lauren's parents married? Is her mother coming too?" Heyward asked.

"They're divorced. Her father lives in Birmingham, Alabama, and her mother lives just outside of Philadelphia. They don't get along too well and never come down here at the same time."

"Well, I don't know if your father-in-law is going to be too happy with me or Horace Parker if you don't close the boat business. I expect Horace thought I was going to recommend selling this place. Guess he will be in for a little surprise, but old Horace can handle surprises okay, I suppose."

"By the way, Heyward, Lauren was asking about you last night. She said you got a few fishhooks stuck in your finger the other day while you all were fishing," Dan told him.

Lauren asked about me, Heyward thought to himself.

He didn't want to stop coming to the boat plant because he realized that would be his only chance to see Lauren unless, somehow, he and Leland and Lauren went fishing together again. There was no reason for him to be there on a daily basis anymore, but he really hated leaving for good.

"Today's Monday, Dan. I need to go see a sick friend in Atlanta for a few days. Why don't I call you when I get back, just to see if you need me for anything? By the way, Boney did a good job of sanding the top of my old desk and revarnishing it for me. I appreciate you having him do that for me." Heyward had explained earlier to Dan the story about Kevin Pasko scratching his old desk up. Dan sent a few of the workers to pick it up from Heyward's house and fix it in the shop.

Dan was about to say something when his cell phone rang. He lifted his eyebrows in a polite way to let Heyward know he was not trying to be rude by taking the call. He could hear part of Dan's side of the conversation and then heard him ask the other party to hold on a minute.

"Heyward, I really hate to ask you this, but I'm all tied up, and Lauren needs to get her car out of Hewitt's Repair Shop today. Would you mind running her over there for me? Our house is not too far from here, and Hewitt's is pretty close too."

CHAPTER 36

▼

Heyward was embarrassed with himself. Here he was in his early sixties, and he felt like he had just won the lottery all because he was getting to drive a beautiful woman to pick up her car.

When Dan asked him to pick up Lauren and run her by Hewitt's, it was all he could do to keep from jumping with joy. *So what if I've got a crush on her?* he thought. *It's no big deal and happens to people every day. Besides, nothing could ever come of it.* Lauren was young, probably younger than his own daughter, but still, he was thrilled to just be around her.

It reminded him of when he was in the third grade. He had been infatuated with his teacher, Miss Herring, couldn't get enough of her and even at nine years old, imagined them being married one day. Miss Herring sensed Heyward had some kind of special feelings for her; it had had happened before with other students, and she was wise enough to let it just play out until Heyward was promoted on to the fourth grade.

Dan drew out a rough map on how to get to their house on Cypress Lane, which was at the most, five miles from the plant, and told him Lauren would wait for him out in the front yard.

"I really appreciate you doing this for me, Heyward. I'm swamped here today," Dan said.

No, thank you. I can assure you the pleasure's all mine, Heyward thought to himself.

On the way over to pick Lauren up, Heyward dug around in the console of the Jeep and found some quarters. He stopped at the first self-serve carwash he could find where he quickly vacuumed the floor of the car. Peaches always seemed to bring a lot of sand into the Jeep from the beach when they went on their afternoon walks. He even considered running the car through the wash, but with the canvas top, there always seemed to be little pools of water here and there in the car every time he washed it. *Besides,* he thought, *that might just be too obvious.* It wasn't like they were going on a date or anything like that. He did wish Peaches hadn't shed so much in the car when he took her to the beach for her walks; her fur was definitely going to get on Lauren.

He followed the map Dan had sketched out for him, and he found their house on Cypress Lane easily. Lauren, true to Dan's promise, was waiting for him in the front yard and waved as he pulled into the circular driveway. She opened the passenger door and climbed into the seat. Heyward was a little relieved that she had done that without his help; on his way over to her house—after he vacuumed the car—he had wondered if he should get out and open the car door for her. A gentleman, particularly a real Southern gentleman, would do that, would help her in the car, he reasoned, but on the other hand, it might overdramatize a simple act like picking up a friend.

It seemed she was even better looking than the day they went fishing.

"Good afternoon, Heyward. Thanks for picking me up. How's your finger where you stuck yourself with that fishing hook?"

Heyward held up his right hand with his fingers close together but bent his index finger down so that only the bottom of the finger could be seen from her seat. "Not too good, they had to cut it off," he said, and they both laughed out loud. Heyward had played that same trick on his grandchildren three or four times, and he knew it was a corny thing to do, but it did make him feel good to hear Lauren laugh.

They had gone a few miles down the road when she looked around his Jeep and said, "How do you keep this thing so clean? I thought you took your dog to the beach in it every day."

Hewitt's Car Repair was only about ten miles from her house and they chatted briefly about fishing and car repairs. Heyward drove as slowly as he could without looking like he was doing so on purpose, and they took the road that wound along the marshes.

"I like this Jeep, especially the big tires and those lights you have across the top of the windshield," she said. "Do you have any special equipment on it like a wench or a souped-up engine?"

The road had brought them around a curve, and right by the pavement were some mudflats that were visible since the ocean happened to be almost at low tide. Out on the mud was a large flock of birds, and they were pecking around for sand fleas, a type of small crustacean that was exposed only at low tide.

"Special equipment? Check this out," Heyward said and reached into the glove box. "Watch." He pushed the button for the hidden air horn.

At the sound of the horn, thousands of birds scattered, all at the same time and all calling and cawing. There was a multitude of birds on the flats one moment, and the next, they were all in the air.

Lauren giggled.

They went on another couple of miles when Heyward saw a familiar sight on the island. A series of movable warning signs had been set up on the side of the road advising motorists that there was some type of construction work being performed up ahead, usually for utility work or road repairs. Drivers had to watch out for them and slow down.

Sure enough, a utilities repair crew of four men, all burly, heavyset, and wearing orange hard hats, were milling around a hole that had been dug out on the side of the road. As was the case with most crews that worked on road repair, only one man was actually working; he was digging with a shovel while the other men were propped against the handles of their shovels, intently watching the lone man work.

"Lauren, if you thought the birds were funny, you'll like this," Heyward said as they drove by the utility workers. Before she could stop him, he pressed the button and the horn erupted in sound.

One fat man was so startled he actually fell down. Two others dropped their shovels and jerked back as if suddenly yanked by an invisible rope, and the fourth man, the heaviest of the lot, didn't, or couldn't, move other than to turn his head towards the Jeep.

Heyward sped on past the group and glanced in the rearview mirror after they had gone a hundred yards or so down the road. "When you drive home, Lauren, you may want to go another way."

Despite her nervousness at being a part of something so reckless, Lauren laughed. "Heyward, you're crazy."

"Crazy as used to describe excitement or crazy as in mentally unstable?" he asked.

CHAPTER 37

▼

Neither Heyward nor Elizabeth looked forward to driving the seven hours back to Atlanta, and neither looked forward to seeing Leon in such bad circumstances. Still, they felt it was the only right thing to do, convenient or not.

According to his ex-wives, Leon was confined to a bed, totally paralyzed on his left side; he could not or would not talk, and it seemed like he had stopped trying to get better and made no effort when the therapist tried to get him to do his therapy. Jean said it was as if he was just lying there waiting to die.

As they crossed the South Carolina line into Georgia, Elizabeth told her husband, "I'll tell you one good thing out of all of this. I've gotten to know Leon's ex-wives, at least gotten to know them on the telephone. They seem like saints to me, looking after him like they do. Leon is lucky. Well, he's lucky in that sense of the word."

Heyward was only half listening to his wife. About the time she was telling him that Jean and Gina were saints, they passed the spot where Heyward had gotten his speeding ticket, the one he crumpled up and threw away on the day Leon got sick. Now, he was driving that same car with the same license plate. He couldn't help but speculate if the Georgia State Patrol sent out some kind of radio signal to their troopers that a traffic violator who hadn't paid his fine was in the area and to be on the lookout for him.

He thought it prudent to keep the Camry close to the speed limit, or just over it. They were in no great hurry to get there, and it made no sense to get caught speeding with Elizabeth in the car. They would probably be taken to a county jailhouse as the result of his unpaid speeding ticket, and she just wouldn't quite see any humor in that, he felt almost certain.

He was generally apprehensive of seeing Leon laid up, unable to move or speak, and he wasn't completely sure how he would react when he saw him again. Not only that, he didn't know if Jean and Gina, if they were in one of their sassy moods, might make some type of veiled tease in front of Elizabeth about his retirement gift from Doreen Shumar, the way they did when he first arrived at the hospital when Leon got sick. In the car on their way to Atlanta that afternoon, Heyward, for the life of him, couldn't remember the exact phrase Jean had greeted him with the last time, but he knew it had the word *titty* in it somewhere.

Heyward tried to imagine which would upset Elizabeth more: getting hauled off to some bumpkin jail because he had defied a speeding ticket or hearing that a supposed lesbian had rubbed her breasts in his face. After deliberating for a few miles, he was confident that being put in jail would make her the most aggravated since jails supposedly didn't have real clean or private bathrooms.

On the other hand, he was looking forward to staying with Tootie and her family. Tootie and Josh had come with the grandchildren to visit a couple of times since they had moved to Wexler Island, but it seemed Charlie and Hannah were growing up quicker between their trips than he could handle. Josh had won some type of big lawsuit on behalf of one of his clients, a woman who found a roach or beetle or some crawling bug in her hamburger at a fast-food restaurant, and from his share of the award, bought Tootie a brand-new Lexus. They had driven it down on their last trip. Tootie insisted that her father take the car out for a drive, but he begged off, reasoning that if he drove her Lexus he might never be happy driving his Jeep anymore; the real truth was that the car was gray, of all things, and he simply couldn't bear to get in another gray car, Lexus or Buick.

Heyward and Elizabeth knew that the grandchildren would be upset that they didn't bring Peaches with them, so they bought several books on seashells that they would give to them to hopefully divert their attention from the dog. They left Peaches at a new upscale kennel, advertised as a "spa vacation for dogs," so Peaches would be spending her time lounging in luxury on Wexler Island instead of being dressed up like Mary Poppins by the twins.

When they were about a half hour from Peace Manor Nursing Home, the facility Leon was in, Elizabeth called back to the island and checked to see if there were any messages on their home answering machine. She pressed twelve or fourteen buttons on her cell phone and then listened to the one message that had been recorded on the machine; in fact, she listened to the message three times to make sure her ears weren't playing tricks on her before she closed her cell phone.

"Oh hell," she said.

Heyward glanced at her quickly. He was beginning to get into some heavy traffic and didn't want to divert his attention, but Elizabeth had sworn again, and he knew something big was on the recording machine. "What?"

"I don't believe it. Your cousin, Dewey Sikes, called. He and Louis want to come to the island and do some fishing. They want to stay with us. Oh hell."

*   *   *   *

Leon's ex-wives looked weary and pale, but they both lit up when they saw Heyward and Elizabeth at the door. Leon looked all but dead and had no reaction, or none that anyone could tell, and just stared up at the ceiling.

They stood by his bed for a while and talked to him, but he didn't seem to hear anything they said. Under his left arm was a stuffed toy, a large penguin.

"It holds his arm up so the blood won't pool in it," Gina said when she saw Heyward looking at it.

After a few minutes, the four walked outside the room and into the dimly lit hallway.

"Boy, he looks bad, worse now than he did when he first got sick," Heyward said. "Does he move at all?"

"No, and he's not trying to either. We think he's given up. The people here work with him and fuss at him, but he just lays there. Don't you think so, Jean?"

Jean nodded her head. "Maybe you can make him do something, Heyward. Make him try. We're worn out, but worse than that, it's just too depressing to come over here and see him. It's tearing me up, and Gina too."

Heyward went back into Leon's room for a few minutes, and then he and Elizabeth left for the evening to go stay with Tootie and her family.

CHAPTER 38

▼

Tootie, Josh, Charlie, and Hannah were thrilled to see them. Tootie regularly sent pictures of the grandchildren to Elizabeth over the Internet, but they didn't do justice to how beautiful they were, at least in their grandparents' eyes.

It was good to see Tootie and Josh too. Heyward liked his son-in-law; their relationship was unlike the one between Dan Jackson and Thomas Pennington. Heyward made sure he always deferred to Josh when he was in his house because, after all, Josh was the one paying for it and working hard to support his wife and children. Heyward liked that about himself, how he respected Josh's position as head of his own family, and because of that, he maintained a low profile whenever they visited his home.

As soon as they walked through the front door, Tootie said, "Charlie and Hannah want you to fix up their playhouse while you're here, Daddy. They saw the pictures of the one you built for me when I was their age, and they want you to make theirs look like my old one, if you can."

"We want you to paint it purple," Charlie added.

Heyward promised he would look into it in the morning, if that was all right with Josh, and told the two grandkids that if they wanted their playhouse to be purple, he would paint it purple, just for them.

Elizabeth and Heyward had agreed not to tell anyone, their children Tootie and Lucas and their families included, that they inherited a great deal of money from Heyward's long-lost uncle. It was just something that no one needed to know about for the time being. They did catch up on all the other news though, and they gave the grandchildren the books on seashells, then everyone went to bed early.

*   *   *   *

The next morning, Josh went to his law firm and Heyward drove back to Peace Manor to see Leon again.

Neither Jean nor Gina was there, but he didn't expect them to be, so Heyward went in and saw Leon, who had not changed positions from the time he'd left the night before. Heyward made small talk with the assisted-living staff when they would come in to adjust Leon's medicine or change his sheets. Not knowing what to do with himself, he walked around the facility, went out to the flower garden a church group had planted in the middle of the courtyard, and finally sat down in a lawn chair someone had placed under some trees. There was an elderly man resting in one of the chairs, taking it easy, like he had all the time in the world to do nothing but that.

"Not much to do here, is there?" the man remarked.

"I guess not. My friend is in here. Had a heart attack and a stroke. He just kind of lays there," Heyward replied.

The man told Heyward that his wife was a resident in Peace Manor, she wasn't doing well, it cost a lot to keep her there, and he didn't have anything much else to do but come over and rock under the shade tree on nice days. The man was pleasant enough, but it was depressing just being around him and listening to his sad, old voice.

Heyward excused himself, got into the Camry, and drove away. He had no idea where to go or what to do. Eventually, he ended up in a novelty store where he bought a large foam-rubber pad, like the penguin the nurses had propped Leon's arm on, except this one was printed like an oversized dollar bill. *Maybe this pad's a little more appropriate since Leon was more of a banker than a nature lover,* Heyward thought.

When he couldn't kill any more time, Heyward went back to the nursing home and stood by Leon's bed.

He took the big foam rubber penguin from under his left arm and put the dollar bill in its place. It seemed to fit fine, and since it was new, a groove had not yet been worn in it. Actually, Heyward thought, it supported Leon's arm a little better than the penguin.

Heyward thought he saw Leon's little finger, the one on his right hand, move a bit and walked around the bed to see if his eyes had played a trick on him. Just moving around the bed gave him something to do and ate up some time, even if it could be measured in seconds.

He touched Leon's little finger. To his alarm, Leon seemed to grab at his hand, which made Heyward step back in shock. A few seconds later, some kind of sound came from Leon's mouth, and Heyward could see Leon's eyes move from looking straight ahead over to the right. Leon moved his eyes three times like that and again, tried to say something.

Just like he did with his uncle Walter Jennings, Heyward leaned over and put his head close to the bed.

"K … ill meeeeeee," Heyward heard him rasp. Then, in a whisper, he said, "End … end it."

Heyward jerked his head back. "What? What?"

Leon tried to say the same words once more. Heyward lurched backwards and stumbled into a nurse walking through the door. "Is everything all right in here?"

Heyward shrugged his shoulders to the nurse and didn't say anything. She checked a few vital signs and left the room. Heyward leaned over and looked Leon in the eye. Leon squeezed both his eyes open and shut, but he never relented in his deep stare into Heyward's.

"Did you say what I thought I heard?" Heyward asked him. Their eyes were locked on each other's. Leon squeezed his eyes shut and opened them again.

Heyward left the room and just like he did the night he went to his uncle's hospital room in Sheridan, found a men's room, went inside, and threw up.

CHAPTER 39

He had heard Leon and was pretty sure he understood exactly what he'd said, but Heyward didn't like it, didn't like what it inferred, and didn't appreciate Leon asking that of him.

What Leon asked him or ordered him or begged him—Heyward was not sure which applied—was totally out of the question. Regardless of whether Leon was suffering terribly or not, he shouldn't have even brought such a thing up. In fact, Heyward was pissed. *Pissed* was the about only word he could think of to describe what he felt about the idea that Leon would put something like that on him. They were friends, yes, best friends, but Leon stepped over the line, and it wasn't a line that he or anyone else should cross.

It was a totally different thing to get in a fight on the beach or threaten a jerk like Kevin Pasko or even to not pay a speeding ticket. What Leon posed could land him in jail or prison or if he got the wrong jury and was convicted, he could get a "rope necktie," at least he thought that's what they used to call a hanging back in the old days. They didn't just give out financial punishment for that sort of criminal behavior. It went far beyond that.

For the rest of the afternoon, Heyward drove around, and eventually, he ended up in a public park where he spent an hour or so sitting on a bench, just thinking and clearing his head. He thought about himself being sick and lying in the bed like Leon; he wouldn't want to live that way, if it could be called living at all. Both he and Elizabeth had signed living wills and instructed their family not to revive them under dire circumstances or give them food or even water to drink. But surely, Leon was not at that point in his illness. Physical or occupational therapy probably could help him, if he only tried.

As hard as he tried to fight it, Heyward began to sense his old feelings of questioning himself. Feelings that he'd let himself and everybody else down welled up in him as he sat on the park bench. Those thoughts hadn't visited him in months, but now, having been asked to commit such a terrible act brought a feeling of powerless to him, the sense of failure that he couldn't do what was asked of him. If the tables were turned, *he* would want Leon to put him out of his misery; he would expect Leon to put him out of his misery if he asked; and Heyward knew Leon would actually be strong enough to go through with it.

In the late part of the afternoon, he remembered that he was supposed to go with Josh to a hardware store and pick up some supplies so that he could fix Charlie and Hannah's pirate ship playhouse. Listlessly, he left the park and went on to his daughter's house. He would have to let Leon down, but he couldn't disappoint his grandchildren.

"You stayed a long time with Leon. Is there any difference?" Elizabeth asked him.

"No, it was kind of depressing." There was no way Heyward was going to tell her that Leon actually tried to speak, much less the content of those few words he did say. Then, too, there was no real reason for him to tell her that he actually spent very little time with Leon in the course of the day; they had driven seven hours to be there, and it seemed almost foolish that he spent most of the day avoiding his sick friend.

Josh came home from his law office and suggested they go on to the hardware store after dinner, so that everyone could spend some time together first. Hannah had made a list of the things she wanted to add on to the pirate ship playhouse, things like a bell and a steering wheel. Most important, she wanted it to be painted purple too, she reminded him.

After eating, Josh and Heyward left for the hardware store in Josh's car, a blue Honda. *Thank goodness,* Heyward thought to himself, *the subject of riding in Tootie's gray Lexus never came up.*

At the hardware store, Heyward was able to find everything he needed: two quarts of bright-purple paint, an inexpensive drill, screwdrivers, pliers, a crescent wrench, and several boxes of nails, bolts, screws, and nuts. Josh tried to pay for the supplies, but Heyward insisted; however, he liked the fact that his son-in-law didn't automatically assume that a grandfather always pays for everything like he had heard some of his friends complain at times. Josh was a good son-in-law, that was a fact, but he was also a good husband to Tootie and a good father to the twins.

By the time they left the hardware store, the sun had fully set, and it was dark outside. Josh asked Heyward if they could drop by Tanglewood Mall on the way home so he could exchange a pair of shoes that Tootie had bought earlier; it seemed they were a little tight, and he wanted to exchange them for a roomier pair.

"If we can find a parking place, let's stop, if you don't mind. Parking can really be a problem at this mall, even on a weekday night," Josh said.

They drove around the parking lot for five or six minutes, trying to find an open parking place when an old, yellow Plymouth failed to yield coming out of a row of parked cars. The old Plymouth cut them off and almost clipped their front bumper; if it had been a second later, they would have collided.

To Heyward's surprise, Josh didn't seem to get upset. His son-in-law simply overlooked it and went on cruising up and down the rows of cars looking for an open place to park. *That must have something to do with having little kids around all the time,* Heyward thought. *A young father can't get mad over every little thing or else he'd be upset all the time.*

Finally, a spot opened up, and Josh eased the Honda in. From their parking place, through two rows of cars, Heyward saw the yellow Plymouth wheel into one of the open handicap parking places. Two healthy, vigorous-looking men got out then slammed their doors shut. As they more or less strutted over to the mall's main entrance, one of them shoved the other in front of a pair of middle-aged women walking out together, causing one of the ladies to drop the shopping bag she was carrying. The men from the old Plymouth shrieked with laughter.

"Can you believe that, Mr. Jennings?" Josh almost never called his father-in-law by his first name. "Those boys parked in that handicap zone. I can't see a handicap sticker or tag on their car. Did they look handicapped to you?"

"They looked in good physical shape to me," Heyward said.

Josh looked around the parking lot for mall security. "You never see one of those mall cops when you need one." On their way into the parking lot, Heyward had noticed a mall security policeman riding around the lot in a golf cart with an amber light flashing on the roof and had wondered if it was fun to drive around all day in a little cart like that.

Seeing the obviously healthy young men park in a handicapped spot reminded Heyward of some earlier event, something that had happened before that had made him angry, but he couldn't quite remember when or where it was.

Then, as Josh opened the driver's door, he remembered, and he remembered how he'd felt. The day he bought his Jeep, a gold Mercedes sports car had taken up two parking places, and he couldn't park his new car. He loosely remembered the car had some type of fancy license plate, something about a "Mrs." or "doctor," but he clearly remembered what he had told James Rimini that day. "Somebody ought to do something about that."

Heyward sat back in his seat and thought about what he had said to James. *Somebody ought to do something about that.* He also remembered what he thought to himself when he got hit on the beach by Michael Castillo. *It just doesn't hurt that much.*

"If you don't mind, Josh, I think I'll just wait here in the car. Take your time; I'm in no great hurry. I just want to sit here and think about how I want to fix up that old pirate ship for the twins."

Josh promised he would be quick about exchanging the shoes and closed his door. As soon as Heyward saw him enter the mall, he reached into the shopping bag from the hardware store and took out one of the cans of purple paint. Then he dug around until he found a paintbrush and, after that, ripped a screwdriver from the sealed plastic pack. Heyward stepped outside the Honda and using the screwdriver, pried the top off of the paint can and stirred the contents a few times with the barrel of the tool.

Heyward knew exactly what he was going to do. He knew it was dangerous, and he knew it was breaking the law. Still, he had no emotion of guilt as he stirred the paint. He had no feeling of fear, no concern if he was right or wrong. It didn't matter.

Once the paint was stirred, he walked towards the yellow Plymouth.

He dipped the brush into the paint can, leaned over the hood of the parked car, and unhurriedly, with long, flat strokes, painted "NEEDLE DICK" in big, purple letters. He stepped back and looked at the word. Satisfied, he calmly walked around to the back of the car and, in the same lettering style, wrote "BUG FUCKER" on the top of the trunk.

When he was done with the outside of the car, Heyward reached through one of the open windows and sloshed paint across the dashboard, over the front seat, and across the back seat. When the can was empty of paint, he dropped it on the floorboard, among several crushed beer cans and empty cigarette packs.

He walked back over to Josh's car, as cool and composed as he had, just moments before, to the Plymouth. It was not until he had closed his door that he began to comprehend the magnitude of his deed and with that understanding, slightly began to lose his nerve.

But it was done. And now that it was done, he was satisfied with himself, proud, just as he had felt in the shower after his fight with Michael Castillo on the beach.

CHAPTER 40

▼

The two boys in the yellow Plymouth came out of the mall before Josh did. Until they were about five feet from their parking space, they hadn't noticed anything unusual with their car.

For a few seconds, neither comprehended exactly what was wrong, but they both knew something wasn't quite right.

It didn't take long before they began screaming and cussing and threatening to kill whoever did that to their car. When the driver looked in the interior and saw the bright-purple paint splashed all over the seats and dashboard, he became so violently angry that he began pounding his fist on the hood of the car parked in the space next to the old Plymouth. When he was through pounding that car, he went over and, in absolute frustration, punched his companion in the face, which knocked him down on the pavement.

It was about that same time that Josh came out of the mall. He first heard then saw the commotion and instinctively ducked around a row of parked cars. By the time he'd made his way back to his Honda, mall security police had been called and were trying, unsuccessfully, to calm the raging men.

Josh opened his car door and quickly got in.

"Did you see what happened over there?" Josh said. "I think somebody wrote some dirty words on their car." Josh was looking at a growing crowd milling around the scene. "Looks like they painted it."

"Josh, let's go. Pull out and head the other way," Heyward said.

By now, he had control of his own fear and tried to act as calm as he possibly could. He had once read in a management book that it was imperative never to show fear in front of one's employees. Josh wasn't an employee of Heyward's, but he was his son-in-law, and so he felt it wise to follow the counsel of the management book, employee or kin.

"Agreed. Let's get the hell away from here before they start shooting at somebody." Josh was definitely rattled; he was not accustomed to being around any type of altercation or even loud arguments, much less wanton vandalism or seeing two men—supposedly friends—punching each other.

Josh drove almost a mile from the mall before he was stopped by a red traffic light. Under the glow of the light, Josh noticed purple paint smeared on Heyward's hands.

"Hey, you've got paint on your hands." It took him a moment or so before he comprehended just what that meant. "Oh no, don't tell me! Don't tell me you messed up that car. Please, oh, God, tell me you didn't do that!"

Heyward had not totally calmed himself. He was certainly not as calm as he was when he first walked over to the Plymouth, but considering things, he was calm enough.

"If it makes you feel any better, Josh, I'll tell you I didn't paint that car. But the truth is, I did. I painted their car, and I sloshed paint all on the inside too."

"Oh, Lord. We're going to get shot." Josh was breathing hard. "If not shot, we're going to get arrested and thrown under the jail. You've got me in big trouble, Heyward. I could lose my license to practice law."

Heyward noticed that his son-in-law called him Heyward, not Mr. Jennings. He thought that odd. Up until this point in their relationship, Josh had always called him "Mister."

Josh was beginning to panic, and as his fear increased, so did his speed.

"For goodness sake, Josh, slow down. You're going to get us pulled over for speeding. Let me drive. I'm okay."

Josh slowed down. "Damn it. What's wrong with you?" he shouted at Heyward.

"You need to get a grip on yourself, Josh. You weren't involved in this, so you couldn't get in trouble anyway."

"Maybe somebody could identify you, Heyward. They could get my license plate number and track us down. There could be policemen at my house right now."

"I doubt that," Heyward said and reached over in the back seat. He put their license plate on the console between them. "I took this off your car before I did anything. In fact, why don't you pull over and let's put it on before we go any further."

Josh looked down at the license plate. Without a word, he wheeled into an empty parking lot, and Heyward got out and screwed it back in place.

"Don't say another word to me, Heyward. When we get home, I want you to leave. I don't care where you go, just leave and don't say a word about this to Tootie. This would tear her up. You know, I always respected you, but this puts you in a different light for me." Josh looked directly at Heyward. "You're a damn nut job."

They drove the rest of the way home in silence. Heyward felt strange about what he had done but even more peculiar that he didn't seem to be too worried about it. He wasn't even worried that his son-in-law called him a nut job. *This is getting to be a regular occurrence,* he thought to himself. Josh had called him a "nut job," Lauren said he was "crazy," and Kevin Pasko had said he was "mentally unstable."

*   *   *   *

When they pulled into his garage, Josh turned the engine off and looked at Heyward.

"Look, I've thought about it, and you can't leave. It would upset Tootie and the kids, not to mention Mrs. Jennings. Just clean your hands off out here and go in like nothing happened. Not a word about this to anyone, not one word. But stay away from me."

Heyward looked at Josh. "I don't think you can get in trouble over this, Josh. If anything ever comes of it, you're my lawyer, and I confessed to vandalizing that car to you, so you're probably covered by that attorney-client-confidentiality thing. Besides, like I said, you're an attorney. Start acting like one if the you-know-what hits the fan."

Josh glared at Heyward. "Just stay away from me."

"Okay, Josh, but let me ask you one question before we go into the house. Of all the colors that Lexus offers, why did you and Tootie have to get a gray one?"

CHAPTER 41

▼

There was nothing on the late-night local news about a car being vandalized in the Tanglewood Mall parking lot and nothing in the newspaper about it the next morning either.

Heyward wasn't worried about seeing news about the car, but he was more than concerned there might be a breaking news bulletin about a killing, at worst, or a shooting, at best, at the mall. He wasn't bothered that he had painted the car; the driver deserved that for parking where he did. It didn't even bother him that the two men ended up fighting each other; maybe they'd learn a lesson or two. It would have bothered him, though, if they'd killed each other or some innocent bystander.

But for the rest of the night, Josh was extremely restless. There were a few times he imagined some noise on the street in front of his house, and every time he thought he heard something, he would look out the front window through the curtains or blinds to see if it was a police car there to arrest him or a beat-up old Plymouth idling in the driveway. Josh felt sure the men in the car would want to seek their pound of flesh in revenge should they ever found out who ruined their car and insulted their manhood.

Heyward spent the next day fixing Charlie and Hannah's pirate playhouse, and when it came time to paint it, he was careful not to waste one drop of the purple. The single quart that was left from the shopping trip the night before was just enough to cover everything with one coat. He knew he didn't want to go back to the hardware store, or any store for that matter, to buy more paint on the slim chance hardware stores had been advised by local police to be on the lookout for gray-haired, purple-paint buyers.

＊   ＊   ＊   ＊

Heyward and Elizabeth went to see Leon one more time as they were leaving Atlanta on their way home to Wexler Island. Neither Jean nor Gina was at the nursing home when they stopped by, and when they got to Leon's room, he was lying in the bed just as always, neither moving nor talking.

Elizabeth held Leon's hand for a few moments and spoke to him in her soft voice, but he didn't respond or even look at her. When she started to tear up, Heyward suggested she go outside for some fresh air while he said his good-byes, then he would meet her at their car.

He waited until she was out of the room and waited a few more minutes until he was sure enough time had passed that she wouldn't change her mind and come back in. What he wanted to tell Leon he didn't want anyone else to hear, not Elizabeth, not his two ex-wives, and certainly not an employee of the nursing home who might happen along at any time.

"Leon, listen to me." Heyward took Leon's hand and leaned over the bed, just over his friend's face. "Leon, can you hear me? Can you understand what I'm saying to you?"

Leon cut his eyes over and met Heyward's eyes. He blinked twice.

"Leon, you need to try and get better. I heard what you asked me two days ago, but that's out of the question. No, I won't do it. You must try to heal yourself by working with your therapist."

Heyward squeezed Leon's hand hard. "Listen to me. I want you to understand. No, I will not do what you asked me to. Now, you do your therapy."

Heyward laid Leon's hand on the bed and looked into his eyes. It would bother Heyward a very long time the way Leon's eyes seemed to be pleading, begging him to end his suffering. "Good-bye, Leon."

He walked out of the room, down the hall, and out into the parking lot where Elizabeth was waiting. About that time, Gina drove up and the three of them stood in the parking lot.

"I was afraid you all would get gone before I got here this morning. I just wanted to thank you both for coming," she said. "Heyward, I guess you couldn't talk any sense into Leon, could you? I mean, about his therapy and all?"

Heyward pursed his lips and slowly shook his head. "I doubt it, but then, who's to say? I'm just concerned that the longer he lays there, the harder it's going to be for him to ever get better. It's almost sadder than I can bear."

Gina reached into her pocket and took out a small box. "Anyway, I made you something, Heyward. I'm taking a class in how to make jewelry, and I made you this little guardian angel." She held up a small gold pin that was in the shape of an angel with outspread arms. "I figured you needed something like this in case you get in one of your fights on the beach."

"Thanks," Heyward said as held the trinket up and looked closely at it. "I think my fighting career is over, brief as it was, but I'll keep this close to me. I really appreciate you looking out for me."

Neither Heyward nor Elizabeth spoke as they made their way to the interstate and then out of Atlanta. They drove along many miles before Elizabeth said, "It's too bad about Leon. It's almost like he is just laying there waiting to die."

"Well, what would you do if that were you instead of him?" Heyward asked.

"For one thing, I would do my therapy. Jean said he wasn't even trying. How else is he supposed to get any better if he doesn't try?"

Heyward thought a moment then said, "I read in some magazine that strokes sometimes cause a person to have a change in personality. Maybe it affected him that way. I, for one, wouldn't want to live like …" but he got too choked up to finish. Remembering the pleading in Leon's eyes was almost more than he could take.

They drove on in silence for almost a full hour, Heyward fighting the image of Leon and Elizabeth fighting a similar image except it was Heyward incapacitated instead.

Their gloom was broken by Heyward's cell phone.

It was Leland Tiller. He wanted to know if Heyward wanted to go fishing the next day, when he got back from his trip to Georgia. Leland explained that a lot of people were catching quite a few fish and it might be a good time for them to have some luck too. "You might be too tired to go, Heyward, you know, from traveling and all, but folks are catching fish now, and I thought about you."

"We'll be getting in before too late, so, yes, I think I would like to go tomorrow," Heyward said and then hesitated a moment. *I wonder if Lauren Jackson might just happen to be going too,* he thought to himself.

"Leland, my cousins from Lost Springs, Georgia, called, and they want to come down soon and go fishing too. Um, they probably won't be coming down tomorrow, but, uh, if they do, is there room on the boat for them?"

Heyward knew it was a dumb thing to ask, but it was the only thing he could think of in the spur of the moment and he surely wanted to know if Lauren was coming with them.

He didn't want to come out and ask Leland directly about Lauren, he felt that Leland *might* get the wrong idea about his interest in her or he might think that Heyward didn't want to go with him by himself. He definitely didn't want to bring up the subject of Lauren in front of Elizabeth; he was sure *she* would get the wrong idea.

"Yeah, there's plenty of room if your cousins want to come. Right now, it's just you and me going."

Heyward knew better, but he really was disappointed. *But then, why should she go fishing with them every time the boat went in the water?* he thought. She couldn't be expected to want to spend all her time fishing with two old men; she had her own life, and besides, she was too busy to spend it with men old enough to be her father or maybe even her grandfather.

When Heyward closed his cell phone, he glanced over at Elizabeth who had a very curious look on her face. "Why, Heyward, would you think that Dewey and Louis Sikes would be visiting you tomorrow? You haven't even called them back yet."

Heyward may have asked Leland a dumb question but recovered his wits by the time Elizabeth asked her question.

"You know how it is with those two, Elizabeth. They might be sitting on our front porch right now waiting on us. You can never tell what they're going to do."

Heyward was pleased with himself for his quick mental recovery. His satisfaction turned to sadness, though, when he remembered the look in Leon's eyes.

CHAPTER 42

▼

To Elizabeth's immense relief, neither of the Sikes cousins were waiting for them on their front porch when they got home, and they hadn't left a new message on their answering machine either.

As they had planned the day before, when Leland had called Heyward's cell phone, the two men met for an early breakfast at Sunny's Diner before they started fishing. Heyward got to the restaurant early, before Leland, and asked Mazelle on his way past the cashier's counter to have some coffee sent over. He took a table near the windows where Leland liked to sit. While he was waiting on Leland, several boat company workers came over and made small talk and related some gossip before heading to work with their ham biscuits and coffee in paper cups.

"Thanks for getting a table over here," Leland said waving his hand at the open windows when he walked in. "I appreciate it, your remembering I don't want to sit in that old alcove. I take it your cousins didn't show up."

"Not yet. Of course, the day isn't over." Heyward had not given any thought to Dewey or to Louis, but after mentioning they might be coming for a visit just to see if Lauren was taking up a space in the boat, he needed to at least play it on out.

Leland talked about some of the fishing spots he would like for them to try on the river that day, and he talked about some of the bait and lures he brought. Heyward had gone to Dilly's Bait Shop and bought another rod and reel, one he could use in fresh water. He was now the proud owner of one of the best surf fishing rods and reels, thanks to the people at FMSB, and a good spinner reel on a six-foot rod he would use on the river.

About the time they were ready to leave the restaurant, Dan Jackson rode up on his bicycle, by himself, much to the disappointment of Heyward. It would have been nice to see Lauren this morning, he thought, and maybe she would have changed her plans and gone with them.

"Hello, Heyward, I just wanted to let you know I have enrolled in some basic accounting courses over at Hoover," he said. Hoover was a community college located in Marshfield, which was the county seat and the closest thing to a real town to Wexler Island. "I'll be starting in a couple of weeks."

"Really?" Heyward was surprised Dan was actually taking his advice regarding the accounting courses. He thought the young man already had an advanced degree in archeology or maybe even a doctor of philosophy; entry-level accounting courses had to be something of a big step down for him.

After a few minutes of conversation, Dan went inside for breakfast and Leland and Heyward got in Leland's pickup truck and, with the boat in tow, headed for the public boat landing.

It was an ideal day for fishing. The sun was bright and warm, but it was not too hot, and there was a pleasant breeze kicking up from the west. It was days like this that made Heyward wonder how he could have lived in a big city for so many years. Leland had a small trolling motor on the back of the boat and used it to push the boat along the riverbank. Both men cast their lures around the edge of some cypress trees which grew in shallow water at the river's edge. After a while, they caught a couple of smallmouth bass, none of which would challenge any local records but were nice sizes nonetheless. Leland sat down on a cushion and got a bottle of water from a cooler that was built into the center console of the small wooden boat.

"You haven't said much about your sick friend, the one you just went to see," he said.

"Well, Leland, there's not much good to say about it. Leon, that's his name, he's not doing very well, just kind of lays there. It's like he's given up on living. Won't try his therapy and doesn't seem to care about anything," Heyward said, and they both sat in the boat and watched some leaves caught in the river's current.

For a long time, neither man said anything. It was like they were thinking about what it would be to be living like Leon.

"I guess I can understand that, in a way. If I couldn't come out on this old river fishing and feel the sun and breeze, I'd just as soon call it a day," Leland said.

Heyward thought about Leon asking—or telling—him to kill him. Here he was, out on a beautiful river, in what he hoped was perfect health, coming and going as he well pleased. Even at the age of sixty-one—he had had his first birthday as a retiree—he felt good and had no real physical complaints. His physical condition seemed to be good and for the most part, so was his mental state. His reoccurring feelings of letting himself and others down came and went, but they were still hanging around.

Heyward knew his feelings didn't make any sense, at least not any sense to an outsider looking in on his life.

Still, he had been called "mental," in one way or another more than once in the last few weeks. Kevin Pasko said he was mentally unstable, and his own son-in-law called him a nut job. Even Lauren had called him crazy when he blew his air horn at those utility men who were working on the side of the road, but he thought, or at least he hoped, she meant it in a good way.

"Leland, at the risk of you thinking bad of me, let me tell you something I did in Atlanta—something I did that some people would call real stupid. Probably some people would it say it was insane. I'd like to get your take on it."

Heyward related the whole story of the car painting incident to Leland, from the time the gold Mercedes sports car with the vanity tags made him mad by taking up two parking places in the bank parking lot to the painting of the yellow Plymouth to Josh's animated exchange with him in his garage. Leland let him finish the entire story without interrupting him once. Both men had stopped fishing for the time being.

"My question to you, Leland, is do you think that's a sign that I've gone crazy?" Heyward said as he finished.

Leland started to say something but stopped himself and chuckled first. "Actually, I'd like to congratulate you. I've wanted to do something to inconsiderate idiots like that before, but never did. I guess everybody would, if they had the nerve. But they don't do anything; everybody just talks about it." Leland chuckled again. "Those two words you wrote on the car, what were they? Needle dick and the other one? Why those?"

"Bug fucker. My friend, Leon, once used them to describe somebody we worked with that neither of us liked. Besides, I like the way they sound," Heyward said. "Old Leon had some good phrases he used from time to time."

"To answer your question: Crazy? No, like I said, everybody wants to get even with bad people; they mostly don't do it, though, for whatever reasons. Why did you do it, Heyward? You told me before you always played by the rules and never made any waves, you know, gray Buicks and those sorts of things. Why, after all that, did you do it?"

Heyward looked at the river and thought for a few moments. Turning, he looked directly into Leland's eyes and said, "I really don't know why."

CHAPTER 43

▼

They fished on in silence for a long while, each man thinking his own thoughts. Around noontime, Leland reached into a cooler and took out a couple of sandwiches and soft drinks.

"My wife used to make my sandwiches before she passed on. I hope you like peanut butter and strawberry jam spread between two pieces of plain white bread. It's about as far as my cooking skills go," Leland said as he passed it and a drink over to Heyward.

"Perfect with me. But then, anything is fine with me sitting on this river, out in this sunlight. Leland, you mind telling me about your family?"

Between bites of his sandwich, Leland told Heyward he was seventy-two years old now and about his wife, Margaret, passing away twelve years ago with cancer, "the bad kind," he said without elaborating. Heyward thought all cancer was bad but didn't interrupt him for more explanation. They had one child, a son, Frank, who was married and lived up in Delaware and was in the electrical supply business. Their son and his wife had two children, Sandra and Joey.

"Sandra is a nurse, and she is doing real well up in Delaware," Leland said and then paused. "Joey lives here on the island with me. He's twenty-one years old."

"What's that like, I mean, what's it like having a twenty-one-year-old living with you?"

"Joey's got some problems. My son and his wife thought it might be good for him to come down here and stay with me for a while. I was kind of hoping he could take over my lumber business for me one day, but I don't know."

Heyward studied his sandwich before taking another bite. He sensed Leland had something on his mind about his grandson and he didn't want to interrupt his train of thought.

Leland hesitated a long time. "Joey got into some drugs when he lived up with his folks. I'm trying to keep him straight, but I don't know … it's really weighing on me. I've got him working out in the woodlot right now, pulling lumber orders and riding on delivery trucks with my men."

"Does your company have drug tests? Your drivers take drug tests?" Heyward asked.

"Yeah, I make all my drivers take drug tests. I do it because I feel I need to, and besides, my insurance carrier insists on it anyway. Joey's not a driver, so he doesn't have to take the test. Right now, I'm still trying to work with him, and I think if I make him take a drug test and he fails it, well, then I'm backed up in a corner with him."

Leland cast his bait out by the limb of a dead tree that was lying in the edge of the river. "All I can say is that I'm really working on him. I'd like to quit the lumber business, but things have gotten so complicated with him and some other things, I just can't quit."

They didn't say anything for a while, each man once again lost in his own thoughts.

Finally, Leland said, "Heyward, you told me about how you messed that car up in Atlanta and asked me what I thought. I might want to ask you for some advice on something I've gotten myself into that I don't know how to handle. I'm not ready to talk about it right now—I hope you can understand that—but if I can't figure it out for myself, I'd like to talk to you about it, get your opinion … in confidence, of course."

"Sure, Leland, I'll be glad to be of any help I can to you. Whenever you're ready, just let me know. Until then, I won't bring it up. And remember, anything you tell me in confidence remains in confidence."

They didn't catch any more fish that afternoon and motored back to the loading ramp. Heyward tried to settle up with Leland for the gas for the boat and the bait but Leland wouldn't let him pay for anything.

"You pay the next time, if you want to," Leland said. "If you don't want to clean the fish you caught, I'll give them to a lady down the street from me who would like them for her supper." Heyward had told Leland on their first fishing trip together that he didn't really like to eat fish at home. For some quirky reason, the only place he liked to eat fish was at a restaurant.

"By the way, Heyward, what's that shiny thing on your hat?"

Heyward took off the baseball cap he was wearing. The hat was a gift from Edna over at Dilly's Bait Shop, which she gave to him when he bought his rod and reel, the one he only used in fresh water. On the front of the hat, Edna had her embroider sew *Dilly's* in big letters and then, under Dilly's, had the words *World-Class Baits* stitched in italics. "You know, Mr. Jennings," she said when she gave him the hat, "I thought about having the words *Master Baiter* sewn on instead, but I don't think that shows much class, do you?"

"Oh, this is a guardian angel pin that one of Leon's ex-wives made for me. I thought it might be good to wear it on my fishing cap."

*   *   *   *

After Heyward helped Leland load the boat back on the trailer at the boat ramp, it occurred to him that Edna over at Dilly's might be onto a good idea about giving away embroidered items to her customers as a way of saying "thank you" for their loyalty. A hat was a good thing to give to fisherman, and he liked his so much that he put his guardian angel on it.

He decided to stop by and run an idea by Dan Jackson for South Island Boat Company. Why not give some type of gift with the boat company's name on it to anyone who bought a boat, particularly a gift that could be used by an entire family? By doing that, the company could build loyalty in existing customers and encourage their children to remember to buy a South Island boat when they grew up. *It wouldn't cost much, and besides, you can never start building brand loyalty too early in the next generation of boat buyers,* he thought.

Besides, Lauren might be there and hear the idea and from that, think he was the smartest, brightest man in the world, along with his good sense of humor in scaring birds and utility workers on the side of the road. *You can never really tell what might impress a woman,* he thought.

Heyward felt like there should be plenty of time to stop, talk to Dan for just a minute or two, and get home by dinnertime. As he drove his Jeep, he flipped down the sun visor over the driver's side and checked to see if the day of fishing had improved his tan any, that, and to make sure he didn't have any bait smudges or fish scales on his face, just in case Lauren *happened* to be there.

When he drove up to the South Island Boat Company's office, he was surprised to see a sleek-looking black BMW 740 parked out front. *There're a lot of people on this island that can afford a car like that,* he thought, *but none of them would want to buy a small wooden fishing boat with the minimal amount of creature comforts they offered.* As he got out of the Jeep, he noticed the expensive car had an Alabama license plate on it.

Walking into the office, he overheard Dan talking, in a voice much louder than he had ever heard him before, except when he was trying to be heard over a saw or sander out back in the production area. He couldn't clearly grasp what he was saying, but he did sense that Dan was not particularly happy.

In a few moments, a huge man walked out of Dan's office in something of what Heyward considered to be a huff. The man was tall, well over six feet, and had a massive chest and arms, like he was some kind of linebacker on a professional football team. Although Heyward could tell from his face that he was at least his own age, the large man's hair was dark brown, and from the way he walked, he could tell the man was in good physical condition, either through regular workouts in a gym or, if he was very fortunate, in good shape from good genes.

Even though the man was a good bit larger than himself, him being on the slender side and all, Heyward, for some reason, did not feel the slightest bit of intimidation; maybe his fistfight with Michael Castillo had something to do with his self-confidence or maybe he was just getting to the point in his life that he simply didn't care.

"The office is about to close. What do you want?" the man asked.

"I'd like to see Dan Jackson, if he's got a minute. I'm Heyward Jennings."

"So you're the famous Mr. Jennings," the man said. Heyward detected a hint of sarcasm in his voice. "I'm Thomas Pennington," the man continued but didn't offer to shake his hand. "Dan will be out here in a minute. I understand you've been giving him some advice on certain things. How much are they paying you?"

"I'm not sure that's really any of your business, but since you asked, the answer is nothing. I'm not being paid anything, but then, like I said, I don't think that's really any of your business." Heyward really felt good talking to the big man that way; it gave him a sense of freedom, like he had never driven a gray Buick in his life.

By this time, both Dan and Lauren had materialized from Dan's office. "I see you two have met," Dan said. Heyward sensed that Dan was uncomfortable, nervous in a way. "We're going to walk out back, Heyward. Why don't you walk with us?"

CHAPTER 44

▼

Dan led the way back to the production area, followed by Thomas Pennington, then Lauren, with Heyward bringing up the rear. Once they were in the connecting hallway between the office and production, with her father out in front of her, Lauren turned around to Heyward and held up her hand. She playfully made an exaggerated wave then frowned, put her hands on her hips, and smiled as if she was making fun of her father.

"Well, hello there, Heyward," she said. "Scared off any birds or chubby men leaning on shovels lately?"

Despite himself, Heyward imagined himself being young again and actually having a chance with someone like Lauren, then he remembered that when he was that young, he probably didn't have the self-confidence to talk to a really beautiful woman like her. *One thing about being old,* he thought, *it allowed young women to flirt with an older man without any worry of consequences.*

"Can't say that I have scared anybody lately. Well, maybe I scared a few really small fish today." Heyward like the way she laughed at his lame jokes.

Once Dan opened the door from the hallway and the hulking Thomas Pennington walked into the production area, all conversation stopped. Everyone looked at him with considerable suspicion; they all knew he wanted to close the plant and were afraid of the man. Most of them turned away, and those that didn't avoided eye contact with him. Monroe even dropped a box of screws on the floor, and a couple of people jumped to help him pick them up. It reminded Heyward of when he was a child at Rawlins Elementary when the school bully felt like beating another kid up and went looking for an easy mark.

Pennington strutted by boats in various stages of construction, and when he passed one that had just received its final coat of paint, he touched the finish and then looked at the fresh paint that smudged his finger. The drying paint on the boat had a blotch about the size of a half-dollar on the otherwise smooth surface. Pennington grabbed a cloth from a pile that had been gathered for cleaning and after he wiped his finger, threw the rag back on the pile.

Heyward saw Dan look at the ruined finish and then at Vermille Bolineau; Vermille had just spent the better part of the afternoon painstakingly applying the paint to the boat. Dan frowned as he looked at the frustrated woman.

Dan, Lauren, and Heyward followed Thomas Pennington out through the back warehouse door onto the lawn that separated the building from the marsh. At that time of the day, in the late afternoon, the view was exceptional.

Pennington turned to his daughter and completely ignored the men. "Lauren, can't you talk any sense into your husband? Look at this view," he said, waving his arms across the vista. "You couldn't make enough of those stupid wooden boats in a hundred years for what you could get for selling this property in one hour. You all would be set for life without ever having to work another day if you didn't want to. Danforth doesn't seem to have any common sense. He may know a little something about dinosaurs and old bones that don't mean squat to anybody but a bunch of academics."

Lauren looked at her father like she didn't understand exactly what he was trying to say. Heyward got the definite impression she had practiced the expression before, like a person sometimes does when they are practicing a speech or a joke they would have to tell in front of a convention or a group of people.

"Well, Daddy, don't the big oil companies care about dinosaurs and old bones? Don't they pay somebody like Danforth a lot of money to find out where those bones are so they can drill for oil?" she asked. "I may be wrong—and you know I have been wrong many times before—but I think a couple of those oil companies wanted to hire him to help them find some of that old oil."

Thomas Pennington walked away from them and stood at the very edge of the marsh. It was almost like he was calculating how many condominiums could be built where they were standing. He walked back over to the group and pointed his finger directly at Heyward.

"And you. Horace Parker told me that you had some good sense and showed sound judgment. He thought you would talk them into selling." Pennington was still pointing his finger at Heyward. "I swear, that sorry-ass Horace has his mind on that girlfriend of his so much it's a wonder he gets any goddamn thing right."

"Well …" Heyward said. He slowly took a tube of lip balm from his pocket. Ever since he had moved to Wexler Island, it seemed that he always had chapped lips, and he never went anywhere without having at least one tube of the soothing salve in his pocket and a spare tube in the Jeep's glove compartment as a backup. "Well, old Horace may always have his mind on Gracie, but at least he was right about a couple of things. He always thought it was impolite to point your finger like you're doing to me, and then, too, he was right when he told me you were a world-class son of a bitch."

In the silence that followed, Heyward calmly applied the balm to his lips.

CHAPTER 45

▼

Heyward felt pretty good about the way he'd handled himself with Thomas Pennington, not that he was able to change the way the man thought but that he wasn't the least bit cowed or intimidated by him. It was the first time he had ever met a "world-class financier"—as Horace had first described him—but, to Heyward, he just seemed like an arrogant, spoiled child. Maybe the man was a genius at international finance and maybe he did have his daughter's best interests at heart, still, all in all, he was a bully, and Heyward wasn't going to be pushed around by him, not in this stage of life.

Any good feeling Heyward had about seeing Lauren or calling Thomas Pennington an SOB faded when he pulled the Jeep into his driveway. It was almost completely dark outside, and even though he thought Elizabeth was supposed to be home, there were no lights shining through the windows of the house. He didn't remember her telling him that she had planned an afternoon shopping trip that might have extended through dinnertime, and if she was running late, she would've called him on his cell phone to meet at some restaurant instead of her cooking after being out.

He closed the garage and went through the side door and into the dark kitchen. Peaches was there waiting for him, and as he fumbled for the light switch, he could hear her tail wagging in the dark. He didn't hear any other sound in the house.

He called out Elizabeth's name, but she didn't answer. Without turning on any more lights, he walked into the den to find her sitting in the dark. The kitchen light threw a little illumination in the den, just enough for him to see her.

"Elizabeth, are you all right? Is anything wrong? You're sitting here in the dark."

In all of their years of marriage, Heyward could never recall any time his wife sat in a dark room. The first thing he thought of was that she had heard some very bad news and was sitting, stunned and unable to move. Then it occurred to him that she might have suffered some type of horrible medical problem, like Leon did with his heart attack and stroke.

"Elizabeth? Elizabeth?" he asked again. She turned her head towards him but didn't say anything. "Elizabeth, what's the matter?" In the faint light, he could see she was holding some tissues in her hands, as if she had a bad runny nose or had been weeping.

"Charlotte Ann called me this afternoon crying," she said. Heyward knew something serious had happened if Elizabeth was calling Tootie by her birth name. "I've been crying ever since she called."

"Oh no, did something happen to the twins? Are they all right?" Heyward felt almost panicked at the thought of something bad happening to his grandchildren.

"Charlie and Hannah are fine. I can hardly talk, Heyward, I'm so upset with what she told me. Did you vandalize a car when we were in Atlanta? Write some very ugly words on it with paint? I just can't believe what she told me."

Heyward felt like he had been kicked in the stomach and could feel the blood draining from his head, making him almost light-headed. Somehow, standing in the den of his home on Wexler Island, far from the mall parking lot, his act of vandalism seemed almost psychotic. At the time of the incident, it seemed so proper, so justified. Here, in the peace of his home, he couldn't put his actions into any sensible context.

Elizabeth continued, "Josh told her about it. He said he couldn't hold it in and that she needed to know about how crazy her father had become. Is it true, Heyward? Is it true? Did you do it?"

Out of nowhere, his feeling of anger returned. The brief instant he'd just had of shame and guilt evaporated, and the feeling he'd had toward the boys who parked in the handicapped parking place rose in him, there in his den. He paused just a moment, trying to sort out his rush of feelings. Months ago, he definitely would have felt overwhelming remorse, mortified that he had lost control at the mall. Now, there was no remorse, only anger.

"Yes, I did it, and I'd do it again. Those two little jerk-offs should've been shot for taking up the parking spot of some old helpless person. I just gave them a taste of what they really deserved. And by the way, I feel like giving a piece of my mind to that back-stabber of a son-in-law we have for telling Tootie about it." Heyward paused then said, more as an afterthought, "He shouldn't have said anything to her about it."

Elizabeth burst out crying, sobbing, like she had just been told her husband had died. Heyward let her cry a while before he tried to stop her. "Okay, Elizabeth, that's enough. It happened. I'm fine. Josh is fine. Tootie and the kids are fine, and you're fine. It's over and done with."

"First, you quit your job without any warning, just up and quit. Then you buy your Jeep and put that crazy horn on it. You get in a fistfight, my God, Heyward, a fistfight, on the beach. Now, you ruin that car. You could go to jail for that, mister. And those words, those ugly words you wrote on that car. Josh told Tootie what they were."

"To tell you the truth, Elizabeth, I thought those words were kind of funny sounding." Heyward was, to a large extent, becoming pleased with himself. At least for now, she didn't mention anything about him bashing Robert Fortson's computer with a baseball bat or, heaven help him, anything about Doreen Shumar's little retirement present.

"What's happening to you, Heyward? Why are you changing from the sensible man I knew, the stable one, the one I understood?"

Heyward sat down beside her and patted Peaches' head. "I don't know what's happening to me, Elizabeth; maybe it's some kind of chemical imbalance in my brain or something like that. I feel like somehow, I've been a failure my whole life—you know, I wasn't even supposed to be hired at the bank—and I've been feeling like I was a failure as a father and a husband. I've stood by my whole life without doing anything about the things that made me mad. Like I said, maybe it's some kind of chemical imbalance."

He thought a moment and then added, "Then again, maybe I just drove one stinking gray Buick too many."

CHAPTER 46

▼

Heyward and Elizabeth sat in the near darkness of the den for almost a full thirty minutes. The little lamp Heyward had turned on in the kitchen when he first came in didn't throw out much light; he could see her in the dimness, at least her profile, and not once did she look at him. Mostly, she just stared straight ahead and occasionally wiped the edge of her eyes with her tissues.

After a while, Peaches started whining just a bit to remind Heyward it was time for her supper. Under different circumstances, he would've suggested to Elizabeth that he understood exactly what Peaches was trying to say from her high-pitched drone—that she wanted some of the dog food out of the red can, not the blue one, and wanted Heyward to put some cheese on it. Normally, if that kind of thing didn't annoy Elizabeth just a little, he would wait until the dog whined one more time and then tell his wife that the last message meant Peaches wanted the cheese melted first then poured over her dog food. Heyward thought it was laudable of him that he somehow reminded his wife of the smart-aleck students she usually favored. But tonight was *not* the time for that sort of nonsense.

Even though he knew that he should have some kind of remorse or regret, perhaps even a large degree of shame, about painting the yellow Plymouth, he had none. If someone had told him a year ago that he would do such a thing, he would have been aghast at the very thought; this evening, in the near darkness of his den, he was actually quite pleased with himself. He did make a mental note to talk to Josh about his big mouth at the very first opportunity that presented itself.

His immediate problem, the one at hand, was that he could tell his wife was deeply upset and confused. He had not ever seen her so disturbed, almost to the point that she sat catatonic on the couch.

"I guess I should get up and feed Peaches," he said. "Just curious, but do you have anything fixed for my supper yet?"

"Heyward, how can you even think of food at a time like this?" she pleaded. The last few words were more crying than talking.

"Well, it's my mind that may be messed up, not my stomach. I'm hungry, and so is Peaches." With that, he got up and fixed the dog's food, making sure that he melted some cheese and poured it on top, just the way she liked it.

While Peaches was eating, Heyward fixed himself a peanut butter and strawberry jam sandwich, the second one he had eaten that day. Just as he had made a mental note only minutes earlier to talk to Josh about betraying him to Tootie, Heyward made another note to suggest to Elizabeth—at a more appropriate time—to buy some bread like Leland used on his sandwiches, the one he had eaten for lunch on the river that same day.

After Peaches had eaten her food taken from the red can, with the melted cheese on top, Heyward decided to take her for a walk around the block, which was not only good exercise for the dog but would give Elizabeth some time to gather her wits and calm down a bit.

"We'll be back in about twenty minutes or so. Would you like to go with us?"

"I'm not hungry, and I'm not in the mood for a walk," she said. "Try not to vandalize any of the neighbors' cars or beat up anybody while you're out, if you can control yourself that long." For the briefest of moments, she felt good enough to be sarcastic with him—definitely a good sign, he thought—but then she lapsed back into her desolation as she sat in the darkness.

Heyward and the dog had not been gone ten minutes before the telephone rang, and Elizabeth, thinking it might be Tootie, or even Lucas, answered the call without checking the caller identification window. She was sure Tootie would tell her older brother about what their father had done and that she would absolutely insist that Lucas drive all the way from Knoxville to Wexler Island to check on his state of mind. Tootie liked the fact that her husband, Josh, would earn a great deal more money in his lifetime than her brother, but in the time of a rare family crisis, she relied on her big brother to make everything turn out just right.

"Hello," Elizabeth said into the mouthpiece of the phone, trying her best not to sound like she had been crying.

"Hello back. Who's this?" The voice on the phone sounded familiar to Elizabeth, but she couldn't immediately place it.

"This is the Jenningses' residence. To whom do you wish to speak?"

"Elizabeth, is that you? This here is Dewey Sikes from Lost Springs, Georgia. I'm Heyward's first cousin, you know. His mama, Ruth Sikes, and my daddy were brother and sister, but both of them have passed on now. Do you recall me?"

Elizabeth wondered what else could go wrong. Her husband was acting certifiably crazy and becoming some sort of senior-citizen delinquent, and now his redneck cousin, a man she regarded as quite crazy himself, was actually shouting at her on the other end of her telephone.

"Dewey, this is Elizabeth. Of course, I remember you. You don't have to shout. I can hear you just fine. I guess you want to speak to Heyward, but he's out walking the dog right now. Would you like to call back in a few minutes or do you want him to call you?"

"Good enough. Me and Louis, Louis Sikes—he's my brother, you know— we're flying down to Orlando tomorrow—that's in Florida, down about midways state. We was thinking about flying to that island of yours on the way back home, since we're already out and all. I think I've flown in that airport once, long time ago."

On her end, Elizabeth heard Dewey cover the phone's mouthpiece and got the impression he was talking to someone else in the background.

She heard his muffled voice say, "I did. I did done it. I flew there before."

Then, from somewhere, faintly, "You ain't. You ain't done it."

"I did done it."

Dewey blew on the mouthpiece as if to clear it off and spoke directly into the phone. "Don't pay no attention to my brother, he don't know nothing. Anyway, we'll call back in about an hour, give or take. Now, you tell old Hick don't go blowin' that Jeep's horn in my ear when I call back, ya hear?"

CHAPTER 47

▼

Dewey Sikes called back in an hour, just as he had promised, and Heyward invited them to stay at their house. Elizabeth was already upset with him about his behavior in general, so he felt like he really had nothing to lose at that point by asking them to stay at their house as guests.

There weren't many times when Heyward and Elizabeth had arguments or got upset with each other over the course of their marriage, but when she was angry at him about something, he would proceed to tell her right then of anything else he might have done—or not done as the case may be—that would have eventually displeased her and get it all over at one time. "Ride the storm out all at one time," he used to say to himself.

Not long after Heyward had hung up with Dewey, Leland called.

"Heyward, I thought I'd call you. It's not too late, is it?"

Heyward assured Leland that it was not too late for him to call, without explaining that it would be hours before Elizabeth would let him go to sleep, her being upset with him about ruining the yellow Plymouth *and* inviting his cousins to stay with them and all.

"Well, I was at Knobby Creek Marina this afternoon, and I saw a boat for sale I thought you might be interested in buying. It's a thirty-two-foot Sea Ray, the kind you were talking about the other day."

"Really?" Heyward said. For less than a second, he thought about asking what color the boat was painted but decided a question like that, right off the bat, was a rather nitpicky thing to ask his friend.

"I know you said you wanted to buy a brand-new boat, but this one is as good as new. I feel sure the guy selling it wants to unload it as fast as he can. One of the marina dockhands told me the owner is planning on getting a divorce and wants to hide as much cash as he can from his wife before any divorce proceedings start."

"Thanks, Leland. I appreciate you thinking of me about it. I'll go see about it tomorrow morning. By the way, I was going to call you. My two cousins, the ones I mentioned to you, are flying in tomorrow afternoon for a few days. I'd like to take them fishing, some kind of fishing that they normally don't get to do, and I was thinking about taking them on a charter boat. See if we can hook up a marlin or a sailfish, something like that. Since you seem to know about these things, can you recommend a charter service to me?"

Leland gave Heyward the names of two charter fishing boats that fished out of Knobby Creek Marina, which was on Wexler Bay, not a far distance from Heyward's house or from the island's small airfield. According to Dewey, he and Louis should be landing on Wexler Island early in the afternoon, so he should have time to check into chartering a fishing boat and see about the Sea Ray as well before they arrived.

*   *   *   *

By the next morning, Elizabeth seemed to be almost back to her normal self. "Heyward, I'm going to put Dewey in the bedroom in the front, and Louis in the one on the side. Do you think they can share a bathroom all right? I mean, they do use indoor bathrooms, don't they? Not outhouses?"

"Very funny, Elizabeth. Remember, they are my cousins," he said, and he kissed her good-bye as he left to go to see about his errands at the marina.

Knobby Creek Marina was the largest marina on Wexler Island. It had in-water berths for about a hundred boats, offered both gasoline and diesel fuels at the dock, pump-out stations and repair and maintenance services, and had a short-order restaurant attached to its small general supplies store and offices. Knobby Creek was situated on the westernmost edge of Wexler Bay, about twelve miles from the Atlantic Ocean. It could be accessed from the bay by going through a narrow channel protected on each side by jetties.

The jetties were man-made, constructed of massive chunks of granite rock, and extended a full mile out into the ocean itself. All boats entering Wexler Bay from the ocean had to pass between the jetties, and the same was true for all boats leaving the bay and going into the Atlantic Ocean.

Two freshwater rivers, the Black Oak, from the north, and the Willow, from the south, emptied into Wexler Bay. The two rivers mixed with the salt water of the Atlantic Ocean and made the water in the bay brackish, neither completely fresh water nor completely salt water. Consequently, with all that water constantly flowing in from the rivers, coupled with the ebb and flow of the tides from the Atlantic Ocean, there was always some type of current to be negotiated by boats traveling on Wexler Bay.

Leland had given Heyward the berth number where the Sea Ray boat for sale was tied up. Walking along the wooden docks, he found it without any trouble. There was no one on the boat for him to talk to, but there was a "For Sale" sign attached to the aft railing with a telephone number for interested parties to call.

The boat, the Sea Ray, was beautiful and seemed exactly as Leland had told him, almost brand new. Heyward dialed the number from the dock and left a message on a voice mail that he was interested and left his cell phone number as a contact.

After he made the call and could finally stop himself from walking around the boat, admiring everything about it, especially the blue-painted hull, he walked back to the marina office to see if he could locate one of the charter boats Leland had suggested.

There was a pleasant-looking woman behind the counter. Lottie was her name, he discovered as she introduced herself with a firm handshake—Heyward liked her immediately, of course. She wrote down the berth numbers of the two charter boats on a small sheet of scratch paper.

"I think you'll be pleased with either one of these captains. I do think that this one," she pointed to one of the berth numbers on the paper, "Captain Johns, is booked for tomorrow. Try Captain Carlson, he's got a nice Bertram, and folks are generally pleased with him."

Heyward thanked her and then asked, "Lottie, can I ask you something else? Do you know anything about that Sea Ray for sale over in berth C-36? I might be interested in buying it, and if I do, I might want to keep it docked here." He thought of what he had just said, then added, "And I might say, I *may* be interested in it." He didn't want to seem too eager to buy the boat in case the woman had some sort of financial interest in any transaction that happened in the marina.

Lottie, just as pleasant as she was when he first walked up to the counter, looked out the window to make sure exactly which boat Heyward was inquiring about.

"Oh, yes. That's Dr. Bowen's boat. He's kept it here ever since he bought it last year, and I can tell you, he keeps that boat maintained well. That's one fine boat." Then she leaned over the counter and looked left and right to make sure no one else could hear her. "I hear Dr. Bowen wants to sell that boat fast. You know, rumor has it that he's getting a divorce and wants to hide the money from his wife's lawyers. But then, I've met her, and I'd divorce her too, you know, if I was him."

CHAPTER 48

▼

Heyward took the scratch piece of paper that Lottie had given him with Captain Carlson's berth number on it and walked along the docks until he located the big Bertram fishing boat. He was immediately satisfied with the look of the boat; everything that he could see was clean and well scrubbed. He always used the appearance of someone's office at the bank as an indicator of the quality of a person's work; a clean, well-organized office generally meant clean, well-organized results, and Doreen Shumar's office, for one, was always clean and well organized.

He didn't see or hear anyone on board the charter boat, *The Battleboat*, and he didn't want to just step over onto the deck in case that sort of behavior violated good boat etiquette or invoked some kind of bad omen to a captain. Heyward knew from his coast guard days that some captains were superstitious and from reading in boating magazines that quite a few boat owners had certain idiosyncrasies that other people didn't have. If he bought the Sea Ray, he thought, he'd have to think up some kind of special eccentric quirk that people could gossip and go on about when he wasn't around.

"Hello, anybody aboard *The Battleboat*?" he called out. Standing on a dock yelling at a boat made him feel a little foolish, but he could think of no other way to hail the captain or crew if anyone was onboard.

Heyward was about to call out again when a young man, he couldn't have been more than twenty-five years old, stepped out of the cabin door. The man was nice looking, with blondish-colored hair, and had a certain presence about him; he carried himself a certain peculiar way. It occurred to Heyward that he had seen him before, or if not actually in person, in a picture or on television or in a movie. There was something about the man, but Heyward couldn't quite make a connection.

"I'm Captain Carlson. Can I help you?" the man said. Heyward caught himself actually staring at the young captain.

"Yes, I am looking to book a fishing charter for myself and two other guys tomorrow morning."

Heyward's curiosity got the better of him there on the dock. It was like an insistent itch that had to be scratched or else he wouldn't be able to concentrate on the task at hand. "I'm sorry, and I really hate to be rude," Heyward said, "but has anyone ever told you that you look like somebody else? Have we ever met before?"

"Well, I hate to be rude back to you, but how old are you?" the captain said. He moved to the edge of the boat closer to Heyward.

"I'm sixty-one or sixty-two. Sometimes I forget my exact age."

"Let me guess, you think I look like Jerry Lee Lewis, the rock and roll guy, when he was young? Everybody your age says that," he said and smiled. "Come on board."

Twenty minutes later, Heyward had booked *The Battleboat* for a fishing expedition the next morning and had given Captain Carlson specific instructions that he, and he alone, would pay for the charter regardless of what Dewey or Louis might insist.

"Of course, if my cousins want to tip you and Hector," Heyward nodded at Hector, the first mate, who had come out on the deck and introduced himself, "that's okay with me, and I expect they'll do that, but make sure I pay everything else. Oh, just so you know, one of my cousins is a huge admirer of Jerry Lee Lewis, a big-time fan. I'm going to tell you that now in case he starts acting a little weird or something."

They all shook hands, and Heyward stepped back on the dock. He looked back at the captain; then and there, he decided not to say anything to Dewey about how much the man resembled his hero. It might be interesting just to wait and see if his cousin said anything about it.

He had noticed on the captain's watch—since Heyward never wore one anymore—it was almost eleven o'clock. He needed to pick his cousins up in a couple of hours. Then, as he was walking to his Jeep, his cell phone rang.

"Yes, this is Jimmy Ratterree. I think you called about the Sea Ray?" the voice on the other end said.

"Yes, I called about the boat. I thought a Dr. Bowen owned that boat?"

"He does. I'm the broker that's selling the boat for the good doctor," he said. "When would you like to take it out for a sea trial? I'm leaving for a trip tonight and will be gone for a few days. Doc Bowen wants to sell it quick for reasons that he alone knows. Can you meet me this afternoon at the marina and look it over today?"

For reasons he, the doctor, alone knows, Heyward thought. *Half the world seems to know why he wants to sell the boat quickly.*

They agreed to meet at three o'clock. Heyward reasoned that Dewey and Louis would probably enjoy getting out on the water themselves for the test run, despite having flown from Florida that morning.

"Dang," he said out loud to himself when he closed his phone. "This is going to be one busy day."

✳   ✳   ✳   ✳

When Heyward got to the small airfield, his cousins' plane was already there, backed in one of the hangers, facing outward. *They must rent hangers out like hotel rooms,* he thought. He was reminded how beautiful the plane really was; even parked it seemed graceful, as if it was a work of art, a sculpture skillfully hammered out of metal by an especially gifted artist.

Just thinking of how difficult it must be to fly such a plane, Heyward was embarrassed just a little that he sometimes didn't fully appreciate his two cousins. After all, it was he who had a college education, and he would never be able to learn such a complicated thing as to fly a twin-engine airplane. Dewey and Louis had barely received a high school education, and yet, they were qualified pilots and were able to fly all around the country.

"Hick," someone yelled across the polished hanger floor, "over here!"

Louis Sikes walked across the hanger, and they shook hands then made a very awkward attempt to hug, neither wanting to be too enthusiastic about it in case someone was watching and might get the wrong idea about them.

Louis pointed at the back of his plane where the steps had been lowered. "Dewey should be coming out of there in a second or two. We had to clean the inside up in Orlando, and he's just making sure we got everything."

Heyward looked at the doorway of the plane and saw the rear end of a fat man bent over, backing out of the hatch. The man's pants had slipped down, and Heyward could see at least half of his butt crack. It reminded him of a show he'd seen on television that made light of a plumber working on clogged pipes in some snobby, high-society woman's kitchen.

Dewey backed fully out of the plane's door before he turned around. In his hand was some crumpled-up paper towels and a spray bottle that looked like disinfectant or cleaning solution.

"It's always the men that throw up, always the daddies. The bigger they are, the more they puke, and the more they puke, the worse it smells," he said and edged down the three metal steps.

Dewey rubbed his palms hard on his pants several times before sticking his hand out to shake Heyward's. Dewey never made an attempt to hug him like Louis always did; Heyward always assumed a man who owned a bar like The Bitch could never afford to show too much affection to another man.

"Hick, like I said, it's always the daddy that throws up. Louis and me flew this nice little girl and her parents down to Orlando this morning. The little girl's got some kind of affliction that I can't pronounce and my fat-ass brother can't say neither." Dewey looked at Louis for confirmation, but his brother acted like he was inspecting the landing gear and conveniently ignored him.

"Anyway, we had smooth air all the way down, but her daddy got sick anyways. Puked up all kinds of stuff—little roast beef chunks—in the bag we gave him, but he missed once and some got on the floor." Dewey held up his hand, and in between his thumb and finger, he was holding some kind of small circle, no bigger than a dime.

"Never seen this before. The man threw up a Cheerio, and it stuck to the wall. Can you believe that? A whole Cheerio, stuck right on the wall? Didn't even chew it one time before he swallowed it."

Louis entered the conversation now that the subject of the little girl's medical condition had passed. "We wanted to make sure it was real clean inside the cabin and didn't smell bad. Me and Dewey thought that this late afternoon, Elizabeth and you might like to take a little flight over the island and see it from the air. It should be real pretty for her at sunset."

His cousins never failed to amaze him. Louis closed up the stairs leading to the cabin of the plane, and Dewey flicked the unchewed Cheerio into the nearest trash can.

CHAPTER 49

▼

Heyward's cousins from the hills and mountains of Georgia seemed genuinely excited to be invited on the boat inspection with Heyward. It seemed they liked the ocean as much as they liked flying, and they liked flying a lot.

Elizabeth, on the other hand, was not thrilled; in fact, she was terrified at the thought of flying with the Sikes brothers at twilight or any other time. As far as she was concerned, it would have been something short of a miracle if they could read and write much less pilot an airplane and even more of a miracle if they could fly a plane with two engines.

"Look, Elizabeth, they really are pretty thoughtful." He had to wait until his cousins had sat down to order lunch at the Knobby Creek Marina Restaurant before he slipped out and called his wife.

"It will be as safe as sitting on the living room couch. I mean, the plane has two engines so you'd still be okay in case one quits working." He cringed when he said that. That was not a particularly wise thing to say to her or anybody else about to go flying. "Come on, I promise you'll like it. Have I ever been wrong before?"

"It depends on what you call 'wrong,' Heyward, but, yes, I can list plenty of times you've been wrong. Where would you like me to start? Would you like it in alphabetical or chronological order?"

Before they got off the phone, Elizabeth agreed that it was thoughtful of them and further agreed that she would go on the plane ride, but only after she had recounted several instances of when her husband had been wrong before. Heyward patiently listened to her without any interruption or attempt at explanation; he assumed it to be the price he had to pay to get her to take the plane ride.

*   *   *   *

Jimmy Ratterree, the boat broker representing Dr. Bowen, already had the Sea Ray's engines on and humming when Heyward, Dewey, and Louis walked down the docks to berth C-36. After everyone introduced themselves and shook hands, Jimmy walked them around the boat showing them all of the highlights and features he thought would interest them.

After the walk-through, one of the marina dockhands untied them from their mooring, and Jimmy headed the boat out toward the Atlantic Ocean.

Heyward stood at the helm with the broker as he put the boat through its paces, running the engines at different RPMs and taking the boat on and off its plane. There were often swells in Wexler Bay, depending on the currents and wind direction, and the boat handled them well. Dewey and Louis ambled around the boat while they motored out to the Atlantic, and then, finally, they both sat on the front deck and took their shirts and tank-top undershirts off to catch the rays of the sun. They both had pronounced farmer's tans.

When the boat sliced through the bay's swells, Heyward and Jimmy observed Dewey's and Louis's stomachs, uncovered, jiggle back and forth with the movement of the boat.

"Ugh. Now, that's one sight I could've done without, friend," the boat broker said after watching Dewey's midsection joggle left, right, up, and down.

He cut the engines back as they moved through the jetties. "You want to always be real careful here and stay in the middle of the channel. The end of the jetties are marked with flashing lights, red and green, depending if you're entering or leaving the ocean." He pointed to the blinking lights. "Right now, with it being almost low tide, you can see the rocks; that's not a problem. But when it's high tide, the water covers the rocks on the jetties and you can't see them. You have to always, *let me repeat that*, always, be careful to go well beyond the end lights before you start your turn."

Heyward looked at the huge boulders that made up the jetties on each side and then located the flashing warning lights. It seemed simple enough to him.

"About once a year, some fool forgets where he is and turns over the rocks when it's high tide. Never fails to happen, at least once a year. That's when the coast guard gets an emergency call that a boat is sinking because the rocks tore out the bottom of the boat." The broker thought just a minute and then added, "You wouldn't believe how stupid some people can be when they get out on the water, especially if they've been drinking. Fools."

Heyward really liked the boat. He liked the way it handled, the layout of the living and little kitchen area, and he liked that the hull was a deep blue. While they were alone at the helm, he asked what the doctor would actually take for the boat and felt the price quoted back to him was reasonable.

"Doc Bowen wants to sell this boat quick," the broker added.

After they had been out for a while, Dewey put his shirt on and walked up to join them at the helm. Heyward excused himself and wandered around the boat, just trying to get a feel for things.

Eventually, he sat down by himself at the stern and felt the breeze blowing on his face as he listened to the steady hum of the engines. Suddenly, the engines were throttled back, and he could feel the boat's transmission shifting to neutral. Dewey climbed down the ladder from the helm.

"I've got to take a piss," he said. "You can't buy any boat without pissing off the back of it, whether it has a head or not. Louis!" he yelled towards the front of the boat. "Pissing contest. Come on back here."

With Jimmy Ratterree still standing at the helm and keeping the boat turned into the wind, the two brothers and their cousin stood at the stern of the boat and urinated as far out as they could into the blue Atlantic Ocean.

After about two hours on the water, they tied back up at berth C-36 with the help of one of the dockhands. Dewey pulled Heyward to the side.

"Hick, I know you like this boat. Hell, I love it myself. But, if you don't mind, I'm going to give you some advice. Don't buy it. Don't buy it at any price. I talked to that broker while you were sitting back here by yourself."

"Why don't you think I should buy it? You're right, I do like it a lot," he asked.

"The doctor's going to have some tax problems, trust me. It's not his wife's lawyers he needs to worry about; it's Uncle Sam's taxman. Believe me, I know about these things. If what I think the doctor is trying to do taxwise happens, the IRS might could seize this boat, whether you bought it on the up and up or not. You'd be out of the money but have no boat." Then Dewey added, "If what Jimmy tells me is true, the doctor's not as smart as he thinks he is. Trust me, I know about these sorts of things."

Heyward told the boat broker he liked the boat but would have to think about it for a while before he made any decision, even though he knew the doctor wanted to sell the boat quickly and knew that he, the broker, was going out of town for a few days.

They all shook hands, and Heyward, Dewey, and Louis walked over to his Jeep.

"Thanks, Dewey. I won't buy that boat. I owe you one."

*   *   *   *

Elizabeth was visibly nervous when she met the three men at the airport. She hugged Heyward's two cousins and welcomed them to the island, but Heyward could tell that she was talking a lot faster than she normally did and seemed to giggle any time someone spoke with her. *That's a sure sign of nervousness,* he thought.

Louis held her hand as she mounted the steps, and Dewey, who was waiting in the plane, guided her through the narrow aisle between the seats. "Elizabeth, why don't you sit up in the front right-hand seat? Louis will sit in the left seat and fly the plane, and I'll ride in the back with old Hick."

"Don't you need to sit up here and help him fly?" she asked and then giggled uncontrollably.

"Oh no, he's just fine by himself. You can see much better up there, and we'll make real sure that you're comfortable, temperaturewise and all that. Louis is a real respectable pilot, but if you feel the least bit uncomfortable, let us know and we'll take care of it right away."

Louis sat down in the left front pilot's seat. Elizabeth sat beside him, and Heyward and Dewey sat in the back. There were two empty seats behind them.

Heyward noticed that when Dewey pulled up the retractable stairs at the back and closed the cabin door, the plane seemed to be extraordinarily quiet, almost as quiet as one of the special soundproof booths he had been in when he once got his hearing tested. He himself didn't especially like to fly, even in big commercial jets, much less a small private plane. The image of the uneaten Cheerio came into his mind as Louis started the engines and taxied the plane onto the apron and then the runway.

Heyward looked up in the cockpit and saw Louis pointing out some gauges to Elizabeth, who apparently had asked him a question, and then they both laughed. Heyward couldn't hear the joke over the idling engines, but he felt better now that Elizabeth seemed a little more relaxed.

Louis ran the throttles up, and they lifted off the runway, climbed over the Atlantic Ocean, and turned north over Wexler Bay, where they had just been a few hours earlier. Heyward looked over at Dewey who was grinning. He gave Heyward two thumbs up. It seemed Dewey could enjoy himself in just about any circumstance, he thought, and wondered how his two cousins could afford such an engineering marvel as their airplane.

After fifteen minutes, Elizabeth looked behind her over her shoulder at Heyward to get his attention. She pointed down to a point on the ground. "Heyward, there's our house. See it?"

The sun was beginning to set, and the view from the air was amazing. Louis dropped down in altitude and flew over the beach, over the stretch of beach where Heyward walked Peaches and where he'd been in the fight with Michael Castillo. The entire time, Elizabeth was looking all around and pointing out landmarks to Louis.

It was almost dark when they landed. As they taxied back towards the hanger, Elizabeth took off her headset, turned back to Heyward, and said, "Did you see them, Heyward? Did you see those two whales swimming up the coast?"

CHAPTER 50

▼

After the airplane flight, Dewey and Louis insisted on taking them out to dinner so Elizabeth wouldn't have to be bothered cooking for them. They suggested they go to her favorite seafood restaurant, the Wexler Island Fishery, where everyone ordered the restaurant's signature seafood specialty, King Neptune's Adventure, which was a huge platter of local fried fish, oysters, scallops, clams, and crab cakes.

Halfway through the meal, Elizabeth put her hand on Dewey's arm—he was sitting next to her—and exclaimed, "Oh, my gosh! I almost forgot! Danforth Jackson called while you all were out test driving that boat and invited all of us to a big fish fry he's having for his company tomorrow night. Everyone that works at the company is going to be there, and he went out of his way to invite you, Dewey, and you, Louis, once I told him you were visiting us."

Heyward said, "So, I take it we'll be eating seafood again tomorrow night?" That was perfectly acceptable to their guests. Heyward had begun to experience a little "sinking spell," like a tiredness or slight drop in blood pressure, as he sometimes did after being out on the water in the fresh ocean air, but he quickly recovered at the thought of seeing Lauren Jackson the next evening.

That night, as Dewey and Louis were settling in their rooms, Elizabeth told Heyward, "You know, I've enjoyed having your cousins here. You really ought to make a point of inviting them more often."

✳   ✳   ✳   ✳

They were to meet Captain Carlson and Hector at *The Battleboat* at five-thirty the next morning, and Heyward woke up early, excited to see Dewey's reaction when he first saw the Jerry-Lee-Lewis-look-alike captain and almost as excited at the thought that he would see Lauren again later that same evening.

I hope Elizabeth and Lauren don't get in a fight over me tonight, he thought to himself, just to make himself feel good, as he pulled the Jeep from the garage. He knew Elizabeth probably wouldn't think he was worth fighting over, and Lauren wouldn't have a clue why she should fight anybody over him, unless they said he'd done a bad job working with her husband at the boat company.

When the three men got to the dock, their charter boat and crew were ready to go. It was still dark when they all made their introductions to captain and crew, but Heyward noticed that Dewey *did* stare at Captain Carlson and that he was uncharacteristically quiet on the trip out of the bay and through the jetties.

It was not until they began trolling and had a wahoo hit their bait midmorning that Dewey asked Captain Carlson where he was from.

"I was born and raised on Wexler Island and lived here pretty much my entire life except for a year I spent down in Savannah," he said. The captain waited a few seconds for Dewey to look a little disappointed, which he surely did.

Then he added, "Some of my kinfolk came here from North Carolina and some from the state of Louisiana. Most of my Louisiana kin were on my daddy's side of the family."

Dewey Sikes's eyes lit up.

Whether or not the man really had relatives that settled on Wexler Island from Louisiana or whether he was just playing up a possible tie to the ancestry of the rock-and-roll legend, Heyward didn't know, nor did he care. The important thing to him—more important than if they caught fish or not, more important than if they did or didn't get seasick—was that Dewey and Louis had a good time.

And both Dewey and Louis did have a good time fishing that day, even though Dewey did remain strangely quiet as if he was lost in his own thoughts. When Louis suggested they have a rematch of the pissing contest off the back of the boat, Dewey told him he didn't think it would be respectful of the boat's crew and declined to participate.

When they returned to the marina, Hector unloaded the fish; they had caught a few nice ones, and he packed them in ice for their trip back to Georgia. Dewey asked the crew if they minded if he took some pictures of them and the boat so he could show his wife when he got back to Lost Springs. He specifically asked Captain Carlson if he minded standing beside him at the helm of the boat and had Heyward take a picture of them together. The photograph ended up on the wall of The Barkin' Bitch less than a week later, framed in an especially tasteful casing.

Both cousins discreetly gave the captain and Hector a wad of cash for a tip and shook their hands as they all left.

It was not until they were about five miles from the marina, on their way to Heyward's house to clean up for the South Island Boat Company's fish fry, that Dewey made any mention of the likeness of the young captain to his idol.

"You boys may not believe this," he said, "but that captain was a direct blood descendant of Jerry Lee Lewis. Heyward, is there anywhere we can get this film developed today?"

✳   ✳   ✳   ✳

If the two cousins from Lost Springs made a favorable impression on Elizabeth Jennings, they were an absolutely wild sensation to the employees of the South Island Boat Company.

Most of the workers at the boat plant had never been on an airplane before, and the two men regaled them with their flying exploits, each story of them flying through lighting storms and dense fog and turbulence growing scarier at every turn.

Dewey talked of some of the catfish he had raised on his commercial catfish farms, how the fish grew so big that sometimes, it took three grown men just to pull them from the dirty water. Mazelle DuPont from over at Sunny's Diner was there, and Dewey told her that one time, he raised a giant catfish from just a little "kitten fish," and furthermore, he and the fish eventually became friends, good friends at that.

"That durn catfish used to follow me home sometimes," he said. "It'd scrap with my huntin' dogs and always win."

Boney had been listening intently to the story as he munched his way through a paper plate full of fried fish and hush puppies. In between bites, he asked Dewey whatever happened to the big catfish.

"Well, strangest thing, Boney, I was playing checkers with it one day, and I finally won a game. That catfish got so mad at losing, he jumped back in the water, and I never saw him again." Everyone, including Dan and Lauren, howled with laughter.

The highlight of the night was when Louis grabbed one of the bicycles parked at the side of the building and rode around the parking lot with Dewey perched on the handlebars. Louis soon ran over a pine cone, and the two men fell off the bike into some bushes, and when they got up—neither one was hurt—Dewey had ripped his pants right down the seam of his butt and had to walk around the rest of the evening with his white underwear showing through.

Lauren idled over and spoke to Heyward. "Well, I must say, Heyward, your cousins are quite a hit tonight. Did they get their sense of humor from you, or did you get yours from them?"

Heyward pulled out his lip balm. "Well, what do you expect? Everybody related to me is talented, one way or another. Me, I didn't get any sense of humor from anybody, all I got was my good looks." They both laughed.

"Speaking of someone with a sense of humor," he asked her, "is your father coming to the fish fry tonight? I expect he and Dewey would get along real well."

"No, he's at a condo he owns on the island. He's putting some big deal together and can't be disturbed, something about making international phone calls and time zone differences and all that. I think he's driving back to Birmingham tomorrow."

CHAPTER 51

▼

Everybody enjoyed the fish fry.

Dan cooked flounder over a huge propane gas grill set up behind the boat plant, and under the ancient oak trees, the same oak trees that may have been witness to George Washington himself, everyone had their fill of fried flounder, potato salad, and coleslaw. Almost all of the South Island Boat Company employees came up to Elizabeth at one time or another during the evening and told her how much they enjoyed working with Heyward the brief amount of time he'd spent there.

Lauren, in particular, made a point of making her feel welcome. She asked her all about their two children and their grandchildren, asked her how she liked living on the island, if she was making friends there, and if she missed Atlanta at all. They briefly talked about Heyward, about how much he had helped Dan and how upset he was over Leon's condition. Heyward had told Dan about him, and Dan had told Lauren.

"Is Heyward as witty at home as he is when he's working here?" Lauren asked.

"Witty? Oh, yes, Heyward is a regular comedian at home. He's like being around clowns at a circus," Elizabeth replied. "Problem is he likes to be especially witty when I'm aggravated at him, and he does that just to annoy me."

"Well, we all just love him here and his sense of humor. I mean, how many men his age drive a Jeep with those big tires on it? And that loud horn?"

Elizabeth frowned. Why would Lauren know about the air horn that Dewey had installed on Heyward's Jeep?

Before she could ask Lauren how she knew about Heyward's horn, a couple of people came over to meet Elizabeth and the younger woman excused herself.

Elizabeth looked over at Heyward, who was talking to Leland Tiller, and scowled at him. She would definitely have to ask him about that, and as she always did, she would ask him at the least opportune time, when he least expected it, just to catch him off-guard.

The cousins from Lost Springs planned to fly home early the next morning, so they, along with Heyward and Elizabeth, left the get-together before too late, but not before Dan and Lauren had elicited a promise from them to come back and see them any time they came to Wexler Island.

"And bring one of those big catfish with you, Dewey. I think Boney would like to have one as a pet," Dan said as they left.

✳   ✳   ✳   ✳

Heyward drove the two men with their box of iced-down fish to the airport in Elizabeth's Camry just as the sun began to break over the horizon. The flight back to the tiny Lost Springs airport was less than two hours flying time, but, as Louis said, "If we don't leave here soon, we might begin to like this place more than we already do and have to move down here."

They began to load up the plane with the fish they caught the day before when Heyward's cell phone rang.

"Heyward, this is Dan. I really hate to ask you this, but it's urgent. Do you think your cousins might fly Thomas Pennington to Birmingham on their way home?"

Dan went on to explain that the investment deal his father-in-law had been working on had reached a critical stage and the man had to be in Birmingham by noon to meet with his attorneys and sign some papers or else the whole deal would be called off.

"He's tried to book a flight out of Charleston, but nothing will get him there on time, and he's called around trying to charter a plane just to fly him home, but there is no one available that can meet his deadline, for any amount of money. I don't think Birmingham is too much farther for them, and I'm sure he would pay them. He could be at the airport in just a few minutes and ready to go."

"I'll ask them about it and call you back in a minute," Heyward said.

Heyward told Dewey and Louis about the urgent call from Dan. He explained who Thomas Pennington was in the international field of finance and his relationship to Dan and Lauren.

"I'll tell you both this, he's a real piece of work. Neither of you are going to like him."

Louis spoke first. "I don't have any problem flying to Birmingham this morning. But if he's a jerk, why should we help him out?"

He and Dewey talked a minute or two, and then Louis said, "We'll do it with a couple of conditions. He has to make a donation to the Lost Springs Charity Fund, and we'll determine the exact amount he has to give after we see how big of jerk he really is. Then, next time we come down here, he has to pay for us to stay in a first-class condominium for a week. Dewey and I talked last night, and we want to bring the wives with us next time, so we'll have to drive down since they won't fly with us. We'd stay at one of them fancy condos right on the beach so Elizabeth don't have to go to a lot of trouble for us."

Heyward called Dan back and told him that the boys would fly Pennington to Birmingham and their conditions. He held on while Dan told his father-in-law. "He'll be there in less than twenty minutes," was all he said.

Exactly twenty minutes later, Thomas Pennington drove up in his big BMW and introduced himself. He was already dressed in a suit and carried a black briefcase that was embossed with his initials on it. He looked directly at Dewey and ignored Louis.

"Which one of you is the pilot?" he asked in a firm tone. Dewey pointed to himself. "Are you absolutely sure you can have me there by noon today? Are you positive you can do it?"

Dewey told him to go ahead and get on the plane; they would be there in plenty of time for him to make his meeting. Then he asked him, "What're you going to do about your car? You going to just leave it here?"

"You don't need to worry about my car. You just worry about getting me to Birmingham on time," Pennington told him. "My car is not your problem."

Dewey shrugged and walked around the plane, checking the tire pressure and making sure the ailerons and flaps moved freely, the way pilots always do.

Thomas Pennington pulled Heyward by the sleeve, away from the plane and away from the two cousins.

"Are you sure that fat man can fly this plane? He looks like some kind of hillbilly to me, like he doesn't have enough sense to pour piss out of a boot. Plus, he's so overweight, he can't be healthy." Then he pointed at Heyward's chest. "And don't you forget, I still remember you recommended Danforth not to sell that boat company." He turned and climbed up the steps of the plane and disappeared into the cabin.

Heyward walked over to Dewey and Louis, who were standing just behind the plane, signing some type of sales receipt for fuel and parking with the airport supervisor.

"You old boys come back here anytime you want to. It was a pleasure doing business with you," the man said and went back to his office.

Dewey and Louis shook Heyward's hand. Louis made the same weak attempt to hug him as he did when they first got there, and they all said their good-byes.

After the cousins began to walk up the plane's stairs, Heyward called them back.

"Hey, Dewey and Louis, could y'all do me a big favor? On the way to Birmingham, could you somehow scare Pennington real bad for me? I mean, scare him really bad?"

CHAPTER 52

▼

Heyward watched as the plane taxied out of the hanger and onto the only runway of the small Wexler Island Airport. He could see Louis sitting in the right-hand front seat, the one Elizabeth had watched the two whales swim up the coast from, and Louis gave him a thumbs-up in response to his wave. He could see the profile of a man in one of the back windows; it had to be Thomas Pennington, but he didn't wave back.

Standing by the hanger, he was again struck by the graceful outline of the air-plane. As Dewey gunned both engines for the takeoff roll down the runway, Hey-ward wondered—as he always did—how something that weighed as much as a plane could not only take off, but actually fly. They climbed up over the Atlantic Ocean, banked to the right, and started towards Alabama; he watched until he could see it no longer.

Heyward decided to go to the Knobby Creek Marina and walk around the docks and look at the moored boats for a while, just for the sake of it. He knew Elizabeth would be cleaning house and Peaches would be napping, both of them trying to catch up on their respective duties after Dewey and Louis had gotten them off their normal routines.

Lottie was standing outside the marina office smoking a cigarette.

"How'd you like Dr. Bowen's Sea Ray? That's a nice boat, isn't it?" she said. When she talked, little puffs of cigarette smoke came out of her mouth with her words.

"It really is, Lottie." Heyward was pleased he could remember her name. "It's exactly what I thought I wanted, but now, I'm not so sure. I think I may wait a while."

They could see the docked boat from where they leaned on the wooden safety railing that kept anyone distracted or preoccupied with other thoughts from accidentally walking off the dock into the bay. While Lottie puffed on her cigarette, Heyward debated to himself if he ought to venture any further explanation why he didn't want to buy that particular boat; certainly mentioning, even off-hand, anything about the doctor and any potential tax problems he might have wouldn't be appropriate. It would, Heyward thought, make for some good gossip, but he had just met Lottie and didn't know her well enough to offer Dewey's professional prediction.

"You know, after I took the boat out for a test run, it occurred to me that I just like to be around the water and out in the fresh air and sunshine. Honestly, I just like hanging out here at the marina, around boats. I hate spending that kind of money for a boat if I'm not sure of everything, if you know what I mean."

"Well then, if you want to hang out around the marina, I'll tell you something you might be interested in. In a couple weeks, we're going to be hiring a part-time dockhand, mostly just for the weekends." Lottie looked at Heyward. "Somebody just to help tie up boats when they come in and work the fuel pumps, help people around the dock, that sort of thing. It only pays minimum wage, though." Then she added, "But the dockhands do get tips and some of them are pretty good."

She finished her cigarette and tossed the butt in the fast-moving current. "Course, I doubt you need the money."

Heyward watched the butt disappear and after a few seconds said, "I appreciate you bringing the job up to me, Lottie. I very well may be interested in that kind of work, if they would hire me. I could be around boats all day and out in the fresh air and sunshine at the same time."

Now wouldn't that be something, he thought. *Go from driving gray Buicks in Atlanta to docking yachts on Wexler Island.*

"I'll tell the old man you're interested. He'll like that. He always worries that these young dockhands will get doped up and get hurt on a boat then sue him."

✳   ✳   ✳   ✳

Less than two hours after the plane had taken off, Heyward's cell phone rang.

"Heyward, this is Louis. We've got a big problem. Seriously. Are you at your house?"

"What kind of problem?" Heyward said. "I've just left the marina, and I'm in my Jeep right now."

"Go home. I'll call you on your house land-line telephone. I don't want to talk about it over a cell phone; you never know who may be listening in. Twenty minutes, okay?" Louis abruptly hung up.

Heyward noticed Louis called him by his real name, not his nickname. That alone worried him, much less the fact that Louis was calling him less than two hours into a flight that should have taken much longer.

He pulled into his driveway and to his relief, saw that Elizabeth's car was not in the garage. At least he wouldn't have to explain a call on their home phone from Louis, who right now, should be airborne somewhere over Georgia or Alabama—at least not have to explain for the time being.

Heyward answered the telephone on the second ring.

"Heyward, this is Louis again. That asshole died on the plane."

Heyward heard his cousin talking, but the words didn't register with him. "Who died?"

"Your buddy, Pennington, died." Louis paused to let the news sink in. "Me and Dewey tried to scare him like you asked us to. When we was taxiing out, he asked me if I could fly the plane too, and, for fun, I said, 'No, just Dewey flies.' Then I told him that I had some kind of medical problem with my inner ears and had a hard time keeping my balance. He asked me if we ever thought of going on a diet. Can you believe that?"

"What happened, Louis? What happened?"

"We was up near Augusta when Dewey starting making himself sweat—you know he sweats like a pig if he's not standing in front of an air conditioner. Then Dewey started acting like he was gasping for breath and grabbed his chest like his heart hurt, so I started freaking out like we were all going to die. Then he faked like he got unconscious or passed out or was dead. I'll tell you, old Dewey ought to get some kind of Hollywood acting award."

Heyward listened as patiently as he could compel himself to and instead of urging Louis to hurry to the conclusion, forced himself to let Louis ramble.

"Of course, Pennington couldn't fly a lick so he got scared too, thinking Dewey had died and we were all going to crash. I had no problem working the controls with my knees where Pennington couldn't see, so I made the plane dip and dive. You've got to remember I'm a good stunt pilot. All the time I was screaming that we was going to crash and crying out for Jesus to save us."

Louis paused just a moment, trying to get a mental picture of what he must have looked like from the back of the plane, then continued, "For a minute there, I almost scared myself, Dewey acting dead and all and me acting like I'd gone crazy with fear."

Heyward got faint and then realized he was beginning to feel as if he was about to have a heart attack *himself.*

Louis went on. "I couldn't really see him good from where my seat was, but after a few steep dives and me making the plane shudder, I guess Mr. Pennington had a real heart attack and dies on the spot. When Dewey and me realized what was happening to him, it was too late to do anything about it. We landed as quick as we could at a little airport just north of Augusta. No matter, the man was dead, and some local EMS boys took him away in an ambulance."

"Ambulance? Where's Dewey now?" Heyward asked.

"Dewey's real shook up right now, and truth is, me too. He's okay, but he's shook up." Louis didn't seem particularly shook up to Heyward, as much as he could tell over the telephone.

"We're a little worried that the FAA might get involved with this. If they do and have some type of radar records of the plane going up and down, we're going to claim all that's from us trying to get to the back of the plane to give the man some medical attention."

Then Louis added, "We didn't even get a check from him for the Lost Springs charity. He told us before we took off that he would pay us once we landed in Birmingham. Can you believe that?"

Heyward didn't say anything.

"I hate it for that nice lady we met last night, I forgot her name now, but I hate it that her daddy died because of our fooling around. 'Course, he was an ass-hole."

"Lauren," Heyward said. "Her name is Lauren."

CHAPTER 53

▼

Heyward couldn't think. It took all of his mental power, all of whatever will and self-discipline he had just to concentrate on his breathing, in and out, in and out.

He more or less remembered promising Louis that he wouldn't tell anyone that what happened on the airplane occurred because they were playing a joke on Thomas Pennington. "We could all get in some serious trouble with the law over this if people knew what we did. If not in trouble with the law, trouble with the FAA. Not to mention, we all could get sued by the family, I feel sure," Louis said, or Heyward thought he said; he just couldn't remember clearly.

It was only supposed to be a joke, a practical joke, a trick on somebody whose only fault was arrogance. Now the man was dead, and the young woman he had begun to care so much about had lost her father because of him.

Holding his hand against the wall, Heyward struggled to walk out of his little office and into his bedroom where he closed the shades and pulled the curtains together to make the room as dark as he could, even though the sun was shining brightly outside. He pulled back the covers of the bed, climbed in between the sheets, and tugged the bedding over his head. He didn't even bother to remove his clothes, although he did manage to kick his shoes off onto the floor beside the bed.

So this is what it feels like when you want to die, he thought.

*   *   *   *

He stayed in bed for three days, only getting up briefly to use the bathroom, and he slept most of those three days and the nights in between.

"Heyward, you have to get up," Elizabeth told him. "You've got me worried sick." Nothing she said seemed to have any effect on him that she could tell. "It's not like you killed the man himself; he had a heart attack and died and that could have happened to him anywhere. You only saw that he got a ride on that airplane, and from what I understand, him being on that plane was a big favor to him—businesswise, I mean."

Nothing she said helped.

Elizabeth called Tootie, and Tootie called Lucas. Both of them tried to talk to their father on the telephone, but Heyward refused to speak to them.

"If he's not out of bed tomorrow, I'd call the EMS people and have him taken to the emergency room of the hospital," Lucas advised. "Make them forcibly take him if they have to, Mom."

It was only when Elizabeth told Heyward that Lucas was leaving Knoxville for Wexler Island that he got out of bed. "Call Lucas back. Tell him not to come, that I'm all right," he said. Then he added, "Better call Tootie and tell her too. Knowing her, she'll come and then start complaining about missing her appointment to have her nails done."

"Just so you know, I had flowers sent for the funeral," Elizabeth told him. "The funeral was today in Birmingham, Alabama. It was on the national television reports that Mr. Pennington died. I didn't know he was such an important man."

"They didn't interview Dewey or Louis, did they? The national news people, they didn't have any interviews with my cousins on television, did they?" Heyward asked her and asked her in a way he hoped didn't sound nervous.

"Not any interviews that I know of," she said. "I really doubt Dewey wants any more attention than necessary, you know, with all the tax stuff you told me about him over the years."

Elizabeth heated up some chicken noodle soup for him, and after three days of fasting, he ate all she had cooked and then asked her to make some more.

"In all the time I've known you, Heyward, I've never seen you this upset. You weren't this upset when your own parents died."

Heyward shuffled to the bathroom to take a shower. *Well,* he thought to himself, *I didn't kill my parents, now did I?*

CHAPTER 54

▼

When Heyward got out of the shower, Elizabeth stuck her head in the bathroom.

"Leland Tiller is here to see you, so don't go back to bed," she said. "In fact, don't go back to bed anyway, whether Leland is here or not."

It amazed Heyward that Leland always seemed to be dressed the same way, khaki pants, a long-sleeve khaki shirt, and low-cut work boots. The only time he had ever seen him dressed any differently was at the fish fry Dan Jackson had put on. Leland was dressed the same as he always was except, on that one occasion, he wore a short-sleeve plaid shirt instead; still, he wore the same khaki pants and his work boots that evening.

"I understand you've been in hibernation, like an old mountain bear, the last three days. Are you all right, Heyward?"

"I'm fine. I guess the shock of Thomas Pennington's death threw me for a loop. You know, I saw him at the airport when he got on the plane. He was dead an hour after that."

"Those things happen in life, I suppose," Leland said, and they all talked for a while about all the television coverage about his life and how important he was in the financial world. Leland said he was glad to have met his two cousins, Dewey and Louis, at the fish fry and that they seemed to be a lot of fun, something Heyward didn't deny, but he certainly didn't go overboard talking about just how much they liked to have fun. *Some things are better not talked about too much,* he reasoned.

"Anyway, I heard you were down in the dumps and wanted to know if you'd like to go fishing in the morning? I could meet you at Sunny's Diner at seven. We could get some eggs and bacon and then go fishing?" Leland said.

When Heyward seemed to hesitate in giving him an answer, Leland added, "Dan and Lauren have gone to Birmingham and won't be back for a couple of weeks. Dan told me they had some things to tie up, personal things, you understand, and then they were going to take the ex-Mrs. Pennington back to Philadelphia or wherever it is she lives now."

In a low voice, like a person might use at a viewing at a funeral home when they didn't want to be overheard or wanted to sound especially respectful, Elizabeth asked Leland, "How's Lauren doing? Does she seem to be holding up?"

"Oh, yes, she seems to be doing fine. From what I have understood all along, her father aggravated her and Dan all their married life, and Dan once told me that she never really forgave him for divorcing her mother and causing her a lot of heartache. Still, the man was her father."

After Heyward and Leland agreed to meet at seven the next morning and then after breakfast, go fishing on the Black Oak River, the telephone rang and Elizabeth went to answer it. Leland left in his dark green pickup truck that had a faded bumper sticker that read, "Trees Are America's Renewable Resource." Heyward watched him drive off and thought to himself that Leland was a perfect depiction of a lumberman: khaki pants, khaki shirts, work boots, and driving a dark green pickup. Even his name, Leland, sounded like it was connected somehow to forests and woods, if you thought about it.

Elizabeth walked outside on the driveway. "I'm glad to finally see you up and about, Heyward. You had me worried for a moment there."

Heyward picked up a twig that had fallen on the concrete and threw it in a small stand of trees by their house. He didn't really feel better about things, being responsible for Thomas Pennington's demise and all the pain he felt it would bring the man's family, but he couldn't stay in bed any longer. *This,* he thought to himself, *this is even more to bear than feeling like a failure at work or as a father.*

Logic could sometimes overrule those feelings; he could look at his bank account and know, at least on an academic level, he hadn't been a failure at his profession. His two children were normal and healthy, and they loved him. He wasn't a failure in *their* eyes. But this was real; he had caused Thomas Pennington's death. If it hadn't been for his suggestion to scare him, the man would still be alive.

Elizabeth took his mind off his guilt for a moment. "You just had a call from a Lottie at Knobby Creek Marina. You have a job interview Monday morning at nine o'clock. Did you forget to tell me something else?"

*   *   *   *

Once they were anchored in the river, after their fishing lines were thrown out but before their first sandwich, Heyward asked Leland something he had meant to ask the day before.

"Yesterday you told me you'd heard I was down in the dumps, Leland. Who told you that?"

"Your son, Lucas. He called me at home that morning. Apparently, Elizabeth had talked to him about you staying in bed all that time, and he must have asked her if you had any friends on the island that could help her out. She gave him my name, and he called me." Then Leland added, "He seems to be a good boy. You must have done a pretty good job raising him."

"Thanks, but I have to give credit where credit is due, and that credit really should go to Elizabeth. But thanks, and I want you to know I appreciate your friendship."

They sat in the boat for a while without saying anything. The tide in the Atlantic Ocean was still flowing out; it was not yet low tide, and that affected the current on the Black Oak, it being a coastal river. Because of the enormous amount of water involved between the interaction of the river, Wexler Bay, and the Atlantic Ocean, it took about three hours for the waterway to fully feel the pull or push of the ocean.

After a while, Leland spoke. "Well, I consider you my friend, Heyward. If a friend won't help you out, who will?"

Heyward thought of Leon the moment Leland said it. Leland was becoming a good friend, but Leon was his best friend, a friend that had asked him a favor, a repulsive favor, but a favor nonetheless. Still, Heyward had told Leon to follow his therapy, and that was the biggest favor he could do for him, he thought.

"Leland, do you ever have anything that really bothers you? I mean, you're a little older than me and you still own your own business, so you've been around the block once or twice before. Yet, you seem pretty much on an even keel all the time."

"I suppose it's very few men our age that doesn't have something that bothers them, at least a little bit. Obviously, it bothers me that my grandson has had problems with drugs from time to time." Leland turned the handle a few times on his reel to reposition his bait. "You know what bothers me sometimes now? I was married to Margaret for almost fifty years, and I never really told her how much I loved her, well, not until she got sick, then it was almost too late. I guess it was always understood between us, but I feel bad some days now that I didn't tell her every day."

Heyward was about to say something when Leland started talking again. "I'll tell you something else that I regret. I never spent the money to drive a really nice car, I mean, a really nice car. I was always a little too practical, I guess, and didn't want to spend the money on it. But I'll tell you, I'd liked to drive one of those big Jaguars just once. Just to see what it's like to ride down the road in style, big-time style. Not a Mercedes, not a big Cadillac—a big, black Jaguar."

Almost as an afterthought, he added, "Everybody ought to drive a Jaguar at least once in his lifetime."

Leland set his rod and reel down on the seat beside him. "What's really bothering you, Heyward? You don't strike me as the type that stays bothered too much of his time."

Heyward set his fishing line down too. "Bothered? Me? How about this: Before that plane took off, I asked my two cousins to scare Thomas Pennington on their way to Birmingham. Try to teach him a little lesson in humility, put him in his place, that sort of thing. I guess you could say that I was responsible for killing him and that bothers me. Wouldn't that bother you too?"

CHAPTER 55

▼

Leland let out a low whistle, almost exactly like the man from Eastern Shipping and Trucking did when he saw that someone had scratched the top of Heyward's desk.

"Damn, for a conservative old banker, you continue to surprise me. First, you mess up those boys' car on your trip to Atlanta, then you accidentally send one of the top financial wizards in the world off to meet his maker. Who'd've ever thought it?"

Heyward didn't answer, but Leland wasn't making him feel any better. "Who knows, Heyward, he probably would've had a heart attack sooner or later, with his lifestyle and all. Maybe you and your cousins just speeded up the process a little."

"You can never tell anyone about that, ever, Leland. In fact, if my cousins even knew that I told you, they'd probably take me for my own little plane ride myself, if you know what I mean. It's really eating on me, and I guess it will bother me the rest of my life."

Leland stood up and reeled his line in. After inspecting his bait, he cast it out again and sat down.

"Heyward, one day, maybe even on a day like this one, when we're fishing, I'll tell you a few things about me that might surprise you, burdens I carry around with me all the time. But I think we've had enough confessions for one day. Some other time, if you don't mind."

＊   ＊   ＊   ＊

They didn't speak of any more secrets or worries or bothers the rest of the day, and the few small fish they caught, they threw back in the river.

After they loaded the boat on the trailer in the afternoon, Heyward asked, "Leland, I've never seen your lumber business before. Why don't you take me by there one day and show me around? I'd like to see where South Island Boats gets their wood from too."

"Well, if you've got the time, let's go by there now. You can meet Joey at the same time. He's supposed to be there."

The Tiller Lumber Company was almost as Heyward had pictured it in his mind, maybe a little bigger in some ways. Out front, there was a small clapboard office building with a tin roof and behind that, on a paved lot, were rows of stacked lumber of different types of wood, all segregated by grade, length, and thickness. This lumber was only protected by tin awnings built over the racks.

There was a large metal-sided building that housed an equal amount of lumber as was outside, but this wood was completely protected from the elements.

"We keep certain types of lumber in here," Leland said, pointing to the neatly stacked wood. "Most of this product will be used for finishing work, you know, inside walls of houses and offices, trim work, cabinets, that sort of thing."

Behind the building that stored the inside lumber were three metal shipping containers. Heyward had seen these kinds of containers on pictures of ocean-going freighters used to ship cargo overseas. They were then off-loaded onto rail cars or trucks. He remembered Leland telling him once at Sunny's that he didn't like to go in because of his claustrophobia. "Why do you all have these green shipping containers here? I thought you got most of your lumber locally or from sawmills around the state?"

Leland pointed to the containers in question. "We get shipments of exotic wood from overseas in those things. Special woods that are used in high-end building projects that you see in some of these multimillion-dollar homes they build around here. You wouldn't believe some of the wood these architects call for in some of these houses."

"It looks like you've got a good business here, Leland."

"We've had our ups and downs over the years; that's for sure." Leland put his foot up on the tire of a forklift that was parked under the shade of an awning. "Three years ago, you may remember, the economy cooled down, and there was a big lull in construction. A year or so before that slowdown, I had decided to expand some and got a little overextended during the slump." He looked down at his work boot and wiped some dust off the toe. "Earlier today, we were talking about things that bothered you, Heyward, remember? During that time, when I got the business overextended, I had to take in a partner, a silent partner with some cash, just to make it through. I made a mistake then, and I'm paying for it now. But keep that to yourself, if you will."

About that time, one of the lumberyard workers walked up to them. Leland introduced him to Heyward as Alonzo Purvis, and they shook hands.

"Hate to bother you, Mr. Tiller, but I thought I better tell you as soon as I saw you," Alonzo said, looking like he was exasperated. "Joey's done gone for the day. He told me you said it would be okay with you if he left early."

Leland wiped the rest of the boot with his hand. "Thanks for letting me know, Alonzo."

CHAPTER 56

▼

On Monday morning, three days after he last went fishing with Leland and three days after he confessed he had a hand in Thomas Pennington's death, Heyward Jennings went to his first job interview in at least thirty-five years.

"I can't believe I'm actually a little nervous," he told Elizabeth as he was getting ready. He had changed from his starched khaki pants to business dress pants then back to the khakis, which, in the end, seemed more appropriate to wear to a marina. "What if they don't hire me?"

"I guess if they don't hire you, you can do what you normally do every day: Wake up whenever you want to, go on your morning walk, try surf fishing, take Peaches to the beach, then lay on the couch and watch The Weather Channel for a couple of hours straight. You know, what most working people would give their right arms to do every day without having to go to their jobs," she said. "It's not like we'll go hungry or become homeless. By the way, just how much is minimum wage these days?"

"I think you are looking at all of this wrong, Elizabeth. Docking boats at the marina may be a whole new career for me, and who knows, if I'm hired, I may get to wear one of those Knobby Creek T-shirts that has 'CREW' printed on the back." Then, just to dig her a little about the minimum-wage remark, he added, "Besides, I'll get some tip money, and I bet some of those wealthy boating ladies may give dockhands some special tips at that, if you know exactly what I'm talking about." For a split second, he thought of Doreen Shumar and her special style of tipping.

Heyward left their house early, allowing himself plenty of time to get to the marina before nine o'clock, the time of his appointed job interview. He'd washed his Jeep on Sunday afternoon, washed it inside and out. He paid extra attention to cleaning the wheel rims and made sure the blackwall tires were gleaming. You just never know, he reasoned, whoever was doing the interview might drive up to the marina at the same time he did and a clean vehicle might be considered a good personality trait by a perspective employer.

He entered the marina office just before nine, punctual, but not excessively early—he didn't want to convey the impression that he liked to waste time—and greeted Lottie who was standing behind the counter.

"Right on time, I see. Man, you're looking dapper this morning. I think you could shave with the creases on those khaki pants. You might add a little class to this place," she said. "Let's step outside. I need to smoke myself a cigarette before the big interview."

Heyward felt a little uncomfortable being outside with Lottie. It wasn't that he didn't like her, he did, in fact, but he had taken a lot of trouble with his appearance that morning and he felt like the humidity might take some of the sharpness out of his starched pants or, at the very, very worst, a seagull might fly over him and feel like making a deposit on his dark blue polo shirt. He had seen that sort of thing happen to a tourist once, and the unfortunate man had to walk around with gull guano on him for a while, despite his wife's best efforts to spot-wash it off.

"Mr. Mickey is going to talk to you this morning. He and his brothers own the marina, among other things around here," she said as she exhaled a lungful of smoke. "You'll like him, but I'll tell you this before y'all talk. He doesn't say much, and the little he does say is exactly what's on his mind regardless of who's listening. He doesn't mince words."

Lottie threw her cigarette butt in the water again, just as Heyward had seen her do before. Apparently, either littering wasn't a big concern of hers or she simply felt like the butt would be swept out into the ocean with the tide and be of little consequence to a body of water that big.

They went back into the store of the marina, and she escorted him into a small, paper-strewn office located at the rear of the building. There, Lottie introduced him to a fidgeting, impatient-looking man, Mickey Wickliffe, who, to Heyward, seemed to be in his mid-forties. He had an enormous beer belly, like he had ingested an entire bowling ball and it had settled at his midsection. The man had a cigarette in his left hand and motioned Heyward to have a seat in a folding canvas chair that had the marina's name screen-printed on the back. Lottie took the seat beside him, as if she was expected to be part of the interview process.

"D'you buy Doc Benton's Sea Ray? I understand you were looking at it. Doesn't matter. D'you have any experience working around boats?" he asked before Heyward could venture any answer about the Sea Ray.

Heyward explained that he had done a stint in the coast guard a long time ago, but he had no current experience in boats or boat handling except for a limited amount helping a friend, Leland Tiller, with his fishing boat on occasion.

"You know Tiller? Good man," he said, but again, before Heyward could answer, Mr. Mickey started talking again. "Just how old are you? Lottie said you were no young pup."

Heyward was a little surprised at the question. To his understanding, an employer could not ask the age of a perspective employee, it was against some type of federal law to do so, he thought. In fact, at one time, FMSB issued bank personnel a guideline of questions and topics that were forbidden to be discussed, not only during any hiring interviews, but in any conversation between supervisors and the rank and file of the bank's staff. Every employee had to sign a form that they had read the guidelines and understood them completely. Heyward was reasonably sure Mr. Mickey was breaking the law somehow.

"Sixty-one."

"You got any physical problems? Dockhands have to push and pull boats all the time and lift heavy things and carry them around … I mean, you being a lot older than most folks we hire." The man blew the smoke out of the left side of his mouth, like he was trying to keep it from getting on Heyward.

"I'm in good physical condition, and I feel like I can handle the physical side of the work without any problems. I've watched some of the dockhands for a while, and I can handle what I've seen them do."

"You're not one of those religious nuts, are you? We work seven days a week around here and that includes Sundays, and I don't want to have to worry about you wanting to take off and go to church. Don't want you giving out any of those religious handouts to any of our customers neither."

Heyward shifted in the canvas chair. He remembered they were called director's chairs by some people. "No, I'm not a religious nut, and I can work on Sundays. I guess I've been to church enough to last the rest of my life anyways and don't plan to go again until my own funeral."

"But you're not planning that funeral to happen anytime soon, are you? Do you use drugs? We're a drug-free workplace here, and you'd have to pass a drug test before you're hired on."

"No drugs, and I'll be glad to take a drug test anytime," Heyward said, now in the same clip, the same cadence of speech that his interviewer was using.

"It's a minimum-wage job, no benefits."

"No problem."

"Lottie vouched for you. You seem okay to me, a little on the old side, but we'll see about that. Any questions?" Mr. Mickey didn't wait for Heyward to answer before he continued, "She'll schedule you a drug test. We may need you to work more than just weekends. If you don't have any questions, we're through." He stuck his hand out and shook Heyward's hand, and a firm handshake it was. "Pass the drug test, and you're hired. Welcome aboard."

Lottie pointed to the door, and Heyward followed her out into the marina store.

"Like I told you, Heyward, he says whatever is on his mind. I think he just about violated every law there is asking you those questions. Come on, let's get that test scheduled."

CHAPTER 57

▼

"You'll have to drive to Marshfield for the drug test," Lottie said. "Mr. Mickey likes to use a lab down there. One of the lab's owners keeps his boat here, and Mr. Mickey likes to keep things 'in the family' as he calls it. Is there any day that's not good for you?"

"No problem driving to Marshfield," Heyward said in the same tempo of speech that his interviewer had used. Then, just for fun, he said, "Sunday's good."

Lottie started to say something—Heyward already knew she was going to say the lab wasn't open Sundays—then caught herself and laughed. "Maybe you can give the lab technicians one of those religious handouts when you go."

His drug test was scheduled for the next day, Tuesday, at two o'clock in the afternoon. Lottie explained to Heyward that he didn't have to fast before the test. "It's not that formal," she told him. "Just show up and pee."

Heyward felt pretty good. It wasn't like he had beaten out several other job applicants for a top-level position for brain surgeon, but he did get the job, even if it was minimum wage, without benefits. There was always something to be proud of in being hired at a new job, as if it was a stamp of approval that a person had value and worth to an organization, he felt. Ever since Horace Parker III told him that his father had not planned to hire him, it bothered him to think Horace Junior didn't value him enough to hire him in the first place.

He hadn't planned anything specific for the rest of the day. He knew there were two things he *needed* to do, even if they weren't things he *wanted* to do, and he wanted to get them over with before he started his new job.

*   *   *   *

Heyward left the marina and drove directly to the South Island Boat Company. He had not spoken to Dan or Lauren Jackson since the death of Thomas Pennington, and he felt like he needed to do so, in person, regardless of the sympathy card and flowers that Elizabeth had sent.

The boat plant looked like it normally looked on weekdays; the lights were on, the large windows in the production area were open to catch the breeze, the bicycles were parked on the side of the building. He saw a couple of people walking around in the shipping area. Just seeing the plant as it had been when he had consulted there settled him slightly, but still, he found himself a little nervous of how the Jacksons might think of him. One thing he had learned in his life was that a person could never predict how anyone would react to an event, particularly a death in the family.

Of course, Leland Tiller had told him that Lauren seemed to be all right after her father's death, but still, he felt apprehensive about seeing them.

When he walked into the office area, he could hear Dan Jackson talking on the telephone. Since there was no receptionist in the small lobby, he waited until he thought Dan had gotten off the phone and knocked on his open door.

"Dan, have you got a minute?" he said, sticking his head into the office.

Dan welcomed Heyward into the office and moved some papers off a couch he kept there.

"I just wanted to say how sorry I am about your father-in-law. Dan, I feel awful that he had a heart attack on my cousins' plane. I'm just sick about it, especially for Lauren."

"Goodness, Heyward, you shouldn't feel bad about anything. He would've had his heart attack if he'd been on that plane or not. You all were doing him a big favor trying to get him to Birmingham," the young man said. "In fact, we were going to call you when Lauren got back from Philadelphia and come see you, just to make sure that you were feeling all right with things."

"Well, I just feel real bad about it. How's Lauren taking his death?" Heyward asked.

Lauren was holding up well, according to Dan, and she had mentioned on the telephone in their conversation the night before that she wanted to write a nice thank-you note to Dewey and Louis for trying to help her father out by taking him to his meeting.

"She especially wants to do something nice for you, Heyward. She said if it wasn't for you, her father might have been driving his car, racing to get to that meeting, when he had his heart attack and wrecked and killed somebody else too."

"I still feel bad that he died on my cousins' plane."

"You don't need to feel bad about that, Heyward. It's not like you were responsible for his heart attack or anything like that," Dan said.

✳   ✳   ✳   ✳

At first, his visit with Dan Jackson, even though he and Lauren seemed grateful to him, made Heyward feel a little like going back to bed for a few more days. But after a few moments of guilt, he decided that he'd had enough of that to last him a lifetime; he may feel guilt later on, but he couldn't do anything about it now, and like Dan said, what if Thomas Pennington was going to have a heart attack anyway and what if he had crashed his car and hurt or killed an innocent bystander? Somebody like Dewey, when put that way, actually did the world a favor by scaring the man to death.

So, feeling a little better—although he knew he hadn't done the world a favor—he went home and called his uncle Walter Jennings's lawyer, Matthew Rabon, to have a word or two with him.

CHAPTER 58

▼

Elizabeth was pleased for Heyward that he got the job as a dockhand at the marina, even if it was only minimum wage. At their stage in life, she couldn't care less how much money he made, or didn't make in this case; the important thing was that he was happy, and he would be more physically active, two vital ingredients she felt would add years to his lifespan. Not only that, his new job had no stressful management responsibility, unlike his banking job, and he would be out of the house more often and therefore, out from under her feet.

Most importantly, he wouldn't lie around on the couch for hours watching The Weather Channel and worrying her about temperature inversions or the rainfall shortages in places like Montana or North Dakota, not that he had any real idea what a temperature inversion was or why a rainfall shortage would be detrimental to those states in particular.

When he got back from his interview with Mickey Wickliffe, he asked her about riding with him to Marshfield the next day.

"Why don't you go with me to Marshfield tomorrow when I go take my drug test? It shouldn't take me long to do what I have to do, and we can spend the rest of the day shopping and looking around." Then he added, "You might even find a blue sweater like that lady on The Weather Channel wears sometimes."

Ordinarily, Heyward would never suggest a daylong shopping trip, but in some ways, he felt he owed her something, as if he needed to somehow show her some gratitude for not badgering him about the Atlanta car-painting incident. She had let the whole thing drop, as if it never happened, and not once had she mentioned it since she confronted him that one night after Tootie first called her about it.

Not only had she all but let the whole Atlanta episode drop, she had gone to great lengths to make Dewey and Louis feel welcomed at their home, and he appreciated that. His cousins were his last connection to his childhood and, in many ways, his last tie to his parents and grandparents, and those were things worth holding on to as long as he could.

*   *   *   *

They left for Marshfield early the next morning. Heyward remembered Leland Tiller telling him just the week before that he missed his dead wife and regretted not telling her until she was mortally ill that he loved her, so Heyward made a point to tell Elizabeth during their morning shopping that he was enjoying himself and was having a good time being with her.

Within limits, Heyward knew he could tell Elizabeth certain things, and she would be glad to hear them, maybe a little surprised, but glad. But to tell her how much he loved her, out of the blue, would be pushing things quite a bit, he felt. Even though he reminded himself of Leland's regret, Heyward knew that any uncharacteristic declaration of his undying love for her would shock her so badly it would verify he was definitely out in left field somewhere, mentally speaking. This trip, he would tell her he enjoyed being with her; on the next trip, maybe he would tell her he loved her.

A little before two o'clock, Heyward dropped Elizabeth off at the Atlantic Fashion Outlet and drove on to the Marshfield Comprehensive Medical Laboratory. As he parked Elizabeth's Camry and went inside, he thought all the while what a good mood he was in and how nice the day was going.

The laboratory waiting room was similar to others that Heyward had been in over the years; it was a small, depressing room with padded chrome chairs and no personality. On the wall opposite the entrance door was a window with a sliding-glass panel, and behind the glass sat a bored-looking receptionist. He signed in, sat down, and waited for his name to be called.

It struck him as odd that almost all of these laboratories-for-hire had waiting rooms that seemed almost identical. It was as if a person who wanted to open a lab simply picked out the same room from the same brochure with the only choice being the padding on the chrome chairs, either nauseating green or revolting orange.

As he waited, Heyward could almost picture a distinguished-looking doctor thumbing through the pages of the brochure and then excitedly pointing to a picture and saying, "That's the one I want. That one—the one with the green chairs and boring lamps on Formica tables. And if it's no extra charge, make sure that some pads on the chairs are already ripped too."

Just thinking about how clever he was to dream up a person picking something like an outdated waiting room from a brochure put him in even more of a good mood.

In a few minutes, his name was called, and he walked through a door being held open by a dour, sad-looking woman in a nurse's uniform. The woman was about as cheerless a person as he had seen in some time and seemed even more bored than the receptionist, if that was in any way possible.

Heyward, being in unusually good spirits, decided that he was going to make the woman—Mildred Hunsacker, according to her nametag—smile, if not laugh out loud, at least once while he was there.

Nurse Hunsacker pointed to a chair. It was actually more half desk, the exact same kind he had seen in other labs, and she sat down in front of him.

"I need some information from you," she said, her voice neither friendly nor unfriendly, and put a form on a clipboard. "What's your last name, first name, middle initial, and your home address?"

Heyward gave her the information and, in an effort to be helpful, asked if it would be easier if he just filled out the form himself.

"No. I see you're applying as a dockhand at the Knobby Creek Marina," she said, reading some information already noted on the form. "Most of those types can barely read or write, so I do it myself."

"Well, I assure you I am fully literate. I was an executive at—"

She cut him off with a wave of her hand, and that subject closed with her gesture.

For the questions about his general health, Heyward took his time to form concise sentences and used multisyllabic words to give her the impression he was highly educated.

"Excuse me, Nurse," he interjected after one of her questions. "I see your last name is Hunsacker. I was once engaged to be married to a Hunsacker—Nadine Hunsacker from Huntington, West Virginia. By any remote chance, are you any relation to the Hunsackers from around there?"

Heyward had never been engaged before he met Elizabeth, had never met a Hunsacker before, never met any woman from Huntington, West Virginia, and to the best of his recollection, didn't think he'd ever met any woman he knew as Nadine.

The nurse eyed him suspiciously. "It's already been a long day, Mr. Jennings. Are you trying to pull my chain?"

"Oh, no, not at all. Nadine Hunsacker and I were engaged to be married, but unfortunately, a week before our wedding day, she died in a skiing accident." Heyward looked at the floor. "Actually, she was killed in a snow avalanche trying to evade a bear, an angry grizzly bear at that. Very, very sad situation." Heyward frowned.

Nurse Hunsacker looked at him and then back to a list of illnesses on the form attached to the clipboard. "Do you now have, or have you ever had, any of the following illnesses, diseases, or conditions?" She proceeded to read down an alphabetical list of common illnesses.

At each sickness, Heyward responded with a "no" or "never" until the nurse reached venereal disease. At that point, he cast his eyes to the floor and slowly nodded his head once. Softly, he said, "Yes, I caught a case of it from Nadine Hunsacker."

There was no reaction, or none that he could see, from the nurse except that she checked the box for venereal disease "Yes" and continued down her list of illnesses.

When she was finished with her questions, she took a vial of blood from the vein of his right arm, and when Heyward told her that he had not fasted before the lab work, she simply told him that it didn't matter for those particular tests and not to worry about it.

Then she pulled out an inflatable cuff to take his blood pressure. Heyward looked at the cuff, which he knew full well went around the bicep of a person's arm.

Up to this point in the exam, the nurse had not smiled in any sense of the word, even with his story about his dead fiancée or the fact that he once had been infected with VD, thanks to her.

Now, it was becoming a point of personal pride, like a private quest, to make the woman laugh or smile.

Once, when he and Elizabeth first started dating, he took her to the local county fair. There were many couples at the fair, walking around in the sawdust paths, and some of the men lugged around a large stuffed animal, a giant panda. According to one of the men, he'd won the bear for his girlfriend by shooting out a small red dot on a target with an air rifle.

Despite Elizabeth's claim that she really didn't want one, Heyward spent the better part of a week's salary before he was finally able to win her a panda. Winning the stuffed toy became an obsession for him that night at the county fair and making this nurse smile had become an obsession for him too, thirty-something years later.

As the frowning woman unwrapped the cuff, Heyward leaned in to her and said, "Ma'am, if that's supposed to go around my penis, you'll need to get a much larger one."

In a flat, monotone voice, she told him, "No, Mr. Jennings, this goes around the bicep of your arm, not your penis," and proceeded to take his blood pressure reading, which was well within the normal range.

It was not until Heyward came out of the men's restroom and lost his balance on the just-mopped floor, resulting in him spilling his urine sample on the front of his starched khaki pants that Nurse Hunsacker smiled.

"Now that, Mr. Jennings," she said, putting her hands on her hips, "that's what I call funny."

CHAPTER 59

▼

Heyward had to wait out in the lobby for over thirty minutes before he had the urge to urinate again. Nurse Hunsacker gave him a bottle of flavored water she was saving for her midafternoon break. "It's the least I could do seeing how you almost married one of my distant kinfolk," she told him, with an element of disdain he thought, but she let him use the staff's restroom, it being the only one with a hot-air blow-dryer, to dry out the spilled urine on his khakis.

Two days later, Lottie called from the marina and told him to come down and sign his employment forms. Not surprising to anyone, except maybe the dour lab nurse, Heyward passed the drug test.

"Fill these out, and I need to make a copy of your driver's license," Lottie told Heyward as she handed him the forms. "The government wants to make sure you didn't slip into the country illegally. I take it you're not from Mexico or Honduras or Guatemala, are you?"

Lottie issued him five Knobby Creek Marina T-shirts that had the word "DOCK" screen-printed in big letters on the back and then a tan-colored baseball cap with the marina logo on it.

Mickey Wickliffe stuck his large beer belly, then his head, out of his office door. "C'mon back here, Heyward. Need to talk to you." He shook Heyward's hand before motioning him to sit in the same canvas chair he used in his interview.

"Welcome aboard, Heyward. Couple of things: Pinky Pinson will be your boss. He's the dockmaster, but listen to what Lottie says. The woman might as well be my boss too, if the truth be told. Don't take any boats out by yourself. Pinky or me will tell you when you can do that." Mickey eyed him. "I guess I don't have to tell you to keep your nose clean and stay out of trouble, not at your age. Any questions, take them to Pinky." He stood up, and they shook hands again. Lottie showed him where to punch his time card then introduced him to Pinky Pinson.

Pinky's real name was Edward, but Pinky suited him much better. He was tall and skinny and had bright-red hair, which he kept tucked up under his cap. Unlike most people with red hair, Pinky had no freckles at all, not a single one, but anytime he got the least bit hot, his face would become flushed and turn pink. It was his best friend in elementary school who first noticed his color and gave him his nickname, which pleased him to no end.

Heyward guessed his new boss was around thirty years old, give or take a few years either way.

Pinky and Heyward talked out on the dock in front of the office for a few minutes, and every now and then, Lottie would chime in when she wasn't puffing on her eighth cigarette of the day. "So, Pinky, what are you going to call your new hire? Heyward? Mr. Jennings?" she asked.

Pinky looked a little embarrassed and began to turn a slightly reddish hue. "Well, I feel a little strange calling a man who's fifty years older than me by his first name, but I don't want to call you Mister Jennings either. How about I just call you Mr. J., and you call me Pinky?"

Heyward started to tell him that was the same nickname James Rimini had given him but decided not to bring it up; his life at FMSB had long passed.

The young dockmaster showed Heyward around the marina and introduced him to the other employees. By far, he was the oldest person working there, but everyone made him feel welcome and told him they'd be glad to be of any help to him, if they could.

Viewed from an airplane flying over, the marina looked sort of like a squared-off pitchfork. There was a long walkway that extended from the parking area over a hundred yards or so of marsh to the main office where Lottie and Mickey worked. In the marina's office were all types of marine supplies, drinks, and a small assortment of groceries. Lottie always kept hot dogs cooking on a small wire rotisserie. Adjacent to the office were the diesel and gasoline fuel pumps.

In front of the office was the main dock, which paralleled the shoreline, and from that dock extended five more docks where the boats were actually moored. Connected to the middle dock, the one right in front of the office, was a dock used for temporary boat tie-ups. All totaled, the marina berthed ninety-five boats.

"Don't worry about picking all of this up at once, Mr. J. Take it one day at a time, and it'll all make sense after a while. All I want you to do at first is hang out with Ron Simmons and help him. He'll show you how to moor boats properly, how to fuel them up, and that sort of thing. Once you are comfortable with that, we'll move you on to other jobs." Pinky looked at Heyward to see if he had any questions. "Oh, one thing, real important, I guess Mr. Mickey already told you, but if he didn't, don't move any boats by yourself. All that'll come later, but not now. We don't want you banging up anybody's boat or ramming one of the piers."

Heyward spent the rest of the day working with Ron Simmons, a likable young man in his middle twenties. He called Heyward Mr. J. too, since Pinky introduced him that way. Ron was patient and showed Heyward how to tie off lines, how to run the fuel pumps, and the sorts of things that were basic to being a dockhand. He was interested in what Heyward did before he retired to the island and thought it was amusing that he went from an executive with his own secretary to a dockhand. Ron described how he'd lived his whole life there and how he supplemented his marina job by catching and selling crabs to some of the local seafood restaurants.

At the end of his first day, Pinky caught up with Heyward as he was coiling up some rope that had been lying on one of the piers.

"How'd it go today? Think you'll show up tomorrow for work, or was it too hard?" he asked. "Ron said you picked up on things real well."

Heyward told him he enjoyed the day and appreciated Ron helping him like he did. "I really feel kind of lucky to have this job. I think I'm going to like everything about it, just being outside in the fresh air and being around the water and boats and all."

"You know, I feel pretty lucky working here too. But then, that's the way I've always been." Edward "Pinky" Pinson then proceeded to explain to Heyward that he'd been born on February 29, in a Leap Year, and when he got old enough to understand certain things, one of his great aunts, who was a very superstitious woman, told him that anyone born on a date that only came around every four years would have exceedingly good fortune their whole life. The same great aunt added that since he had red hair, which to her was a sure indicator of good luck, he had more than double the chances of being lucky his entire life.

"That's how I met my wife, Dee Dee," he continued, "Just pure good luck."

They both agreed that good luck was a blessing, then Heyward proceeded to counsel Pinky that he was only thirty or thirty-one years older than him, not fifty.

CHAPTER 60

▼

By the end of his second day at the marina, Heyward was beginning to feel like he was at home.

When Ron Simmons was not showing him the different ways to tie a boat off on a dock cleat or the proper way to fuel a diesel yacht or even how to empty a boat's holding tank of waste, sewage, or "product" as Ron called it, Heyward began to memorize every boat in the marina and in which slip it was moored.

Ron and Heyward walked along the docks, and the younger man would point out what kind of boat each one was. There were huge fishing boats over sixty feet long, boats just for pleasure cruising, some of which cost well over a million dollars, sailboats, and small center-console day boats. There was even a boat, about thirty feet long, that looked just like a tugboat, but on a smaller scale.

He was surprised at how many boat manufacturers there were: Hatteras, Bertram, Luhrs, Parker, Sea Ray, Boston Whaler, Scout, Silverton, Tiara, Carver, Mainship, Triton, Rinker, Fountain, Chris-Craft. He only saw one South Island Boat Company wooden boat, and it looked like it was out of place among the bigger, more expensive fiberglass and steel ones. Pinky later explained to him that South Island boats were usually considered work boats and were tied up at commercial fishing and crabbing docks.

He even saw Captain Carlson, the skipper of *The Battleboat,* and with a grin, the young captain asked him how his two cousins were getting along and when were they coming back to fish again.

Once, Mr. Mickey came out and talked to him. "You getting all this, Heyward? You're not running boats around by yourself yet, are you?" the owner asked and then turned around and left before Heyward could answer.

"I doubt he's ever given anybody time to answer a question yet," Ron said. "About the only person he ever really listens to around here is Lottie, I guess."

On the third day, Heyward met Warren Spearman. Warren didn't actually work for the marina as an employee but was an independent contractor who hired himself out as a specialist, performing tasks and jobs that fell out of the normal range of marina responsibilities.

One thing boat owners would hire Warren for was to scrape the bottom, the hull, of their yachts of anything that might attach itself to the underside of their particular boat's hull, like barnacles or algae. Those sorts of things would grow below the waterline of the boat despite the fact that the hull bottoms were painted with special growth-repelling paint. Warren could only manage that by using a machine that pumped air through a thick rubber hose to his facemask. With that apparatus, he could stay underwater, and therefore under the boats, for extended periods of time, while he scraped off the growth using a tool that looked something like a painter's putty knife.

"You wouldn't believe some of the things that swim by me while I'm under there. I see huge fish, bigger than me, and eels, rays, all kinds of scary-looking things," he told Heyward. "But then, those things keep me from becoming soporiferous."

Later on, Ron let Heyward know that Warren liked to use big words that no one else knew the meaning of. "I guess that keeps his mind occupied while he's down under those boats by himself. You'll sometimes see him studying a list of complicated words—kind of like Greek words—while he's sitting on the side of the dock. He memorizes them then makes up sentences with them while he's working under the boats."

Then he added, "But that's just Warren. He likes to 'elucidate,' he once told me, or at least I think that's what he said." Ron frowned at the thought that he couldn't remember if that was the exact word or not.

Heyward couldn't imagine how dark and lonely it must be for Warren working by himself in the murky, brackish water that constantly flowed under the boats. Although he couldn't see himself doing the same work, he could imagine some of the sea creatures that might be sizing Warren up as to whether or not he was part of their food chain.

"Why do you do that, Warren, go under the boats and work like that?" Heyward asked him.

"Well, let me ask you something first, Mr. J." Heyward noticed that everybody was starting to call him by the nickname Pinky had given him. "What did you do for a living before you signed on at the marina as a dockhand?"

"I was a banker." Then he added, "I was a banker because, the truth be known, that's probably all I was good at."

"Same here," Warren said as he picked up his scraping tool and pulled his facemask over his head.

*   *   *   *

Heyward's days began to fall into a loose routine. Mondays, Wednesdays, and Fridays, he worked at the marina from early morning until just after lunchtime, then he would drive home, gather up his fishing gear and beach chair, and spend the rest of the day surf fishing; although he was still largely unsuccessful at catching any fish off the beach. After he finished fishing, or more accurately, sunning himself in his folding chair, he would go home and wake up Peaches from her long afternoon nap and take her for a walk on the beach or around one of the golf courses in The Three Oaks development.

Saturdays and Sundays, he would be at the marina most of the day but would still find the energy to walk his dog before eating his evening meal.

On Tuesdays and Thursdays, he didn't work at all and either went surf fishing or fishing on Black Oak River with Leland Tiller. Unless he got home after dark, Peaches expected him to take her for a walk, and according to Elizabeth, it didn't matter if they went to the beach or around the golf course, as long as she had her required walk.

Other than the fact that Leon Campbell was not doing well—Heyward would call either Gina or Jean weekly to check on him—and that he still felt bad about having a hand in Thomas Pennington's death, Heyward thought these days were the best in his life.

Heyward couldn't decide what bothered him more: just that Leon was sick or that he had asked him to kill him, an act that he, Heyward, would have no part in. Either way, the situation troubled him whenever he thought about it, and so he tried not to think about it as much as possible.

Leon Campbell and Thomas Pennington would just have to be his "crosses to bear," as he liked to put it. He still had some flashes of his old feelings about being a failure and his unspecific guilt, but those feelings came rarely now and left as quickly as they came, like a bird that might land on his shoulder, peck his head to torment him just a moment, then fly away as quickly as it came.

Even Josh seemed to no longer harbor any ill will towards him for his shocking stunt in the Tanglewood Mall parking lot. Whenever Heyward called to talk to Charlie and Hannah, Josh would chat with him about fishing or his part-time job at the marina. Neither ever mentioned the car-painting incident.

Lauren Jackson sent a very nice thank-you note to Heyward and Elizabeth for the flowers they sent to her father's funeral and said she hoped to see them at the next fish fry, whenever her husband arranged one. She added a few sentences of how appreciative she was that Heyward and his cousins had done her father such a big favor in trying to get him to Birmingham that day, although it had not ended as planned.

In the recesses of Heyward's mind, he just added her handwritten thank-you note to Thomas Pennington's piece of the cross he was bearing and let it go at that.

✳   ✳   ✳   ✳

On the Wednesday of his third week, Pinky was waiting for him as he entered the marina office to punch in on the time clock.

"Hey, if you feel up to it today, I want to start teaching you how to run boats around," he said.

"Really? That sounds kind of like a promotion to me," Heyward said as the time clock clunked.

Pinky grabbed an ignition key from a wall cabinet that held copies of keys for all the boats moored at the marina. It was a marina requirement that every owner supply Lottie with duplicate keys for their boats in case the marina staff had to move boats around to fuel them or to change berthing slips or, in cases of emergencies like a boat fire, move the boats out of harm's way.

"We'll start with *The Rear's Near*. It's an easy boat to dock and a good one to learn on. Besides, Dr. Morton wants me to run his engines since he hasn't been out for a while." Pinky went on to explain that the doctor was a proctologist that lived upstate and that he had something of a weird sense of humor about his chosen profession.

The Rear's Near was a twenty-five-foot fishing boat with two outboard engines.

Pinky was a patient teacher. He spent a long time telling Heyward about how the tides and currents and wind affected a boat trying to dock, how the propellers sometimes pushed or pulled a boat in unusual ways, and how even the slightest change in the RPMs of the engines could be used in the docking procedure efficiently.

"We have some owners that never can seem to back their boats into their slips when they are moving *with* the current. Almost anybody can dock a boat *against* the current; it's with the current that can create a problem," Pinky said. "You've already helped some of those folks when you and some of the other dockhands pulled them in place with their lines."

Heyward remembered helping several boats dock when someone on the boat tossed him a rope as he stood on the finger piers. He felt like the captains were having a hard time controlling their boats and figured out on his own that the currents were the real culprits.

In a couple of weeks, by practicing every day he worked, Heyward could run a boat into its slip, by himself, as if he was doing it in his sleep.

CHAPTER 61

▼

There was only one thing that Heyward didn't like about working at the marina and that was when thunderstorms rolled in off the mainland, usually in the late part of a hot and humid afternoon.

It was one thing to be in a thunderstorm when he was working at FMSB in his office at the corporate tower. There, through the windows of his office, he could see lightning flash and know that he was completely safe, thanks to the marvels of modern building engineering. Safe in his office, even during the worst storms, he was only an observer.

Working on the docks when storms came in, he was a participant.

Invariably, a captain would try to bring his boat in as a storm began to crank up, and Heyward and the other dockhands had little choice but to stand out on the piers, just feet away from Wexler Bay's waters, in the open, as lightning flashed around them, and tie the docking boats in their berths. Heyward didn't mind the rain, and he didn't even mind it when it started hailing pea-sized hail one time, but he did mind the lightning.

It amazed him that sometimes, the people on the boat wouldn't even thank the dockhands, much less offer them a tip when the wind and rain died down. It bothered him not so much for himself, but for the younger dockhands, some of whom had families to support.

"If and when I buy me a big boat, I'm going to give out big tips to everybody for helping me, especially if I'm dumb enough to come in during a storm," Heyward told Ron Simmons and Warren Spearman after one cloud came up. Ron had tugged on Warren's air hose as a storm was approaching to get him out of the water; it was usually so dark under the hulls of the boats he was scrapping, Warren couldn't really tell if it was day or night. Still, lightning or not, Warren helped Heyward and Ron moor a big Egg Harbor fishing boat, even though it wasn't his job.

"I heard you were going to acquire Dr. Benton's Sea Ray, him wanting to liquidate it quick?" Warren asked him one day. Warren wanted to use some more complex words than "acquire" and "liquidate" but couldn't think of any on the spot.

"Decided not to. I think his wife's divorce lawyer may end up with it," Heyward told him, even though he thought to himself it might be the IRS that actually would get it first. The inheritance from his uncle Walt was still sitting safely in the bank getting some good interest thanks to some special rates on certificates of deposit that the Island Bank was offering. Besides, he hadn't seen any other boat he wanted to buy.

A few days after Warren asked him about the doctor's boat, it was gone. Nobody at the marina saw anyone take the boat; when the sun came up one morning, it had just vanished, as if in thin air. *The IRS, like God, works in mysterious ways,* Heyward thought.

Not long after that, Pinky informed Heyward he was getting a raise, fifty cents an hour.

"Well, in that case, let's celebrate. My wife, Elizabeth, and I are going out to eat tomorrow night with my friend Leland Tiller, and I think his grandson is coming along too. How about you and Dee Dee go with us?" Heyward asked. Then he added, "It's our wedding anniversary, and I'm buying."

Pinky agreed that they would go. "I know Dee Dee would like to meet you all. You say Mr. Tiller's grandson is coming. Is his name Joey Tiller?"

CHAPTER 62

$$\blacktriangledown$$

They all showed up at Oscar's Fish Camp for their anniversary celebration, including Joey Tiller.

But on the drive from their house in The Three Oaks to Oscar's, Elizabeth fussed at Heyward a bit for not promptly fastening his seatbelt and then fretted a little more that her hair was getting mussed because he insisted on driving the Jeep, with his window open at that. She had just caught him earlier putting melted cheese on Peaches' food and made a snide remark about him spoiling the dog.

"You know you should have your seatbelt on before you leave the driveway, Heyward. And you are fully aware that cheese isn't good for Peaches. After all these years of marriage, it seems like you would know how I feel about those things." Then she added, "Do you even remember how long we've been married?"

It vexed him he couldn't recollect the exact number of years, but then, he sometimes even forgot how old he was. Still, it was their anniversary, and he felt like he should have remembered, at least on this one night, how many years they had been together.

Leland and Joey were already sitting at a large table when Heyward and Elizabeth arrived. Leland introduced them to his grandson. Joey was in his early twenties and a normal-looking, polite young man. Heyward couldn't help himself from thinking that he didn't look like a drug addict, or whatever a drug user was called, and wondered if Nurse Hunsacker could tell just by shaking his hand.

Pinky and his wife, Dee Dee, showed up not long after, and they all ordered iced tea and shared appetizers of crab dip, onion rings, and a specialty of Oscar's: fried pickles.

Heyward had described Pinky to Elizabeth the first day he was hired on at the marina, so she had some idea of what to expect of him. But neither Elizabeth nor Heyward could possibly have expected how homely Pinky's wife, Dee Dee, was.

There was no way to kindly say it, Heyward thought, but Dee Dee Pinson was about as unattractive as any woman he'd ever laid eyes on. It was as if the poor girl had been somehow cursed at birth with bad looks. Her eyes didn't go with her nose. Her nose didn't match her mouth, and her mouth didn't agree with the overall shape of her face.

Later on, however, Heyward realized she had a very pleasant personality, she seemed to be exceedingly cheerful and, to her credit, had impeccable table manners too. Nevertheless, he avoided looking directly at Dee Dee, particularly when he was chewing or swallowing food or taking a sip of his iced tea.

All of them had a pleasant time talking and getting to know each other. By the time their seafood platters arrived, everyone seemed to be enjoying themselves, Heyward included, even though Elizabeth had earlier annoyed him about the seatbelt and his spicing up Peaches' food with the melted cheese.

But, Heyward's mood changed from good to bad when a group of eight men came into Oscar's and was seated at a round table next to the Jenningses' anniversary party. He didn't really notice them coming in until one of the men bumped the back of his chair. That, in itself, irritated Heyward, but when the man didn't apologize or even acknowledge his discourteous manners, it aggravated him even more.

He immediately pegged the group as golfers from out of town. Wexler Island was a golf destination, and it was common for people, usually men, to come to the island for several days just to play golf or take golf lessons at some of the resorts that had teaching golf professionals. Usually, most golfers behaved and understood that while they were on the island only temporarily to play golf, there were many residents who lived year-round on Wexler and worked and raised their families there, which included eating at the same restaurants as the vacationers did.

On occasion, there were problems between the golfers and the residents, particularly when the golfers, or beach vacationers like Michael Castillo, had been drinking, and quite a number of golfers liked to drink while they were away from their wives' scrutiny.

At first, the eight men talked with voices Heyward considered louder than necessary but still not so loud it couldn't be tolerated. But as the waitress continued to bring round after round of drinks, they seemed to Heyward to grow louder and brasher, as if each man at the round table was trying to be heard above everyone else.

It seemed they didn't disturb anyone at Heyward's table but him. Elizabeth and Dee Dee chatted like old acquaintances, while Pinky explained at length to Leland and Joey why the rising cost of diesel fuel wasn't hurting the marina's business.

Heyward, earlier annoyed by Elizabeth's fussing and having his chair bumped with no apology, sat quietly and listened to the growing uproar behind him. From bits of what he heard, he was able to ascertain the group was from the state of Ohio, a few of them served in the army, a couple of them got drunk the night before, and one of them was having prostate trouble. Something about their accents and the way they laughed out loud began to grate on his nerves, like somebody dragging his fingernails across the surface of a chalkboard.

Elizabeth began to notice her husband was ignoring her and their dining partners' conversations. He had a look on his face that she had never quite seen before, as if he was focusing all of his concentration on a dilemma apparent only to him.

Heyward thought he heard one of the men say something about somebody being so ugly her face would stop a clock. Was he talking about Dee Dee?

"Heyward? Heyward? Are you all right?" Elizabeth asked him. When it appeared he hadn't heard her, she asked again, this time with a louder voice, "Heyward? Are you getting sick?" She feared he might be in the first stages of a stroke.

He snapped out of his preoccupation. "Are they bothering you, Elizabeth? Maybe I ought to speak to the waitress or the manager. Tell those guys to hold it down some?"

"Who? Hold what down?" she asked. "Are you all right?"

"Don't you hear them? Those people behind me, aren't they bothering you?" he demanded. Before she could answer, he motioned for the manager, who was standing by the hostess's podium, to come over to the table.

Heyward requested—later, he told the police he'd used a very polite tone—that the manager talk to the table behind him and advise them to lower their voices. The manager furrowed his brow as if he didn't fully understand what he was saying, so Heyward pointed the index finger of his right hand over his left shoulder.

"Them. Tell them to hold it down some," he demanded and continued to point over his left shoulder. Even then, as agitated as he was at the time, Heyward thought of the irony that he was attempting to correct someone's impolite behavior, while he himself was rudely pointing his finger. Horace Parker would certainly be disappointed in him.

Leland, Joey, and Pinky stopped talking about diesel fuel prices and looked at Heyward.

He was sure he'd heard it again. One of the golfers said something about an ugly woman, and the others laughed raucously. *A man who said something like that would be the same kind of man who wouldn't let a person have the desk he wanted so badly or think nothing of parking his car in a handicapped spot, whether he needed it or not. A man like that would cheat his own hard-working brother in a land deal or throw an empty beer can at a little dog that nobody wanted to adopt.*

Then, one of the golfers tipped over a drink. "Goddamn it." Was it the same man who was making fun of Dee Dee?

Heyward Jennings, the conservative and reserved banker, a respected man who once never dared to break the speed limit, shoved his chair back, stood up, and shouted at the man sitting directly behind him. "You sorry motherfucker! There're proper ladies at this table. How dare you use cuss words in front of them."

He hit the man as hard as he could with his balled-up fist.

CHAPTER 63

▼

The moment he hit the man, Heyward knew he was in trouble, big trouble. One man against eight was not a wise bet.

The advantage of surprise disappeared, and in less time than it took to sneeze, two of the golfers sitting at the round table—Heyward later found out they *were* actually from Ohio—jumped on him and proceeded to wrestle him to the wooden floor. A few punches were thrown by Heyward and by the men, but they were mostly wild swings that didn't connect with flesh or bone, and eventually, the parties that had been sitting at both tables pulled them apart.

In twenty seconds, it was all over. Leland and Joey held Heyward back, and some of the calmer men at the other table penned their two fighting friends on the floor until they promised they'd had enough. The immediate area around the fight scene looked precisely like a brawl had occurred: Pieces of fried seafood and French fries had been mashed on the floor, broken plates and silverware were scattered about, and the floor was sopping wet where iced tea glasses had fallen then broken. Someone's foot had smeared a mixture of cocktail and tartar sauce on one of the walls, and the top of a saltshaker had been kicked off. Salt was beginning to stick to the floor where a ketchup bottle had emptied.

In a bit of plain bad luck, the manager had taken a weak but direct punch to the side of his face. He later claimed it came from Heyward.

Aside from one of the food servers repeatedly saying, "The cops are on their way," the restaurant was quiet except for Heyward's labored breathing and a couple of the Ohio golfers cussing under their breaths.

Finally, people started moving around. A few employees began to pick up chairs that had been knocked over, but no one, not even the families sitting on the far end of the room, tried to finish their meals.

$$*\qquad*\qquad*\qquad*$$

Officer Wayne T. Chow and Officer Annette M. Wright from the Wexler Island Police Department responded to the call of a 10-31, which was the police code for some type of altercation, but not a domestic dispute. Domestic disputes were 10-32s and nearly all police officers hated to respond to them because they were typically more risky, mostly due to the unstable emotions of the combatants.

Weeks later, when, as he was coiling a rope on one of the docks, just out of the blue, it struck Pinky as amusing that a police officer actually named Chow was called to the restaurant that night. He laughed out loud at the irony, standing there alone, and he quickly looked around to see if anybody was watching him laugh for no apparent reason.

Officer Wright called for an ambulance for the first man Heyward hit, who complained that his teeth hurt.

"You son of a bitch, I'm going to sue your ass for everything you're worth," he snarled as he shook his fist at Heyward. No one standing there was exactly sure that was what he said though because one of the EMS technicians was holding a small white towel filled with crushed ice to his mouth, and the words came out more muffled than clear.

Heyward growled back at him, "I thought I warned you about that cussing," as Officer Chow escorted him outside. Heyward simply glossed over the fact he'd said "motherfucker" just before he hit the man.

Eventually, the two police officers had written all of their notes as to what happened and had recorded all of the names and addresses of the witnesses.

"We're going to have to take you in," Officer Chow told Heyward. "You might want to have Mrs. Jennings follow us so that she can post bond for you."

"Are you going to arrest me?" Heyward asked. "I've never been arrested before."

"I want to talk to the chief first, and we'll sort it out," Officer Chow said. "But you are in for a lot of trouble, either way."

Heyward looked around the room but didn't see Elizabeth. He remembered seeing Pinky and Dee Dee standing together, both of them kind of in shock, right after the fight, but he couldn't remember seeing Elizabeth.

"She left, Heyward. Elizabeth left," Leland told him. "I tried to stop her, but she was crying so bad I could hardly get her to talk. What in the hell got into you tonight?"

Before he could answer, Officer Chow opened the back door of the police cruiser, and Heyward took a step toward the car. He saw the restaurant manager holding an ice pack to his eye.

"Look, Mr. Oscar," Heyward more or less shouted out to him, "I want you to know I'm sorry for what happened here tonight, and I'll take full responsibility for everything. Just let me know how much everything cost, not just the damage, but everybody's meals I ruined. I'll pay for those too."

The manager walked over to the police car.

"My name's not Oscar; it's Houston. I can assure you that you'll pay for all of this, sir, and more. You'll be hearing from my attorney as soon as I can get him on the telephone tonight."

*   *   *   *

Leland Tiller told Heyward that he and Joey would go to Heyward's house and check on Elizabeth while the police took him downtown, wherever downtown Wexler Island was. Heyward shouted over to Pinky that he was sorry he ruined a nice evening for them and that he enjoyed meeting his wife. "Oh, I'd like to take a couple of days off from the marina. I may need them to get all of this stuff straight, the stuff that I caused here tonight."

Pinky thought it would be a good idea for him to take a few days off too. "I don't think Mr. Mickey will look too kindly on this sort of thing, but I don't think he'll fire you over it. He's been in a few tussles himself over the years," Pinky said. Then he added, "But he was a lot younger than you at the time."

*   *   *   *

Since they hadn't formally arrested him, Officers Chow and Wright didn't hand-cuff Heyward when they put him in the back of the cruiser. After they pulled out of the parking lot and got on the road, Heyward leaned forward and through the wire screen separating the seats, asked them if they knew Officer Roberto Ramirez.

"He's an island policeman too. Seems like a good guy to me," Heyward told them.

Officer Wright spoke into the car's two-way radio. Somebody responded, but Heyward couldn't make out the words over the static.

The female officer said, "Wait one," then turned around and looked at Heyward. "Officer Ramirez wants to know how your little dog is doing?" she said.

CHAPTER 64

When they pulled up into the police station parking area, Police Officer Chow opened the car door for Heyward. "Watch your head on the door," he said as he helped him from the backseat.

"Mr. Jennings, I've heard every reason in the book for why people do things, but I've just got to ask you something. You weren't drinking tonight. I understand it's your wedding anniversary. You seem to be a levelheaded man. Why did you hit that guy in the first place, especially when he had seven other men with him?"

Heyward looked him in the eyes. "I heard him call my friend's wife ugly, and that's reason enough for me. Wouldn't you want me to kick somebody's ass if they insulted your wife?"

After a long discussion between the arresting officers and the police chief, they decided not to arrest Heyward, although they did issue him a ticket for disturbing the peace.

"You'll have problems enough when all those people's attorneys come after you. Besides, if you've been married as long as you say you have, your wife will string you up, if she's anything like mine," the chief said.

After the chief had had his say with him and let him go, Heyward realized he didn't have a way home. He certainly didn't want to call Elizabeth to come get him or trouble Leland or Pinky any more than he already had. It occurred to him that he could call a taxi, just as he did the day he decided he would no longer drive FMSB's Buicks, and just as quickly, thought of Leon.

I wonder what old Leon would think of me tonight, getting in a fight and all, he thought. Then it really occurred to him, the real question: *I wonder what the man*

I was back then in Atlanta would think of me now, the man I was for so many years, not even ever getting a speeding ticket because I didn't want to break the rules. In less than two years, I've been in two fistfights, vandalized a car, caused a man to have a heart attack and die, and now, I'm going to have my rear end sued off me. My wife will probably be divorcing me too.

"Actually, it feels pretty good," he said out loud in the station hallway. "Feels pretty damn good. Who's a boring old man now?"

A voice answered him, "What feels good, Champ?"

Officer Roberto Ramirez had walked up behind him. "What feels good, Mr. Jennings? This is getting to be something of a habit for you, this fighting obsession you have."

They shook hands, almost as old friends do, then the policeman drove him home in his squad car. "Don't worry," he told Heyward, "I remember where you live."

✳   ✳   ✳   ✳

Leland, Joey, and Elizabeth were talking in the den when Officer Ramirez dropped Heyward off. Leland made up an excuse about them needing to be up early in the morning and quickly left but not before telling Heyward that if he needed anything, like a ride to the emergency room, just to let him know.

Heyward and Elizabeth were left alone in the den.

"Before you say anything, Elizabeth, I want to tell you something, then you can give me all the hell you want. I've been thinking about it for a couple of weeks now, and I don't want us to keep the money I inherited from my uncle—not buy a boat, no new cars, no stereos, nothing like that."

He waited a moment, expecting her to make some kind of comment, but when she didn't say anything, he continued, "I've been thinking about it. I want to use all the money to set up a college scholarship in the names of my mother and father and my sister, Barbara. We can set one up in your parents' names too, if you'd like. I want that money to be used for something good." Heyward was beginning to ramble. "I want the money to be used for college scholarships. You know, the money I inherited from my uncle, the money that was sent to us by Matthew Rabon? You do remember Matthew Rabon's name, don't you?"

He sat down in his chair across from her. He winced from a pain in his side due to a blow he'd taken in the fight.

Elizabeth looked at him as if he was from outer space.

Heyward asked her again, "You do remember who Matthew Rabon was, don't you? My uncle's attorney? He told me my uncle earned his money in some dishonest ways, and I don't want to keep it."

Finally, she spoke. "Heyward, have you absolutely lost your mind? Have you completely lost your senses?"

"No, of course not, I haven't lost my senses. I'd've thought you'd like to set up scholarships so some needy kid could go to college, put bad-earned money to some good. We don't need it, and I thought you, being a teacher after all, would like to see it used for somebody's education."

Elizabeth erupted. "Not the money, you crazy idiot! I'm not talking about scholarships. I'm talking about what you did tonight at Oscar's Fish Camp. *Got in another fight, again.* In the middle of our meal, in the middle of a restaurant—a family restaurant—and they had to call the police on you! You started a fight for no reason and got arrested. Doesn't that sound like you've lost your mind?"

"Strange enough, Elizabeth," he said with a smirk, "I didn't get arrested after all. The chief let me off if I make restitution to everybody. And on top of everything—you're absolutely not going to believe this—it was Officer Roberto Ramirez that brought me home tonight from the police station. He remembered where I lived from the time before."

Elizabeth started to say something but started crying despite her anger. After a few seconds, she collected herself. "Heyward, I know it's our anniversary today, but I want to tell you this, if you don't see a doctor, I'm going to leave you." She stopped and let it sink in to him.

"Elizabeth, I'm okay. I just got hit once or twice, nothing bad. Those guys can't fight very good, and I scraped my knee on that wooden floor, but other than that, I'm fine. I don't need to go to a doctor for that."

"Not that kind of doctor, Heyward. I'm talking about a psychiatrist. You have some serious mental problems, and if you don't get help for them, I'm going to divorce you."

CHAPTER 65

▼

Having his wife tell him she was going to divorce him if he didn't see a psychiatrist startled Heyward. He recognized the fact that from the day he walked away from the bank, he had changed from the person he had been his whole life—the person his wife knew and married—to someone else. But no psychiatrist on earth was going to change him back to the same man Elizabeth wanted; as far as he was concerned, he'd rather be divorced.

The next morning, Elizabeth declared she was going to Atlanta to stay with Tootie, Josh, and the grandchildren and Heyward was not invited to go with her.

"I'm going to give you time to think about what I told you last night," she said. "You'd better give some serious thought about seeing a doctor that can help you or else."

"Well, while I'm thinking about that, you think about what I said about setting up some scholarships with that inheritance money from Uncle Walt," he told her.

Elizabeth had thought about setting up scholarships, but with her husband like he was, her priority was getting him back to the man she married.

"You be careful driving to Tootie's, and call me when you get there. I'll think about going to a psychiatrist, but I'm pretty sure it won't do much good for me."

Elizabeth closed her car door and lowered her window. "The closest one is in Charleston, and there's plenty of them there. I strongly suggest you make an appointment with one of them before I get back from Atlanta."

*   *   *   *

Heyward was sore all over from the fight, but his left ribcage hurt more than anything else. He attributed it to the fact that one of the golfers from Ohio must have connected with a lucky punch, but he couldn't remember any specific knocks he had taken. Sore or not, he showed up for work at the marina on time.

Pinky was the first person he saw on the docks that morning. "I didn't think you were coming in today and wanted to take a few days off." Before Heyward could answer, Pinky started up again. "By the way, Dee Dee said Mrs. Jennings was a very nice lady and that you were lucky to be married to her."

"Oh, yeah? What did she say about me, Pinky?"

"Not much good. Let's just put it this way, she asked me not to hang out with you after work. She thinks you might be a bad influence on me, truth be known."

About that time, Warren Spearman walked up and said, "I see the Wexler Island pugilist showed up after all. I've been waiting to use that word, *pugilist*, for a long time." Then he added, "You do know what that means, don't you?"

"Glad to be of service, Warren, and yes, I know what it means," Heyward told him.

"Look, I'm glad you're here after all, Mr. J.," Pinky said. "Mr. Mickey wants to see all the marina employees, you too, Warren, in his office this morning. Something's bothering him, but he didn't tell me what it was. You know him, he's not going to say much, one way or another, and even Lottie didn't know what the meeting's about."

Mickey had Lottie make a little sign to hang on the marina office door that they would be in a meeting for fifteen minutes. Anyone who wanted to come in and get some supplies or, if they were hungry, get one of the hot dogs she cooked on the rotisserie all day would just have to wait.

All the dockhands were there, along with Lottie, Pinky, Warren Spearman, and some of the waiters that worked in Mr. Mickey's restaurant next door.

"Okay, everybody's here. Wanted you to hear this too, Warren, even though you don't work for the marina. I got a call last night from Mason Thornhill. Most of you already know him, the little prick. Anyway, Thornhill's yacht, *The Golden Touch*, is coming for his annual stay and will be docking in a few days. For those who do know him, it won't surprise you that he's fired his captain and crew and they'll be leaving the boat once here. Thornhill's going to stay at the marina until he hires a new captain—whoever that unlucky bastard will be—so everybody be aware of what's going on and stay out of his way. Any questions? No, then let's get back to work."

Heyward raised one of his sore arms for a question, but Mickey ignored him. After everyone cleared out of the office, Mr. Mickey told him, "Heyward, I'll get Pinky to fill you in on our guest. Didn't want to say any more about him than I already did in front of everybody."

Mickey started to walk away then turned around and added, "Try not to start any fights around here today. Got enough to worry about without that."

✻   ✻   ✻   ✻

According to Pinky, Mason Thornhill might as well be the devil himself. In fact, Heyward sensed Pinky was even a little nervous talking about the man, even to him in private.

"He's in all kinds of businesses, most of them shady. But he's never been convicted of anything that I've ever heard about, or no one here has ever heard of him going to jail or anything like that," Pinky said. "Just know that Thornhill has a real bad temper and always causes some kind of problem when he docks here. Usually, he just stays a night or two, then *The Golden Touch* moves on out to other places."

Pinky thought a minute and added, "*The Golden Touch* is a huge yacht, probably the biggest that ever came to this marina, and, as you well know, we see some big boats here from time to time. Thornhill's boat was custom built in Italy, to his specifications."

Pinky lowered his voice. "There's rumors that he's had some people he didn't like killed on it. 'Course, nobody knows anything about that for sure. I will tell you one thing about him, though: Thornhill has some real good-looking women on that boat sometimes, although they're a little on the skanky side for me. Skanky."

With a homely wife like Dee Dee, Heyward had to wonder what standard Pinky used to describe good-looking women by.

"Well, Pinky, why doesn't Mickey just tell him he can't tie up here if he's so bad?" Heyward asked. "No matter how mean this Thornhill is, he's not going to kill him for that, is he?"

"He'd like to tell him that, but he can't. No one tells Mason Thornhill what he can or can't do. It doesn't surprise me a lick that he's already fired his crew."

CHAPTER 66

▼

A couple of days after Mr. Mickey's meeting about Mason Thornhill's expected visit, while Elizabeth was still in Atlanta, Leland Tiller called Heyward.

"Heyward, I need your help. Joey hasn't shown up for work at the lumberyard in the last couple of days, and no one knows where he is. Would you help me look for him?"

Heyward felt bad he didn't get to spend much time with Leland's grandson the night he got in the fight at Oscar's and felt even worse, when he considered it, that what he'd done hadn't set a good example for Joey. But then, he thought, starting a fight at a restaurant, particularly where families were eating, didn't set a very good example for anyone, even if he was defending Dee Dee's honor.

Once Heyward arrived at the lumberyard, Leland explained that Joey had driven off in his pickup truck, the green one, the morning after they had been at Oscar's and no one had seen him since.

"I'm getting worried about him. He's been gone before, but he always calls his friends or somebody and talks to them … but no one has heard anything from him, nobody," Leland said. He pointed to spot on a map of the county roads. "He may have gone over to this place, Sandy Point, to go fishing. How about you go there and see if you can find him, and I'll go down to this place, Angie's, to see if he's there," he said, pointing to another spot on the map.

"Call me on my cell phone when you get to Sandy Point, Heyward. If you don't see anything of him there, would you look around a spot a few miles behind Dilly's Bait Shop and see if he's there? It's called Yancy's Inlet, and Joey has fished there before."

They talked a few minutes more about other places where Joey could be, then Heyward took the map and walked towards his Jeep.

"Heyward," Leland called after him, "I appreciate you helping me. I hope you know that."

There was no sign of Joey at Sandy Point and no sign of Leland's truck. Heyward walked around and talked to a few people fishing off the point, but no one had seen Leland's grandson or his vehicle.

Three miles from Sandy Point, heading due west, a glint of light caught Heyward's eye as he passed through an out-of-the-way place called Harmon Swamp. The road itself was a seldom-used county road that had only been paved a few years before and was built on a type of levy, or berm, just a few feet above the swamp. Harmon Swamp was little more than a thick grove of old oak and cypress trees mired in stagnant, algae-filled water that nothing much could live in.

Heyward drove on down the road until it occurred to him that something in the swamp had to cause the reflection; it wouldn't naturally happen. He braked and backed up the road to where the glint caught his eye again. There, when he looked for it, he could see that the grass on the sloping side of the road embankment had been crushed and mashed down.

Slowly, he climbed out of the Jeep and walked over to the side of the road where he'd seen the reflection. Once his eyes became adjusted to the shadows thrown by the tall trees, Heyward could just barely make out the profile of a pickup truck's cab, although it was hardly visible in the motionless water.

Against all his instincts, Heyward slid down the embankment and waded out into the water, to chest height, and after he slogged on through the mire, he saw through the murk the bumper sticker he had seen many times before, "Trees Are America's Renewable Resource."

He didn't want to go any further, but nonetheless, he pushed himself to half-swim, half-wade over to the truck's cab and look in.

Joey Tiller was dead, slumped over the steering wheel, and in the heat, it appeared that he was starting to become bloated. Heyward slowly made his way back through the bog to his Jeep and called 911. He told them there was no need to hurry. After about ten minutes, to give the ambulance a head start, he then called Leland with the bad news.

Joey Tiller was the closest Heyward had ever been to a dead body. It was the first time he'd come upon a wreck like this, and the first time he'd ever had to call a friend with news that a family member was dead. It took a while for everything to register with him.

As he sat there alone, it dawned on him that he'd seen a plastic bag floating in the water next to Joey's body. Heyward looked up and down the deserted road then contrary to his better judgment, waded back into the swamp and over to the partially submerged truck.

Trying not to look at Joey's body, Heyward reached into the cab and plucked the floating plastic bag from the water.

The bag was filled with what he believed to be some type of illegal substance, some kind of drug, and some objects he thought might be called drug paraphernalia, although he had never personally seen or handled anything like that before. He was smart enough to know that whatever he was holding wasn't good and wasn't legal.

He made his way back to the road embankment and with the plastic bag in his hand, walked a few hundred feet down the road in the direction the truck had been traveling. Heyward found a small stick in the grass, punched a couple of holes in the plastic, and then threw the bag out into the swamp, on the opposite side of the road from the sunken truck.

The bag settled in the green water and disappeared from sight. Heyward felt sure that anybody investigating the wreck wouldn't look on the other side of the road and wouldn't look that far ahead in the direction the truck was traveling.

Fifteen minutes later, a deputy sheriff drove up in a patrol car, followed by an ambulance.

"He's in the water, over there," Heyward said and pointed towards the submerged truck.

Five minutes after that, Leland arrived.

CHAPTER 67

▼

Joey's parents decided to bury their son next to his grandmother, Margaret Tiller, in the Mount Zion Baptist Church's cemetery. The cemetery was situated on the mainland, just off Wexler Island, and was the highest elevation around and really the only suitable place for a burial ground around those parts. The island itself was just too low, only a few feet above sea level, and the water table was just too high.

Elizabeth cut short her visit with Tootie and her family to attend the funeral with Heyward.

Dan Jackson closed the South Island Boat Company for the day of the funeral so all the employees could attend if they wanted to. Almost everyone there, Boney, Monroe, and all the others, had known Leland all their life, and most had eaten meals with him at Sunny's Diner. Some of them had even gone fishing with him on the river. Leland had been to funerals of their own family members over the years too.

Mazelle Dupont closed the diner for the afternoon out of respect for Leland, and she managed to get a photograph of Joey and kept it by the cash register for a week after the funeral. One of the cooks found a black ribbon and wrapped it around the corner of the picture.

Lauren Jackson was at the funeral, and despite the circumstances, Heyward couldn't help but think how good-looking she was and how much he missed going fishing with her. Since Thomas Pennington's heart attack, Heyward felt uneasy being around her; he still felt so guilty about his connection to his death, he thought that somehow, Lauren might sense his guilt—like some kind of osmosis—and come to hate him for it.

She and Dan did come up and speak to Heyward and Elizabeth as they were milling around outside the church with everybody else after the service.

"Isn't this the saddest thing you've ever seen?" Lauren asked them. "Joey was a good person, but he just fell in with the wrong crowd." Then she asked Elizabeth, "Did you ever meet him? Did you ever meet Joey?"

"Yes, I did. I met him a few days before his accident," Elizabeth replied and looked directly at Heyward. "We went out to eat with him and Leland, but we didn't get to spend very much time talking. I would've liked the chance to know him better, but Heyward, here, thought he needed to end the evening earlier than we'd planned."

"Yes, I've heard a little about that," Dan said. "Miss Mazelle was telling me about Heyward deciding to take on half the state of Ohio, all by himself. I must say, the folks at the plant are quite impressed with you, Heyward."

To Heyward's relief, before Elizabeth could bring anything else up, one of the black men softly began singing some type of hymn, a song about the comforting hand of Jesus, and almost all the other black people joined in at some point. Sung a cappella, it was a beautiful thing in itself, and the words were comforting and reassuring, even to Heyward. He had been to many funerals before but had never witnessed the spontaneous singing of hymns. It was touching and sad at the same time. Not only that, it distracted Dan and Elizabeth from talking about the fight at Oscar's Fish Camp, and Heyward was grateful for that intervention.

After the song, Heyward and Elizabeth excused themselves from the Jacksons and went over to express their condolences to Leland, who standing in the churchyard, was inconsolable. Heyward knew he was close to his grandson, but to him, Leland appeared more distraught than Joey's own grieving parents.

There, under the tall pine trees that framed the small Baptist church's grounds, Leland broke down when Heyward and Elizabeth came over and hugged him.

"You all never even got to really know him. He was a good kid, and you'd've liked him," Leland sobbed.

Then he said something that neither Heyward nor Elizabeth understood. "I'm responsible for that boy's death. It's like that truck wrecked in Harmon Swamp by my own hand."

With a promise to check on him after his children left, Heyward and Elizabeth left, neither saying much on the short drive home.

*   *   *   *

"I take it you haven't made an appointment with a psychiatrist yet?" she asked him once they got home.

"Not yet, Elizabeth. I'm still deliberating about the whole thing. I know I've acted just a little off base lately, but I don't think it's been crazy enough to see a shrink."

She started to say something, but Heyward interrupted her. "I haven't ruled it out completely, but I don't want to have to drive all the way to Charleston just to have some doctor tell me what I already figured out on my own."

Elizabeth knew she had backed him into a corner by threatening to divorce him if he didn't see a psychiatrist. But she felt like if he didn't, she might be attending *his* funeral sooner than it should be and maybe somebody else's too. "Well, what have you figured out on your own then?"

"It's pretty simple. Up 'til now, I've lived a boring life—boring, like those gray Buicks. I'm just kind of making up for lost time, if you know what I mean," he declared.

"No, I don't know what you mean. And get off those Buicks, why don't you? I'm going back to Atlanta in the morning. Make that appointment soon, or I might just stay there for good."

CHAPTER 68

▼

The Golden Touch, Mason Thornhill's yacht, was everything Mickey and Pinky had said it was. On a calm, cloudless day—just days after Joey Tiller's funeral—the huge yacht motored in to Knobby Creek Marina and was moored at D-01, the only berth large enough to handle a boat that size. It took Pinky, Heyward, and two other dockhands to tie the boat up.

The yacht had its own distinct look about it. Pinky described it as having a European look, but no one else knew why he said that other than that it was designed and built in Italy. Warren Spearman, never at a loss for unusual words, said *The Golden Touch* had a certain "cachet." The boat was painted a brilliant white, so white that Heyward had to wear sunglasses any time he walked on the dock around it lest the glare give him a headache. Thornhill, at the time it was constructed, insisted that florescent gold stripes be painted along the side of the upper structures to emphasize the boat's name.

On the stern, two Jet Skis were secured to the deck, sharing the space with an oversized Jacuzzi. Towards the front, a small outboard boat was strapped to the first level of the outside deck.

"That's a dingy, Heyward. The owner uses that boat when he anchors the big yacht out in a bay and uses it to get back and forth to land," Pinky said, unaware that Heyward already knew exactly what a dingy was and what it was used for and had for well over forty years.

Heyward wasn't insulted by Pinky's remark; he just attributed it to him being overwhelmed at having such a magnificent yacht tied up in the marina. Pinky, as the dockmaster, felt like it somehow was a positive reflection on him.

Once the boat was tied up and secured, the soon-to-be-fired captain motioned Heyward to the side of the boat. "Would you ask the marina's owner, a Mr. Wickliffe, to come aboard, if you please?" The captain had a pronounced British accent and was wearing a starched white shirt and matching long pants. There were some gold insignias on both sides of the shirt collars.

Mickey Wickliffe was standing right next to Heyward at the time. There was no way he was going to let a yacht the size of Mason Thornhill's come into his marina without personally supervising the mooring.

Mickey told Heyward to come with him, and the two stepped onto the main deck. The captain shook their hands and introduced himself.

"I'm Captain Penfield. I have been relieved of duty, as has my first mate and all of the ship's staff, by the owner, Mr. Thornhill. The owner will not be available to board the vessel for a fortnight. He has asked me to turn the ship over to you until his arrival." And with that, he handed Mr. Mickey a small leather briefcase and a key ring with several keys.

Heyward didn't say anything at the time, but he thought the captain's manner was the epitome of formality and decorum, while the keys to the multimillion-dollar yacht looked almost identical to his Jeep's key ring. His Jeep, even as proud as he was of it, cost way less than the little dinghy Pinky was so excited to point out to him.

Captain Penfield escorted Mickey and Heyward over every inch of the yacht, from the engine room through two sitting rooms, three staterooms, and the galley. All of the staterooms were bigger and grander than the master bedroom in Heyward's expensive Wexler Island home, and the bathrooms looked like something out of the finest hotels in the world.

When they reached the helm of the boat, the captain asked Mr. Mickey to insert one of the keys in an ignition lock, then he, the captain, pushed a button next to the key, and the two diesel engines started. After they had run for a minute or so, he turned the engines off and gave the key back to Mr. Mickey.

"As you, Mr. Wickliffe, and your assistant can see, I'm leaving the vessel in excellent condition. If the owner ever puts forth a claim that I somehow left it in any condition other than it is, I will call upon you to swear in your courts of law that the boat was left in perfect condition. Now, at the request of Mr. Mason Thornhill, I am leaving his employment, as are the first mate and the two ship's stewards." With that, the captain turned and walked back through the boat with Mickey and Heyward trailing him.

Outside, standing on the dock in white uniforms, were the first mate and the two stewards. The first mate looked callous and less polished than the captain;

the stewards, both women, were blond and looked to be in their mid-twenties. For some reason, Heyward got the feeling the first mate originated from one of the former Soviet-Bloc countries, but he didn't know why he felt that way; the man neither spoke nor looked in his direction. Wherever he was from, Heyward could tell he was angry about something.

Once the captain stepped off the boat and onto the dock, they all picked up the few suitcases and bags they had and walked away. They had only gone a few steps when the first mate turned back and unhooked one of the marina's plastic trash cans from the bungee cord holding it to the dock. He lifted it above his head and tossed it onto the main deck of *The Golden Touch*. Heyward couldn't decipher what the man said when the trash can hit the boat, but he was pretty sure that, translated from his native language into English, it would have been something along the lines of "son of a bitch."

"I guess they're all pretty angry at being fired," Mickey said to Heyward and Pinky, who had now joined them on the dock. "Anyway, we'll need to take good care of this boat until Thornhill gets here in a fortnight, however long a fortnight is."

About that time, Warren Spearman walked up to them and looked at the big yacht. "A fortnight?" asked Warren. "*Fortnight* is one of my favorite words, but I never get to use it around this old place. It means fourteen days."

CHAPTER 69

▼

The next morning, Lottie caught Heyward as he was punching in on the time clock. "Mr. Mickey told me that he wants to see you in his office as soon as you came in today. He's in there now, I think."

Heyward looked at Lottie's watch. He was on time for work, not a minute late or a minute early. He knew that the marina owner had been upset with a few of the other dockhands because they occasionally clocked in early and then sat around and talked to Lottie for a few minutes while she was putting fresh hot dogs on the rotisserie as she did every morning.

"Burning minutes off the clock at my expense," Mickey would tell her but never actually do anything about it. He liked to act gruff and crabby in front of most people, even customers, but everyone knew it was just an act. Privately, he liked the dockhands chatting with Lottie in the morning as she went about her routine; they would sometimes tell her things that were going on around the marina that they wouldn't necessarily tell him—things he liked to know. Lottie would run the news through her personal filter and tell him what she thought was in his best interest to know or leave out bits of information that might worry him unnecessarily.

"What does he want to see me for, Lottie?" Heyward asked. "Am I getting a big raise or something? Maybe a bonus?" Despite the fact that he and Elizabeth— if she stayed married to him—had more money in the bank than they would ever spend in their lifetime, Heyward still respected the fact that he could be fired at any time, for any reason, and he didn't want that. It always made him apprehensive when the boss wanted to see him, retired and financially comfortable or not.

"He wouldn't tell me if you were getting a raise or not, even if you was. He always keeps that sort of thing to himself, you know, so the other employees don't know about it," she said and added, "but he always tells me when he's going to fire somebody. Today isn't your day, just for the record." Lottie put another hot dog on the grill and went outside to smoke her first cigarette of the day.

Mickey Wickliffe was on his fifth cigarette of the same day, but he didn't bother himself to go outside and smoke. After all, he owned the place. Heyward followed the smoke trail back to his office.

"Come on in, Sit down," Mickey pointed to a vacant captain's chair. Pinky was in the office too and was fanning cigarette smoke away from his face. "Pinky thought it'd be a good idea if we assign one person to take care of Thornhill's yacht while we all wait for him. I think it's going to be a couple of weeks before we see him."

Pinky coughed, and after he cleared his throat, he said, "A fortnight, remember? Warren said that was fourteen days."

Mickey looked at Pinky but didn't say anything. He took a deep drag from his cigarette and continued talking to Heyward. "I think Pinky's right. Neither of us trusts Thornhill as far as we could throw him, so we want to make absolutely sure nothing happens to his boat while no crew's living on board. I don't want to be sued by him if some bird craps on the deck and he gets pissed off about it."

"What could he sue you for? He's the one that fired his crew and had the boat moored here with no one on it, not you," Heyward asked.

"Doesn't matter. In case you didn't know this at your advanced old age, Heyward, this here's America, the good old United States of Litigation, where people can sue you for anything if they get a wild hair up their ass about something. Doesn't mean they can win, just means they can force you to do what they want you to do or make you spend a fortune in lawyer's fees defending yourself. Mason Thornhill has enough money to pay a thousand lawyers to sue somebody just for looking at him the wrong way."

Heyward shifted uncomfortably in his seat. *This Thornhill guy is going to be a problem,* he thought to himself.

"All right, Heyward. Pinky thinks you would be the most responsible person to look after *The Golden Touch* until the little emperor, 'Mason the Magnificent,' hires a new crew. I want you to scrub the boat down every day, make sure it stays clean inside, don't let anyone on it, that sort of thing."

Mr. Mickey reached in a drawer and pulled out the key ring that Captain Penfield had given him the day before. "Here's the keys for everything. Suggest you check 'em and keep everything locked up." He looked over at Pinky. "I think the diesels should be started up every other day and run for an hour or so, don't you?" True to form, he didn't give the dockmaster time to answer.

"Under no conditions, Heyward, let me repeat, under no conditions, do you untie that boat from where it sits right now. Don't care if Moses himself comes down off the mountain and tells you to untie it, don't do it, understand?" Heyward nodded that he understood. "Oh, one other thing, just in case you get the notion to spice things up a little in your love life, I don't want you and the missus trying out one of those big staterooms, if you know what I mean."

*   *   *   *

For the next couple of days, Heyward familiarized himself with *The Golden Touch*, tried out every key on every lock, cleaned out both of the huge refrigerators of any food that could spoil, and ran the dishwasher every day, even though there were no dirty dishes to wash. He arranged all of his cleaning supplies, water hoses, mops, squeegees, and toilet brushes the way it suited him. The boat even had two vacuum cleaners, and Heyward used both of them daily.

Once he had everything organized exactly to his satisfaction and had established a cleaning routine, he and Pinky worked out a schedule to start the boat's diesel engines. Pinky wanted to always be on board when the engines were started, just to help monitor all the gauges and dials and make sure no weird noises came from the machinery.

On the fourth day, with Mickey's permission and blessing, Heyward lowered the dinghy from the front bow and ran it around Wexler Bay for a good thirty minutes or so. Heyward explained to the marina boss that the small outboard engine that powered the little boat needed to be run periodically, just like the big diesels did, if he really wanted to keep everything maintained. Mickey already knew that, but he was glad that Heyward was at least thinking for the two of them.

Heyward almost made a bad mistake when he lowered the dinghy. The davit, which in reality was a miniature crane, was the only thing that could lower or raise the little boat, and Heyward, never having used a davit before, swung the dinghy out from the yacht too fast. Before he could react, the dinghy whirled around and its propeller came less than an inch or so from scratching the polished white side of *The Golden Touch*. Fortunately for Heyward and fortunately for everybody at the marina, no actual contact was made between propeller and yacht, so there was no damage done. Almost as good, at least for Heyward, no one saw him nearly foul up.

CHAPTER 70

▼

That very evening, Heyward took the small guardian angel, the one Gina Campbell made for him, off his old Dilly's Bait Shop hat and put it on the marina hat Lottie gave him his first day on the job. It bothered him that he'd had such a close call with the dinghy's propeller almost crunching into *The Golden Touch*, and with what happened to Joey Tiller, he felt that having a little angel resting on the side of his head couldn't be anything but a help. He didn't suppose Mickey would judge him to be a "religious nut" or put the little angel in the same category as handing out religious flyers should the boss see it on his hat.

Pinning the tiny angel to his hat reminded him to call Gina, as he did every two weeks or so, just to check on Leon's condition and see how she and Jean were holding up through the ordeal. It occurred to Heyward on more than one occasion that Leon's ex-wives were still—in a manner of speaking—acting as if they were married to him with their constant care, while his own wife threatened to divorce him over a matter as simple as him seeing a psychiatrist. Of course, Heyward conveniently neglected to remember why she wanted him to get psychiatric help.

"No change, Heyward. He just kind of lays there staring at the ceiling. They're feeding him through a tube now, and he's losing weight," Gina said when he called her. "Are you coming here to visit anytime soon?"

"I will in a couple more weeks, Gina. Believe it or not, I'm tied up looking after a big yacht right now, but I'll get there as soon as I can," he said. Then, after a few seconds, he said, "Gina, I just wanted to thank you for the little guardian angel you made for me. It may not have meant a lot to you at the time, but it means a lot to me now, and I just wanted to say again, thanks for everything."

Heyward promised again to come see Leon soon, and they said their good-byes; he felt sure that Gina was tearing up a little when they hung up. Heyward fed Peaches and took her for a short walk around their neighborhood and then, with Elizabeth still in Atlanta, he decided it might be a good time to go visit Leland.

It had been well over a week since Joey's funeral, and even though Heyward had talked to him on the phone once, he hadn't actually been to see him since the day of the burial. Leland's son and daughter-in-law, Joey's parents, had stayed the week on Wexler Island with him, tying up all the loose ends of their son's affairs and trying to comfort each other. Now, they had gone home to Virginia, and Leland was by himself.

"I don't know, Heyward. This thing with Joey has bothered me more than when my wife, Margaret, died. Margaret had lived a long and good life, and I guess I knew her time was up. Somehow, I feel like I should have done something more for Joey, you know," Leland said as they sat in his den.

They talked about Joey and about the wreck and how he must have gone to sleep at the wheel after a night of fishing. Heyward said nothing of the plastic bag he'd taken from the truck and thrown on the other side of Harmon Swamp; no one would ever know anything about that.

"I'm glad it was you who found him, Heyward, not just some stranger passing by or a highway patrolman, nobody like that." In the soft lighting of the room, Heyward could see Leland smile for a moment. "You want to know something? You really made an impression on Joey."

"Me?" Heyward caught himself. He almost added he'd only met the boy once but thought better of it. He knew Leland had been disappointed on more than one occasion that Joey didn't show up to go fishing with them, and the one time Heyward went to Leland's lumber company, Joey had sneaked off his job early.

"He liked that you started that fight at Oscar's. Eight against one." Leland smiled. "Joey admired that although it did scare him a little. Scared me too."

"Well," Heyward said, "it scared Elizabeth all the way to Atlanta—scared her enough to tell me if I don't go see a psychiatrist, she's going to divorce me."

Leland stood up, walked over to a bookcase, and picked up a picture of his family taken when Margaret was still alive at a family reunion long ago. He stared at the faces for almost a full minute then carefully put the picture back in place.

"You don't need to go to any head doctor. I think you're just making up for lost time. Nothing wrong with that as far as I'm concerned, and on top of everything, Joey died thinking you were a pretty tough old man."

Leland eased himself back down in his recliner. "Heyward, I want to tell you something. I've decided to close down my lumber company and sell this house. I'm going to move up to Virginia to be near my son, Frank, and his wife. I've already told Dan Jackson about my plans, and he wants to buy Tiller Lumber, but I'm not going to sell it to anybody—personal reasons." He turned his head and looked back at the picture he had just held.

Leland continued, "I've sold all the inventory of lumber sitting in the yard to a company near Marshfield, and they'll be sending trucks soon to pick it all up. I think my employees will be able to find jobs without too big of a problem. Who knows? Maybe Dan'll open up his own lumberyard and hire them."

Heyward didn't say anything. He'd probably do the same thing, if put in the same set of circumstances.

"I'm going to keep the property since it's in my name only. The way these developments are going up around here, one day, that land will be real valuable and worth something to my son and his wife."

Leland took a deep breath. "I told you some time ago I took a partner on a while back. I'm not going to worry about him in any of this; he'll find out soon enough. But I do want you to do me a favor, if you will."

"Sure, Leland, just ask. Anything I can do."

Once again, Leland stood up, but this time, he walked over to a small writing desk his wife had bought when they first were married. He opened one of the drawers and pulled out a manila envelope that had been sealed with tape. "I want you to hold this for me, Heyward. Don't open it, just keep it for me. One day, I'm going to want it back from you. Will you do that for me?"

Heyward took the envelope. "Yes, sure, I'll hold it for you. Just let me know when you want it back. Is there anything else I can do?"

"Yeah, one more thing: I want you to take my fishing boat since I won't need it where I'm going. I've already signed the title over to you," Leland pulled out a folded piece of paper from his shirt pocket and handed it to Heyward. "It's been notarized so you shouldn't have any kind of problem about that." Then he smiled. "You just might get Lauren Jackson to go fishing with you.

"So, I guess that's about it, Heyward. If you don't mind, I'm pretty tired now and want to go to bed. I haven't slept well since Joey died." Then he added, "I think that trailer hitch you have on your Jeep will work fine to haul the boat and trailer around. Go ahead and take it with you tonight, if you will."

They shook hands. Heyward thanked him for the boat and hooked it up to his Jeep. He went straight home and put the manila envelope in his dresser drawer.

Not once did he hold it up to the light to see if he could read any of its contents.

CHAPTER 71

▼

The first time Heyward met Mason Thornhill, he didn't seem to be the evil man or the devil incarnate Pinky had said he was. He seemed smaller than Heyward had imagined in his mind and younger; Thornhill wasn't tall, he only came up to Heyward's shoulders and couldn't have weighed much more than 140 pounds soaking wet. Heyward placed him to be in his early forties at most. Other than arriving at the marina by private helicopter, he seemed just like most of the people that came there, only a little smaller and a lot richer. Later on, Heyward noticed that Thornhill's helicopter kicked up some small pebbles that dinged the paint of the Jeep's front grill.

"Don't say anything to him about those nicks, just let 'em go. That pilot looked like he was in the Mafia or something and wouldn't take too kindly to you complaining to Thornhill about 'em," Pinky told him. "They scratched up my car too, but I'm not saying one durn thing about it to him."

Mickey and Pinky escorted Thornhill over to *The Golden Touch*, and after the owner had inspected the boat inside and out, Mickey called Heyward over.

"It looks like you took better care of my boat than my last three captains did," Mason Thornhill told Heyward. The boat's owner didn't make any attempt to shake his hand, but he did pull out a box of cigars from a cabinet and handed them to Heyward.

"These cigars are Cubans. They tell me this is the same brand that Fidel Castro smokes himself," he said as he passed the box to Heyward. "I want to give you these as a token of appreciation for looking after my boat so well." Pinky was standing next to Heyward on the stern of the yacht, but Thornhill didn't offer him any, and no one brought up the fact that Cuban cigars were illegal in the United States.

Later that day, a nervous Mickey called a staff meeting with all the marina's employees, which was done and over almost in the time it took him to light up a cigarette. "For the next several days, Mr. Thornhill will be interviewing captains and crew on his boat. Keep everybody out of his way, yourselves included." Mickey was so upset he actually lit another cigarette before his first one was burned halfway down.

Over the next couple of days, the dockhands did see people go and come from *The Golden Touch*, but nobody spoke to them, and no one ever seemed to stay on the boat very long.

Late one afternoon, Heyward and Pinky were standing by the fuel pumps talking about the price of gasoline, when a stylishly dressed woman walked by them and boarded *The Golden Touch* without as much as glancing at them. Heyward noticed that she was wearing high heels and that every few steps, one of her heels got caught up in the spaces between the dock's planking; Pinky saw that she had a coat of heavy makeup on her face and her dress was cut low in the front. Both of them took in the fact that, apparently, she had had some serious breast augmentation done at some point.

"See? See what I told you before?" Pinky quietly but excitedly asked. "I told you Mason Thornhill likes his women skanky-looking."

The fact that Thornhill was around seemed to cast some kind of pall over the whole marina. Heyward noticed Lottie began smoking her cigarettes in Mickey's office and not out on the dock in front of the office like she normally did.

✳   ✳   ✳   ✳

Elizabeth, meanwhile, decided she couldn't stay upset at her husband or in Atlanta for too long and came home.

To her surprise, Leland Tiller's fishing boat was parked in their driveway, and to her greater surprise, Heyward had actually tried to make an appointment with a psychiatrist down in Charleston.

The issue of the boat was fairly easy to handle. "Heyward, you know you can't leave that boat in the driveway. The neighborhood association will only allow you to keep it there less than a week, I think, so you'll need to find some place to store it away from here," she told him. He already knew that fact but didn't much care what the association thought at the time.

The matter of making an appointment with a psychiatrist was a little more complicated, both for Elizabeth and Heyward. "According to the receptionist that answered the phone when I called the psychiatrist's office, a person has to be referred by another doctor. It has something to do with health insurance regulations, she said. Since I don't have another doctor to speak of, I can't make an appointment with the shrink."

Elizabeth started to say something, but Heyward held up his hand and continued, "Before you say anything, I called for an appointment with a general practitioner in Marshfield for an overall physical, but he can't see me for another month because they're so busy. Believe it or not, I went ahead and had them schedule me in. So, after I see the general practitioner next month, I can get him to call the psychiatrist's office, and probably a month after that, I'll see the crazy-man doctor."

Elizabeth was pleased. "Well, all right, I guess," was all she could think to say.

*   *   *   *

"Did you think about what I asked you?" Heyward asked Elizabeth the same night she came home from Atlanta. "You know, did you think about setting up some scholarships with the inheritance from Uncle Walt?"

"As a matter of fact, yes, I did, Heyward. I actually thought about it a lot."

"Well, what about it?" Heyward wasn't too sure how Elizabeth was taking anything about him, for the time being, until he saw the shrink.

"First of all, Heyward, let me tell you this. I do think you have some mental issues going on right now with all this defacing cars and all of these fights you've been in," Elizabeth said.

"We're not talking about that stuff now. Like I told you, I'm going to see the psychiatrist as soon as I can get an appointment. And for the record, it wasn't *cars* I defaced, it was *a car*, singular," he said.

"I know, I know. I just wanted to remind you that I think you have some problems going on right now. But that said, I think your idea to set up some scholarships with the money is perfectly fine with me and shows me you haven't hardened your heart as much as I thought—or totally gone off the deep end."

Then she added, "We don't need the money for ourselves, and I'm concerned that if we try to give it to the kids, it will just bring problems to them somehow. They'll be just fine without it, anyway."

"All right, then," Heyward said. "Let's decide whose name we want to put them in. Definitely one in the name of my sister, Barbara, and I was thinking about one in memory of Joey Tiller too. Maybe some of the production folks that work at South Island Boats can send their kids to college."

CHAPTER 72

▼

The next afternoon, Mickey interrupted Heyward as he was tying off the lines of a boat that had just docked at the marina.

"I'll take care of this boat for you, Heyward," he said. "Mr. Thornhill wants to see you. Don't know why, just go now."

"What does Thornhill want with me?" Heyward asked. "Does he want to hire me on as his captain? Hey, maybe he wants to write me a check for the damage his helicopter did to my Jeep's paint job."

"Look," Mickey said. "None of that funny stuff with him. He's not like that sourpuss nurse over at the lab where you poured piss all over your pants. Compared to Thornhill, she's a regular comedian."

Standing there on the dock, it was easy to be glib with Mickey, but on the inside, Heyward was uneasy about being summoned by Mason Thornhill. He remembered the comment that Pinky had made earlier—although he'd scoffed at it then—the comment about rumors Thornhill had people killed on his yacht. Heyward had no reason to believe the rumors were true, but then he had no reason to believe they weren't either. Besides, the way the helicopter pilot looked, gangster-like, didn't make him feel any better.

Heyward boarded *The Golden Touch* on the stern and knocked on the main salon door. Thornhill was sitting in one of the plush leather chairs with a drink in his hand. He made no move to get up and didn't make any effort to shake hands.

"Come in. Sit down on that chair over there where I can see you," he said. "What was your name again?"

"Jennings. Heyward Jennings."

"You did a good job looking after my boat. That captain and first mate were incompetent, and I'm going to make sure they never work on a yacht this size again. They'll be lucky to get a job on a trash scow after I finish with them." Thornhill took a sip from his drink and stared at Heyward.

Heyward shifted uncomfortably in his seat. Maybe Mickey was right; he definitely shouldn't try to be sarcastic with this man.

"You look too old to be doing this kind of work. What's your story?"

Heyward cleared his throat. As concisely as he could, he related how he'd worked in a bank in Atlanta most of his adult life, raised a family, and eventually retired to Wexler Island. He explained that he was working at the marina only because he liked the work. Heyward left out the fact that he'd been in a couple of fights since he'd moved to the island or that he'd vandalized a car or that he was responsible for Thomas Pennington's untimely death. Even though Heyward was proud that he'd thrown away the speeding ticket from the Georgia Highway Patrolman, he didn't think that one small instance of defiance would impress Mason Thornhill. *Hell,* he thought to himself, *this guy's probably killed a cop just for fun.*

"You lived in Atlanta? Good town, bad traffic. I don't like bankers, though," Thornhill said. "They're too cautious. Bankers want everybody else to take chances while they sit back and watch. Maybe that's not all bad. They let other people take all the chances, and if they fuck up, the bankers take the collateral."

Mason Thornhill stared at Heyward. "Do you take chances, Mister Ex-Banker from Georgia? Chances like you and that pink-faced dock boy did yesterday?"

Heyward shifted again in the chair which was beginning to get real uncomfortable. "I'm sorry, I don't think I understand what you just said."

"You and that pink-faced boy, did you leer at my girlfriend? Red dress, black hair, big tits? Sharona said you did. Said both of you gave her the eye and made some unkind remarks to her. Said Pink-face whistled at her."

"I can tell you we never did that, none of that. Yes, we saw her walk down the dock, but we didn't leer at her. And we certainly didn't say anything to her, and Pinky, uh, Edward, didn't whistle at her," Heyward said. Then he added, "I was concerned that her high heels would get caught between the wooden planks on the dock, and she would get hurt; that's all."

Thornhill took another sip from his drink but never took his eyes off Heyward.

"I believe you mister-conservative-banker. Sharona can be a lying bitch when she's mad about something. Doesn't care who gets hurt. Tell that dock boy what I just told you, and while you're at it, tell that fat-ass marina owner to get my bill ready. I'm getting ready to leave this godforsaken place with or without a captain."

"Without a captain?" Heyward asked. He never imagined Thornhill to be a capable seaman.

"Anybody can pilot a boat like this. The electronics do all the work, and a captain does nothing more than turn them on. Most captains are either drunks or too damn lazy to get a real job anyway."

Heyward stood up and walked to the salon door.

Thornhill called out after him, "For the record, Sharona's not my girlfriend. She's just a hooker." He paused. "A high-priced hooker at that."

CHAPTER 73

▼

"Did you tell him? Did you? Did you tell him I didn't hardly look at his girl-friend and sure didn't say anything to her or whistle?" Pinky frantically begged.

Heyward had just relayed to Mickey and Pinky what Thornhill had just told him.

"Seriously, did you tell him? I don't want any trouble from a man like that. Maybe I should go talk to him myself or write some kind of note to him explaining everything?"

The three of them went into Mickey's office and closed the door.

Heyward forced himself to calm down after his meeting with Mason Thornhill on *The Golden Touch*, just as he did after vandalizing the car in the parking lot. But Pinky became more upset with every passing minute, just as Josh had done that night at the mall.

"No, don't do anything, Pinky." Heyward tried to reassure him. "I explained everything to him, and it's fine now. In fact, it would only make matters worse if you said anything to him. Just get out of sight if you see Sharona on the docks again, though."

Mickey sucked in a drag from his cigarette. "You say his boat is leaving soon, in a couple of days?"

Heyward looked through a cloud of smoke. "With or without a captain, he told me."

"Son of a bitch. Without a captain …" was all Mickey could say.

*   *   *   *

Late that same afternoon, as the marina office was about to close for the day, Heyward, standing outside, looked through the plate-glass window and saw Lottie closing out the cash register. Pinky, who was still shook up from the thought that Thornhill was angry at him, opened one of the cooler doors and took out a bottle of root beer.

Heyward dialed the marina office phone number on his cell phone and from where he was standing outside, saw Lottie reach for the phone.

"Hello, Knobby Creek Marina. This is Lottie speaking, how may I help you?" she answered.

"Lottie, it's me, Heyward. Don't say anything yet. Just tell Pinky that a Sharona is on the phone and wants to speak to him."

Peering through the window, Heyward could see Lottie hold out the telephone and say something to Pinky. Pinky seemed to take a half-step back, then he disappeared from sight. Heyward opened the office door, and when he went in, he saw the young dockmaster spread-eagle on the floor, his head resting in a puddle of root beer.

"He's fainted," Lottie said. "Pinky's done fainted."

*   *   *   *

When he got home that evening, Elizabeth was packing her suitcase again. "Heyward, you're not going to believe this. I've got to drive back to Knoxville in the morning. Lucas called and said Samantha's broken her leg, and they'll need me for a week or so until her mother can get there."

CHAPTER 74

▼

The next morning, Elizabeth left for Knoxville, and Heyward went to his job at Knobby Creek Marina.

"Just so you know, Dee Dee wanted me to tell you that you're in hot water with her," Pinky said when he punched in on the time clock. "First, you get me caught up in a brawl at Oscar's Fish Camp, then you cause me to faint and hit my head on that potato chip rack yesterday evening."

"Dee Dee didn't think that was funny? My wife thinks it's hilarious when I get hurt. In fact, she encourages me to injure myself any time I can," Heyward said. He watched Lottie put the first hot dogs of the day on the rotisserie. "Has anybody died from eating one of those hot dogs yet, Lottie?"

"Nobody that I know of, Heyward," she said. Lottie never called Heyward "Mr. J." like everyone else did. She didn't think it was dignified for a man his age.

"No kidding, Dee Dee's kind of mad about it. She had to come pick me up last night because I was too dizzy to drive home," Pinky said, trying to change the direction of the conversation away from hot dogs and back to his ailment. "She's not happy about having to come get me, and then your old friend almost ran into the side of her car out in the parking lot."

"Whose friend?" Heyward asked.

"Your friend. That fellow from the lumber company, Mr. Tiller ... you know, the one whose grandson was killed when his car ran off the road. Apparently, Mr. Tiller isn't much of a better driver himself. She said he wheeled out of here like a madman."

"Is she sure it was him? Sure it was Leland Tiller?"

"He was driving an old blue truck with the lumberyard's name on the side. Dee Dee said she wanted to yell something mean to him for almost hitting her car, but she didn't. She's a nice person that way."

That's strange, Heyward thought. Leland Tiller never came to the marina, as far as he ever knew or had any business there. Surely, Leland would have called him if he needed to talk to him. Maybe he changed his mind and wanted his fishing boat back and just came to the marina to tell him in person.

Heyward's thoughts were interrupted by Mickey. "Let's quit burning dollars off the time clock and get to work, everybody. If you don't have something to do, I can find something for you." Lottie, Pinky, and Heyward all went to work.

The rest of the workday was routine and uneventful, but Pinky and Heyward both avoided working anywhere near *The Golden Touch*; it made no sense to push their luck with Mason Thornhill, they both thought. Around three in the afternoon, Elizabeth called to let Heyward know she had arrived safely in Knoxville. Samantha, she said, was in a good bit of pain with her leg, but the doctor had given her some strong prescriptions and she should be fine before long.

It was when Heyward got home around six that afternoon that things began to change, and not necessarily for the better.

*   *   *   *

Not long after he had fixed himself and Peaches dinner, Heyward got a phone call.

"Mr. Jennings, this is Sharona. I want to dump little Thorny and take up with a real man like you." Heyward recognized the number on the caller ID and knew the call was coming from Pinky's cell phone. Heyward also recognized the dockmaster's voice, though he was trying to disguise it with a falsetto tone.

"Is that right, Sharona? Well, right now, I'm with the dockmaster's wife, Dee Dee, but as soon as I get through here, I'll come over and see you," Heyward said as seriously as he could.

"Ha, ha. Very funny. I guess you saw it was me calling," Pinky said. "By the way, Dee Dee's still mad about you making me faint and hit my head on that potato chip rack." Sometimes Pinky—like Elizabeth—just wouldn't let some things rest.

"Anyway, I just wanted to tell you that I saw your friend, Mr. Tiller, just leave the marina with Mason Thornhill. Thornhill looked none too happy, but then, neither did Mr. Tiller."

"Really? That's strange," Heyward said.

"That's why I called you. You seemed to be interested that Mr. Tiller was leaving the parking lot last night like he was upset or something. I know he's your friend and all."

Heyward thanked Pinky for calling and as an afterthought, added he was just kidding about being with Dee Dee at the time. He had hardly ended Pinky's call when the phone rang again. This time, he didn't recognize this caller's area code or phone number.

"Mr. Jennings, this is Frank Tiller, Leland Tiller's son. You and I met at my son's funeral. I know you and my father sometimes go fishing together, and I was wondering if you minded helping me?"

Frank Tiller went on to tell Heyward that he was worried about his father, and while everyone in the family was devastated at Joey's death, his father seemed to be taking it much harder than anyone else, even worse than he and his wife, and they were Joey's parents.

"I can't get him to answer his telephone. I'm up here in Virginia, and it would take me at least seven or eight hours to get down there. Would you mind looking for my father, and if you see him, have him call me immediately. We're real worried about him."

"Frank, I'm worried about him too. I know he took the recent events real hard," Heyward said. "I'll tell you, I hate to see him leave down here, but it probably will do him a lot of good when he moves up near you and your wife."

There was a long pause before Frank Tiller spoke again. "Move up here close to us? He hasn't said anything about that to me. I wish he would, but he said over and over he'd never leave that island."

As soon as he hung up the phone, Heyward went into his bedroom and from his dresser drawer, took out the manila envelope that Leland had asked him to hold for him. On instinct, whether it was the right or wrong thing to do, Heyward tore the envelope open.

There was one sheet of white typing paper in the envelope and on that paper, written in a labored hand, was a letter:

> To whom it may concern, I, Leland J. Tiller, write this letter to explain. I caused my grandson, Joey Tiller, to die, because he had a drug problem and I made it worse for him. Even though I did not know that from the start.
>
> Back when my lumber business fell on hard times, I needed some money so I took in a partner against my better judgment. That partner was Mason Thornhill.

Unknown to me, Thornhill had drugs shipped from some places in South America in those metal shipping containers that were supposed to only have special wood shipped in them. Once the shipping container went through customs and was delivered to my lumber company, somebody would come get them from Thornhill's organization to sell to people like Joey. The customs people never seem to inspect those containers for some reason. Maybe Thornhill has the custom people on his payroll. Joey was a good boy. He just had some problems and I made them worse for him. I am sorry for what I have done and I should have stopped it from happening.

The letter was signed "Leland J. Tiller." Heyward read the letter three times then ran it through Elizabeth's shredder.

CHAPTER 75

▼

He knew it was useless to try, but Heyward called Leland's cell phone and home phone. Just as he expected, no one answered.

Heyward knew the sun would be setting in less than an hour. There would be a short period of twilight, then darkness would fall suddenly. If he had any real chance of finding Leland, and with Leland, probably Mason Thornhill, he had to move quickly.

He first drove to Leland's small house, which, like the homes of most long-time Wexler Island residents, was situated on a patch of land under a spread of old oak trees. There was no sign of anyone when he drove up. He parked his Jeep in the driveway and knocked on the front door then the back door and walked around the house. Other than the lawn being cut and the bushes trimmed, there was no real indication that anyone still lived there.

From Leland's empty house, Heyward drove to Tiller Lumber Company which was no more than five miles away. The lumber company was located out by itself on part of the island that had seen little development; it was in such an isolated spot that it probably still looked like it did when Thaddeus Wexler had been thrown off his ship several hundred years before. As he drove through the woods, Heyward's thoughts went to what Leland had said just days earlier. The land he owned would be worth a fortune in a few years, if not before.

The sight of the deserted lumberyard shocked him. The last time he had been there—the day Joey had left work early—the yard was full of cut lumber and workers. There had been thousands and thousands of boards, all neatly stacked on pallets. That day, months before, there had been several cars in front of the small office building; forklifts were loading flatbeds and a truck had been making a delivery on the loading dock.

In the fading light, Heyward was taken aback; the lumberyard looked like a ghost town. Every bit of the cut planks, boards, and lumber was gone. There was not one piece of wood anywhere that he could see. The doors to the warehouses were closed and locked, and all of the windows were shuttered. Off to the right of the parking lot, the swinging doors of the three overseas shipping containers, the ones that once held the exotic woods, were thrown wide open and the containers empty.

Heyward parked his Jeep in front of the wooden office building and cupped his hands together to peek through the windows. The small office was completely dark, and from what little Heyward could see, all the furniture and desks had been removed. On the front door was a notice stating, "NO TRESPASSING UNDER PENALTY OF LAW," signed by "Leland Tiller, Owner."

Not finding any sign of life at the lumber company, Heyward drove back down the small road, through the woods, and out onto the island's main two-lane road.

It was completely dark when he drove to the South Island Boat Company, Sunny's Restaurant, and then to the boat ramp where together they had launched Leland's—now his—boat to go fishing. There was no sign of a person anywhere.

Frustrated, Heyward drove to the Knobby Creek Marina. The marina office was closed, and there was no one on the docks. Sometimes, a boat owner spent the night on his boat, but in the middle of the week, there were no lights on in any of the moored boats. Heyward walked around a dark *The Golden Touch*. No one was on board, not Thornhill, not Leland, and not even Sharona, Thornhill's skanky hooker.

Heyward walked back to his Jeep. *If* he found Leland and Thornhill, *if* everything turned out where everyone was safe and sound, and *if* Mickey was not in one of his normal moods, he decided he was going to recommend that Mickey hire a night watchman or put up some security cameras, or at the very least, put one of those locking gates over the boardwalk leading to the boats. A person on the wrong side of right and wrong could get on any one of the boats and steal almost anything they wanted. On the boats at the marina, there had to be hundreds of thousands of dollars worth of electronics worth stealing, and they were just sitting there. There might as well be a sign on them that said, "Take Me." You didn't have to be a big-time bank executive to realize that, he thought.

Sitting alone in the marina parking lot, Heyward tried to imagine where Leland could be. Surely, he thought, Leland and Thornhill weren't out together at a restaurant, enjoying a meal and talking about how profitable the illegal drug business was.

The only place left that Heyward could think of was Sandy Point, or more precisely, Harmon Swamp, where Joey had run off the road. Leland had placed a small wooden cross on the side of the road, and he remembered someone—he couldn't remember who—had heard that Leland had placed fresh flowers there every day since the funeral.

With no other ideas, Heyward cranked the Jeep and headed for the narrow county road where he had found Joey.

It's going to be real dark out there, he thought as he flipped the Jeep's headlights on.

CHAPTER 76

▼

Heyward was right; it was dark on Sandy Point Road, so dark that even his head-lights seemed to barely cut through the blackness. It was dark and deserted; once he got on the narrow road, he didn't meet or pass another car the entire time. The road, narrow at best in broad daylight, seemed no wider than the breadth of his car at night.

Heyward drove out to Sandy Point, just like he did when he looked for Joey, but no vehicles were parked in the small lot, nor was there anyone fishing on the point. With no further ideas of where the two men might be, he turned around and headed home. It was only after he'd started back down Sandy Point Road and entered Harmon Swamp that he saw the dull glow of a headlight just off the right side of the road, in the stagnant water. He was almost in the exact place where earlier, he'd found the green pickup truck with Joey Tiller's dead body inside.

Heyward pulled his Jeep to a stop. In the darkness of the swamp, he couldn't see much more than what appeared to be a dying headlight. He turned the Jeep, angled it in the road, and threw the switch to the spotlights bolted to the roll bar just over his head. Their brilliance illuminated the night, and he saw the partial silhouette of a vehicle. Nervous at the thought of seeing another wrecked truck, he opened the glove compartment, avoided the air horn button, and took out a flashlight.

Anxious, Heyward stumbled down the embankment and waded into the black swamp water. The soft mud pulled at his legs, and only by his dogged effort was he able to make his way over to the light, the whole time dreading what he might find. Standing chest high in the water, he shined his flashlight into the truck's cab and saw Leland Tiller's body in the driver's seat, with most of his head and body underwater; there was no doubt that he was dead.

On the passenger side of the truck, Mason Thornhill was groaning. His head was above the water and was slowly twisting back and forth. His face was covered in streaks of blood, and Heyward could see his left eye was completely swollen shut.

Heyward edged himself around the front of the truck, momentarily breaking the beam from the one working headlight and over to the passenger side door. He reached through the open window and lightly shook Thornhill's arm. Thornhill jerked his head back and slowly following Heyward's voice, turned his head toward the window.

"Can you tell how injured you are?" Heyward asked him. "It looks like Leland's dead, and I need to get you out of this water or you'll die too."

Even though it was in the waning days of summer, the swamp water was beginning to chill Heyward, and he knew that anyone in the water long, especially injured and in shock, could succumb to hypothermia quickly. Snakes and alligators were also still active, and even though he didn't want to think about either of them in the area, Heyward knew that they would be very interested in all three of the men.

Mason Thornhill moved his lips, but he couldn't talk. Heyward attempted to wrench the truck door several times before it finally opened, and carefully, he pulled Thornhill from the cab into the water. It took Heyward a few seconds to realize Thornhill's hands were bound together with duct tape.

Buoyed by the water, Heyward managed to pull himself and the injured Thornhill around the truck and towards the road. More than once, the man shouted out in pain, but Heyward forced himself to ignore the shrieks and dragged him out of the water and onto the bank. There was nothing he could do for Leland.

"I think we'd better get to the hospital immediately. You can't wait for an ambulance to get here," he said. Heyward boosted him up and with great effort, laid Thornhill in the passenger seat of the Jeep. "I'm sorry I don't have a jacket or blanket to put around you. Just try to hold on, and I'll get you there as fast as I can."

He turned the spotlights off, cranked the Jeep, and started for the only emergency clinic on the island which had to be at least ten miles from the site of the accident. As he wound through the gears, Heyward heard Thornhill murmur something, but he couldn't understand him. His passenger definitely had sustained internal injuries. When he'd touched Thornhill's abdomen as he pulled him from the wrecked truck, he'd cried out with pain. He also thought his lower left leg might be broken because it seemed to be at an odd angle. Leland's truck had crashed through some trees, and from the little Heyward could see when he was in the swamp, the truck looked like it had left the road at a very high rate of speed.

Thornhill groaned, and Heyward realized he was trying to say something so he leaned over as far as he could and still drive at the same time. "I'm going as fast as I can. We'll be there real soon so just try to hold on and don't try to talk," Heyward said.

"That man tried to kill me." Thornhill sat up a bit. "Untie my hands."

"Let's get you to a doctor first; he'll cut that tape off your hands. Just hold on," Heyward said.

"Cut them off me now. I'm Mason Thornhill, and I'm telling you what to do," Thornhill hissed.

Heyward came to the stop sign at the end of Sandy Point Road and turned onto the main road which would take them to the island's clinic. They were less than three miles from medical help.

"I said, cut this tape from my hands. Do what I say."

Heyward heard but ignored him. Up ahead, he could see the glow of the clinic's florescent sign.

"Cut my hands loose now, and do what I say. Have you lost your mind?"

There were those words again. Once more, someone was questioning his sanity, Heyward thought. He backed off the accelerator, and the Jeep slowed down.

"Funny you should ask that question. Have I lost my mind? I ask myself that from time to time, and I've had several people ask me that recently too," Heyward said.

He could see Thornhill's bloodied face in the glow of the instrument panel. "Maybe I have lost my mind. Then again, maybe I haven't. Thing is, I just can't tell one way or another. The important thing is I don't much care anymore."

Heyward braked to a stop and made a three-point turn away from the emergency clinic. He started toward the Tiller Lumber Company.

In what seemed like a very short time to Heyward, he pulled into the deserted and dark lumber company. Heyward drove through the lot and stopped in front of the three metal shipping containers, the very same ones that Thornhill or one of his employees used to ship drugs into the country. The headlights lit up the inside of the empty metal shells.

Heyward got out of his seat, then jerked Mason Thornhill from the passenger seat out the door and dropped him on the ground. The injured man squealed in pain. Once on the ground, Heyward dragged him by his bound hands into the middle shipping container.

Thornhill screamed. "What are you doing? This isn't the hospital."

"Scream all you want to. Nobody's going to hear you way out here."

Heyward leaned over and took Thornhill's billfold and keys. "You're right," he said with his mouth pressed against Thornhill's ear. "This isn't the hospital, but it is where you're going to die. My friend, Leland, you remember him, don't you? The man with you in the swamp tonight? The man whose grandson died because of your drugs? Well, he was afraid to step foot in these containers. Said he had claustrophobia or something like that."

When Heyward thought of Leland and Joey dying because of this man, he stepped on Thornhill's fingers and pressed down hard. He heard one of his knuckles splinter and even in the heat of the moment, thought it sounded like a pecan shell cracking.

"Let's just see if you die of claustrophobia yourself, that is, if your injuries don't get you first. Maybe those won't kill you, after all. When the sun comes up in the morning, and it gets hot in here and you don't have any water to drink, maybe that'll do the trick. Either way, you're going to die in a hard way, and you're going to die alone."

Heyward closed and latched the gate doors of the container. In the light cast by the headlights, he closed the doors on the other two containers.

He walked around to the back of his car and unlocked a padlock Leland had given him to use whenever he hauled the boat and trailer. "Put this lock on the trailer's hitch," Leland had told him. "That way, no one can steal your trailer when it's hooked up to your Jeep."

Heyward put the lock on the container that Thornhill was in and locked it. Then, he removed the key and threw it in the woods.

"Damn straight," he said to the closed container door. "Damn straight. I *have* lost my mind."

CHAPTER 77

▼

Heyward knew what he had to do, and it had to be done that night. He smiled grimly to himself and thought that while *he had* lost his mind, he hadn't lost his senses.

Careful not to drive in a way that would attract the attention of the police, Heyward drove home, took a quick shower to wash the swamp water and filth off his aching body, and put the soaked clothes in the washing machine. Elizabeth was in Knoxville; there wasn't anyone at home to question him.

With an old towel, he wiped down the seats of the Jeep as clean as he could and hooked Leland's boat—now his—to the Jeep. Quickly, he got his fishing rods, his tackle box, and the few remaining bits of frozen bait he'd bought at Dilly's and put them all in the floor of the boat and covered them with an old green tarp.

It was well after ten o'clock, so there was virtually no traffic on the back roads as he trailered the boat to the launch ramp, the same one he and Leland had used many times before. There were no other cars or pickups at the landing, no fisherman launching or hauling in their boats for some night fishing, and thankfully, no young couples were in the deserted parking lot, using it as a lover's lane.

Without much trouble, Heyward backed the boat off the trailer into the river, tied it to the small floating dock by the ramp, and parked his Jeep with the empty trailer in the parking area. That done, he cranked the small outboard engine, turned the boat's running lights on, and motored out into the Black Oak River, towards Knobby Creek Marina, which by water, was less than six miles away from the boat ramp.

On the horizon, in the distance, Heyward could see flashes of lightning, but he couldn't yet hear any thunder over the sound of the little outboard engine. He studied the pattern of each streak and before too long, realized the storm was headed in the direction of Wexler Bay and that, in short order, he would be in the middle of a summer thunderstorm; it should provide him some cover for what he was going to do.

Heyward was able to manage reasonable speed from the boat, even in the dark, and after about twenty minutes, he reached the outermost ring of light of the marina and cut the engine back. The marina only had soft yellow lights, waist high, that only lit the wooden planks of the docks and nothing more. The first time Heyward worked past nightfall at the marina, he had been surprised that the docks and walkways were not lit any more than they were; there was just enough light to see where he was walking, but beyond that, the water around the marina was dark.

"We only have low lights so people can see where they're walking and nothing more," Pinky had told him when he'd asked about it. "Some people like to take their boats out at night, and anything brighter that this would kill their night vision. Besides, lights use electricity, and you know how tight Mr. Mickey can be with cash."

The marina was quiet and completely still, the storm still a ways off when Heyward guided the outboard boat alongside *The Golden Touch*, which was still moored at the outmost finger pier. He cut the engine and tied the little boat to the stern of the big yacht and quietly jumped on the back deck. It was the same place where he'd first met Mason Thornhill, where the man had given him the box of Cuban cigars.

From the ring of keys he'd taken from Thornhill after he'd dragged him into the metal shipping container, Heyward located the key he'd used many times during the two weeks he was looking after the boat and opened the back salon door. He strode through the deserted yacht and up to the helm, where he inserted the ignition key in the master switch.

Heyward paused for a minute and considered what he was doing. There was still time, not much, but still some time, to get Mason Thornhill out of the container and take him to the hospital before he died. Thornhill, if he lived, would surely accuse Heyward of trying to murder him—murder him as Leland had tried when he crashed his truck in Harmon Swamp. But it would be Thornhill's word against his; after all, didn't Heyward rescue him from the wreck and the swamp? There was still time to save himself from his horrifying act.

Heyward turned the key and started the yacht's big diesel engines.

The surge of electricity generated from the engines activated the boat's electronics: the global positioning system, the radar, the radio, and the depth finder. The glow from the dials lit up Heyward's face.

The storm was fast approaching from the west, and Heyward could feel the yacht begin to sway slightly in the breeze and tug against the lines holding it to the dock. Quickly, Heyward left the helm station, the diesels beginning to idle, and went through a side door and dropped down on the pier. He untied the lines holding the boat, and the yacht began to drift away from its berth.

Heyward jumped on the boat and back at the helm, pushed the throttles. *The Golden Touch* eased forward with Leland's boat in tow.

Just as he was about to clear the marina's entrance, Heyward spotted a green light on top of a piling immediately to the boat's front starboard side, and he realized he was much too close. As it moved ahead, *The Golden Touch* brushed the side of the piling. Heyward could feel a slight jar as the boat hit the support. Collision or not, the yacht continued moving and cleared the marina.

Heyward stuck his head out the starboard door and looked behind the boat. The piling he rammed was noticeably leaning, but it was standing, and the green directional beacon on top of it was still working.

It was ten nautical miles from the Knobby Creek Marina to the entrance of Wexler Bay, then past the jetties and into the Atlantic Ocean. Heyward pushed the throttles forward again and picked up speed a bit, but he was careful not to go so fast as to swamp the little boat he was towing at the stern. The channel was well marked with buoy lights, and Heyward had no trouble heading towards the open ocean, even though the storm was about to catch up with him and the yacht.

Before too long, Heyward spotted the beacon lights of the man-made jetties, which formed the narrow entrance to the ocean from Wexler Bay. He clearly remembered the warning from the Sea Ray boat broker, Jimmy Ratterree. "Be careful … around the jetties … rocks tore out the bottom of the boat."

CHAPTER 78

▼

Once Heyward spotted the blinking warning lights of the jetties, any nervousness he might have had, if he had any, left him. For a man who had just committed murder—if not murder itself, at least voluntary manslaughter—and was in the process of stealing a multimillion-dollar yacht, he was remarkably composed. Even when the thunderstorm caught up with him, Heyward felt a sense of total peace and contentment.

While Heyward was calm, Wexler Bay was becoming anything but tranquil. Even though *The Golden Touch* was the biggest yacht that had ever graced the Knobby Creek Marina, it was beginning to pitch and roll in the wind and building waves generated by the powerful storm. Rain began to lash across the deck, and after a few minutes, Heyward could clearly hear small pellets of hail bouncing off the windows and the deck panels above his head. Every time the lightning flashed, he momentarily lost his vision, like a person sometimes does when the light bulb of a camera catches them unaware.

Heyward eased back on the throttles and cut the yacht's speed. He wasn't worried about being manhandled by the storm; he just didn't want to swamp the little boat that was in tow. He needed it to get home.

Less than a mile from the jetties, Heyward shifted the throttles to neutral, and the boat's forward motion slowed then stopped. Almost immediately, the howling wind turned the boat broadside and began pushing it towards the shoreline.

He left the helm station and made his way to the master stateroom. Flashes of lightning illuminated the way. There, he took Mason Thornhill's billfold from his pocket and put it in a drawer built into one of the closets. That done, he groped his way to the stern of the yacht to check on Leland's boat.

The little boat was still tied to the yacht and was bobbing in the waves, even though, as best as Heyward could tell, it was beginning to fill with water from waves sloshing over it and from the driving rain.

With *The Golden Touch* still being pushed sideways by the wind towards the shore, Heyward fought his way to the bow of the yacht. The whole time, rain was stinging his exposed face and hands. He tugged his shirt up to cover his chin and pulled his hat down hoping to afford his eyes some protection.

Once on the bow, he removed the latches holding the dinghy, the same one whose propeller almost dug into the side of *The Golden Touch*. With the help of a gust of wind, he pushed the dinghy off its cradle and into Wexler Bay. Another gust knocked him down and blew his hat from his head, exposing his face to the full fury of the wind. When a streak of lightning flashed, Heyward could see the dingy floating away on the roiling bay.

Back at the helm, Heyward eased the throttles forward, turned the yacht into the wind and away from the shore, and headed in between the left and right jetties. Soon, when he had the boat lined up just where he wanted it, he pushed the throttles forward as far as they could go, and the big yacht quickly picked up speed.

Forty seconds later, Heyward drove *The Golden Touch* onto the rocks that formed the right jetty.

The impact knocked Heyward off his feet and threw him into the control panel, which knocked the breath from his lungs. The diesel engines continued to run at full speed, and the yacht freed itself for just a second and lunged forward until a huge rock tore a massive hole in the hull. One of the spinning propellers struck something solid, and the heavy engines tore from their fittings.

Heyward, injured with a few broken ribs, fumbled his way to the stern and managed to untie Leland's boat. He was able to start the outboard engine and slowly backed the partially filled boat away from *The Golden Touch*, which began to break apart as the waves pounded it on the large granite boulders that made up the jetty.

*   *   *   *

Eventually, the storm moved on out into the Atlantic Ocean, and Wexler Bay began to calm. Heyward, his ribs aching, bailed water from the motorboat using an old plastic bait bucket and slowly made his way back across the bay.

He skirted around the marina as close to the opposite shore as he could and then up Black Oak River towards the boat landing and his Jeep. After he got his second wind, Heyward arranged the rods and reels and fishing equipment around the boat, just in case he happened upon a game warden or if the coast guard stopped him.

He would be just an old man with gray hair out night fishing under what was then a calm, starry sky.

CHAPTER 79

▼

The next morning, as Heyward had expected, his telephone rang. He just didn't expect it to be as early as five-thirty, though.

"Heyward, this is Dan Jackson. I really hate to call you, but I wanted to let you know as soon as I found out."

"Don't worry, Dan, about the time. Elizabeth is in Knoxville, and I was planning to get up early anyway, even if it's my day off," Heyward said. "What's the matter?"

"Leland Tiller was found wrecked in the swamp this morning, same place you found Joey. Leland's dead, Heyward. I'm sorry to have to tell you."

Heyward acted stunned then thanked Dan for letting him know. They briefly spoke about how upset Leland had been about his grandson's passing and how it seemed to have changed his personality.

"The highway patrol thinks Leland may have run off the road on purpose there at Harmon Swamp ... where Joey did, you know, as a suicide attempt," Dan said.

Heyward got up and took a shower. A big bruise was starting to form on his side, and his ribs hurt terribly when he twisted his body certain ways, but other than that, he was fine, physically. Mentally, he had never felt better in his life.

After lunch, he gathered up his rod and reel and beach chair and put them in the back of his Jeep. He looked around for his marina hat but remembered it had blown off in the storm, so he found his old hat, the one the old woman at Dilly's Bait Shop had given him. He put it on his head and put a dab of suntan lotion on the bridge of his nose and cheekbones; it was going to be hot on the beach surf fishing.

About the time he was ready to get in the Jeep, Heyward heard the mailman beep his horn then wave and put something in his mailbox before driving off. He walked slowly down the driveway to the mailbox, favoring his injured side; maybe there was a letter from his grandchildren.

There was no letter from Charlie or Hannah, but there was an envelope from a law firm addressed to him. He had worried so much before at the bank about being sued by Robert Fortson over the computer-bashing incident and his physical threat to the man. Now, after all this time, was it going to finally happen?

Standing there on the driveway, he tore the envelope open and began to read the enclosed letter: "Mr. Jennings, this notice is to advise you of legal action, taken on behalf of my client, Mr. Jonathon Burroughs of Cleveland, Ohio …"

Heyward was being sued for damages caused by the fight at Oscar's Fish Camp. As he walked to his Jeep, he tore the letter up and threw the pieces into the garage trash can.

✳   ✳   ✳   ✳

Once on the beach, Heyward realized that he didn't bring any bait with him. Still, he unfolded his chair, drove the spike he'd bought at Dilly's into the sand, and put his rod and reel in the holder, leaving the hooks and sinker wrapped tightly around the fishing rod.

"This is a good day just to sit on the beach and enjoy the sun and watch the waves," he said to Peaches. Heyward never went to the beach—fishing or not—without his dog.

Sometime later in the day, a man and woman walking at the edge of the water stopped at his chair. The man had a hairy chest, skinny legs, and an enormous beer belly, even larger than Mickey Wickliffe's. The man's wife, Heyward assumed she was his wife, was wearing an old-fashioned bathing suit, the kind that women wore in the 1950s and had her hair wrapped in a matching scarf.

"Why don't you have your line in the water?" the man asked Heyward. "They're catching fish up and down the beach, some kind of a bass-like fish. I even saw one guy pull in two fish at one time," he said.

"He said those were redfish, Gordon," the woman interjected. Heyward couldn't see her eyes because she was wearing large sunglasses that looked like the lenses were tinted extra dark.

"You're not going to catch anything just sitting here with no line in the water," the man, Gordon, said again. "The tide's right, the wind's right, and the fish are feeding like crazy. You're wasting perfect conditions, just sitting there like that."

"Well, I appreciate your concern for my opportunities, but, Gordy, you know something? Sometimes, it's better just to sit and enjoy the sun."

Heyward thought of Mason Thornhill. He wondered how hot the sun was making the interior of the metal shipping container that he'd left him in. Surely, with the sun baking the metal, it had to be unbearable inside—if he was still alive.

The man with the skinny legs and considerable beer belly, Gordon, and his out-of-fashion wife said nothing more and walked on down the beach.

Before they were out of sight, Heyward spotted a man, tall and thin, with a flushed face and wearing a black T-shirt walking towards him. He was carrying something in his hand, but Heyward couldn't make out what it was.

The lanky man called out, "Some people have it made, that's for sure." It was Pinky Pinson.

"I thought I'd catch you out here fishing. Look here, Mr. J., I know it's your day off and all, but I wanted to tell you something. I tried calling you on your cell phone and home phone, but nobody answered," Pinky said.

"I decided not to bring my phone out here with me, Pinky. It's just so nice out here—I didn't want to be bothered by it today."

"Sorry, but I wanted to tell you something. Mason Thornhill's gone. So is his yacht, literally. Broke up on the jetty and sunk," Pinky stated.

"Really? Sunk?" Heyward asked.

"Yep, sunk. The coast guard thinks he tried to take his yacht and leave by himself, you know, all the big talking he was doing about not needing a captain and all. Anyway, the fool must have accidentally run up on the jetties then drowned when the boat broke apart. The coast guard is searching the bay and ocean for him now."

"I'll be durned, Pinky. But, you know, he *was* as arrogant as they come. I guess having all that money does that to some people," Heyward said. "Thanks for letting me know."

"Oh, by the way, I was out on the bay this morning helping them look for Thornhill's body and came across *The Golden Touch's* dingy floating along, just as pretty as you please. I guess it broke loose when he hit the rocks, or maybe Thornhill tried to get off his yacht with it, you know, when it was breaking up. No matter, this's your hat, the one with that little guardian angel pinned to it. I found it in the dingy and thought you'd want it back."

Pinky handed the hat to Heyward.

"Thanks, Pinky. I appreciate that," Heyward said and put the hat on. It was still wet. "I probably left it in the boat when I was cleaning it up."

Heyward reached into his front shirt pocket and pulled out two cigars. "Pinky, how would you like one of these cigars? They tell me they're the same kind that old Fidel Castro himself smokes."

"Thanks, but I've got to get back to the marina. Some people still have to work, you know."

Pinky turned and started walking back toward where he'd parked his car.

Heyward called out after him, "Pinky, hold on a minute. I was wondering if I might be able to take a few days off?"

"Sure," Pinky said. "Anything wrong?"

Heyward lit the cigar. "No, nothing's wrong. I'm going to be heading to Atlanta tonight. There's a favor I want to do for an old friend of mine."

978-0-595-45956-8
0-595-45956-0

Printed in the United States
97187LV00003B/139/A